The
PRINCESSES
of IOWA

The PRINCESSES *of* IOWA

M. MOLLY BACKES

CANDLEWICK PRESS

Copyright © 2012 by M. Molly Backes

First edition 2012

Library of Congress Cataloging-in-Publication Data

Backes, M. Molly.
The princesses of Iowa / M. Molly Backes. — 1st ed.
p. cm.
Summary: After being involved in a drunk driving accident in the spring, Paige Sheridan spends the summer in Paris as an au pair and then returns to her suburban Iowa existence for her senior year of high school, where she begins to wonder if she wants more out life than being popular, having a handsome boyfriend and all the latest clothes, and being a member of the social elite.
ISBN 978-0-7636-5312-5
[1. Conduct of life—Fiction. 2. Popularity—Fiction. 3. High schools—Fiction. 4. Schools—Fiction. 5. Iowa—Fiction.] I. Title.
PZ7.B13222Pr 2012
[Fic]—dc23   2011018622

12 13 14 15 16 17 BVG 10 9 8 7 6 5 4 3 2 1

Printed in Berryville, VA, U.S.A.

This book was typeset in Fairfield.

Candlewick Press
99 Dover Street
Somerville, Massachusetts 02144

visit us at www.candlewick.com

To the Backes Girls:
Mama, Megan, and Natalie

Prologue

Everyone knows you're not supposed to drink and drive. I mean, *obviously*. They start telling you that in fourth grade and you nod along, wide-eyed, because you can't imagine ever being stupid and awful enough to drink at all, much less drink and drive. You make posters about how dumb it is, drinking and driving, and they hang them in the elementary school hallway. You tell your parents to stop smoking and accuse them of being alcoholics if they have a glass of wine with dinner more than once a month, and in health class you take tests on drugs, where every single drug is listed with a bunch of outdated slang and possible side effects, which all include death. Tobacco (butts, heaters, cancer sticks): lung cancer, emphysema, DEATH. Alcohol (booze, hooch, sauce): impaired judgment, loss of consciousness, DEATH. Marijuana (ace, grass, hay): disorientation, paranoia, DEATH. Heroin (boy, horse, smack): euphoria, convulsions, coma, DEATH.

For the next few years, you basically assume that you'll drop dead the second you're even in the same room as someone drinking a beer, and you solemnly swear that you'll never be that stupid. But then in eighth grade you're hanging out at the park shelter, waiting for something interesting to happen, and your best friend pulls out a cigarette she's stolen from her mother and dares you to smoke it, and you do because the cute boy from your math class is there watching, and you feel brave and strange and grown up, even though you're half convinced that you'll be addicted within seconds of your first puff. If not dead. But nothing happens, except that the boy's eyes widen slightly and your best friend looks at you with new interest, like you have all kinds of potential she never saw in you.

And then maybe you have another cigarette at a party later that spring, standing out beyond the lights of the back porch, talking to a different cute boy, and he offers you a sip of his beer, and you don't die, you just giggle a lot. And you start to suspect that all the stuff they told you in fourth grade was a little exaggerated—not that you'd ever do *heroin,* but maybe shrooms or something—because you probably wouldn't die. Your teacher made you believe there would be trench-coated junkies hanging around the school yard, but then she always used articles with drugs, like "the marijuana," and belted her polyester pants just under her ribcage, so in retrospect she maybe wasn't the best source of information about illegal drugs.

But obviously you shouldn't drink and drive. They start

telling you again in high school, making you watch videos in driver's ed where a kid piles fifteen of his best friends into a big yellow van and then drinks half a PBR and drives off a cliff, killing everyone but himself, and then lives with that guilt for the rest of his awful life. They tell you that you shouldn't give in to peer pressure, and they make you role-play ways to say no when someone hands you a joint. You can throw your hands up and say, "No, thanks, I'm cool." You can pass it to the next person in the circle without saying anything. Or you can make some snotty remark that only works on sitcoms, like "I get high on life."

What they don't tell you is that sometimes you might not care about the side effects, that they might not be such a bad trade-off if it means you get to get the hell out of your own head for a little while and let go of the breath you're always holding, the tiny bit of pudge on your belly you're forever sucking in, if for one stupid night you can stop worrying about what people think about you and stop watching every word you say. And maybe that night, as you're holding an ugly plastic cup and listening to everyone have the exact same conversations as last weekend and you're inside your head thinking all the same thoughts, and sometimes you kind of hate your friends, sometimes you really kind of hate *yourself,* and maybe you wouldn't mind getting hurt or going into a coma or something. Something.

And what they don't tell you in fourth grade is that if everyone's drunk and the least drunk person offers to drive, it will make a kind of crazy sense, and everyone might even congratulate themselves on how responsible they are to make the car owner sit in back and not drive her own car. They don't tell you that the whole impaired judgment thing means that you'll make decisions you'd never make sober and you'll think they're good ones, or maybe you'll know they're bad, but you won't even care anymore, because it was such a stupid night and you just want to get home. Because maybe your best friend was making a total slut of herself with a college guy and then disappeared for an hour, leaving you to make small talk with her brother and drink the rum and Cokes he keeps handing you until you can hardly see straight and you can't stop thinking about what a stupid whore your best friend is, and what if you're actually no different because you're the one who agreed to go to a college party even though your boyfriend had to go to a funeral in Kansas this weekend and what if he comes back on Monday and hears rumors about what happened at the party even though nothing did, it was a total bust, you sat there and talked to your best friend's brother while everyone else paired off in dark corners and you sat on the couch getting drunker and drunker and listening to him talk about some Boy Scout trip he went on in ninth grade, no kidding, he will not shut up about hiking in Philpot or something, like anyone seriously cares, and about how he found God or something, though actually when you think about it, it's kind of sexy to hear a guy talk about God, and the way he's describing the desert sky at night is amazing, seriously, just beautiful, and you really don't mean to kiss him but it just sort of happens.

And then suddenly she's standing over you with this look of horror, gleeful triumphant horror, and she's your best friend but what if she calls your boyfriend to tell him what she just saw, even though it was seriously nothing, it's not like it meant anything, but she saw it and you can see it in her eyes, she's going to tell him, because she's always had a crush on him, even though she denies it, and then you're running through the house to find your other best friend because you are not going to stay in that house a minute longer, and when you finally find her, your other friend, she's half dressed and barely conscious and you grab her purse and keys and shirt and drag it all out of the frat house with your other best friend, the bitch, at your shoulder, saying, "What about Jake? How could you do that to him?" and obviously you shouldn't drive, *of course* you shouldn't, you're all drunk, but you don't even care anymore, you just want to get home, and if you all die in a horrible fiery crash then fine, great, because you cannot let her tell your boyfriend about what did not just happen, and it's all so fucking pathetic and tedious and awful.

They don't talk about that part in fourth grade.

But maybe they should.

chapter ONE

I didn't want to go to Paris. Not that I had a choice or anything, but if someone had bothered to ask me how I wanted
to spend the summer before my senior year, I would have
voted to take all my closest friends to an amazing beach
house in California or Florida or something and spend the
summer lying out and having fun. Realistically, though—
because while my family is comfortable, we're definitely
not beach house comfortable—I would have opted just to
stay with my best friends in Willow Grove. Lacey, Nikki,
and I would spend our days in the good chairs at the pool
(now that we were seniors, we could claim the best spots)
and nights hanging out together with our group of friends.
And on the weekends, when he was free from his intern-
ship at his father's law office, Jake and I would go anywhere

we could be alone, whether that meant hanging out in his basement or on the golf course behind his house or even just driving around the dark country roads. Because even though Iowa isn't the most exciting place in the world, I would rather be with my friends at home than be all alone in stupid Paris, where I'd been treated like slave labor and everything smelled bad.

Seeing as how I wasn't given a choice, though, I have to admit there was a tiny part of me that had hoped Paris would work its magic on me, and I'd come home at the end of the summer all Sabrina-ed up, transformed from prom queen runner-up to elegant, worldly Audrey Hepburn–esque homecoming queen. Not that I was mad at Lacey for winning prom queen last spring — we were best friends, so her winning was almost as good as me winning. I just figured that it was my turn to be in the spotlight, and if Paris could help, then at least I could get one good thing out of my summer.

But even though the only fashion choices I had made involved choosing new clothes for the baby after she'd pooped through her diaper, up to that last morning in Paris, I kept a small shred of hope that the city would transfer some of its elegance and allure to me.

Ten minutes into my triumphant return to Iowa, that plan did not seem to be working.

Instead of sweeping across the jet bridge into the airport as I'd imagined — fresh, cool, newly adult — I hobbled behind an old man who had smashed my toes with his cane. The flight from Paris to Chicago had been bad enough—I'd been pinned between the window and an enormously fat man, my shoulder pressed against the plastic airplane wall in an effort to make myself as small and contained as possible to avoid any further contact with the masses of flesh hanging over our shared armrest. Our plane circled Chicago for almost an hour, sweeping out over Lake Michigan and back, due to traffic on the tarmac or who knows what, but by the time we finally landed, I had to sprint across the airport in four-inch heels, push my way through customs, jump on a stupid train thing to get from the international terminal to the whole other side of the airport, and then run all the way to the end of the concourse. I arrived sweaty, panting, and bruised from where my bag kept hitting me as I ran, only to be seated directly in front of a screaming baby whose every breath gave me PTSD flashbacks to the summer, with Mrs. Easton crying and Mr. Easton yelling and the baby screaming its red little face off. Getting stomped on by Gramps was a fantastic finale to the whole hideous thing.

When I finally limped past security, looking less like Sabrina and more like an escapee from the asylum, I was almost happy to see my mother. At least she couldn't dump me on the spot, as I was sure Jake would do if he saw me in this state. My mother stood at a slight angle, the Leaning Tower of Jacque, with one tanned arm perched on her hip and one hanging down casually at her side, holding a trendy bag. She wore Jackie O sunglasses ("My

3

namesake!" she always said), and her hair was swept up in a neat summer do. She looked less like a mom and more like a cool older sister.

"Hey," I said, reaching her. "Where's Lacey and Nikki? Where's Jake?"

"What happened to you?" She held me at an arm's length. "Did you have to ride in the baggage hold?"

I sighed. "There were fat people and screaming babies and running . . . I'm just tired."

"Oh, honey," my mother said. "It's always a good idea to stop in the restroom to freshen up before you leave the terminal."

"I know." I did know. I'd been flying with my mother for seventeen years, and each flight required a stop to freshen up. I should have gone directly from my flight to a sink and mirror, but after traveling for eighteen-plus hours, I was so tired that my fatigue seemed to take on physical properties of its own, like it could stand beside me and pull at my hair and clothes.

She glanced around. "This airport is so small, you never know who might see you. You can't take any chances right now. Not after —"

"Mom," I said. "I know."

My mother wrapped her arms around me loosely, raising her voice almost imperceptibly. "I'm so happy you're home! I missed you! My little girl is all grown up!"

"Okay," I said. "Seriously, though, where is everybody?"

"I thought we could spend some time together, just the

two of us," she said. "Plus, the Austins' barbeque is tonight. I'm sure they're helping with it."

Helping? My friends? I loved them, but I wouldn't exactly call them helpful. Well, Nikki maybe, even Jake, but if Lacey was doing anything but lying out I would eat my boarding pass.

My mother pulled away and started walking toward the baggage claim. "Let's get your luggage and then go get some lunch. I'm just dying to hear all about Paris."

I stopped. "What?" She didn't notice, and I had to kind of shuffle-jog to catch up with her. "You're dying to hear about Paris?"

The people from my flight had positioned themselves around the baggage carousel. Baby McScreamy was peacefully snoozing in a hippie sling across its mother's chest. The old man who'd crushed my toes was sitting in a wheelchair at the U-turn. Probably looking for someone else to maim.

"Of course, honey!" My mother planted herself strategically behind a giant linebacker-type guy. "The lights, the museums, the food! The men!" She winked at me, then checked her skinny gold watch. "I hope this doesn't take too long."

"What are you talking about?" I asked. "Lights? Food? I spent the whole time babysitting."

"Paris is so romantic," my mother said, and the linebacker turned to give her a smile.

"Romantic?" My mind played a slide show of my summer

in Paris: Nights lying as still as possible on a tiny twin bed, waiting for the ancient fan's breeze to sweep across my face. Borrowing the baby's diaper cream to treat my own heat rash. The time the Eastons left for the opera together and came home separately, an hour apart, both so drunk they were practically crawling, and so hungover the next morning that I had to take the baby on my day off. The man in Aix-en-Provence who had lifted his little daughter over a street planter so she could pee, and how she smiled hazily at passersby as it trickled down between her legs. The time Mrs. Easton threw a piece of expensive china at her husband's head and it flew straight out the window, only to hit a pigeon on the next rooftop and knock it flat dead. "Are you joking?"

"What girl wouldn't kill to be an au pair for the summer?" The linebacker turned around again, and my mother asked him, "Am I right?"

"Sure." He looked her up and down and turned to me. "Listen to your sister."

My mother giggled. "Sister! This is my daughter."

"No way," he said. "You can't be a day over twenty-five."

"Oh, you!" my mother said, and turned to me. "Every girl dreams of spending the summer in Paris. Being an au pair will look so great on your college applications, all that responsibility and international experience!"

"Mother. I was not an au pair! For one thing, au pairs get paid. I was not paid." The baggage carousel grumbled to life, and the first bag tumbled down the ramp.

"They fed you. And housed you! In Paris!"

"What's your bag look like?" the linebacker asked.

"In exchange for slave labor," I said. "It was in their best interest to keep me alive so I could continue to do everything for them."

The linebacker said, "This one's mine," and scooped up one of those gigantic hockey bags, slinging it across his shoulders.

My mother rolled her eyes at me, and winked at the linebacker. "Teenagers."

"For another thing," I said, "au pairs are supposed to have days off. Like, regularly! Every time I tried to take a day off, Mrs. Easton would cry and beg me to take the baby 'just this one time.'"

"Oh, there's your bag!" My mother pointed, and the linebacker grabbed it and swung it off the carousel in one clean motion.

"Where are you parked?" he asked my mother. "I could carry this out for you."

She put up a token fight but quickly demurred when he insisted. "And they say chivalry is dead!"

He followed her out of the terminal, trotting like a puppy. I thought about calling Lacey or Nikki to pick me up and hiding in a bathroom until they came and rescued me. But my cell phone was still at home in Willow Grove, probably still resting in the top drawer of my mother's dresser, where she put everything she took away from us, and I was so tired I just wanted to go home, crawl into my bed, and sleep until everything melted away and I could wake up brand-new at the beginning of my senior year and shake the whole summer off like a long bad dream.

So I followed her, as I'd done my entire life. Nothing, really, had changed.

chapter TWO

My mother talked the whole way home. I tuned in and out, hearing snippets of gossip and updates about her job and something about someone's cat, but mostly I was looking out the window, trying to see every single leaf on every single tree before we passed it. Paris had been beautiful at times, like one night when I'd managed to slip away from the stuffy apartment and walk through the streets alone and ended up on this stone bridge and everything was quiet and I could see the Eiffel Tower lit up in the distance. But I'd missed Iowa, more than I'd even realized: green as far as you can see, the horizon stretching all the way to the sky without a single building interrupting it.

"And I thought we could do our annual shopping trip to Chicago this weekend, even though I'm sure you picked up tons of great clothes in Paris, because I want to take you over to campus and show you the sorority house and maybe see if we can introduce you to some nice girls who might have some insights about the application process. . . ."

We drove across the bridge just outside of town, broad concrete rather than narrow stone, but the river beneath us was wide and clean and sparkling in the August sun. After the bridge it was just another two miles into Willow Grove, first the chain stores on the outskirts and then the cute little shops around the central park downtown.

". . . started thinking about what you're going to wear on the first day of school? Because you really need to make a strong impression after what happened last spring. But, of course, if you remind everyone you spent the summer in Paris, that should help people forget—"

"We have a stoplight now?" I asked.

My mother glanced up at the red light over the intersection, seeming surprised. "Yes, I suppose they did just install that in June. I'm so used to it already!"

"Why didn't you tell me?"

She laughed. "It's just a stoplight, sweetheart."

I slouched in my seat. "It would have been nice to know, that's all."

The light turned green and we rolled forward, heading down Main Street. The houses were a familiar assortment of one-story ranches, small square boxes, cute bungalows, and nice big Victorians, but my eyes were peeled for any other changes my mother had failed to mention: new siding on this house, a stump on that corner where there used to be a tall oak tree. When we finally pulled into our own driveway, I stiffened. "You painted the front door."

"Don't you love it? I know red is such a bold choice, but Stella said it would improve our curb appeal, and as usual she was right!"

"I think it sucks." I got out of the car and slammed the door behind me, leaving my bags in the trunk for my mother to deal with.

I felt more human after a much-needed nap, shower, and luxuriously long primping session in preparation for the Austins' barbeque. I wouldn't make the same mistake twice in one day: the first time Jake saw me would be perfect. The sounds of my mother and sister yelling at each other floated upstairs, and I listened idly as I pumiced my feet. While I was gone, Miranda had gotten her driver's license, cashed in four years of babysitting money for a beater Honda, dyed her hair burgundy, and changed her name to "Mirror." I'd left behind a gangly, geeky freshman and came back to find an angry alternateen.

The yelling seemed to wear itself out with a few last slammed doors, and I gave myself a final appraisal in the mirror. My hair was darker than it had been in years, thanks to a summer away from my colorist, but it was kind of working. I pursed my lips thoughtfully. I might pull off the Audrey transformation thing yet.

My mother seemed relieved to see me looking more like myself. "Isn't that so much better, honey?"

"I love my shower," I said. "I love my bed and my closet and my window, but mostly I love my shower."

My sister stood in the corner, scowling. "What's so great about it?"

"Water pressure is a beautiful thing, Miranda, my dear. In Paris—"

"My name is Mirror." Her voice was a shard of glass. "Can I go now? I'm picking up Jeremy, and the movie starts at six."

"You know, honey," my mother said, ignoring her, "if you'd just take a little rejuvenating spritzer on the plane with you, like I suggested, your skin wouldn't look so sallow after traveling."

I felt my shoulders sag. "I know that, Mother. But I didn't have—"

"Can I go?" my sister asked, interrupting me again. We had been on the same team as kids, us against Mom, until about middle school, when all the things our mother had nagged us about over the years—*stand up straight, you don't want to look cheap; don't frown, you'll get wrinkles; brush your hair, it looks like a rat's nest; no more cookies, you don't want to get fat; smile, you never know who might be falling in love with you!*—suddenly made sense to me. Seemed important. I wanted in on my mother's secrets. The triangle shifted its balance and I allied myself with our mother, leaving Miranda out in the distance, the lonely isosceles angle.

My mother sighed. "Fine. But I want you home by ten. And please say goodbye to Daddy before you go."

Miranda gave me a superior look. "Have fun at the Austin Freakshow."

"What does that mean?" I asked. I hadn't seen Jake since June. It was stupid, but I was nervous to see him again. What if things were weird? What if I didn't live up to his memory of me? Had I embarrassed myself in the letters I'd sent him? I'd filled up an entire notebook with letters to him and to Lacey, but I'd gotten only postcards and short notes in reply. But that was because they were busy—normal people didn't have time to write long letters anymore, not unless you were stuck all by yourself without a cell phone or email in a country where you didn't even speak the language.

"Like you don't know," my sister said. "Stella can't even move her face from all the botulism she gets injected in it—"

"It's called Botox," my mother interrupted. "And it's not cheap."

I had a brief pang of jealousy that Miranda had seen Jake all summer. Of course my mother would have dragged her over to the Austins' when Stella needed help with the latest wedding. Not that I imagined they were suddenly best friends—I doubted they'd even talked—but she got to be in the same room with him while I would have killed just to be in the same country.

"—and Jake's dad is always pulling weird macho head trips on Jake, challenging him to play H-O-R-S-E or whatever, putting him in headlocks, calling him a pussy if he doesn't want to go hunting with him," Miranda continued. "Major creepers."

"Whatever, Miranda. He's just messing around."

She shrugged. "Okay. And I'm sure he'll be just messing around when he ties some gay kid to the back of a truck and drags him down the highway."

"God! Exaggerate much?"

"Miranda!" my mother snapped. "The Austins are good people. If you can't say anything nice, don't say anything at all."

My sister rolled her eyes. "Sorry, Mommie Dearest." She spun lazily and headed up to her room, stomping each foot as she went.

"Well!" My mother flashed me a brilliant smile. "Don't mind her; she's going through a difficult phase!" She reached up to untuck a strand of hair from behind my ear and style it casually around my face. "Anyway, it's been hard for her, trying to follow in your footsteps. She looks up to you, Paige."

"She does?" I could smell my mother's perfume, lemony and light, and I had a sudden impulse to hug her.

"Of course she does." She finished pulling at my hair and stepped back, scrutinizing her work. "It can't be easy to follow her perfect older sister."

"I'm not perfect."

"You know what I mean." She glanced in the hall mirror, which hung above a faux-antique, faux-French writing desk, straightening first the collar of her shirt and then the mirror itself. "Stand up straight, honey; slouching adds five pounds."

My mother timed our arrival at the party so we weren't the first ones there, but we weren't the last, either. The long driveway was lined with cars, like beads on a necklace, and we had to walk a ways to get up to the front door. My heart pounded with a mix of anticipation and nerves. Automatically, I glanced at his bedroom window, but it was empty. From the front, the house looked nearly abandoned, save for the catering truck parked near the garage on the side of the house. Everyone would be gathered around the pool in back.

The Austins' house was on a small hill overlooking a golf course. The neighborhood was shaped like a saucer, with the houses perched around the rim and the golf course in the sunken middle. The homes all had huge yards bordering the course, and Jake's yard was the largest, dropping sharply down from the pool into a terraced retaining wall and then to a long, manicured green space that blended seamlessly into the fourteenth hole. Thick stands of trees on both sides blocked direct views of the neighbors, though on a nice day you could stand right at the edge of the terrace and peer around the curve of the course to see Lacey's house up by the eleventh. Nikki lived in an older, slightly dumpier development near the front entrance of the course. My mother had been scheming to move us out to this neighborhood since she first started working for Stella Austin, but sometimes I suspected she secretly loved our strange, sprawling Victorian in town.

Mrs. Austin greeted us at the door, kissing my mother on both cheeks and my father on the mouth. "Just give that to the bartender," she told him, gesturing to the bottle of wine my mother had spent twenty minutes agonizing over in the store. "Paige!" She kissed me on both cheeks. "How was Paris? Did you make it to the spa I suggested?"

"I didn't really have . . ."

But she had already turned to my mother. "Jacque, I'm so glad you followed my suggestion! Paige seems so mature now! And what girl wouldn't kill to be an au pair for the summer?"

My mother nodded. "Oh, I agree completely." She turned to my father and mimicked Mrs. Austin's tone. "Dear, why don't you take that back to the bartender?"

Mrs. Austin looked at me for a moment, appraising. "A summer in Paris," she said at last. "Oh, to be young again!"

"I know!" my mother agreed. "I would love to be an au pair! Free room and board, and the best part? You get to give the baby back at the end of the day!"

Mrs. Austin laughed and waved toward the back of the house. "Everyone's out by the pool, dear. Please remind Jake to reapply sunblock; I can't have him peeling in the church directory pictures next week."

As if I were already gone, Mrs. Austin grabbed my mother by the arm and dragged her toward the kitchen. "Now, about the McIntyre wedding. . . ."

Before stepping through the familiar glass doors into the Austins' backyard, I sweet-talked the bartender into a glass of pinot grigio, glancing around to be sure my father had already wandered off in search of Jake's dad. One thing I could say about the Eastons: they taught me how to appreciate fine wine. I got only one good sip, though, before Nikki screamed my name and hurled herself through the open glass doors, crushing me in a hug and spilling the rest of my wine in the process.

"Oh my God, Paige, how are you? When did you get back? Why didn't you call us? Look at your hair! Did you get it cut in Paris?"

"Hi, Nikki," I gasped, untangling myself from her hold. "I literally *just* got home."

"How was Paris? Was it so amazing? You are so lucky; I wish my mom would send me to Paris! Did you get this skirt there? I love it! And you look so skinny, you bitch!" She hugged me again.

I blinked. Nikki was the one who looked skinny, scary skinny. She must have lost fifteen pounds since I'd seen her last. Her legs weren't much thicker than my forearms, and that they could hold her up seemed a miracle of physics. "You've lost weight. . . ." I ventured.

She glanced down. "Whatever, I'm such a tub! I'm

starting a new diet next week, though. I've been so busy all summer; things have been so crazy! I've been working super hard on this thing . . ."

Behind her, Jake and Lacey appeared at the same time, coming around the corner from the side yard. His hand was on her back, but before I could even feel jealous, I realized why: she was walking with a cane. A cane! She leaned on it with every other step, like a World War II vet. My cheeks felt hot and the back of my throat cramped up. Why hadn't anyone told me about the cane?

They saw me at the same time. Jake crossed the flag-stones in two strides and swung me up in a hug. I wrapped my arms around his neck, closed my eyes, and concentrated on the scent I'd been attempting to imagine all summer long. He was taller than I remembered, and thicker, and so much more real. When the scent of his skin threatened to overwhelm all my senses, I pulled back, looking at him, drinking in every cadence of texture and light in his face, every detail. My Jake. He smiled indulgently at my scrutiny.

All summer I'd rehearsed what I would say to him when I finally saw him. I would say all the things that I couldn't write in a letter, all the things that sounded cheesy on paper but that would sound just right with my voice in his ear, his hands around my waist. I would tell him how important he was to me and how hard it was to fall asleep at night without him on the other end of my phone, his breath growing steadier as he fell asleep with me, cradled in the palm of my hand. But now, confronted with the real Jake, I couldn't think of a single sentence. "Hi," I said finally.

"Hi yourself."

Lacey reached us a moment later, leaning on the cane. If I was at a loss for words with Jake, I was utterly speechless when it came to Lacey. I wanted desperately to ask her what had happened. But I had a bad feeling that I already knew—and the fact that nobody had thought to mention this to me made me quake inside.

With no other option, I went with the time-honored tradition of pretending nothing was wrong. "Lacey! It's so good to see you!" I wrapped my arms around her gingerly. "I missed you so much!" She felt fragile in my arms, even more than skinny Nikki, as if her bones were made of something finer than the rest of ours.

"Thanks." She reached up and pulled at the tiny gold cross on her necklace, sliding it up and down the thin chain.

"You look really great," I said.

"Yeah, right." Her mouth tucked itself into a flower of disapproval, and I shrank a little inside. The look had been directed at others hundreds of times; at me, almost never.

We were all quiet for a moment, staring just past one another, until Jake suggested we girls go sit by the pool and offered to bring us drinks. Lacey flashed him a grateful smile, brilliant in comparison to the frown I'd earned. Nikki clapped her hands. "Yay! Just like old times! Girl talk!" She skipped over to Lacey, wrapped a bony arm around Lacey's waist, and managed to contain her bounciness all the way to the far end of the pool. Left alone, I squeezed my eyes shut and took two deep breaths before fixing a giant smile to my face and following them.

My parents would be the last to leave the Austins'; my mother would be hostessing alongside Stella until the end. She was one of the primary planners for Jake's mom's business, Stella Austin Events. They did weddings and graduations and fiftieth anniversary parties and bar mitzvahs and any other event the residents of central Iowa could dream up for themselves. She'd been waiting for a promotion to partner for years, but something always came up that got in the way: an audit, a slow year, a bad wedding. "You know how the business world is," she'd tell us over dinner, her eyes glistening in the light from the candles she lit. "The rat race and all. What really matters is the dreams I can help make come true."

I claimed jet lag around ten, angling for a ride home from Jake so we would have some time together at last. All evening he'd been solicitous to Lacey, offering to bring drinks and then a blanket from the house after the sun went down. He was a good guy, I told myself, and I was awful for wishing that he weren't quite so devoted to poor, crippled Lacey. But I did.

I'd hoped to use the ride home to talk to Jake, find out what he'd been up to over the summer—his letters had been vague—and get him to explain what, exactly, was wrong with Lacey, but I'd underestimated the impact his driving would have on me. It was the first time I'd ridden with anyone but my mom since last spring, and though I hadn't anticipated it, I was scared. There were so many things that could go wrong: a moment's distraction, a fraction of an inch in the wrong direction, a half pound of pressure on the accelerator instead of the brake. I didn't breathe until he pulled his silver car into my dark driveway.

We were quiet for a moment, and he reached forward to turn up the music. "I love this song."

Even through the wide windshield, the Iowa stars were sharply defined against the low black sky. The moon hung in a crescent above the neighbor's garage. I took a breath. "Jake?"

"Yeah?" He put his hand on my knee, rubbing his thumb against my bare skin. I shivered.

"Is Lacey—I mean, is she okay? I mean, obviously not, but . . ."

Jake's thumb slowed against my leg. "Well," he said. "She had a rough summer."

I sighed. "Who didn't?"

He shot me a look and I immediately felt like a jerk. "She was the last to get out of the hospital, and by then you were long gone. I think it was hard on her that you left without saying goodbye."

"I didn't have a chance to! I—"

"Okay, but it still hurt, babe." He didn't look at me, and

I wondered if he was talking only about Lacey. "The fact that you got to go to Paris—"

"Got? My mother dumped me on the Eastons so she could do damage control. I spent the whole summer working my ass off taking care of their disgusting baby. At least Lacey got to hang out by the pool."

"Paige, Lacey had to have, like, seven hours of surgery on her leg, and for a while they were worried that she might lose it. They didn't even know if she would walk again! She was in physical therapy all summer."

Ugh, poor Lace. Why hadn't anyone said anything in their letters?

"Plus, she was grounded the whole summer. Her parents were really freaked out."

Nikki had been the one driving, but Lacey's parents must have freaked out for the same reason my parents did: Thou shalt not mar thy parents' reputations. "Well, at least she wasn't bound, gagged, thrown in a trunk, and driven across state lines in the middle of the night."

He looked at me. "Bound and gagged?"

"Basically."

I waited for Jake to laugh, or at least smile. He didn't.

"You know what I mean!" I exclaimed. "I didn't even get to say goodbye to anyone! Not even you! I had to spend the whole summer with crazy people! You don't even know how much I wished I could trade places with Lacey or Nikki or you or anyone!"

He shrugged. "I know, babe, but all Lacey sees is that she got crippled and you got to go to Paris."

Crippled? Wasn't that a little melodramatic? I bit my lip and looked out the window. It was my first night back, and I didn't want to fight. Why were we talking about Lacey anyway? I wanted to talk about us. Or better, not talk. The tip of the crescent moon dipped behind the garage roof, and I wondered how long we'd been sitting here — and how long it would be until he kissed me. From the moment I'd settled myself into the plane bound for Paris, the only thing I'd wanted was to get back to Jake. Every night in Europe I dreamed that I was next to him, and every morning I kept my eyes closed an extra moment, trying to capture the feel of his fingers on my skin, the weight of his arm across my chest.

Now here we were, alone under a blanket of dappled shadows created by the streetlights shining through the trees. Half turning in the plush seat, I looked at Jake's face. Shadows fell across the hollows of his eyes and throat, but I could still see his smile. "Hi," I said quietly.

"Hi yourself," he said. There was a long second where we both just looked at each other. Then he reached across the gearshift and pulled me toward him, his wide hand on my back. "Come here."

It had been twelve weeks, but the minute he kissed me it was like no time had passed: his slightly chapped lips against mine, his tongue wandering across my bottom lip and the tips of my teeth, his fingers winding through my hair. I smiled into the kiss, loving him as much in that moment as I ever had. "Hey, princess," he whispered.

"Hey," I whispered back. Even with my eyes closed, I could sense the speckled shadows fall across my face as I kissed him.

His hand slid under my shirt and I shivered. His kisses trailed down my neck, along the line of my jaw, and his hands fumbled with the clasp of my bra. I pulled back slightly, waking as though from a trance. "Hey," I murmured, reaching for his hand. "A little fast. . . ."

He pressed his mouth against the side of my face, half kissing, half whispering. "We've gone farther than this before."

"Yeah," I said, waking up a little more fully. "But not since last spring. Can we just take it slow?"

Jake buried his face in my shoulder and traced his lips across the hint of skin at the top of my collar. "I missed you so much, Paige."

"I missed you, too, Jake." For a scary second, the words didn't sound true, so I repeated them until they did. "I missed you so much."

chapter THREE

School started the day after Labor Day, and it was cold. I stood at the mirror in the bathroom I shared with my sister, carefully wiping the mascara wand on the inside of the tube so it wouldn't clump. Lacey and Nikki and I were planning to meet outside the school, just as we always did, to make our grand entrance into senior year together. That is, Nikki and I were planning to—I hadn't actually talked to Lacey, but I was sure she would join us. Walking in together on the first day was a tradition going back to middle school. Jake's words played in my head. *She got crippled and you got to go to Paris.* His voice was the bass line beneath Lacey's treble, laughing as Nikki told a story about their summer. *Oh, Paige doesn't care about that. She was in Paris.*

The mascara wand slipped and stabbed me under the eye. I sighed, reaching for a tissue. I actually hadn't talked to Lacey at all since the barbeque, but it had been only a week, and I'd been gone for most of it, in Chicago with my mother for our annual girls' shopping trip and then fishing at Lake McBride with my father. When I was little, we used to go on family trips all the time, fishing or hiking or canoeing, but as I got older, my social life and his job both began to take more and more time, until we rarely saw each other at all. I agreed to fish with him before school started because I had a strange feeling that this might be my last chance. And anyway, I like my dad, and spending the day out on the boat was peaceful—and great for my tan. Plus, I caught a fish.

As soon as school got started, everything would be back to normal. I was sure of it. I capped the mascara, dropped it into a drawer, and gave myself one last layer of lip gloss before leaving the bathroom. It was 7:30, and I hadn't even heard Miranda yet. I wondered if she was still asleep. In my bedroom behind me, the TV chattered on about the unusual weather. "This," the cheery weatherman informed me, "is the coldest it has ever been on this day in September, as long as the University of Iowa has been keeping track! Brrrr! So all you gardeners better bring in your begonias, and for all you kids getting ready for your first day of school today . . . take a jacket!"

"Ha," I said, clicking him off and heading out the door. But then I paused and turned back, reaching in my closet for a sweater. School didn't start until 8:05, but I was supposed to meet Lacey and Nikki in the parking lot at 7:40. My mother stopped me on my way to the front door. "Is that what you're wearing, Paige?"

I glanced down at my outfit, a short white skirt with a pale-yellow top and bright-orange heels. The girls and I were coordinating but not matching for the first day back. "Does it look bad?"

She tilted her head. "I don't know. I can't see it under that granny sweater."

We'd had an uneasy truce since I'd been back: if I didn't mention my awful summer, she wouldn't bring up my awful spring. Instead, she'd put all her energy into helping me get ready for my senior year, when I'd be homecoming queen, just like she'd been, clear evidence of our family's success. I'd sit atop the parade float and wave away any damage to our reputation with a swoop of my scepter.

"I just bought this sweater," I said. Outside the front window, the leaves of the ash tree shivered in the early morning air.

"I bought it," she corrected, "and it's supposed to go with that striped V-neck, not with this." She softened. "Honey, you have only one chance to make a first impression, and Lacey and Nikki won't be wearing sweaters. We've been planning this year for a long time." She reached over and whisked a minuscule speck of dust from my shoulder.

I brushed at my sweater self-consciously. "It's freezing out, Mom."

"I know, sweetheart, but people will be looking to you to set an example for the rest of the school. The way people see you today will stay in their minds all the way through to homecoming. And after last spring, you can't afford to have a single hair out of place." So much for the tacit agreement. Automatically, she glanced at herself in the hall mirror, lightly touching the tip of her finger to the corner of her lip to fix some tiny imperfection in her lipstick. "Anyway," she said brightly, "you won't be outside; you'll be inside!"

"What if I take it off when I get to school?"

There was a clatter on the stairs behind us, and my mother's eyes jumped to my sister's feet stomping down the stairs. Her steel-toe boots came first, followed by long black corduroy pants, a merlot-colored tank top, and a black hoodie. Before my mother could say anything, Miranda said, "Let me guess: 'Is that what you're wearing? All that black?'"

My mother pursed her lips. "Miranda—"

"It's Mirror," she said, and pushed past me into the chilly morning. "Better hurry up, *princess.*"

"So," my mother said, turning back to me. "You're not really going to wear the sweater?"

Twenty minutes later, I stood in the parking lot, rubbing my bare arms to stay warm. Where were they? I'd been standing there since 7:40, but it was five to eight and people were giving me strange looks as they hurried past me toward the school. Most of them were wearing sweaters *and* jackets.

"I'm sorry, I'm sorry, I'm sorry!" Nikki came hurtling out of nowhere and plowed into me, nearly knocking me over. Had she always been this clumsy? I couldn't remember. "You look so great, Paige! I'm sorry I'm late!"

"Where's Lacey?" I asked.

Nikki bit her lip. "She's inside already. She didn't want to do the grand entrance thing with the cane."

"I've been standing here for like fifteen minutes already and I am freezing, and Lacey was inside the whole time?"

Nikki grabbed my arm. "I know. I'm sorry! But Lacey was just so . . . She thought people would laugh at her, so I helped her. . . ."

I pulled out of her grasp and started walking toward the school. "Great. Thanks for letting me know, you guys. So much for our grand entrance."

"Wait, Paige!" There was a clopping behind me, and Nikki caught up, crooking her elbow through mine. "It's not too late, see?" She matched her steps to mine and we headed for the front doors, arm in arm. "Welcome to senior year, bitches!" she screamed. A few people glanced at us, but mostly the crowd flowed around us, heading for lockers and classrooms and the beginning of a new year. So much for a first impression.

• • •

Later that day, I sat in the first student council meeting of the year, listening to Lacey give orders. Even with a cane, she still had the power to make things happen. "You guys," she said seriously, addressing a table full of the school's most well-connected and influential kids—the student council social events committee. "Homecoming is the senior class's chance to give back to this school. WGHS has given us so many opportunities, and we can finally give something back, by helping to keep our school spirit high. It's our job to make this year the best year ever." Around the table, heads nodded.

"That is so true, Lacey," said Geneva Barrington, the junior class president. "You guys are a really great class, and what you do for homecoming this year is really going to raise the bar for our class next year."

I rolled my eyes. Lacey wouldn't stand for such blatant ass kissing. She herself was the master of the subtle apple-polish, and Geneva would never gain the favor she craved if she kept sucking up so obviously. For God's sake, the girl had made a giant bedsheet-size sign for Lacey and hung it in the room where the student council met. WELCOME BACK, LACEY! AN AMERICAN HEROIN!

When we'd walked into the room, I had immediately looked at Lacey, waiting for her to double over in laughter and possibly make a Kurt Cobain joke. Instead, she'd clasped her hands to her heart and then waved at her eyes, Miss America–style, so her mascara wouldn't run with her tears. I'd been shocked speechless.

And now, Lacey was just encouraging her. "Good point, Geneva." She tugged at her necklace, swinging the tiny cross along the chain.

"Also," Geneva said, "can I just take a moment to say that we all really admire your bravery and courage over the last few months? You have been such an inspiration to all of us. And you're a true model for the whole school." She looked around the room. "Can we get a round of applause for Lacey Lane?"

Oh, Jesus.

I waited for a cheesy Slow Clap, but thankfully everyone started to clap at a reasonable tempo. "Thank you all so much," Lacey said, biting her bottom lip. "It really means a lot."

"We love you, Lacey!" another junior cried.

Lacey gave her a smile, and then she turned serious. "Seniors, we have to remember that not only do we have a legacy to create, but we're also the role models for hundreds of students in the junior, sophomore, and freshman classes. We have a duty to them to make this the best homecoming Willow Grove High School has ever seen." More nods, more murmurs of approval. "Okay, y'all, who's with me?"

As always: everyone.

After the meeting I hurried to catch up with her. "Lacey," I said, raising my voice as much as I dared in the crowded hallway (*Princesses never yell, Paige*).

She was surrounded by a gaggle of girls, sophomores who adored her and juniors who hoped to become her. "Pajama Day is kind of played out, don't you think?" someone was asking. "What about Toga Day?"

I tried again. "Lacey."

"No," someone else said. "Dr. Coulter said no togas."

"Why don't y'all keep track of all your ideas, and we'll vote on them at our next meeting," Lacey suggested.

The crowd murmured its agreement and began to disperse, still discussing Spirit Week. "We should definitely do a day where we make the freshmen dress like babies! That would be so awesome!"

"What do babies have to do with school spirit?"

"What do togas?"

"Hey, Lacey," I said, still a few steps behind her. You'd think it wouldn't be hard to catch a girl with a cane, but she was surrounded by devoted worker bees and impossible to touch.

"Hey babe." Jake appeared out of nowhere, winding his arm around my waist and pulling me away.

"Hey," I said absently, looking back at Lacey, who tossed her hair and laughed before disappearing into her fifth-period class. "Do you think she's mad at me?" I asked. "She was kind of ignoring me back there."

Jake shrugged. "She has a lot on her mind right now. The whole student council thing—and organizing homecoming—it's a big deal."

"I guess."

"Not to mention her handicap."

"She has a *limp*," I said, before I could stop myself.

Jake gave me his Caring, Serious Face. "Put yourself in Lacey's shoes, Paige."

I looked down. "These *are* Lacey's shoes."

He frowned. "You know what I mean. She had a hard summer."

"And I didn't? I spent twelve weeks with a disgusting baby barfing on me every five minutes."

"In France."

"In a tiny, dark, hot apartment with no cell phone or Internet."

"In France," Jake said again.

"Sometimes the baby pooped all the way up its back."

"In France."

"Yes! In France! Jesus!" A kid in a long black trench coat and combat boots gave me a weird look as he walked past, and I realized I was shouting. "Jesus," I said again, more quietly.

"Well?" Jake asked. "That's all I'm saying. Lacey had a hard summer, babe. Go easy on her."

I chewed on my bottom lip, trying to keep myself from saying more. If I kept pushing the issue, he'd keep defending her, and we'd end up fighting about nothing. Ignoring my frown, he leaned in and kissed me, crushing my teeth into my lip, and then strolled off down the hall toward the field house.

• • •

It was cold all week. "Global warming's really a misnomer," our physics teacher, Mr. Berna, told us on Thursday, collecting the first real homework assignment of the year. "They should really call it 'global temperature change' to be accurate."

"At this rate, we're going to be under three feet of snow by homecoming," Lacey said at lunch. She perched on the edge of the picnic table, her bad leg stretched straight ahead of her, her bare arms folded inside the tent of Randy's jacket.

"I hope not!" Nikki said, biting the head off a baby carrot. Her new diet involved only eating things that were orange. "I wouldn't want to wear a coat over my dress on the float. Or mittens."

I laughed. "Mittens?"

"Gloves," Lacey said. "You'd wear gloves. And you could always wear someone's letter jacket." She adjusted the one around her shoulders. "People have done that before."

"Snow might affect the game." Chris Jensen frowned, staring up at the sky as if he could see what the weather would be like a month from now.

Randy ripped cheerfully into one of three cheeseburgers sitting on the tray in front of him. "We could be under ten feet and still kick Newton's ass."

"They've never beat us," Jake agreed. "So you ladies just need to worry about looking gorgeous, and we'll bring the victory."

"Yeah," Chris said. "Just practice that wave. How does it go? Elbow, wrist . . . elbow?"

"Elbow, elbow, wrist wrist wrist," Nikki said. She grabbed his meaty hand and moved it back and forth like a doll's hand, giggling.

Lacey raised an eyebrow at Jake. "Worry? Paige and I have been working on this since middle school, right?" She flashed such an easy smile at me that I wondered if I'd imagined her distance since my return. I smiled back.

"It's true."

Randy stopped waving. "I would worry about tripping in those heely things you have to wear."

"You mean high heels?" Lacey rolled her eyes.

Nikki patted him on the arm. "A true princess never worries."

"Guess you're not cut out to be a princess, dude." Jake elbowed him, and Randy immediately threw him into a headlock. A moment later, they were off the picnic table and wrestling in the grass, locked together like elk.

Lacey said, "Okay, you're both very studly! We get it!" She laughed. "Men!" I tried to catch her eye, share another smile, but she was gazing off across the courtyard.

Nikki looked serious as she popped open an Orange Crush. "It would be harder to be pretty with mittens."

"You'll be fine," I told her.

"Hey!" she said, looking up. "Lacey!"

"Yes?"

"I just remembered that you forgot to mention DIEDD at the student council meeting!"

"Oh, sorry," Lacey said, sounding anything but. "Next time, okay?"

"What's DIEDD?" I asked.

"It's a group to raise awareness about drinking and driving," Nikki said. "I spent the whole summer working on it. After . . . you know."

After last spring. After the first cracks that split into canyons between us, sending me spinning across the ocean, Nikki down the Crazy Diet Rabbit Hole, and Lacey into the Land of Crippled Martyrdom. "DIEDD?"

Nikki nodded. "It stands for Don't let frIEnds Drive Drunk."

"D . . . LF . . . DD," I said, sounding it out.

"The IE comes from friends," Nikki said.

Jake covered his mouth with a hand, turning away and coughing. Lacey tugged on her necklace, staring off into space. "Um," I said. "That's not really how acronyms work."

"There's a double meaning," Nikki explained. "Because it stands for Don't let frIEnds Drive Drunk, but it spells DIEDD, because if you drive drunk, you could have DIED. Like we could have DIED."

It was still ridiculous, but I no longer felt like laughing. "Oh. A double meaning. Yeah, I get it now."

"It's really important," Nikki said. "Lacey, don't forget to remind me to remember it at the next meeting, okay?"

Lacey stood, grabbing her half-eaten apple. "The bell's about to ring."

"Laceeeeeeey . . ."

She sighed. "Fine! But I'm not explaining your acronym."

chapter FOUR

By the second week of school, Jake and I had a routine. Every day, he was there when the bell rang, waiting to walk me to the English hallway. Every day, he'd wind his arm through mine and steer me through the crowded hallways, waving and calling to his friends as we walked. And every day, Jake's friends waited until the last possible minute to walk into the classroom, preferring instead to stand outside and harass people.

Chris Jensen saw me and called, "Ten! Definitely a ten!"

Jake pretended to misjudge the distance and walked into Randy, catching him with an elbow. "Oh sorry, dude, didn't see you there!"

I rolled my eyes. "I'm so flattered." The halls opened up around us as people wandered into classrooms, calling back over their shoulders, giggling, sighing. A gross goth guy pushed a skinny, pale girl up against the cold concrete brick, stealing one last black-lipstick kiss before the bell rang.

Brian Sorenson turned to scold Chris. "Paige is an eleven, at least!"

"Thanks," I said flatly. Sometimes I got tired of putting up with Jake's friends, but I knew I needed to keep their favor if I wanted to be on homecoming court at all, much less become queen. I kissed Jake goodbye and walked to take my seat. I wasn't even supposed to be in this class. I had planned to take film appreciation as my elective, but Jake and his boys heard that creative writing was the easiest A and talked me into switching. So I did, reluctantly, only to find that over the summer Lacey had talked Jake into switching out of creative writing to be in class with her — in film appreciation!

"She was so nervous about taking it alone," Jake explained after I'd sat through an entire class without him. "She didn't know how people would react to her, you know, now. She was worried they might make fun of her."

"So you ditched me?" I pulled on a strand of my hair, wrapping it around my finger. Over at our usual table, Lacey was laughing and threatening to hit Chris with her cane.

"Babe," Jake said, "I knew you'd be fine on your own." He kissed me on the nose and I gritted my teeth. "You're such a strong woman, you don't need me."

"But Lacey does?"

"She would do the same for you or I if our places were switched."

"You or me," I muttered.

"What?"

"Nothing."

He frowned. "Are you mad? Don't be mad."

"We should have just signed up for film appreciation in the first place. I don't know why I listened to you." I had already tried to switch back to film appreciation, but the guidance counselor wouldn't let me. Apparently, it was a very popular class. As was creative writing, she reminded me. I was lucky to get in at all, she said, but she could always switch me into another elective if I wanted: business math, or ag.

"Because creative writing is easier," Jake explained patiently. "That should make you feel better! I'll be busting my ass while you coast through."

"Watching movies," I said, but dropped it. I already felt like Jake and I were fighting all the time. I didn't need to add to it.

And that is why I was now wasting seventh period watching Mrs. Mueller chatter and flirt with the football players when I could have been slouched in the back of film appreciation, napping to the sound track of *Citizen Kane*.

Behind me, Randy whistled. "Now there's a ten." The boys around him erupted in laughter as a tall freshman hurried into the classroom. He ignored them, keeping his gaze on the girl he always sat with, as if he were so intent on talking to her that he didn't even notice the guys hassling him. At the base of his hairline and just before his ears, though, his skin turned slightly pink, giving him away.

"You wanna come to our kegger, Freshman?" Chris asked loudly, laughing before he even finished the question, as if the idea of the Freshman coming to the kegger was just too, too hilarious.

Randy drawled lazily, "Dude, he can't come. He probably has a date with his boyfriend." More snickers.

The class was a joke. Every day, Mrs. Mueller fluttered her hands as Randy and the guys did whatever they wanted. According to Nikki, all they'd done so far in film was watch some black-and-white movie where soldiers stabbed people with bayonets, and a bunch of Ku Klux Klan members galloped around on horses. All Nikki could think as she watched it was, *What if a KKK guy rode under a tree with low branches? Wasn't he worried he'd lose his hood?* Other than that, she said, it was pretty boring.

Still, it sounded better than creative writing. In a week of class, we had spent an entire day listening to Mrs. Mueller explain what a journal is and why we should keep one, read and discussed a poem called "Theme for English B," and watched *Dead Poets Society*. Literally, we spent three entire class days watching Robin Williams yell "Carpe diem!" while in the back of the room Randy and Brian snickered about the faggy kid who wants to play Puck. Maybe film class would have been equally lame, but at least I would have been with Jake.

The Freshman was becoming a daily target of Jake's friends' teasing. He hunched over his notebook with an air of extreme concentration, attempting to convey the message, I assumed, that he was so engrossed in his writing that he didn't even hear the taunts of the jocks. His floppy brown hair fell across his eyes, and he brushed it away with an absent wave. I probably wouldn't have noticed him at all if Randy and Brian hadn't singled him out. We were on opposite ends of the social spectrum. I was a senior and he was a freshman. I was popular and he was an unknown. I was going to be a princess, and he was going to stay a nobody.

I sighed, watching the clock. A minute and a half before the bell would ring to start class. Only two weeks in and I'd already memorized the exact position of the second hand for each period's bell.

Behind me, Randy pretended to sneeze into his fist. "Faggot."

The Freshman's friend, a pretty Indian girl with thick black hair, whipped around in annoyance. "Why don't you go eat some more steroids, dickhead?" she snapped. "Another week or two and you'll grow out of your training bra."

Randy's face turned bright red and his nostrils flared. It was true that his man-boob problem was growing out of proportion, but we all knew better than to say anything to him about it. "Better watch your back, Tonto."

"Yeah," added Brian, "or you might get scalped!"

A look of amused disbelief moved across the girl's face. "I'm Indian, geniuses, not Native American."

Randy crossed his arms smugly. "Same thing."

"No, it's not. My family's from Chennai." She paused, waiting for a reaction she didn't get. "In *India*." She laughed. "You stupid asshole."

I knew her, I realized suddenly. Shanti Kale. I had a random memory of her punching Danny Abbot in the solar plexus during a flag football game in sixth grade. Her family had moved the next summer. In my memory, she looked like a little boy, with super-short hair and baggy clothes. She must have moved back over the summer; I was surprised I hadn't heard anything about it.

Randy's face turned bright red. "What did you just call me?" He slammed his meaty hands on his desk, but the ringing of the bell kept him from descending fully into one of his 'roid rages.

Mrs. Mueller bustled into the room, looking like a monstrous sparrow with her puffed-out chest and her beady little eyes. She stood behind her overly large podium and clapped her hands. "Class? Class . . ." Almost too short to see over the dais, she grabbed its wooden sides and pulled herself up on her tiptoes. "Class?"

Under the low murmur of "Chill out, man" repeating itself in the back of the room like a jock mantra, Randy's breathing quieted until he sounded less like an angry bull and more like an asthmatic pug. The whispering and giggling dulled to a low hum, and Mrs. Mueller chirruped in gratitude. "Thank you, class, thank you." She pushed her glasses up her shiny nose and checked her notes. "For your assignment today, class, I'd like you to pair off with each other—" Everyone started murmuring, securing their preferred partners. I saw Shanti give the Freshman a quick head nod.

"Okay," Mrs. Mueller said. "Listen first, okay? What you're going to do is, in partners, you're going to interview the other person, and then you're going to write some kind of creative introduction to them, okay? And then you're going to introduce your partner to the class, by reading your creative introduction. Does that sound good?"

People started to stand up, shoving desks around to be closer to their friends. I scanned the jocks in the back row, looking for an odd man out, but there was an even six.

"Hold on a moment!" Mrs. Mueller called. "Hold on one moment, everyone! I forgot one thing!" It got slightly quieter, and she announced, "I want you to count off by twelves!"

Everyone groaned. Count off? What were we, kindergartners? I bet I wouldn't be counting off in film appreciation. We did it dutifully, though, and of course we had to find our partner number. I was one. Across the room, I saw the Freshman holding one finger to his lips, as if shushing someone. Behind his finger, he was almost, but not quite, smiling. He raised an eyebrow at me, and I held up one finger. *One?* He shrugged and nodded.

I reached down and grabbed my bag, tucking a strand of hair behind my ear as I headed over to where the Freshman was half sitting on the edge of his desk. His friend—the girl, Shanti—had paired up with my sister's friend Jeremy Carpenter. They settled themselves on the floor near us, leaning against desks. Jeremy said something that made Shanti laugh. She swatted at him as if they were best friends.

"Hey," said the Freshman. "Paige, right?"

I stared at him curiously. His voice was different than I'd assumed it would be, deeper and far more confident. It was the voice of a radio announcer, an NPR reporter maybe, but not a freshman.

"That's me," I finally said.

"Ethan. Ethan James." He held out his hand and lowered his voice, speaking quickly. "Pleasure to meet you, ma'am, my pleasure."

"Thanks." I allowed my hand to be shaken, then looked around to see if anyone was looking. I'd gotten so used to being alone all summer, I still wasn't used to being home, where everything you said, and everyone you said it to, was noticed. "Well? Should we . . . ?"

"Yes, of course," he said. "Step into my office." He gestured to the desk facing his.

"Okay, everyone!" Mrs. Mueller called. "Remember, you're going to interview each other, and then write a creative presentation introducing that person to the class!"

Ethan leaned over his notebook like a cub reporter. "Okay, Miss Paige. I'm ready. Spill it all."

His cheeks showed a hint of shadow, suggesting that if left to their own devices, they'd sport a beard worthy of a coffeehouse rocker in no time. It made him look older than he was, and for a second I saw what he might look like in five or ten years, sitting in the back of some city council meeting with a notebook perched on one knee, a serious look in his dark eyes. If you could ignore the fact that he was a freshman, he was almost cute.

"What do you want to know?"

"The five Ws," he said. "I'll start with the easy ones: Who is Paige Sheridan? What lies beneath the surface? When are you most yourself? Where do you go when you need to get away? Why are you here?"

I shifted uncomfortably in the school-issue chair, determined to keep my face blank. "You forgot *How.*"

"Forgive me, miss. You're absolutely right." He smiled slightly and looked off behind me, speaking lowly. "The dame had class, I'll give her that. You couldn't slip a thing past that razor-sharp mind."

"Has anyone ever mentioned the fact that you're kind of strange?"

Ethan grinned. "Not a one. In fact, it comes as quite a shock. You've cut me to the quick."

"Okay," I said, tiring of his game and unable to resist showing off just a little. "To answer your questions: Who? You're looking at her. What? More than you'll ever know. When? I'm never not. Where? None of your business. And why? Because my boyfriend made me."

He raised an eyebrow. "Made you?"

I'd known it was the wrong thing to say the second before it came out of my mouth. Now I sounded like some pitiful girl whose boyfriend makes all her decisions for her, who can't go against him, who will end up in some crappy marriage where she has to show up at work telling stories about running into doors. And I was *so* not that girl. The idea that the Freshman would assume such a thing about me pissed me off.

"Nobody makes me do anything," I said coldly.

He held up his hands. "Whoa, I didn't say that—"

In the front of the room, Mrs. Mueller clapped her hands, cutting him off. "Fifteen minutes left, everyone, and then you'll present your partner to the class!"

"She took an entire fifty-minute period to explain what a journal is, but she's only giving us twenty minutes for this?" the Freshman asked, with a look that was part apology, part peace offering.

I decided to be charitable. "I know, right?"

He picked up his pen. "Children, this is a pen! Can anyone tell me what you use it for?"

"Seriously," I said.

Mrs. Mueller shrieked over the low chatter of the class;

in the distance, a thousand dogs probably started barking. "If you get stuck, ask about plans for next year! Are you going to college? Where are you applying?"

The Freshman propped his chin on his hand and crossed his legs. "What are your plans for next year? Are you going to college? Where are you applying?"

"I'm going to Northwestern, just like everyone else in my family."

"A legacy, hmm?" He nodded. "I thought about Northwestern, but during the tour this extremely haunted-looking dude grabbed my arm and told me that if I was at all interested in writing, I should stay far, far away, as they would"—he made finger quotes—"eat my soul."

"Weird." Across the room, I could hear Randy telling a story about turning a plastic flamingo into a bong.

"So," the Freshman said cheerfully, "good luck with that!"

"Thanks."

"You must get pretty good grades to get into Northwestern. Or is it one of those things where you can just sort of buy your way in?"

"Jesus," I said, surprised into giving him my full attention.

He shrugged. "Not that there's anything wrong with that, I suppose. Personally, I will be racking up the student loans. The good news is that once it's in your head, they can't come and take it back. It's not like the bank can repossess your brain." He feigned a worried look. "At least, I don't think they can. . . ."

"My grades are fine."

"Dude, it was the best thing ever. We called it the Pink Flaming-go. Get it? Like, flaming?"

"Flabongo," the Freshman muttered.

I looked at him. "What?"

"If you're going to build a bong out of a plastic flamingo, the proper name is Flabongo, not Pink Flaming-go," he said.

I shrugged. "Randy's not known for his great intellect."

Mrs. Mueller screeched, "Ten minutes, people!"

The Freshman snapped into action. "Okay! What did you do over the summer?"

I immediately felt defensive. Every time I said anything about the summer, Lacey rolled her eyes and changed the subject as quickly as possible. "Don't even get her started on Paris," she'd said yesterday at lunch, lounging back against the picnic table where we always gathered. As though my stories about Paris were so glamorous — and as though she'd completely forgotten that it was her fault I'd been exiled in the first place. Well, Nikki's fault, technically. But Lacey's fault, too, because if she hadn't been such a bitch about Prescott, the whole rest of the night would have been different. The whole rest of the summer would have been different.

For a second I thought about lying, about just making something up, but a tiny part of me wanted to dazzle the Freshman a little, to intimidate him. "Actually I was in Europe for most of the summer. Paris, mostly."

He whistled. "Fancy. Must be nice to be you."

I tucked a strand of hair behind my ear. "Whatever."

"How'd you score that?" he asked. "Wait, let me guess: you were on a Fulbright, analyzing cross-cultural movements of taxi-driving poets. Am I right?" There was a challenge in his voice.

"Actually, I didn't have a choice. I was exiled."

"Exiled? Wow, so you must be, what, an enemy of the state? Defending the people's right to assemble?" One of Jake's friends walked by and pretended to trip, kicking the Freshman in the process. A muscle in his jaw jumped. "No, don't tell me. It was an Evita thing. Forced to live in Paris away from your adoring crowds. *Don't Cry for Me, Willow Grove.* Am I right?"

"You don't know anything about me," I said.

Exile, n., expulsion from one's home by authoritative decree. My mother was the authoritative decree: judge, juror, and hangwoman. A week after school ended last spring — a week after the accident — my mother rolled me out of bed in the middle of the night and told me to get dressed. She'd packed her own LeSportsac luggage with my clothes and shoes, and she stood waiting in the doorway with passport and tickets in hand while I fumbled around in the dark for a sweatshirt and flip-flops. She hadn't said a single word to me since the night of the accident, and we drove in silence through the cool June darkness, five hours to Chicago, where she enlisted the help of an airport security man to walk me to my gate and make sure I got on my plane. I was barely awake, but I heard her describe me as a "troubled youth," and a "high flight risk." The guard nodded seriously, accepted the handful of bills my mother shoved at him, and trailed me through O'Hare like a sheepdog until my plane took off a few hours later.

I remember staring out the airplane window as the land disappeared beneath us and we flew into the sunrise. The clouds wisped past the windows, the early light reflected off the plane's wings, and my throat got tight with tears I wouldn't let myself cry. I hadn't even gotten to say goodbye. To anyone.

Suddenly, there were only five minutes before the bell, and the room was filled with the sound of shuffling papers and the heavy scratching of desks moving across the tiled floor. "Well—" Ethan said, but was interrupted by Mrs. Mueller yelling over the din. "We'll have to do our creative presentations tomorrow!"

"Later," I said, and hurried back to my own desk.

Randy and the guys wandered up to the front of the room, laughing and boasting. "What about that chick from Cedar Falls, dude? You could have banged her, if you weren't such a pussy."

"Students! I almost forgot! Students!" Mrs. Mueller called. "Boys and girls!"

The class quieted down a notch, staring at the clock, muscles tensed to leave the room the second the bell rang.

"Your assignment for this week is to go to a literary reading!" She grabbed a pile of flyers from her desk and started handing them out. "All the second-year students at the Iowa Writers' Workshop are giving readings this weekend, all over town! You have to find one to attend! That is your homework!"

Tyler raised his hand. "What if we can't make it?"

"Oh!" Mrs. Mueller said, sounding pleased with herself. "Well! Then you can choose a Shakespearian sonnet and write a three-page paper explaining its meaning and importance in the literary canon!"

The noise level rose again as the class started murmuring about how busy they were, it wasn't fair, this was supposed to be a blow-off class.

Randy crossed his arms. "Fuck that, dude, I'm not writing a paper."

"You shouldn't have said anything," I told Tyler. "She probably just made that assignment up right now."

"You should ask Paige's partner if he has a date yet," Randy said, punching Tyler in the hip.

Chris looked back at the Freshman and laughed. "Hell yeah. Did you have fun with Barbra, Paige?"

"Whatever," I said.

"Dude," Tyler said. "He was probably just using Paige to get close to Jake."

I glanced over at the Freshman, who probably considered himself to be so enlightened and high-minded and worldly and yet had no problem whatsoever immediately categorizing me as a stupid, spoiled ditz. Screw him, anyway. "Yeah, apparently the Spice Girls are getting back together with a new member," I said. "Fairy Spice."

The guys erupted in laughter. "Fairy Spice! That's awesome!"

From across the room, I thought I saw the Freshman wince, but his face went blank again so quickly I wondered if I had imagined it.

chapter FIVE

Thursday morning, I was running late thanks to my mother's morning inspection — as the weeks ticked down to the homecoming vote, she was ramping up her scrutiny of my outfits, hair, makeup, and posture — and by the time I got to our table, my usual place had been taken by some junior girl from student council. Next to her, Geneva sat in Lacey's spot. Our group had been gathering at the same tables every morning since sophomore year, to finish up homework, catch up on any gossip that might have occurred overnight, and delay the inevitable moment when we'd have to submit ourselves to yet another day of classes. Jake patted his lap and I perched on his knee, glaring at the juniors. Who did they think they were? "Someone should tell them not to turn the spray tan setting all the way to Oompa-Loompa," I muttered.

Jake followed my gaze and laughed. "Is someone cranky this morning?" He nibbled at my neck and I smiled in spite of myself. "Anyway, look at the bright side."

"What's that?" I asked suspiciously.

"If they get any oranger, Nikki will eat them, and you can have your seat back." He pretended to chomp down on my shoulder. I laughed and bit him on the arm, and soon we were fighting and laughing like idiots.

Geneva called, "Get a room, you two!"

Just to spite her, I kissed Jake more passionately than was probably appropriate in a public setting. He didn't seem to mind. "I really hate her," I said when I came up for air. "Why isn't Lacey keeping her in check? Where is she, anyway?"

Jake shrugged. "I think she had a rough night last night. Her mom—"

The bell rang, cutting him off. He stood abruptly and I slid off his lap. "What about her mom? Did you talk to her last night?"

All around us, people were yelling and laughing and shoving one another. "It's a long story, and I have to run. I'll tell you at lunch, okay?" He kissed me fast and hurried off toward the math wing. Sighing, I slung my bag over my shoulder and headed the other way.

My first-period class was a sleeper we called Contemptible American History. Mr. Silva wasn't at his desk when I walked in, and I surveyed the room for signs of what the period would hold. No TV, so we weren't watching a movie, but if we were lucky, Mr. Silva might get sidetracked by stories about his time in Vietnam, and the creepy kids who loved guns would keep asking him questions until he forgot all about his lesson plans, and the rest of us wouldn't have to listen at all.

The class was rowdy with gossip. "I heard she had a total breakdown, freaked out, screamed at Dr. Coulter, and stormed out!"

"No, my mom knows her doctor's sister, and she says it's a brain tumor."

"Dude, I heard it was, like, a broken uterus."

"You moron, you can't break your uterus."

I leaned across the aisle to Elizabeth Carr, a pretty girl who was in creative writing with me. "Who has a broken uterus?"

She laughed and adjusted her glasses. "Mrs. Mueller, I guess. I'm pretty sure you can't break your uterus, though."

"So . . . brain tumor? Nervous breakdown?"

Elizabeth shook her head. "All of the above? I really don't know."

"Huh." I leaned back in my chair. A sub was good. Maybe we'd watch more inspiring movies about people writing, and I could catch up on my sleep. I was exhausted. The night before seemed like a cruel extension of the summer, which I'd spent fitfully tossing on scratchy blankets and flipping my pillows, searching in vain for an inch of cool fabric against my sweaty face while Paris thrummed through the open windows and the baby cried in the next room and Mr. Easton tried in hushed tones to talk his wife out of throwing herself into the Seine. Sometimes in the afternoons, I'd wheel the baby's stroller over to the Jardin du Luxembourg and park her in the sun while I stretched out along a bench or on the grass to steal a few quick minutes of precious sleep. Those afternoons were the best part of my summer, until the day one of Mrs. Easton's expat friends, an obnoxious woman from Dallas who despite her best efforts would never pass for Parisian, found me dozing next to the peaceful baby and went into histrionics about how easy it would have been to steal the baby. I'd had an ankle hooked around the stroller, I tried to tell her, but she wouldn't listen. There wasn't much point in trying to convince her that Mrs. Easton would have been happier if the baby had disappeared.

Lacey didn't get to class until a minute after the bell rang, but Mr. Silva just looked at her cane and waved her in. She used the cane to shove people's backpacks aside, clearing a path for herself as she shuffled to her seat in front of mine. "Hey," I whispered, leaning forward. "Where were you this morning? Geneva was being all—"

She didn't turn around. "Class is about to start."

I fell back in my chair, heat flooding my cheeks as if I'd been slapped. A moment later, Mr. Silva cleared his throat and said, "June 25, 1950. Anyone? Did anyone do the reading?" I spent the rest of the period fighting to stay awake, and Lacey kept her back to me the whole time.

• • •

At lunch, Lacey was her usual bubbly self, chattering with the junior girls about homecoming plans and fundraisers and dates to the dance. I kept trying to catch her eye to ask her what was going on, why she'd been late this morning, what was the drama Jake had hinted at last night, but Lacey didn't allow a single break in the conversation until halfway through the period, when she abruptly grabbed her cane, said something about student council, and limped away. Jake was trading insults with Randy and Chris, and Nikki was nowhere to be found, so I spent the rest of the period sitting quietly in the middle of the chaos, utterly alone in the crowd.

When I walked into creative writing later that day, the principal was standing at the dais. "Good afternoon, Paige," he said. "Don't you look pretty today."

"Thanks, Dr. Coulter."

As more people trickled in, I noticed that he greeted Jake's friends by name, but didn't seem to know the names of the other students. "Hello there, Sandy," he said blithely to Shanti as she walked in. Hurrying past him, she made a face in Ethan's direction. When the bell rang, Dr. Coulter rubbed his hands together. "Students, I have good news and bad news. The bad news is that Mrs. Mueller is . . . ill."

"Does she have a brain tumor?" someone called.

Dr. Coulter ignored the comment. "She will likely be out for the rest of the semester."

Low voices rumbled through the room at this, giddy and

wondering. The whole semester? Not only would we not have to hear Mrs. Mueller's screechy voice until Christmas, but also we'd get a sub, thereby guaranteeing that we'd be doing no work for the rest of the term. Yes and yes.

Dr. Coulter cleared his throat. "The good news is that we have already found a substitute teacher to take her place. Students, I'd like to introduce you to your new teacher, Mr. Tremont. We're very lucky to have him here, as he is a part of the Writers' Workshop at the university. He will be filling in for Mrs. Mueller for the rest of the semester, until she gets back on her feet."

The room filled with whispers as this information was digested. The Iowa Writers' Workshop was one of the most prestigious writing programs in the whole country. Why would someone from that program want to sub at Willow Grove? People looked around, searching for the new teacher. Was he standing out in the hallway, awaiting his cue? I didn't think I could stand that degree of cheesiness.

But no, he was sitting in a student desk in the back corner of the room. He smiled and stood up. There were gasps and giggles from some of the girls. The new teacher was unquestionably handsome. Movie star handsome. Dressed in dark jeans and a black shirt, he was a whole different species compared to our other teachers. In the back of the room, Jake's friends muttered to themselves, and some of the lamer girls frantically scribbled notes back and forth.

Mr. Tremont looked around the room, still smiling agreeably. "Thanks for the introduction, Dr. Coulter."

The principal made his way to the door. "Okay, then. Well, good luck, and listen to your teacher, children."

I saw Shanti grin and roll her eyes at the Freshman. He grinned back.

Mr. Tremont clapped his hands together, just once. "Okay, folks, open up your notebooks and let's get started." He spoke with an easy confidence that was almost unheard-of in new teachers. I glanced across the room toward the Freshman, remembering the way he'd mocked Mrs. Mueller. Were we finally going to have a good teacher? He caught my look and raised his eyebrows, giving a little half nod, as if to say, I know!

Without waiting for us to comply, Mr. Tremont continued. "We're just going to warm up with a ten-minute free-write. Don't edit yourself, don't worry about how it sounds; nobody is going to read this but you." He fiddled with a black stopwatch. "Have you guys done this before?"

A girl in the back practically jumped out of her seat, stretching her hand to the ceiling. "No, Mr. Tremont! But it sounds like fun!"

Oh, my God. I tucked my chin into my shoulder to keep from laughing.

Mr. Tremont smiled, but said seriously, "If you're here because you think that writing will always be fun, you're in for a disappointment. Writing—real writing—is among the most difficult work you will ever face in your life. The irony is that the harder you work at it, the harder it gets."

"That doesn't even make sense," Randy burst out.

"If you're not scared while you're writing, you're not working hard enough," Mr. Tremont said. "You'll be afraid, but you have to keep going."

I felt a shiver race up my neck. It struck me that for the first time in our lives, a teacher was giving us neither the convenient version nor the watered-down textbook version of the truth.

"Sounds pretty gay, if you ask me," Tyler muttered. His friends rewarded him with laughter, but Mr. Tremont wasn't amused.

"Out." He pointed to the door.

"What?" Tyler asked.

"I didn't even do anything, man." He looked to his friends for confirmation, and they nodded.

"Yeah, he didn't do anything!"

Mr. Tremont said calmly, "If you're not going to take this class seriously, you may leave now. In fact, the only people who should stay are those who are prepared to work harder in this class than they do in any other." He waited.

Tyler looked like he was going to argue more, but then he shrugged. "Whatever, dude." He gathered his things and walked out the door.

More whispers from the back of the room. Mr. Tremont said, "Ten-minute timed writing. Start with *I remember*, and go from there. Keep your pen moving the whole time. If you get stuck, write *I remember* again, and follow your thoughts. Don't worry about staying on topic; just write whatever comes to you." He paused. "Any questions?"

A girl in the front row raised her hand. "What should we write about?"

"Just write whatever comes into your head," Mr. Tremont said. "Don't censor yourself. You can write whatever you want to. Just keep going. The point of freewriting is to write fast enough to get past the little voice in your head that says, 'Don't write that, it's stupid!' or 'That makes no sense!' You're trying to outrun your editor, because that's how you get to the good stuff, the moments of truth. If you get stuck, and *I remember* doesn't work, try *I see, I wish, I don't remember* . . . Whatever comes into your head, write it."

"Even swear words?" someone asked.

He grinned. "It's your writing, you guys. Follow it wherever it takes you. All you need to do is tell your truth. Get it? Everyone with me here?"

A few people nodded.

"Ready . . ." Mr. Tremont said. "Write."

I put my pen to the page, hesitantly. *I remember* . . .

"Don't think too hard," Mr. Tremont said. "Just write."

I remember . . .

I remember Lacey. I remember Lacey in seventh grade, the first time we made brownies together. I remember turning up the radio in her kitchen, singing along to the Top 40 station, screaming when our favorite song came on. I remember the day at lunch in middle school when Tyler Adams climbed up the big oak tree to get the football they'd thrown up there, and he got stuck coming back down. I remember how the janitor had to get the ladder to get him down, and how we laughed, Lacey and I, sitting against the sunny brick wall at the corner of the playground, laughing and laughing until tears ran down our cheeks and our mascara ran in black trails down our faces. I remember how we ran into the girls' bathroom to fix it and saw Morgan Ellington in there with tweezers, trying to pull a hair out of her chin, and how we looked at each other with giant eyes and squeezed together lips and ran right back out until we could collapse by the pop machines outside the gym, laughing and laughing until we could hardly walk back to class when lunch was over.

I remember . . . I remember her standing over me with that look on her face like she knew she had me good and she wasn't going to drop it. When did she stop forgiving people their mistakes? We used to tell each other every secret, but one day secrets turned into weapons and now we brandish them back and forth to keep each other in check, walking along a perfect straight line, daring one another to fall.

The stopwatch beeped loudly, and I jumped. "Okay, stop," Mr. Tremont said. He was sitting with a yellow legal pad at the front of the room. I looked down at my notebook in amazement. I'd covered more than two pages.

Jenna raised her hand. "Mr. Tremont?"

"Yes?"

"Were you writing, too?" she asked.

"I was," Mr. Tremont said. "It's only fair, right?"

Across the room, Shanti and the Freshman exchanged looks.

Mr. Tremont stood and moved around to sit on the table. "I know I said no one would read this but you, but there's something freeing about reading a raw draft. . . . Anyone feel like sharing?"

"Dude, I will," Randy said.

"Great," Mr. Tremont said, looking around the room. "Before you start, I'd like to remind the class that it takes a lot of guts to read your own work, so I'd ask you to be respectful of anyone who offers to read. In order for this class to work, you have to be vulnerable and open in your writing. And in order for that to happen, we need to establish a sense of trust and safety."

Behind me, Brian Sorenson snorted. "Dude, Tyler was right. This class is totally gay," he muttered, keeping his voice low enough that Mr. Tremont couldn't hear him.

Randy stood and cleared his throat dramatically. His friends cackled. "'I remember this morning, when I waked and baked. I remember how fine Paige looked in that little skirt on the first day of school. She looks hot today, too.

It would be awesome if her and Lacey made out, even though Lacey's like a cripple now. I remember—'"

"That's enough."

Randy stopped, looking pleased with himself. Brian and Chris were still laughing loudly.

"All three of you may go to the guidance counselor to get your schedules changed," Mr. Tremont said evenly.

"What?" Brian asked angrily.

"Yeah man, we didn't even do nothing!" Chris said.

"If you'd like to discuss this further, you may see me after class," Mr. Tremont said. His tone was neutral, his expression calm. "For now, though, I'd like you to leave."

The boys stood and grabbed their stuff, grumbling and muttering their way out the door.

Mr. Tremont surveyed the room. "I said before that the point of freewriting is to get past the voice inside your head that tells you your ideas aren't good enough, your words aren't good enough, you're no writer, and so forth. But getting past your internal editor is kind of pointless if you're just going to treat your own work—or the work of your classmates—as a joke."

The class was quiet, and people seemed to be listening to Mr. Tremont. I saw a couple people jotting notes in notebooks, but most people kept their eyes on the teacher, nodding seriously.

"So basically, our class motto will be the same as Google's was, back in the day: Don't Be Evil. If there's anyone else who can't work within that basic guideline, I'll write you a pass to the guidance office. Anyone?" He surveyed the room, smiling. "Good. Let's get to work."

Our class would follow a similar structure every day, Mr. Tremont explained. The first ten minutes would be a warm-up write, and then we would either discuss a published work, write, or do a peer-review workshop for the rest of the period. Mr. Tremont asked for volunteers for the first round of workshopping, and both Shanti and the Freshman raised their hands. "One more?" he asked. "Volunteer . . . or victim?" The rest of us remained silent, looking everywhere but at him. "My high school Spanish teacher always used to say that," Mr. Tremont said. *"Voluntario . . . o víctima?"* A few people laughed nervously and he shrugged. "Okay, victim. Let's see. . . ." He scrolled down the attendance list. "How about Paige Sheridan?"

A bunch of people turned to stare at me. Shanti gave me a thumbs-up, which I hoped no one else noticed. "Oh," I said, "um . . ."

Mr. Tremont looked right at me and smiled. God, he was beautiful. "You can do it." A pathetic protest got caught in my throat, but he didn't seem to hear. "Paige . . . Sheridan," he said, writing. "Okay, Shanti Kale, Ethan James, and Paige Sheridan are up for workshop next Friday, September twenty-fourth. I'll need your pieces by that Wednesday so that I can make copies for everyone."

I snapped to attention. The twenty-fourth was the day

of the big homecoming week kickoff bonfire, where the members of homecoming court would be announced. The JV teams would spend all afternoon gathering wood pallets donated by local businesses and Bee Boosters and piling them in the parking lot behind the practice fields. Normally it would be held after the varsity football game, but this year the team had a bye that week, so the bonfire was scheduled to start slightly earlier than usual. It would be weird to just show up and immediately go to the fire without sitting through a game first, and some people worried that the break from tradition meant bad luck for the team. Usually the football coach would light the fire after the game, but I wondered if this would be different, too, without the game. Once the bonfire was lit, everyone would gather around the giant fire—parents, teachers, coaches, a few bored volunteer firefighters, and students—and the varsity football coach would stand on a flatbed truck and announce the names of the football players, and then Dr. Coulter would cough into the microphone and announce the names of the court. Lacey and I had a tradition of squeezing hands as Dr. Coulter named the court, as if we could capture the magic of that moment and hold it between us. Regardless of who we were dating or who we'd come with, we'd always find each other and stand together near the truck, hands solemnly clasped. For years we'd been waiting for our turn to hear our names called, to climb the hay-bale step onto the truck bed and stand above everyone else in the flickering, dancing light of the fire. And now, after all these years, suddenly it was only a week away? I had a brief, panicky feeling that time was moving much too quickly, that at this rate graduation would be here before I knew it, and then I'd be in college and then be married and old before I even had a chance to take a breath. These were supposed to be the best years of my life, and they were slipping away in a haze of awkwardness and silence.

I snapped back into the present to hear Mr. Tremont talking about workshopping as a process, and how it was supposed to help you grow as a writer, and I realized that the bonfire wasn't the only thing fast approaching. I was supposed to come up with something for the whole class to read and discuss in a week. Shit. A week? I hadn't written anything other than essays and papers since middle school. Well, except for the freewriting thing, but that didn't really count, since I hadn't known what I was writing about until after it happened, the words just came out of nowhere. And the last part, about us using secrets as weapons—I hadn't even known I felt that, not really, and yet there it was on the page. But it wasn't like I was about to hand these scribbled pages in to the class to read—I had to figure something else out, and soon.

Before the bell rang, Shanti raised her hand. "Mr. Tremont? Before she . . . left, Mrs. Mueller gave us the assignment of going to hear a literary reading during the festival this weekend. Do we still need to do that?"

Everyone groaned. "Jesus, Shanti," I heard Jeremy hiss.

Mr. Tremont watched our reactions with amusement. "Now that you mention it, going to a reading is an excellent idea. So, yes, the assignment stands."

"Way to go, Shan," Jeremy whispered.

"Whatever," she said. "You were going to go anyway."

"That's not the point," he said. "Homework ruins everything." He pretended to pout, and she rolled her eyes and laughed. I wondered when they'd become such good friends, if she'd just moved back. What else had I missed over the summer?

"So," Mr. Tremont said, "I guess I'll see you guys on Monday with some sort of evidence that you attended said literary event? A program? A poet's signature, perhaps? A signed copy of a book?" The bell rang, and everyone filed out, muttering death threats at Shanti.

As I walked past them, I heard a girl say, "For the record, Shanti? You suck."

chapter SIX

After creative writing, I headed straight for my car, completely preoccupied with the assignment. It was weird—I'd had big papers for classes before, and hard assignments, but nothing had ever stumped me like this before. I'd always been a pretty good student, usually getting all As. My friends teased me sometimes, but the truth was we all got decent grades. And if I occasionally put a little more work into school than they did, it was only because I planned to go to Northwestern, which isn't exactly a slacker school. Still, it wasn't like I wanted everyone to see me slaving over the books—it was one thing to get good grades; it was another thing to be totally obvious about it.

But this assignment was throwing me. Not only would I have to work my butt off to have something ready by next week, I'd also have to share it with the whole class. It would be one thing to embarrass myself in front of the teacher, but in front of the whole class — and right before the homecoming vote?

Lost in my thoughts, I got in my car and, for the first time since the accident, turned the key without feeling a hint of anxiety. I headed for the one place I knew no one would find me, where I could get a jump start on trying to write something without anyone watching, where I could freak out in peace. Field after field flashed past me, yellow soybeans and tawny corn, shimmering poplars, goldenrod and bittersweet, red vines twisting around farmers' fences. In the late afternoon light, everything looked golden, and I could almost forget that Lacey was distant, Nikki was wasting away, and Jake suddenly felt the need to be Lacey's knight in shining armor.

I parked at the trailhead that led to my favorite spot in the world: a hidden spring, deep in the woods and far away from everything. A circle of boulders marked the place where the springs bubbled up, feeding into a small pool that spilled in a tiny, perfect waterfall to the stream below. Further on, the stream curved around a bend, wound its way under a wooden bridge, and eventually met up with a large lake. As far as I knew, the only other person who knew about the spring was my father, who had introduced me to this spot when I was still a little kid, back when he spent more time at home than on the road. Though the lake, with its boat launches and beaches, was a favorite hangout for fishermen and drunken teenagers alike, I had never seen anyone else here at this spring in the woods, and I considered it to be my secret.

I grabbed a notebook and pen from my bag. If nothing else, I could always follow Mr. Tremont's instructions: *Keep your pen moving.* As I hiked up the steep path toward the spring, I wondered if I could capture it again, that feeling of freedom and release as my pen skipped across the page like stones over water. The words had come from nowhere, and afterward I'd felt lighter, almost giddy.

The woods were full of dappled sunlight and flashing birdsong. As I walked, I tried not to think about the tangle of my friends and friendships. I did not want to think about Lacey, or Nikki, or Jake. I didn't want to think about my mother, or my sister, or the fact that I'd barely seen my father since I'd gotten home. Instead, I turned my mind to creative writing class, to Mr. Tremont's casual posture against the board as he explained freewriting.

It took me longer than usual to find the little path to the springs, but eventually I found my way. I took a deep breath for the first time in forever and just listened. This. This was what I'd missed in Paris. Green all around me; no cars, no people. Just birds and water and quiet.

I climbed up on a sun-warmed boulder and propped the notebook on my knee, remembering Mr. Tremont's instructions. "Start with *I see,*" he'd said. I stared at the blank page, feeling nervous and more than a little stupid. *I see . . .*

I paused, looked up and around me. What did I see? Trees. Um . . . the sky. *I see the sky. I see a pool and bushes.*

Ugh. I drove my pen through the words. This was stupid. In class, it seemed like someone took over my hand, like the words weren't coming from me so much as through me. I wanted to write something true again, even if it was just describing the woods around me.

Mr. Tremont said it should be difficult. *If it's easy, you're not working hard enough.* I looked down at my legs, my black boots. I wasn't the kind of person who gave up so quickly. At least, I didn't want to be.

I see . . .

I see red sumac, a few leaves beginning to turn yellow. Clear water. A squirrel hopping along a fallen branch, pausing to look at me looking at it. I see . . . my house, the front door painted crimson. I see . . . a girl alone in a strange city, far away from her friends, her boyfriend, the roads and trees she knows. She is lying in her narrow bed, listening to angry voices arguing in the next room. She tries to pretend she's not here. She tries to pretend there was never any reason for her to be here. That when Lacey said, *"Paige, this is not a choice, you have to come to this party,"* she'd said, *"Actually, it is, and I choose to study for finals and work on my tan,"* and then she went home and wrote her boyfriend a long

73

email about how much she loved him, and then the doorbell rang and her best friends showed up saying, *"It wasn't the same without you, so we left the party!"* And they ordered a pizza and painted their toenails and watched stupid teen movies where everyone sings their way through high school and it's easy and happy. And they fell asleep sprawled across the couch, legs tangled with legs and toes in the air to protect their pedicures. And no one got behind the wheel and no one got hurt and the school year ended not with doctors and nurses but with yearbooks and exams, and then the summer stretched out forever, waiting to be filled with trips to the mall and random drives through the countryside and bonfires and stargazing and crazy adventures on the golf course.

If she just believes hard enough, she can wake up in the life she's supposed to be living, in her own bed in her own room in Willow Grove, the sheets soft against her legs, a cool breeze and a clean conscience and no canes and no Paris and no yelling and everything the way it was before. If she just believes —

I was jolted out of my trance by the distinctive *flap flap* of sneakers on wet leaves. I listened, waiting for the jogger to pass on the trail above. It wasn't the easiest trail in the county to run, but every now and then I encountered someone attempting it. I could see feet on the trail above, and a flash of gray through the trees. Instead of turning toward the running trail, though, the feet slowed and turned toward me. My trail. My secret. I'd never seen anyone else down here, ever; the trail was far too steep to run. I froze, waiting for the jogger to realize his mistake and turn around.

But he didn't. Instead, he half climbed, half stumbled down the trail, grabbing at slender tree trunks and sliding on damp leaves. There was a very specific way to get down elegantly, which involved stepping precisely on certain roots and embedded rocks, but he missed it entirely and slid the last fifteen or so yards, landing somewhat miraculously on his feet.

The jogger looked up and I gasped. "Hello, Paige Sheridan. You come here often?"

Dumbstruck, I shook my head.

It was the Freshman from creative writing class, Ethan. "No? You should," he said, looking around. "This place is amazing."

"No, I mean, I do." I hugged my notebook to my ribcage. "I just—what are you doing here?"

"Exploring. I had a rare free moment, so . . ." He shrugged. "I used to do a lot of hiking on the Missouri, around Council Bluffs."

He stepped into the clearing, looking past me to the tiny cave and the spring pool. "It really is nice down here." He seemed different than he had in class. Less weird, maybe. Less staged. But then, I wouldn't know anything about that, right?

"What?" he asked, noticing my wry smile.

"Nothing."

He looked at his legs. "Am I covered in mud? Am I trailing toilet paper or something? Am I breaking out in mint chocolate chips?"

I laughed. "What?"

Ethan shrugged. "Hey, there are countless ways I could be humiliating myself in front of you right now. I need to be ready for any possibility."

"You're not breaking out in mint chocolate chips," I said seriously. "But I think I see a hint of praline pecan on your forehead."

He slapped his hand across his face. "Ugh, it never fails. Run into a girl, break out in pralines."

I smiled and looked away. For a moment it was silent between us, and I could hear the echoes of geese honking on the distant lake.

"So," he said. "I guess this answers one of my questions."

"What's that?"

"Where."

I shifted my weight, looking at him. "Where?"

"You know, from class? 'Where does Paige Sheridan go when she needs to get away.'"

"Oh. Right."

He looked at me. "So you come here to get away, and the new kid shows up and starts peppering you with questions. You know, you should really keep this place a secret."

I raised my eyebrows.

Ethan grinned and held up his hands. "Okay, okay. I promise I'll never come down here again. And I won't tell anyone about this place. I won't even think about it, in case they can read minds."

"No," I said. "It's okay. I mean, I don't own it. You can do what you want. If . . . if you need to get away. It's good for that."

"Well," Ethan said slowly. "Thanks." He took a step toward me, gesturing to my boulder. "May I?"

"Oh." I slid off the rock. "Sure, yeah. I was just about to leave."

"You don't have to do that," he said. "There's room for both of us." He stopped abruptly, eyeing my notebook. "Were you writing? Crap, did I interrupt you?"

He thought I was writing. No one else in the entire school would run into Paige Sheridan and ask her if she'd been writing. I should have rolled my eyes, but instead, I found myself grinning. "No, it's totally fine," I said.

Ethan grinned back. "Are you sure?"

I attempted to get ahold of myself. "Yes. Sure. You—you just surprised me, that's all. But yeah, I was leaving, and so, um, I will just do that now." He watched me for a second and I nodded encouragingly. "Really, make yourself at home."

He shrugged and hopped up on the boulder, pulling out a small notebook from his sweatshirt pocket and waving it at me. "You sure you don't want to stay? I'm a very friendly writing companion."

Why was he being so nice to me? After what I'd said in class—I felt my face getting hot at the thought. I was such an asshole. Unless he hadn't heard me? Unless he thought I was somehow different from my friends? Or maybe he was just a freshman in the presence of a senior, so he wasn't going to pick a fight.

"Thanks, but I have to get going. Good luck with your writing." I turned and made my way up the steep hill to the main trail, stepping carefully from root to stone to root.

Behind me, Ethan said, almost to himself, "Is that how you do it?" Then, as I reached the leaf-strewn path at the top, he called, "Your secret's safe with me!"

I crouched down to see him. "Not if you keep yelling it through the woods, it isn't!" I heard him chuckle faintly, and as I headed up the path, I realized I was smiling.

That night, Nikki came over to help me prep appetizers for my mother. "I should have called Chris," she said, stabbing a toothpick through a bacon-wrapped date. "The way to a man's heart is through his stomach."

"Ha." My sister walked into the kitchen, heading for the fridge. "The way to a man's heart is through his rib cage." She reached out and grabbed an imaginary heart in her claw, bringing it up to her face. "Yum."

Nikki looked slightly horrified. "Ignore her," I said, turning my back to my sister. "She's going through her dark phase."

Miranda grabbed a soda and walked past us. "Ignore her," she told Nikki, nodding at me. "She's going through her artificial phase."

"Go away, Miranda," I said.

"Gladly." She turned and stalked grandly out of the kitchen, calling back over her shoulder, "It's Mirror!"

Nikki sighed. "I wish I had a sister."

"Um, okay."

She was quiet for a moment, staring out the big kitchen window into the dark yard. Nikki was an only child. Her parents were older than everyone else's, and she once told me that she'd been a mistake. In middle school, she'd been obsessed with babysitting, and she kept trying to get Lacey and me to start a babysitting club with her. I imagined her at dinner with her parents, silent but for the noise of a knife scraping across a plate. Poor Nikki. She'd probably spent the summer months alone, trapped in her cavernous house, beating herself up for one bad night. One mistake. No wonder she seemed quieter this year.

When she turned back from the window, her blue eyes looked gray. My heart broke for her, just thinking about all the sleepless nights she'd had, blaming herself for everything that had gone wrong between all of us.

"Do you think," she finally said, her voice quiet and thoughtful, "if I put orange frosting on a cookie, it counts for my diet?"

• • •

Nikki and I made a good team. I pitted the dates while she wrapped them in bacon and secured them with a toothpick. We'd had years of practice, ever since my mother went to work for Stella Austin when I was in middle school. Some Friday nights before a huge event, my mother would appear in the doorway of my bedroom, where the three of us were curled up in our usual spots, painting our toenails and watching movies, and flirt with Nik and Lace until they thought it was their idea to help her in the first place. In exchange, she'd give us each a twenty and talk Lacey's mom into driving us to the mall the next day.

"Where is Lacey, anyway?" I asked.

Nikki's eyes got shifty like they did when she was trying to get out of something, as if she were literally looking for an escape. She was the worst liar I'd ever met, and she couldn't keep a secret to save her life.

"You know something," I accused.

She turned her back to me, grabbing for the box of toothpicks and spilling them across the counter and onto the floor. "Oh, no!" She scrambled to catch them as more and more rolled off the counter.

I ignored her little crisis. "What are you not telling me?"

"What do you mean?" she finally asked. Her voice was squeakier than normal.

I narrowed my eyes. "Nikki . . ."

She didn't look at me. "Hand me the tinfoil?" I pushed it across the counter without saying a word. Nikki was the kind of person who got nervous in silence. Wait long enough and she'd crack, every time. I crossed my arms and leaned back against my mother's designer countertop, prepared to wait as long as I needed to. Nikki's arm moved up and down as she folded and tucked tinfoil into a new baking pan. She was way too skinny, I thought. Her elbow crooked out at an unnatural angle.

"You're staring at me, aren't you?" she asked, still not turning.

I nodded and then realized she couldn't see me. "I'm going to keep staring at you until you tell me what you're hiding."

She sighed and turned, her eyes all squinched up in her narrow face. One eye opened slightly to peek at me. "She's with Jake."

The words rang through the large kitchen, bouncing off my mother's decorative copper pots and shiny appliances, vibrating in the air for nearly half a minute before my brain understood them. "Right now?"

Nikki opened her eyes, looking miserable. "Yeah."

"With Jake?" I repeated. My arms wound tighter around my ribs, cutting into my abdomen.

"Don't get mad, Paige, okay?" Nikki held up the box of foil like a white flag. "Promise?"

"No," I said.

"I'm sure it's nothing," Nikki said.

"But?" My ribs ached, but still I pulled my arms more tightly against me.

"They're at the gym."

My arms fell to my sides. "What?"

"They're doing physical therapy or something. Jake's helping her."

"Physical therapy."

She nodded. "She was in the hospital for like a whole month, and her doctor told her she'd be walking with a limp for the rest of her life, and she refused to accept that. So she got Jake to start helping her with exercises."

Exercises? Jake said Lacey had been in physical therapy all summer, but I'd just assumed it was over . . . I hadn't considered that it might be an ongoing thing. I hadn't asked, though, had I? I'd just tried not to stare at the cane and pretended that everything could magically go back to the way it had been before.

I realized I was staring at the shiny black refrigerator across from me. For the first time, I noticed that it never had anything hanging on it, no cute artwork from when we were kids, no coupons for a free oil change or haircut. No magnets, even.

Jake's voice echoed in my head. *She's got a lot on her mind right now, babe.* "Why doesn't Randy help her? Or Chris? Or Tyler? Or anyone else?"

Nikki shrugged. "Jake took that sports medicine elective last year when the rest of them took bowling. He knows the people at the clinic—"

I interrupted her. "Are you sure that's all? They're not . . . *together?*"

Nikki's eyes glistened in the glow of the tasteful track

lighting. Automatically, she ran a finger under her eyes to catch any stray mascara. "No! Of course not! Jake totally loves you, and Lacey's your best friend. They wouldn't do that to you!"

I felt like choking on the words. "Would you tell me?"

Nikki nodded emphatically. "Yes! Of course!"

"So why didn't they say anything to me? Lacey's barely spoken to me since I got back, but Jake could have . . . should have . . . said something."

She sighed and wiped at her eyes again. "I don't know, Paige. You had such an amazing summer, and you seemed so different when you got back. . . . I don't know. Maybe they thought you'd be weird about it? It's just, with the whole divorce—" She clapped her hand over her mouth, eyes wide. "Whoops."

I was too startled to correct Nikki's claims about my summer. "Divorce?"

"Oh God," she said through her hand. "You can't say anything. She was going to tell you herself. You don't know, okay? Please. Don't say anything."

"Lacey's parents?" I asked. "They're getting a divorce?"

Hand still over her mouth, Nikki nodded. "She's been really messed up about it. Jake's been helping her."

A few years ago, Jake's parents had gone through a trial separation, after his mother discovered his father's affair. Mr. Austin lived in an apartment in Iowa City for a whole summer, moved back in with the family in September, and as far as I know, they never said another word about

83

it. Even in the gossipy country club set, few people knew about it. So it made sense that Lacey would want to talk to Jake. What I didn't understand, though, was why she hadn't said a word to me. "Why didn't she tell me?"

Nikki shrugged helplessly. "You were in Paris when it happened. . . . And when you came back, you just seemed really distant."

Frozen in place, I said nothing. I didn't even blink. Was I so self-absorbed that I hadn't even picked up on the clues? There must have been clues, right? People don't just get divorces out of nowhere. And I practically lived at the Lanes' house — at least I had, before the accident. How I had not guessed? Poor Lacey.

After a time, Nikki set the box of foil on the counter and crossed the kitchen, cautiously putting her arms around me. "I'm sorry, Paige." She whispered the words into my neck, and I thought of all the times I'd held Jake in the same way, speaking my words directly into his skin.

Nikki left with worried eyes. "Promise me you won't say anything to Lacey about the divorce thing, Paige. Please. She will kill me if she finds out I told you."

I walked her out to her car, shivering in the cold night air. "I won't."

"Thanks, Paige." She reached over to hug me, giving me a quick squeeze around the neck before climbing behind the wheel of her giant SUV. Before closing the door, she said, "It's been really hard on her. Don't be mad at her, okay?"

"I'm not mad," I said automatically. But I was, a little. Why hadn't Lacey told me?

"This is our year, Paige. Pretty soon everything will be back to normal, okay? Just like we all planned. It's going to be awesome."

I nodded, swallowing hard. "I know."

"Okay, see you tomorrow!" She closed the door and waved though the window, starting the SUV and backing out of the driveway. She was halfway down the street before she remembered to turn on the lights.

I headed back into the house. My mother stood in the kitchen, wiping the already clean counters. "Where was Lacey tonight?"

"Um." My chest was tight. "She had a student council thing."

"That Lacey! She'll be a legend in her sorority." She ran the sponge under the faucet, squeezing it out carefully. "Did you remember to label the vegetarian trays?"

"Yes."

She checked the fridge to see for herself, and then she nodded in satisfaction. "Did you girls have fun?"

"Yeah," I said, standing in the doorway. "It was great."

My mother turned and looked at me, her eyes thoughtful. I struggled to keep my face neutral. What did she see when she looked at me? When I was little, she seemed to see all, to know everything.

"Honey?"

I swallowed against my closed throat. *Don't ask,* I

85

thought. *Don't ask if I'm okay.* I just wanted to go to my room and call Jake. I wanted to hear it for myself. I would tell him I was cool with it, that everything was fine. Everything *would* be fine, just as soon as I could talk to him. Jake would reassure me and explain everything.

My mother perched a fist on her hip. "Does Nikki look like she's gained weight to you?"

I shook my head. "She's very skinny, Mom."

"You girls are at the age when your metabolism will betray you, you know. It can happen so quickly. You let go for one day, and you're just lost."

"I know, Mom."

"It's just, with the vote coming up, and after last spring . . . well, you girls can't afford to slip again."

"I know, Mom."

"You were lucky, Paige. You got to be away from here while things cooled down. And if we're really lucky, people aren't thinking about the accident when they look at you. Not like Nikki." She clucked in sympathy. "Poor girl. But at least she's out of the running, and it's just you and Lacey, though I don't see how anyone could possibly vote for a crippled queen. On the other hand, the sympathy vote might be big."

I shifted my weight uncomfortably. "I don't think that's true, Mom. Nikki's still very popular."

"Well, you can be popular and not have a shot at being queen. It's not about popularity; it's about being the girl everyone else wishes they could be." She leaned in to check her teeth in the reflective surface of a copper pot. "Nobody wishes they could be a drunk. Or a cripple."

The world spinning toward us, everything dark, Lacey screaming, shattered glass—

My mother kept talking. "The vote's next week?"

I shivered. "Yeah." *Just let me go, Mom. I have to call Jake. I have to make things okay.*

"Are you wearing the yellow dress?"

"Uh, yeah," I said, stepping backward into the dining room. "Yeah. I have a lot of homework, so . . ."

"Okay, honey," she said, still watching herself. "Don't stay up too late now, okay? You need your beauty sleep."

Jake didn't answer. All night. Lacey didn't either. I called them three times each, feeling less forgiving each time I hit the SEND button. Were they together, ignoring my calls? Was Jake reaching across the seat of his silver car, pressing the button to silence Lacey's phone for her? It made me ill just thinking about it.

Divorced. How could she not tell me about that? Mrs. Lane had been like a second mother to me, ever since middle school. She and Lacey's dad always seemed so happy together, not like Nikki's parents, who always seemed overly formal and weird, or my parents, who were incredibly polite to each other but didn't seem to actually like each other that much. Of course, they only spent about three days of every month together, so how they felt about each other hardly seemed to matter. But the Lanes kissed in public, much to Lacey's middle school mortification. What had happened to them? And how could Lacey not tell me?

This was supposed to be our year. For the last four years, Lacey and I had studied *Cosmo* like some people study the Torah, modeling ourselves after the perfect, smiling girls in every toothpaste and shampoo ad. And for what? What's the point of being perfect if your best friend won't even talk to you about what's going on in her life?

The roles we'd carved for ourselves were narrow. I hadn't seen just how narrow until I'd spent the summer in Paris. I'd always taken my life for granted, assumed that the path I'd been traveling was absolutely the correct one. Never gave it a second thought, until last spring. But after the accident, and a summer away, it all seemed narrower than I'd remembered, harder to navigate.

Neither Jake nor Lacey called me back. I sat in the oversize wing chair by the window in my bedroom for hours, trying not to imagine them holding hands across a sticky booth at Perkins, cradled together in the front seat of Jake's car, lying on their backs in the middle of the golf course, looking up at the stars. . . . A thousand images flashed before me, and I tried not to see. I stayed tucked in my chair, unable to sleep, staring through the cold glass as the stars shivered in the sky and the moon rose and fell over the trees.

chapter SEVEN

Ripping myself from my pitiful two hours' sleep the next morning was agony, and I was slower than usual to get out the door. I could have hustled and made it to our usual morning meetup, but for the first time ever I just didn't feel like it. The feeling was strange but not exactly painful, and I probed it like a potential cavity. Instead of speeding to claim my secret spot at the back of the student lot, I turned toward downtown and stopped at the gas station for a large cup of terrible black coffee. Normally we drank faux cappuccinos out of the fountain machines, but black coffee appealed to me and I decided to learn to like it. I wanted to be the kind of girl who drank black coffee and didn't take shit from anyone.

Clutching the coffee to my chest like a security blanket, I wove and dodged my way through the noisy morning hallways to Contemptible American History. Lacey didn't show up until a few minutes after the bell rang, and I used the time to rehearse what I'd say to her. *Where were you last night? I called you three times. Were you with my boyfriend? Do you feel any guilt at all about using Jake?* But when she finally appeared, first peeking timidly through the door and then shuffling into the room, her limp more pronounced than usual, my anger morphed back into pity. My best friend was handicapped and her parents were divorcing, and all I could worry about was my boyfriend? Feeling contrite, I leaned forward to whisper to her. "Lace . . ."

She shot me a death glare. "I'm trying to pay attention, Paige."

"I know, I just—"

Lacey raised her hand. "Mr. Silva?" Her voice went syrupy and meek. "Would it be possible for me to move? I'm having trouble seeing the board."

"Of course, Miss Lane."

"Thank you, Mr. Silva," she said, and grabbed her cane, pulling herself out of her desk. She gestured to her books. "Could someone . . . ?"

"Mr. Jensen, could you please assist Miss Lane?" Chris jumped to attention, practically leaping from his chair to carry Lacey's books to the front of the room. A moment later, everyone was settled and Mr. Silva was droning on about the Gulf of Tonkin and Lacey was across the room and I was alone.

• • •

Lacey wasn't at lunch that day, something that seemed to be becoming a trend. Jake was saving a chair and I slipped into it, dropping my bag on the table.

"Hi babe," he said, leaning forward to kiss me.

I leaned back. "Hey."

Across from us, the juniors were rapid-fire gossiping, punctuating their exclamations with shrieks and giggles. Jake gave me an appraising look. "What's up? Are you mad?"

"I don't know," I said. "Should I be?"

He paused. "Am I supposed to know the answer to this one?"

"Where were you last night? I called you like five times." The chatter around us quieted, and I realized I'd spoken much louder than I'd meant to. I was surrounded by the little chipmunk faces of the stupid junior girls, and they were all staring at me.

Jake stood, offering me a hand. "Wanna walk?"

I allowed him to pull me up and followed him out of the crowded commons and down the little-used hallway toward the art rooms. He stopped and turned, wrapping his arms around my waist and pulling me in. "Hey," he said softly.

"Jake," I said. "Don't distract me."

"But it's so fun." He kissed me on the side of the neck, and I was tempted not to stop him. "Am I in trouble?"

I got ahold of myself. "Yes. I know about the Lanes' divorce."

He stopped nibbling at my skin. "How —? Nikki?"

"Why didn't you tell me?"

Jake pulled away and leaned against the wall. "It's not my story to tell, babe."

"You could at least have answered your phone last night," I said.

He sighed. "Lacey needs . . . I'm just trying to be a good friend to her. We've known each other since we were babies, and she doesn't have anyone —"

"She has me!" I protested. "Or she would, if she would let me know what's going on with her."

"She will," Jake said. "Just give her time, babe." He kissed me until I forgot what else I'd wanted to say to him. For now, he was with me, alone in this hallway, his hand on my back, his mouth on my mouth. For now, this moment was enough.

In creative writing that afternoon, Mr. Tremont had us read this poem about New Mexico that was full of descriptions of foods and plants and landscapes. The poet was homesick, he said, and was writing in the middle of a Minnesota winter. "Green-chile pizza!" he said. "You can't get that in Iowa! Which is too bad, because it's amazing. Look at these other foods: *posole, chile rellenos* — it's these very specific details that make this poem so vivid. Piñon trees! Yucca! Sage! Pigweed! We're not in Iowa here, folks. Or Minnesota."

A girl in front of me raised her hand. "I went to New

Mexico once! It was super pretty! We went in this gondola thing and my mom fainted. . . ."

"Did you eat green chile?" Mr. Tremont asked. "Or *sopaipillas*?"

The girl shrugged. "I think so? I don't remember."

"Oh, you'd remember," Mr. Tremont said. "Okay guys, now it's your turn. I want you to keep this level of specific detail in mind as you describe a setting somewhat closer to home. It could be as specific as your bedroom or as broad as the state of Iowa, but it should be somewhere you know well. Use specific details. Not just *a car* but *a beat-up Subaru Legacy with only one side mirror.* Got it?"

We nodded, shuffling notebooks and pens.

"Cool," he said. "Specific details, somewhere you know well. Beyond that, don't think too hard. Just write."

A place I know well . . . I wrote, then paused. Should I write about my bedroom, or was that too easy? I could write about my secret place in the woods. But what if he made us read them out loud?

"Don't think, Paige," Mr. Tremont said. "Just write."

I looked up guiltily and he smiled, making a writing gesture with his pen. I started again.

A place I know well . . .

A place I know well is my locker. It's mostly bare now, chipping green paint and the numbers on the lock so faded you can hardly see them, but I know them by feel. It used to be decorated, like in the movies, full of cute pictures of Lacey and Nikki and Jake and me, and inspiring words cut out from magazines, tickets from school dances and notes from Jake and little drawings Nikki doodled in the margins of my homework and reminders about student council meetings and parties and papers due. I remember kneeling on the cool tiles in front of my locker at the end of last year, doing one final sweep to make sure nothing important would be thrown away when the janitors came through and cleaned over the summer, when suddenly Lacey appeared, holding up her cell phone like a winning lottery ticket. "You love me!" she announced, and I looked up from the year's worth of junk, debating whether I should bother trashing it myself or whether I should just let the janitors take care of it. "What?"

"Seriously, you should just get down on your knees and kiss my feet."

"I am on my knees," I said. "And kinky."

She laughed and swatted at my head. "Shut up. You know what I mean. Worship the ground I walk on, my friend. You'll never guess what I got."

I stood and looked at her, trying to determine whether she was bluffing. "No you didn't."

"YES I DID!" she cried. "I got us invites to the Sigma party."

"Through Prescott?"

"Please. Through my own amazingness."

I crossed my arms. "What do you owe him?"

"What? Nothing." She fixed her eyes at a point above my head. I waited. Lacey sighed. "Fine! I said we'd wash his car."

"We'd?"

"Well, you. I mean, Nikki and I will help. . . ." She shrugged. "You know he has a thing for you."

Nikki appeared behind us, bouncing like a little girl. "Omigod you guys, hi! We're seniors! Did you tell her, Lacey?"

"Yep," Lacey said, and Nikki squealed, grabbing my arm.

"Isn't it so exciting? The Sigma party is like THE biggest party of the summer!"

A pair of sophomores strolled down the hall-way, hand in hand, with moony kissy faces, like they didn't even notice the sagging Yearbook Dance posters and lemon-yellow cinderblock walls around them. He leaned over and whispered something in her ear, and she turned pink and broke into a run, dragging him down the hallway, giggling. I wondered where Jake was, whether he was already at the visitation, and what that was like. I wondered if he was wearing the same suit he wore to prom a few weeks earlier, and then I wondered if I'd left anything in the pockets of his jacket to remind him of me. We used to do it all the time, leave little notes or tiny paper hearts for each other in surprising places: the pocket of a winter coat, between the folds of a wallet, behind the sun visor in the car.

"I don't know," I said suddenly, my voice too loud in the mostly empty hallways.

Lacey and Nikki spoke in unison. "What?"

"I don't know if I should go. To the party."

Lacey looked at me like I was speaking Chinese. "WHAT? Why not?"

I fiddled with the dial on my locker. "It's just, you know, Jake's out of town, at a funeral, and you know. It doesn't seem right."

"Oh, Paige," Nikki said. "You have to! This is a once-in-a-lifetime opportunity."

Lacey said, "Jake would want you to go. He worries that you don't have enough fun, Paige. He told me."

I looked up. "He did? When?"

"In study hall last week. He's worried you've been spending too much time studying lately."

"I have to keep my 4.0," I said defensively. "My parents will kill me if my grades drop. You know that. If I don't do well on the precalc final, I'm totally screwed."

"Whatever. You'll get straight As like always and make the rest of us look bad! Paige, you've studied enough. You seriously cannot miss this party."

Nikki nodded earnestly. "And plus? There will be so many hot guys there!"

"Yeah, I have a boyfriend?"

She shrugged happily. "I don't!"

Lacey grabbed my hand and locked her cornflower eyes with mine. "Seriously. This is not a choice. You must come."

The bell rang. I jumped in my seat, practically flinging my pen across the room. Thankfully no one seemed to notice, as they were all shoving their notebooks into bags, standing up, chatting about the weekend. Over the din, Mr. Tremont called, "Don't forget Mrs. Mueller's homework this weekend! Literary readings in the city!" Without meaning to, I looked over at Ethan, though I'd been actively avoiding his eyes all through class, irrationally worrying that someone would see and somehow know that we'd been semi–hanging out the day before. But he was engrossed in conversation with Shanti and Jeremy, and a moment later the three of them were through the door, laughing.

I headed toward the parking lot in a fog. The writing thing was so intense, it was kind of freaking me out. When I'd managed to do as Mr. Tremont suggested and stop thinking too hard, it was like my hand took over, and once again I'd been surprised by what my hand had written, as if it had all kinds of things to say that my brain knew nothing about.

As I cleared the lawn and stepped onto the cracked pavement of the student parking lot, I heard a voice behind me. "Paige! Paige, wait up!"

Unmistakably Nikki. I had a sudden strange urge to run away, running like little kids do before they learn to worry about who's watching. But I wasn't a little kid anymore, and I was all too aware of being watched. So I took a deep breath and forced myself to smile even before I turned around. "Hey, Nikki."

She was breathing heavily. "Gotta quit . . . soon . . ." she panted.

"No shit," I agreed.

After another moment or two she managed to collect herself. "What are you doing tonight?"

Friday night. It took me an embarrassingly long time to remember. "Uh . . ." I squinted up at the vivid blue sky, so bright my sunglasses made little difference. "I guess there's a game tonight."

She tugged at the hem of her little sundress. "Are you going to Lacey's party afterward?"

"I don't know. I didn't know about it."

"Of course you did."

I lowered my sunglasses. "Actually, I didn't. Lacey's totally been avoiding me."

"No she hasn't!" Nikki scanned the parking lot. "I'm sure she hasn't. It's just—she's going through a hard time. . . ."

"Right," I said.

"Anyway," Nikki said, "you totally have to come tonight!"

"Why?"

She looked surprised. "Um, because we're finally seniors? And we're going to be princesses? And it wouldn't exactly look good to miss a huge party this early in the year?"

"I'll think about it," I said. "I'll have to talk to Jake."

"Oh, he's totally coming! He told me in fourth." Her nose and cheeks were flecked with tiny brown freckles. "So that means you're coming, right?"

He told her in fourth, but he hadn't said a word to me at lunch? Why? Because he just assumed I'd be there, Perfect Paige making a Perfect Party Appearance? Or because he and Lacey didn't want me there? I bit my lip. "Maybe."

Nikki clapped. "Yay!"

I lowered my sunglasses and raised an eyebrow warningly, a trick I'd learned from my grandmother. "Maybe."

"Okay, right," she said, and held a hand to her mouth, as if to hide a secret. "See you then!"

"Maybe!" I exclaimed, smiling in spite of myself.

Abruptly, she changed the subject. "Have you seen Lacey?"

"In the five minutes I've been talking to you?" I asked. "Uh, no."

Nikki pulled her cell phone out of her purse and checked the time. "Shit, I have a meeting with . . . I have to go!" She spun on her trendy heels and hurried toward the school. Halfway to the door, she turned and yelled back at me. "See you tonight!"

I turned back toward the parking lot, shaking my head. She was a spaz, but I loved her.

Lacey grabbed me just before I reached my car. "Have you seen Nikki? She was supposed to meet me out here."

"Oh, you're talking to me now?"

Lacey's expression was blank.

I sighed. "I just saw her. She was looking for you."

"Well I don't see her now, do you?" Lacey stamped her cane in irritation. It had been painted like a yellow-and-white candy cane, school colors, with girls' names running up and down it. It looked like the work of the dance team, or maybe the juniors in student council.

I looked around. "Uh, no."

When I turned back, she was studying me, her eyes pale blue in the afternoon sun. I noticed that she was wearing white eyeliner, and I wondered when that had started. Strange, how I could remember every detail of her so clearly from one day last spring—her outfit, her hair, every word she said—and put it all on paper, but now every detail of her face looked unfamiliar. "What's wrong with you?" she asked. "Are you stoned?"

My head was still in class. "We got this new creative writing teacher—"

"Yeah, I heard he's a real fag," Lacey said, unwrapping a stick of gum.

"What?" I asked, startled.

"Randy says he's the worst teacher he's ever had."

"Randy's just pissed because Mr. Tremont kicked him out of class." My voice was much louder than I meant it to be. I looked away, embarrassed.

"Whatever," Lacey said, sounding bored. "Anyway, are you coming to my party tonight?"

"I don't know. Maybe."

"Maybe? It's like, the biggest party of the year!"

"No it's not," I said. "What about the post-homecoming party? Or the Halloween party? Or the luau in February? Or—"

"Okay, okay." She quickly checked the car beside mine for dirt before leaning her butt against it. "The point is, it will be big."

"Well, ask Nikki," I said. "I just had this whole big conversation about it with her."

"Fine," she said. We eyed each other warily. There was so much between us, so many years of friendship, and yet we had nothing to say to each other. What could I say, now that I knew how much she wasn't telling me? Finally, I opened the door of my car and slid into the driver's seat. "Well . . ."

She grabbed the top of my door before I closed it, her perfectly manicured nails peeking over the edge. "Hey Paige?" Her voice was low, tinged with a warmth I'd nearly forgotten.

"Yeah?" My heart got fluttery in a moment-of-truth kind of way. My script from earlier waited on my lips. *I'm sorry, too. I know things have been hard—*

Lacey cocked her head to the side. "You're not going to wear that tonight, are you?"

I don't know how long I sat in my car after that, but when I looked up again the student lot was mostly empty. My head was full of stuffing. I had a ton of homework and my parents were starting to harass me about my Northwestern application essay; I'd have to get something done if I was going out tonight. I needed to focus, and gas-station coffee wasn't going to cut it—I needed the hard stuff. Just making a decision helped; my brain felt sharper already. I turned my car toward Starbucks, the only café in town.

Inside, people were scattered at the tables in ones and twos, cups and napkins filling the space between them. I headed toward the counter and then stopped. Ethan was behind the cash register, making change for another customer. I considered backing away, ducking out of the café, but he looked up from his work and locked eyes with me. "Hey, Paige."

"Hey," I said, feeling awkward.

"What're you drinking today?"

I ordered my usual, which I'd inherited from my mother. "Grande skinny caramel latte, extra hot, please." I expected him to smirk at the fussiness of my order, but he just punched it into the computer and asked, "Anything else?"

"No thanks," I said, swiping my credit card through the machine. "I, uh, didn't know you worked here."

He grinned. "Now you do," he said, "and knowing's half the battle."

I looked at him blankly.

"No? G.I. Joe? Eighties nostalgia?"

"Sorry," I said.

"Kids these days." He shook his head. "Are you here to write? Shanti's here." At her name, a dark head in the corner popped up and turned toward us. "Hi, Paige!" she called. She waved, and I instinctively glanced around to make sure no one I knew was in the café before I waved back.

Ethan picked up a marker and scrawled on a cup. "So how's it going?"

"It's . . . whatever."

"Ah," he said. "I see you're taking Mr. Tremont's lesson about specific details to heart."

"Shut up," I said. He grinned, then ducked behind the espresso machine.

I leaned against the counter, feeling awkward. "So," I said, "um, how long have you worked here?"

He spoke over the clanking and hissing of the machine. "Just a few weeks, but I worked at a Starbucks in Omaha, so when we moved here . . . It's just like riding a bike, you know."

"Do you enjoy working here?"

Ethan's head popped up over the machine. "Oh, I get it. We never finished our interview in class. So it's my turn, right?"

"Uh, right," I said, only then realizing that we'd never gotten around to talking about him.

"Do I enjoy working here?" Ethan asked. "I mean, it's a job. It has its moments."

"I've never had a real job." The moment I said it, I knew it was a mistake.

"Must be nice."

"I don't know. Sometimes I think I should get one."

He fitted a plastic lid over my drink. "Well, Freud said that you need a balance of both love and work in your life. *Lieben und arbeiten.*"

"Interesting," I said. "So . . . do you have to have a special work permit to work here?"

He looked amused. "Are you thinking of applying?"

"No," I said. "No, I was just wondering . . . don't you have to be sixteen to get a job?"

Ethan squinted at me. "Technically, I think you can get a work permit at fourteen. But yeah, you have to be at least sixteen to work here." He tilted his head the way my mother does when she's trying to understand me. "Why? How old are you, seventeen?"

"How old are *you*?" I asked.

"Okay," he said. "I'm eighteen. This is an odd conversation we're having."

"You're *eighteen*?"

"Yessss? Is that a problem?"

"But you're—" I felt my face get hot and looked down to hide it. "Are you a senior?"

"Ohhhhhhh," he said. "I get it. You thought I was a freshman."

"No I didn't."

"Yes you did."

"No I didn't."

"Yes you did." He laughed. "You shouldn't believe everything you hear, Paige."

"I don't," I insisted. He laughed again, and I realized how ridiculous I sounded. I smiled tentatively.

And then the door opened, and I stepped back automatically, looking away. Mrs. Austin strode in, covering the distance from the door to the counter in a breath, and by the time I looked back for Ethan, he was hidden behind the espresso machine.

"Well hello there, dear," Mrs. Austin said, and then to Ethan: "My usual." He paused for a millisecond and she snapped, "Triple espresso with a shot of nonfat soy."

"Of course." He passed my cup across the counter. I couldn't look at him.

"What does your mother drink, Paige?" Mrs. Austin asked. "I can never remember." My mother had been working for Mrs. Austin for six years. They'd sat through countless client meetings together, nearly always anchored with Starbucks cups.

"She—"

"Oh well, just make two of the same," Mrs. Austin said, then looked at me. "What are you doing this afternoon, dear? Waiting for Jake to get off practice?"

"They have a game —" I started.

Mrs. Austin pushed her credit card across the counter, and Ethan had to turn the card machine around in order to slide it himself. Mrs. Austin didn't seem to notice. "Ah, young love. What I wouldn't do to be back in your place, Paige. These are the best years of your life, you know. Enjoy them while they last."

"Thanks," I said.

"Are you here studying?" she asked. "It's a good thing that Jake's naturally gifted, because between football and working at the law firm, I don't know when he'd find time to study if he needed to. You're lucky to have long afternoons stretched out in front of you, dear. Plenty of time to focus on your schoolwork."

My fingers wrapped around the cup more tightly. "Yeah, thanks."

"So you're here alone?" Mrs. Austin asked, looking around the café. "I don't see Lacey or Nikki anywhere."

I opened my mouth. "I'm —"

Wordlessly, Ethan passed her cups across the counter to her and she grabbed them, winking at me. "Well, a woman's work is never done. But you know that. Enjoy your luxurious solitary afternoon, my dear."

Without looking at Ethan, I hiked my bag up on my shoulder. "I should go," I mumbled, and followed the trail of Mrs. Austin's perfume all the way to the door.

chapter EIGHT

My mother scolded me into a dress for the party that night,
a little black thing with white accents that I'd picked up on
Michigan Avenue with her before school started. I tried to
point out the obvious fact that before the party, I'd have to
spend several hours freezing outside on the bleachers, but
she was insistent. We had a week before the vote for court,
and people would be paying attention. She pushed me into
a chair and swept my hair into an elaborate updo. In the
end, even I had to admit that the effect was good. I smiled
at myself, tilting my head down slightly so my face was half
in shadow.

"Oh Paige, you look so pretty!" She leaned down next
to me and looked at us in the mirror. Our faces were the
same shape, pale ovals repeating themselves. Her eyes
were a bright false blue, while mine were the scorched

yellow-green of grass in August. During our shopping weekend in Chicago, her college friends kept telling me how much I looked like my mother when she was my age. One of them even called me Jacque, accidentally, and when she did my mother looked at me like I was someone she should know but couldn't quite pinpoint.

I caught her eyes in the mirror and smiled, wondering if she saw herself when she looked at me. She smiled back. "Why can't your sister be more like you, Paige? She could easily be as pretty as you are, if she put forth any effort whatsoever. She has better cheekbones."

My smile faded. "I'll let her know."

Her reflection stared at me. "Just a moment." She turned and clicked down the hallway toward her room. When I was certain she was gone, I leaned toward the mirror until my nose was nearly pressed up against it, staring at the minor imperfections and unevenness of my skin up close. I pulled back again, slowly, until the moment my skin looked perfect again. I squinted, trying to memorize the distance, and made a mental note not to let anyone get closer to me than that. At least, not in the light.

My mother reappeared behind me and draped a necklace over my collarbone, a glittery, elegant piece she'd had as long as I could remember. "Oh yes," she said to herself, "isn't that perfect."

I reached up to touch it with nervous fingers. "Are you sure?"

"Of course, dear," my mother said, fumbling with the clasp at the nape of my neck. "After all, you're a going to be a princess; we can't have you looking like a grungy teenager in public." The clasp caught and my mother pulled back, scrutinizing me in the mirror with the eye of an artist. I watched her watch me, careful not to make eye contact but noticing the tiny wrinkles around her eyes, the long vertical line running down her forehead and ending just between her eyebrows, the puffiness beneath her lower lashes. She worked out with a personal trainer five days a week, spent hundreds and hundreds of dollars on face creams and products that promised dewy youth in a bottle, watched what she ate, religiously stayed under an umbrella in the sun, and yet she couldn't run forever. For a second I saw the strain of trying to stay young etched in her face.

She reached up to smooth an invisible stray hair on my head. "Maybe tonight will be the night."

"What do you mean?" I asked, digging in a drawer for some lip gloss.

"Oh, you know," she said. "Perhaps tonight will be the night that Jake pops the question."

I looked up in horror. "What? The *question*?"

"You look so pretty tonight," she said dreamily.

"Mother, are you insane? I'm not even eighteen yet! We're in high school!" Did she think I was some character in a Salinger novel, a pretty girl in a camel coat to be admired and then wed?

Her gaze was distant. "I had just turned seventeen when Bobby Monroe proposed to me. It was the most romantic night of my life."

"That was a different time, Mom. Like, a whole different *world*. People don't get married after high school anymore."

Her hand patted along the counter until it found a tube of lipstick. She watched her reflection remove the cap and twist the bottom, followed the waxy crimson finger as it traced the lines of her lips in a perfect bud.

"Anyway," I said, too loudly, "you didn't marry Bobby Monroe. Even back then, it was weird. Right? You wanted to go to college, just like I do."

"He's the vice president of a bank now. In *Chicago*." She dabbed the corner of her mouth with the tip of her finger, blotting away the tiny rivers of color that had followed the creases in her skin. "Emily Hamilton said he takes his family to Mexico for two weeks every year." She sounded wistful. "You know, sometimes I wonder if I should have . . ."

"Should have what?" I asked. "Thrown your life away before it even started?"

Her eyes in the glass looked surprised, as if she'd forgotten I was even there. "True love is rare, Paige. The kind of connection you have with Jake—you get it once in a lifetime. Don't take it for granted."

"You love Dad," I said.

She paused for a fraction of a second. "Of course I do, sweetheart."

"I'm going to college, Mother," I insisted, a little surprised

110

at the anger in my voice. A year ago, the idea of marrying Jake would have thrilled me. I'd spent hours doodling our names together in my notebook. Paige Austin. Paige Renee Sheridan Austin. Mrs. Jacob Austin. Jake had his entire future—University of Iowa, then UI Law, then a place in his father's practice—planned out since childhood. His life stretched out before him, always easy. He'd have a beautiful wife, a giant house, and a couple of perfect children, unquestioningly following his father's footsteps the whole way. For years, I'd imagined myself as that beautiful wife, standing proudly by his side, but now the idea clutched at my throat and chest, making it hard to breathe. I loved him, I did, but I wasn't ready to go down that road. Not yet. . . . "I'm going to college," I said again. "I'm going to have a *life*."

"Still," she said, draping a hand on my shoulder, admiring our reflections. "You never know."

The game was a long, dull stalemate, and I was alone on the bleachers, freezing. I had a coat on over my little dress, and a blanket wrapped around my legs, but I was still kicking myself for letting my mother talk me into this outfit in the first place. Lacey was with the dance team, preparing for the halftime tribute in which she would hobble out onto the field and everyone would cheer for her, as if she'd been injured rescuing a houseful of orphaned kittens. Nikki had been sitting with me earlier, but somewhere in the second quarter she wandered off. I thought I saw her down by the fence around the field, leaning against someone much taller and broader than she, but they were half in shadow, and I couldn't be certain.

Out on the field, Jake seemed to be calling every play, and Randy was his go-to man. At least, that's what I thought was going on. I really didn't know that much about football, despite both Lacey's and my mother's encouragement to learn something about each sport in order to better hold a man's interest.

The field was in a little valley, lower than the surrounding land. From where I sat, near the top of the bleachers, the high school was to my left, the student parking lot directly behind me, and the tennis courts, baseball diamonds, and practice fields were off to my right. In front of me, past the unnaturally bright field, past the red track circling the field, past the dark visitor bleachers on the far side, past the farthest fence, the land rose sharply, its horizon defined by a highway. From the highway, you could look down and see the kelly-green field, the tiny players like bright dolls, the stands full of yellow. Drive a little farther and you'd see the back of the high school, the back lot near the auto shop, the windows of the English classrooms, the sad little garden that the biology teacher's homeroom planted and forgot every year.

Looking back from the bleachers, all you could see was the steady stream of white headlights and red taillights, whispering up and rumbling away into the cold September night. Every now and then a semitruck rumbled past, and the *chunk-tunk* of its axles echoed across the valley of the football field, hinting at a world beyond its blazing borders. I sighed, my breath coming out in a little cloud. If I had driven myself, I would at least be able to sit in my car for a while and warm up, but my mother had driven me so I could leave with Jake. Which meant that I was stuck up here on the frozen bleachers, waiting for the godforsaken game to end.

"You look cold."

I jumped, nearly losing my balance on the cold metal. Shanti Kale climbed down from the bleachers behind me and sat down next to me. "Do you mind?" she asked, looking around.

I followed her gaze. The only people sitting this high up were mothers in turtlenecks and old people who attended every single game. "No," I said.

"Aren't you freezing?" I shook my head. She wore white gloves like the ones the cheerleaders wore. Her similarities to the cheerleaders ended there, though. Instead of a snug black-and-yellow uniform, she wore a black wool peacoat and long, well-fitted jeans that draped elegantly over her shoes. Her feet were tiny, I noticed, and once I noticed, I couldn't stop peeking at them. She was probably five four, five five; how did she manage to stand on such little feet?

"I used to go to school here, back when we were kids. I just assume no one remembers me."

"I remember," I said. Maybe she'd moved away in sixth grade, but it was a small school and I wasn't an idiot.

The yellow crowd below us suddenly yelled and stood up. "Go go go!" Down on the field, someone in yellow was running with the ball. The crowd's cheer steadily rose in pitch and volume, swelling collectively, and then turned into a disappointed "Awwww" when the runner was tackled on the twenty-yard line. I had a flash of being at the State Fairgrounds with my father, years earlier, standing near the racetrack. "You hear how the noise of the car sounds higher as it approaches, and lower as it goes away?" he asked. I took his hand, nodding solemnly, awed by the noise and the speed of the cars. "That's called the Doppler effect. It happens with sound waves and light waves, both."

I should ask him for help with my physics paper, I thought idly. If I can ever catch him at home.

"I have to confess: I'm kind of surprised you remember me," Shanti said as the crowd sat back down.

I was taken aback by her boldness, and I studied her in the cold night air. She raised her eyebrows and smiled as if waiting for me to agree. It took me a minute to pinpoint exactly what was so strange about this conversation, but then I realized that very few people outside my circle had randomly approached me in years.

"We were in the same math class in fourth grade. Mrs. Dawson." Shanti reached over and tugged at the blanket around my legs. "May I?" At a loss for words, I just shrugged.

"You're different than you were back then," she said. "Am I allowed to say that?"

"No," I said, vaguely remembering a little girl playing Mercy with the boys at recess. She stood on the far side of the big oak tree, where the teachers couldn't see, digging her nails into the backs of the boys' hands until they conceded their loss. "I mean," I said, "yes. You can say whatever you want. I don't care."

"Okay." She leaned in conspiratorially. "I just didn't know if people knew that you used to be a . . ." She whispered, as if it were a curse word, "A nerd." And then, in a normal voice continued, "You know, now that you're a princess."

I was flustered. "No, I mean—I wasn't exactly . . ."

"It's okay." Shanti grinned. "I'll keep your secret."

"Anyway, I'm not even a princess yet."

"'Yet' being the operative word," she said. "You will be. Obviously. And Lacey. She was popular even when I lived here before, but now that she's crippled? She's like Princess Di."

"Um, she's my friend."

"Really? I assumed it was more like a political marriage, you know, like France and England. Catherine of Aragon and Henry VIII. That kind of thing."

"She was from Spain," I said.

"Ha, I knew you were a nerd!"

I tucked the blanket more tightly around my legs. "I watched *The Tudors.*"

She looked down at the field, seemingly captivated by the action. "They look so little down there, don't they? They look positively adolescent."

She was right. The second string, especially, looked like little boys. Most of them had toothpick legs and shifted their weight uncomfortably, swaying back and forth in their bulky shoulder pads, trying to stay warm. I felt a little embarrassed for them.

"It's weird, you know, how everyone's changed since sixth grade," Shanti said. "Isn't it weird to think that was six whole years ago? Like, it was a third of our entire lives ago. Back then, everyone was basically split into three groups: the cool kids, the totally hopeless loser kids, and everyone else. Now there are like a hundred groups and subgroups, a whole complex hierarchy of coolness and loserdom, and each strata is relative to each other one, you know? Like, there are the cool theater kids who, relative to you and your friends, are probably considered losers, but compared to, say, the marching band nerds, the cool theater kids are like gods. But then there are the less-cool theater kids, the dumpy kids and the awkward kids who don't really make it into shows, or stay in the chorus, and they look up to the cool theater kids, but even those kids are cooler than the tech guys, who are totally hopeless cases, but not to themselves, because in their own minds they're way cooler than the coolest theater kids. You know what I mean?"

"I never really thought about it before," I said. "But yeah, I know what you're saying."

"Really?" She looked at me for a minute, her breath coming out in puffs. "Awesome. No offense or anything, but I don't really like your friends. They were jerks in middle school, and they're jerks now. I mean, Randy Thomas? What a dick. I guess I assumed you were the same as the rest of them — no offense — but then in creative writing . . . you seem different."

I didn't know if I should be offended or pleased. I looked away, pretending to study the crowd. Down in front of the brick building where the announcers stayed warm in their booth, I saw a head of frosted curls bobbing above a leather jacket. Stella Austin. Normally I would make my way down to where she was sitting with Mr. Austin to chat for a bit about Jake's game, but something kept me where I was, hidden high above the crowd.

"You can tell me to shut up if I'm talking too much," Shanti said.

I didn't say anything. She shifted her weight, bouncing her tiny foot against the bleacher seat in front of us.

"You know what I remember?" she asked suddenly, turning toward me. The light caught on her little gold earrings.

I rubbed my bare hands together, blowing little clouds of warmth into them. "What?"

"In fourth grade, you found this little bat at recess. Remember? This little brown bat. It was sleeping on the outside wall of the school, low enough that anyone could touch it, but you wouldn't let them. You stood guard over it for all of recess, and when the bell rang you went and got the janitor to watch it so nobody from the other grades could mess with it on their recesses. You kept saying that if anyone touched it, it would have to get its head cut off, and it didn't deserve that. You said it was just sleeping, and just because it picked a bad place to sleep didn't mean it should get its head cut off."

"Wow," I said. "I forgot about that." My mother had taken us to the Brookfield Zoo in Chicago the summer before, and I'd completely fallen in love with the bats. Miranda was scared and my mother waited with her outside while I stayed in the bat room by myself. I watched them crawl around with their little hooked thumbs, amazed at the contrast between their grace in flight and their awkwardness on the ground. "It's true, though," I said. "If someone had touched it, they would have had to call Animal Control, and it would have gotten its head cut off to see if it had rabies."

"But it didn't," Shanti said. "You wouldn't let anyone touch it."

I was silent for a minute. "I remember you, too," I said at last. "You used to play Mercy with the boys."

She laughed. "I won, too. I kicked your boyfriend's ass. I made him cry." She laughed again, shaking her head. "I had anger issues."

Below us, the crowd stood once more, cheering. Down on the field, a yellow-and-black figure ran ahead of the pack, hunched over the ball in his arms. This time, the crowd's cheer built into a crescendo without falling, as the runner crossed into the end zone.

Shanti stood and stretched. "Well, I better find Ethan. I

left him alone with his notebook. Who knows what kind of trouble he's gotten himself into, without me."

"Oh, is Ethan here?" I asked.

She looked at me. "He is. . . . Were you looking for him?"

"No." I crossed my arms. "I mean . . . no."

"Hmm."

"Well, I'd better go, um, look for Nikki. Because she . . . needs . . . to find me."

"Sure, yeah." She nodded, and then put her hand out as if she'd just had a thought. "Hey—Ethan and I are supposed to hang out tomorrow and write. You want to join us? You're up for workshop next week, right?"

"Oh," I said. "Um, yeah. I mean, I am."

"You should come," Shanti said. "We write every week. Seriously, it would be great."

Surprised, I looked down at my blanket. "Thanks." I fiddled with the edge of fabric, rubbing it between my stiff fingers. "But I . . . um, I can't. I'm supposed to . . . I'm busy."

"Okay," she said easily, "that's cool. But the offer stands. We write every Saturday. You're more than welcome to join us, anytime, okay?"

"Yeah," I said. "Totally. Thanks."

"All right," she said. "Well, I'm going to go find Ethan. Nice talking to you. Seriously. Have a good night."

"Thanks," I said again, though I doubt she heard me; she was already halfway down the bleachers, disappearing into the crowded night.

• • •

After the game, I stood in the parking lot forever, waiting for Jake. When he finally emerged from the locker room, freshly showered and smelling like cologne, my mother's voice echoed in my mind. *Perhaps tonight will be the night.* I shivered.

"Hey, babe," he said, grabbing me around the waist. "Did you see that field goal? Wasn't it amazing?"

"Yeah," I said. "Amazing." The night had gotten colder, and I wore the blanket around my shoulders like a cape.

Jake walked ahead of me, weaving through the remaining cars in the parking lot, occasionally shouting to his teammates. "Dude, you going to Lacey's? Cool, see you there!"

Jake stopped at his father's truck. "Where's your car?" I asked.

"Some fuckwad dinged the bumper." He hopped into the cab without opening the door for me. I took it as a good sign that my mother was wrong. Still, I watched him warily, analyzing his every gesture and word for any hint that he was planning to do something as monumentally stupid as propose. It seemed so completely, unimaginably bizarre — and yet, my mother did work for his mother, planning weddings together, no less. I squinted at him as he lit a cigarette and turned the key in the ignition, still talking about the game. He seemed normal enough, though, and I began to relax slightly.

Jake blew smoke out of the side of his mouth and tapped

the cigarette against the window. "Where were you today? Lacey said she saw you leave."

"Just around," I said vaguely.

He pulled out of the student parking lot, honking at a red Blazer. "Just around? What were you doing?"

I shrugged. "Homework."

He snorted. "It's Friday. You have the whole weekend to worry about that stuff."

I reached across the seat for his cigarettes. Supposedly I had quit when I was shipped off to Europe—even though everyone else there smoked, Mrs. Easton had an incredibly sensitive nose and went psycho at the merest hint of cigarette smoke—but at the moment I felt like I wanted to quit quitting. Without taking his eyes off the road, Jake offered me a light from his Zippo. *He's a good guy,* I thought fondly. I sucked on the cigarette, comforted by the familiarity of self-destructiveness. I could totally marry him. Not now— God, not at seventeen or even eighteen. But after college, maybe. Or someday.

I cracked the window and blew a long stream of smoke into the night air. "Do you ever wonder if there's more than this?"

"More than what?" Steering with his knee, he took my left hand in his, lightly tapping at each of my fingers in turn.

"I don't know." I waved my cigarette toward the fading lights of the high school behind us, the quiet dark street, the familiar glow of downtown ahead of us. "This."

"More?" Jake asked incredulously. He dropped my hand and turned toward me. "Babe, this is *it*. Weren't you watching the game tonight? We kicked Monty's ass. We're finally seniors, the whole school worships us. . . . What more do you want?"

"I don't know," I said, frustrated that I *didn't* know — not well enough to put it into words, anyway. "Never mind. Forget it."

"You and Lacey have been working toward this for years. The vote's next week."

"I know."

"Well? What's the matter?"

For a second I thought I could tell him everything, could confess my fears about us, about him and Lacey, and about me and Lacey. I could let him comfort me, let him tell me it was all in my head. Nothing had changed between us, between any of us. Everything was fine. I could let him convince me.

But I knew I couldn't say everything, couldn't say any of it without sounding like a pathetic, needy girlfriend. Besides, *Princesses don't whine.*

"I don't know," I repeated. "It's nothing. Really."

Jake flicked his cigarette out the window and looked at me, and for a brief second I wondered if he saw it all, if I didn't even have to say the words. "You know what you need?" he asked, reaching his hand across the seat again and patting mine. "You need a drink."

• • •

He was right, I thought, staring out the truck window at the buttermilk moon as Jake sped through the countryside toward Lacey's house. I had everything: the adoration of the school and town, a good chance at princess-hood, a great-looking boyfriend . . . It was everything we'd planned for in junior high, everything exactly as we'd dreamed. Well, except for the accident. But even that was behind us now, except for Lacey's limp, and Nikki's skeletal arms. Other than that, everything was good. Perfect. What more did I want, really?

Jake took the turns tightly, his father's giant extended-cab truck whipping around each curve. The last fireflies of the year slowly blinked in the grasses along the side of the road, fading in and out like fairy lights. I felt surprisingly safe, cradled in the shelter of the passenger seat between Jake's warmth and the darkness outside. I allowed my hand to move across the front seat, to rest on his leg, hoping my touch could say all the things I felt in that moment.

"Can I ask you something?"

"Sure, babe," he said, easing the truck around the last, sharpest turn before Lacey's house.

"You don't . . ." I started. "You never . . . had any feelings . . . for Lacey?"

"What? When? What do you mean?"

"Nothing," I said. "Just—before you and I started dating, like freshman year, you guys used to hang out a lot . . ."

"Where is this coming from?" he asked.

Two eyes appeared up ahead on the side of the road, flashing like tiny yield signs.

"Nowhere," I said quickly. I watched as the raccoon waddled out from the long prairie grasses. "Just, you know . . . you and Lacey seem so close these days. . . ."

Jake suddenly swerved toward the raccoon, and there was a thud as the tiny body bounced against the under-carriage of the truck. "Suicidal little fuck," Jake muttered. I screamed, grabbing at the door handle. *Bloodred moon, wheel wrenched, shattered glass.* The truck slowed slightly, and something rolled from under the seat and hit me on the ankle. Hard.

"Jesus! I can't believe you did that!" I pressed my hand against my chest, trying to suppress the suddenly surfacing ghosts of last spring.

"I know," Jake said. "I hope I didn't fuck up the alignment."

"What? Who are you?" *Screams echo in the car as it swerves sickeningly across the country road . . .* "You could have killed us! Remember last spring? Shit, Jake!"

He slowed slightly as we neared the spot where Lacey's driveway met the road. "Last spring?" he asked.

Was he serious? "Are you drunk?" I reached down and grabbed at the thing that had hit me. It was a can of spray paint, red. What the hell? I threw it behind the seat, see-ing those animal eyes flash before me. *Everything out of control, the car flipping over an embankment and falling an eternity through space to the riverbed below* . . . I couldn't catch my breath.

Suddenly, Shanti's words from earlier echoed through my head: *You stood guard over it until the end of recess.* Jesus. The poor little thing. "I can't believe you did that," I said again.

The Lanes' driveway was long, winding at least a quarter mile through the dark woods up to their faux-country mansion. At the top of the driveway, Jake pulled into a shadowy spot in the trees, gently setting the parking brake before turning to me. "Shh, Paige," he whispered. "It's okay." As if he could hear it still pounding, he brought his hand slowly to my heart, holding it there for a moment as I closed my eyes, beginning to relax. His other hand cradled my cheek before falling to trace my collarbone to my shoulder. Leaning in, he brushed his lips across the hollow just behind my ear, and I shivered. He pissed me off sometimes, but he always apologized. Generally, the apologies were worth the fight. I waited for his reassurance.

"Go easier on your friends," he whispered.

I drew back from him. "What?"

He took my hands in his own, pulling them together like I was praying. "They miss you, Paige. They're worried about you. They need you."

"Um, okay . . ." In almost a year and a half of going out, Jake had never given me advice about my friends unasked. In fact, even when I did ask him for advice, he usually just shook his head and shrugged. Where was my apology? The *I'm sorry I killed an innocent little raccoon back there and sorry I scared you and sorry I reminded you of the accident last spring that got you banished all summer and, while I'm at it, sorry about your ankle.*

He smiled at me. "You ready?" Without waiting for a response, he pulled away from me and opened the door, stepping out into the cool darkness.

chapter NINE

The customary campfire was burning down the hill where the lawn met the forest. Inside the house, the party was going strong, and people kept arriving. It was the usual mix of high school and college people, our friends from school and Lacey's brother's friends back for the weekend from college in Cedar Falls and Iowa City. The second we walked into the darkened living room, a pack of Jake's friends swarmed us, and a moment later he squeezed my hand and plunged into the crowd.

Prescott, Lacey's brother, was spinning in a corner of the room, his state-of-the-art stereo system blasting at full volume. As always, he had a whole mixing board set up, with some of the speakers aimed out the open windows so that the bass line rolled out over the dark lawn, spilling beyond the boundaries of light from the house and bouncing off into the trees. He caught my eye and waved, keeping one hand clutched over his ear, as if his giant headphones might suddenly slip off and ruin the party. It was the first time I'd seen him since the night in June. I blushed and turned away, grabbing a beer from a cooler in the kitchen and heading through the wide French doors down toward the fire.

I'd left the blanket from the game in the truck, and I was already regretting it. The air was cold on my bare legs, and I walked slowly, in part because my strappy heels were hard to handle in the spongy grass. Sparks flew up into the night sky and happy, drunk voices filled the air. A few of the louder ones were chanting, encouraging Hunter Torres, a popular junior, to jump over the fire, while he drunkenly protested that the flames were too high. He was right, but I knew that it was only a matter of time before he would give in and jump anyway, likely catching himself on fire in the process. It was all so damned predictable.

I stayed in the shadows for a while, meditatively sipping my beer. The sensations of heat on my face from the fire and cold on my back danced together, and I closed my eyes for a moment, absorbed in feeling my own skin. Maybe I should find Jake and borrow his jacket. He was an expert at playing the part: the doting boyfriend, the good-times jock, the golf-loving junior lawyer. Any role a situation called for,

Jake came through with panache. At least, he usually did. I heard his voice again, low and mean: *Suicidal little fuck.* I shivered.

The voices of increasingly drunk people wrapped around me like a soothing wall, a barrier between myself and the true silence of the night and the stars. My beer softened the edges of the evening, warmed me up. So Jake hit an animal in the road. It was sad, but it wasn't *evil*.

I thought too much; that was my problem. What I needed to do was relax, take a deep breath, maybe get another drink, and kick it with the people around me, people who, if not true friends, were at least a comfortable and easy group to be a part of. High school was for having fun, after all. Jake was right: What more did I want? What more did I need? I was at the top of the school, and I was in danger of ruining the best time of my life by thinking too goddamn much.

Resolutely, I turned away from the fire, heading back up to the house for another drink. Maybe I'd find Lacey and we'd gossip like old times, sit in the cushy chairs on her patio, smoking cigarettes and giggling. I'd smile at the college boys who flirted with me and laugh at their jokes, then I'd go find Jake and lean against him for a while. I'd drink and dance with my girls. And it would be enough. How could it not be enough? But first, I needed another drink.

Nikki materialized at my shoulder, clumsily carrying three large plastic cups, sloshing liquid over her hands.

"Paige?" Her voice squeaked even higher than usual. "Oh, I'm spilling all over."

I nodded, unable to pull my eyes from the flickering orange fire at the bottom of the hill.

"Paige, is that you?"

I nodded again. "Yeah."

"Have you seen Lacey?" She wobbled on her tall heels, losing her balance and splashing on my arm. I jumped out of the way, grabbing at my dress to pull it as far from her as I could. "Damn it, I keep spilling!"

"Here," I offered, taking one of the cups from her. I sniffed it. "What is it?"

"Um . . ." She giggled. "I don't know. Chris made them for me, special. His special mix."

I took a cautious sip. "It tastes like fruit punch."

Still giggling, she thrust one of her cups out in the air before her. "Let's toast!" She clunked her plastic against mine, sloshing "punch" over my arm. "To best friends!"

"To best friends," I echoed quietly.

"Where's Lacey?" Nikki asked abruptly. She looked around her, as if Lacey might just be standing a few yards away, hidden in darkness.

"I don't know," I said, and took another sip. "I haven't seen her."

"I'm supposed to take her drink to her. Hers and Jake's, both."

"They're together?" I asked, a little too loudly.

"She looked really upset earlier. Something about her

dad, I think." She put the plastic cup to her lips and then pulled it away again, waving to someone down near the fire. "Hey, Jordyn! I like your hair!"

A shadow waved back. "Hi, Nikki! I love your dress!"

"Thank you!" she yelled, and then turned to me. "Yay! Isn't this the best night ever?"

"Nikki, is she with Jake?"

"Oh my gosh, I forgot! She saw you. Don't tell her I told you, okay? But she saw you, and she's mad!"

"What? She saw me when?"

"Tonight! She looked like she was going to cry," Nikki said, suddenly on the verge of tears herself. "That is so sad. Isn't that so sad? I think it's really sad."

"When did she see me, Nikki?"

Nikki focused suddenly. "She saw you talking to Shanti! At the game! That was so not cool, Paige!"

"What? Why not?"

She threw her arm in the air, sending a shower of red liquid down her dress. "Hey, Geneva! I love those shoes!"

"Thanks, Nikki!"

I snapped my fingers in Nikki's face. "What's wrong with talking to Shanti?"

"You know! Because she's . . ." She looked away.

She's what? Not from here? Not white? Not one of us? I waited, almost hoping to hear Nikki say something completely awful, just to give me an excuse to fight. It wasn't Nikki's fault, but suddenly I resented her stupid passivity, her endless peacemaking, her tiresome drunkenness.

131

Wasn't her drinking what got us into this mess in the first place?

Nikki jumped. "Oh my God, where is Lacey? I have to take her this drink! This is her drink! I don't want her to hate me! I have to find her!" Her voice pitched up another few steps. "I hope she's not mad! Or sad!" She nodded in agreement with herself. "I don't want Lacey to be mad OR sad. I want her to be glad."

"Mmm." I should have wanted her to be glad, too. A year ago, I would have. But at the moment, I just wanted to catch her kissing my boyfriend so I could know what was going on once and for all, and then rip her hair out. Even if she was sad.

"Paige, you have to help me. Lacey's going to be so mad if she doesn't get her drink. I want her to be glad. Please!" She reached out and nudged one of the cups against my bare arm. "Please."

Was it evil to want to mutilate your best friend if she was already a cripple? And why was Nikki falling all over herself to get Lacey a drink? She should be getting me a drink. I was the real victim here.

"You're drunk." I put my drink down. "What happened to DIEDD, Nikki? Isn't it kind of hypocritical for a drunk to lecture the whole student body about drinking and driving?"

Nikki stepped back, looking stung. "I'm not driving tonight."

"So you can get as trashed as you want, as long as you don't get behind the wheel?"

She shook her head. "I have to go find Lacey."

I suddenly regretted lashing out at her. It wasn't her fault; Lacey was the one I wanted to punch. "Nik, wait —"

"I have to go."

"Wait, Nikki, I'm sorry —"

She swept past me, catching me in the solar plexus with her elbow. "Ow, shit!" My right ankle twisted awkwardly and I fell sideways, down over the artificial stone wall into the grass below. I landed with a brutal thump, my ankle turning again beneath my weight. "OW! Dammit! Nikki!"

Nikki turned on a wobbly heel. "Paige, oh no! Oh my God!" She looked down at me over the edge of the terrace, her hair lit from behind and her face masked in shadow. "Are you okay?"

"No!"

"Oh my God, Paige! I am so sorry! Are you mad? Don't be mad!" She teetered drunkenly over me. "Hang on. . . ."

I had a vision of her losing her balance and falling down to join me. "Be careful!" I didn't even try to hide the annoyance in my voice. This always happened. I always ended up babysitting a drunken Nikki, and I was tired of it. The meanest and most secret part of me was almost happy to be justified in my annoyance, like Nikki's pushing me off the patio somehow made up for my being a bitch to her, and now she owed me.

"Okay, sorry!" She took a step back from the edge of the terrace. "Are you mad at me?"

I struggled to my feet, clutching the rocky wall for ballast. "Goddamn it, Nikki. . . ." My ankle wobbled fiercely, threatening to give way again. Hesitantly, I leaned a fraction of my weight onto my right foot and was promptly rewarded with flames of pain shooting up through my calf. "Shit!" I swore, grabbing again at the wall. "Can you help me?" I asked grouchily.

No answer. "Nikki?" I managed to stand up and caught a glimpse of Nikki's back before she disappeared around the corner with a tall guy. "Goddamn it, Nikki!"

The party was quieter by the time I managed to hobble my way up the steep slope of Lacey's yard and back into the house. Most people seemed to have reached the contemplative plateau between dancing drunkenness and unconsciousness. They gathered in groups of four and five on couches and chairs, talking quietly. One of Prescott's friends had taken over the music and was spinning a slow, pretty song that made me think of twinkling stars in a wide-open sky. I paused in the doorway, leaning against the jamb to take the weight off my throbbing ankle. I just wanted to find Jake and leave.

"Don't you love the Cure?" An unfamiliar guy with long, well-kept dreadlocks appeared in the doorway next to me.

"No," I said, with as much disdain as possible. Where was Jake?

"They're like, so magical." He closed his eyes, an expression of peace on his tan face. "Listen to that guitar."

"Uh-huh," I said. "Listen, have you seen—?"

"Shhhh," he said. "You have to listen." He took my hand. "Close your eyes."

To my surprise, I did. "Breathe," he said, and I did, deeply. A galaxy of unfamiliar constellations appeared in my dark vision. The muscles in my shoulders relaxed, and my body grew heavier, slumping against the polished wood.

When the song ended a moment later, the guy gave my hand a warm squeeze. "Take care of yourself." By the time I opened my eyes, he was gone.

Lacey's room was upstairs, the final door in an endless hallway of guest rooms, closets, and bathrooms. She kept a myriad of bandages, knee braces, and athletic tape in the top drawer of her dresser. Or at least she did, before. Captain of the dance team, Lacey had been no stranger to injury, even before the accident. If I could just wrap my ankle, I'd be able to put weight on it. The fewer people who saw me limping the better; I didn't want anyone to think I was trying to steal Lacey's cripple angle.

The light was low under Lacey's door, and I could hear murmured voices. My heart pulled against its moorings, beating frantically. *Idiot.* I was an idiot. I'd spent the entire night looking for them all over the house and they were in her bedroom the whole time.

I reached for the doorknob. Inside, the murmurs turned to laughter. I considered just turning around and leaving. I wanted to know the truth, to put a stop to all of the suspicion and sadness that were wearing me so thin, but the thought of actually catching them in the act made me dizzy.

I squeezed my eyes shut against the promise of future pain, from the memory that, once captured, wouldn't fade.

Deep breath. I turned the knob and pushed the door open.

A figure on the bed sat up. "Paige?"

"Nikki?"

She leaned against Lacey's pillows in her bra and panties, her shoes and dress in a pile on the floor. She giggled, brushing her long hair off her face. The guy next to her trailed his hand up her arm, watching me lazily. He looked like a lion who'd just been fed. "Don't tell Lacey, okay?" Nikki asked.

It was last spring all over again: clothes on the floor, older dude in the bed, Nikki half undressed and mostly drunk. Déjà vu. I almost expected Lacey to barge in and drag Nikki out to the car, screaming at me about kissing her brother.

"Okay, Paige? Don't tell."

I backed out of the room. "I didn't see anything." Before I could pull the door shut, the lion rolled over and reclaimed his kill.

Gross. Gross. I hobbled back down the hallway, cringing

with every step. I tried to shake the sight out of my head, her skinny, vulnerable arms, his thick fingers.

And then I found Jake and Lacey. Or they found me.

They were walking up the stairs together, laughing, their shoulders touching with every step. Jake looked kind, protective. Lacey looked drunk.

"Oh!" she said, seeing me. "Paige!"

They were leaning on each other. They were laughing. They were fully clothed, but somehow they seemed far more intimate than half-naked Nikki and the faceless dude had. That just seemed like sex. This seemed like something deeper. Like—I didn't want to form the word, not even in my own head.

My breath came in little bursts. I felt so stupid, so naive. Faced with the truth at last, I realized I'd never really believed that they could do this to me, had never actually thought that Jake was cheating on me with her. With my evil, evil crippled bitch of a best friend.

Lacey and Jake glanced nervously at each other, sharing an entire conversation without saying anything. Somehow that pissed me off more, the notion that they had some shared understanding binding them together. That was betrayal. Jake and I were in love. The understanding was supposed to be between *us*.

Jake looked at me, and for a second I saw the boy he'd been when we first got together, sophomore year. My anchor. My love.

I couldn't breathe.

"Where have you been all night?" Jake asked. "We've been looking for you."

"Where have I been? Where have *I* been?" I gasped for air. I would not cry. Goddammit, I would not cry.

"We couldn't find you anywhere," Lacey said. "We looked everywhere." She paused. "And then we found you here." She and Nikki sounded alike when they were drunk, I thought distantly, like a goddamn Dr. Seuss book.

"Paige? Are you okay?" Jake asked gently. He sounded like himself. He sounded like my Jake.

Instinctively, I moved toward him. "I—"

"Yeah, where were you?" Lacey interrupted. "It's like you disappeared into the darkness! And then you reappeared into the light! Right?"

"Oh, put it on me," I said, trembling. "I'm the one who disappeared. Where the fuck were *you* all night?" I was asking Jake, but Lacey answered.

"Paige," she said seriously, reaching out a wavering hand. "My parents . . . are splitting up." She waited, full of self-important sadness. Her eyes blinked slowly in the dim hall light. What did she want from me, I wondered. What did she seriously expect? Did she think I'd throw my arms around her and cry? Beg her forgiveness? Give her my goddamn boyfriend as a consolation prize?

"I know." My voice was bitter. "But look on the bright side: at least your boyfriend isn't cheating on you with your best fucking friend."

Jake reached for me. "Paige, we weren't—"

Lacey looked shocked. "My parents are getting a *divorce!*"

"We were, uh, talking about our parents. And forgiveness," Jake said.

Lacey smiled at him, nodding solemnly. "Like Jesus."

"Like hell!" I said. "Would Jesus screw his best friend's boyfriend?"

"Baby," Jake said. "We would never—I would never—"

"Jesus wasn't GAY!" Lacey exclaimed.

"Fuck you!" I pushed right through them, forcing them apart, and ran blindly down the stairs.

chapter TEN

Anger is buoyant. It carried me down the front staircase and out into the night, masking the pain in my ankle until I was nearly to the unlit cul-de-sac. With every step I took, the woods bent and creaked, moaning in the night air. My heart pounded in my chest, pushing shards of glass through my veins, tearing at me from the inside. If I could outrun the spasms in my ankle, then I could outrun the gaping holes in my chest where he was supposed to be, where she had been since middle school. But as soon as I slowed down, it all came speeding back—ankle ache and heartache—punishing me for my flight.

The Lanes had a pair of faux-rustic wooden benches at the end of their driveway, perhaps to offset their ostentatious mansion—or perhaps to emphasize it, as if to say, "You think this house is grand? Shucks, this is only our little country cabin. You should see our real house!" Normally I didn't even notice the benches. Lacey and I had long ago stopped objectively seeing the elements of each other's lives. Like family, we saw each other in glances only, no longer truly looking at each other. When I thought about it, I could more easily picture Shanti Kale's face than Lacey's or Nikki's.

I collapsed onto the rough-hewn logs. The woods around me were quieter now, with the faint wheeze of late cicadas and the slight rustle of leaves. There were no cars speeding down the driveway after me, no muffled rubber *thup thup* of sneakers on the pavement. I released a breath I hardly knew I'd been holding.

I dug in my purse for my cell phone. I couldn't call my parents for a ride: my mother would demand to know why I wasn't going to wait for Jake, and her answer to anything I told her would inevitably be advice on how to be properly wifely in order to win him back. My father would come get me if he was the one who answered the phone, except he had an early meeting at the university the next morning, and my mother would kill me for dragging him out of bed in the middle of the night. I flipped through the contacts saved in my phone. Brian, Chris, Jake, Lacey, Nikki, Prescott, Randy, Tyler. No good—they were all at the party behind me, probably all drunk. I scrolled through my list again, looking for anyone not at the party. Dentist. Doctor. Grandma. Shit.

Sighing, I scrolled through again, paused at the *M*s and pushed the SEND button.

It rang three times before she picked up. "What."

"I need you to come get me."

"Do you know what time it is?"

It was on my phone, but I hadn't been paying attention. "Uh . . . no."

"It's fucking one in the morning."

"Look, Miranda—"

"It's Mirror."

I took a deep breath and counted to five. "Mirror. Please. I'm at Lacey's, and I need to get out of here now. Please do this for me."

She hung up without answering. I took it as a yes.

The night was getting colder, and I was dead sober. I should have taken Jake's jacket before I ran.

I shifted my weight on the bench and settled my foot on a fallen log. The blood thrummed through my ankle for a moment and then subsided, and after a few minutes the constant throbbing pain began to subside, too. I closed my eyes, leaning against the branchy backrest.

"Tough night?"

My eyes flew open and my hand tightened around my purse. "Who wants to know?"

A dark figure stepped out from the woods and sauntered over. In the faint glow from the picturesque yard lights lining the driveway, he looked a lot like Ethan. But what would Ethan be doing at Lacey's house in the middle of the night?

"Hello?" I asked uncertainly.

"Hey, Paige." Definitely Ethan. He stood above me for a moment, as if waiting for some cue. Finally he asked, "Is this seat taken?"

"Oh, sorry," I said, awkwardly sitting up. "Sure, sit down."

He settled himself next to me, leaving a few inches of space between us. Through a patch of sky above the street, the moon floated, round and white.

"What are you doing here?" I asked. "You weren't at the party, were you?"

"In fact, I was," he said. "Hard to believe, right?"

"No," I said too quickly. "It's just—you don't seem to, um . . . get along . . . with most of these people."

He nodded thoughtfully. "I don't. But I know Prescott from this summer, and he invited me. I didn't realize it would be so heavily attended by Willow Grove's intellectual elite."

I coughed. "You know Prescott?"

"Yeah, we played Ultimate together. I was taking summer classes at the university. That's where I met Shanti, incidentally." He folded his arms behind his head. "When Pres said he was having a party, I assumed it would be on campus, not some high school thing full of stupid jocks and their asinine girlfriends."

Ethan glanced at me. "Present company not included, of course."

I shrugged, unable to care enough to take offense on behalf of my so-called friends.

"It's funny," he said. "Back in Omaha, my best friend, Aaron, used to wonder obsessively about these parties. Were they as cool as everyone made them sound on Monday morning, or was everyone just reciting some agreed-upon narrative to make themselves feel cooler?"

He glanced at me as if I might have an answer to this question, but I didn't say anything. Ethan went on. "This was back in like ninth grade, when he and I were the two geeky freshman in a math class full of juniors and seniors. Back then, Aaron would have killed to get into a party like this. We both would have, I guess. Now I don't really care either way."

"Huh," I said. I'd been a part of the popular crowd since middle school, and though we'd always relished the idea that the rest of the school looked up to us, envied us, it had always seemed very abstract. I'd never considered that people *actually* sat at home feeling sorry for themselves because they couldn't come to our parties. The idea made me feel strange, kind of sad and responsible and helpless all at the same time, like when you looked at pictures of little otters and ducks covered in oil from an oil spill and felt like somehow you should be there, with gloves and a bucket, scrubbing them down one by one, while concurrently understanding that you would never actually do that,

144

you would just stay in your house looking at pictures and feeling sad and hopeless until you couldn't take it anymore and clicked over to something happy.

"Of course, half the people here tonight think I'm a freshman anyway, so maybe we can still count this as a win for Freshman Ethan."

He looked at me, seeming to expect some reaction. I gave him a wan smile.

"What about you?" he asked.

I sat up a little straighter, trying not to jostle my twisted ankle. "What do you mean?"

"What are you doing here?"

"Lacey's my best friend."

"Okay," Ethan said agreeably. "Which explains why you're sitting on a bench at the end of her driveway."

"I hurt my foot." I gestured lamely to my ankle, which in the dim light looked like it was already swelling. Great.

"So you're waiting for your boyfriend to take you home."

"Well," I said, and shivered. "Not exactly."

"You're cold. I'm sorry, I'm an asshole." He started to pull off his sweatshirt.

"I'm fine," I said, but it was too late. He scooted closer on the bench and draped his sweatshirt around my arms.

"Thanks," I said. His sweatshirt was warm and smelled like campfire. Without thinking, I snuggled into it, catching a trace of a citrusy clean scent beneath the smoky campfire. He was watching me, and I suddenly became keenly aware of his eyes, how dark and rich and endlessly deep they were, deep enough to lose yourself in, and I had a strange, heady sense of falling, and then suddenly I was kissing him.

He was surprised, but he sank into it willingly and kissed me as deep as the dark night woods. I dissolved into the kiss, and the shards of glass in my veins melted back into sand and light.

After an eternity, we pulled apart, and I smiled slowly at him. He reached over, smoothing a strand of hair behind my ear and tracing his thumb down my cheek, my neck, across my collarbone. "You're so beautiful," he breathed.

My smile faded. What the hell was I doing? It was last spring all over again: have a bad night, kiss a random boy. I was so stupid.

A moment later, the too-bright lights of Miranda's old Honda Civic swept the cul-de-sac and stopped in front of us. Gratefully, I grabbed my purse and jumped up from the bench. A flame of pain shot up my ankle, but I kept my voice cool. "That's my ride."

"Oh," Ethan said, rising. "I could have—"

"No, that's okay," I said, and hurried toward the car. "Thanks anyway."

Jeremy Carpenter was sitting in the passenger seat, and I had a moment of total paranoia—he was the editor of the school paper, and for a second I was absolutely convinced that he was spying on me as part of some crazy paparazzo stalker thing, that he would publish pictures of Ethan and me together to sabotage my chances at queen. It took my brain a long moment to realize he wasn't holding a camera, not even a phone, and then I remembered my sister saying something about doing community theater with him over the summer. So now they were best friends? I didn't know why a senior would want to hang out with a sophomore, but as long as no one had seen Ethan and me together, I didn't care enough to try to figure it out.

I opened the back passenger-side door and flung myself inside.

"Hi, Paige," Jeremy said.

I slammed the door behind me. "Let's go."

As Miranda pulled the car around, I looked down, trying not to see Ethan against the dark forest, standing alone.

"Was that Ethan James?" Jeremy asked.

"No!" I said. "It was, um. Some college guy. Just some dude." I covered my face with my hands and realized I was still wrapped in Ethan's sweatshirt. "Shit."

"Rough night?" Jeremy asked sympathetically.

"What was your first clue?"

My sister glanced at me in the rearview mirror, her eyes flicking scornfully from my dress to my hair. "What's wrong, didn't enough people tell you how pretty you are?"

"Hilarious." I leaned down to rub my ankle, which was definitely swollen. It occurred to me that I probably should have taken my shoes off before running away from the party.

Miranda looked at me again, taking her eyes off the road for longer than I liked. "Who said you could wear that necklace?"

I touched it absently. "Mom did."

"That's supposed to be *my* necklace," she said. "Grandma promised it to me."

"Sorry," I said. "I didn't know."

"Like you care!" she snapped. "Like you've ever spent one minute thinking about anyone but yourself!"

"God, Mirror, give her a break," Jeremy said. "She obviously had a hard night."

"Whatever," Miranda said. "Why couldn't Jake give you a ride home, anyway?"

I shook my head and looked out the window. "I don't really want to talk about it."

"What, did he hook up with someone else or something?"

"Mirror!" Jeremy said.

I gritted my teeth. "What part of 'I don't want to talk about it' do you not understand?"

"You're so pathetic," Miranda said. "You and all your friends, your fake little parties, your prancing around to see who's the prettiest. Your life is basically meaningless, you know? You're such a phony. You're such a nothing."

"Screw you," I said, but I couldn't help thinking that she was right. Without Jake, without Lacey, who was I? Nobody. I was an empty, pathetic nobody. I was a stupid little girl who still thought kisses could make things better, when they only made them worse.

"A lame little crown and a picture in the yearbook for losers to jack off to, and that's seriously your greatest aspiration in life?" My sister's voice was relentless. "The rest of us are going to get out of here and make something of ourselves, but you? Maybe you'll be a slutty sorority girl for a few years, and then you'll get married, spit out some kids, and spend the rest of your life trying to get back to your glory years."

A teardrop escaped and rolled down my face. I squeezed my eyes shut and felt another tear splash on my collarbone.

"Oh my God, Mirror," Jeremy said. "I love you to death, but you are being the biggest bitch in the world to your sister right now."

"Since when are you on her side?" she asked.

He glanced back at me, and I shook my head mutely at him. "I'm not on anyone's side," he said. "Just — she's your sister. Give her a break."

Miranda took her eyes off the road to look at him. For a long minute, the only sound in the car was the hum of the wheels on the road, until finally she sighed. "Whatever."

I lay in bed for hours, staring at the black ceiling. Car lights on the street moved shadows of trees across the walls. The night wouldn't leave me. Nikki's thin arms — the sad pretty guitar — Shanti at the game — orange flames circled by dark bodies — the warmth of Ethan's sweatshirt against my bare skin — the bitter tang of alcohol — the blood thrum of my ankle — Prescott's intent face, bent over his mixing board—the raccoon's *thump thump* under my feet—cold air against my skin—Jake's voice—his warmth and scent in the parking lot—his shoulder, pressed against Lacey's—

The first time he kissed me was sophomore year, the night of Prescott's graduation party. That afternoon, we were sitting on the bleachers in the hot June sun, trying to stay awake as the idiotic valedictorian stumbled through a speech cribbed directly from *Chicken Soup for the Soul*, when he leaned over and whispered, "Confession." His breath moved a strand of my humidity-curled hair and I shivered in the heat. We were surrounded by our families, Mrs. Austin's knees pressed into the small of my back, Miranda fidgeting next to me, but somehow that made it more thrilling, that Jake had words just for me. I leaned toward him, my eyebrow lifted the tiniest bit, and he breathed, "I like you." I turned to him, squinting and unsure, but he looked shy and pleased, and a smile bloomed across my face like a timed-release flower unfolding. All day his confession moved between us like electricity, and that night in the Lanes' backyard, under the low bowl of the Big Dipper, he pulled me away from the bonfire and we stood in the misty trees talking about nothing, and then he laughed quietly and I asked, "What?" and he said, "I was just trying to think of an excuse to kiss you," and I said, "You don't need an excuse," and he kissed me.

And tonight? Tonight I imagined him standing under the same trees, whispering to Lacey as she let tears well up in her blue eyes. Had she let herself sink into his arms? Had he kissed her in the wispy moonlight? I squeezed my eyes shut against the thought, shoving my fists into my eye sockets until the screen behind my eyes exploded with stars, yellow and red, and I wasn't kissing random stupid boys at parties, and Jake wasn't kissing anyone but me.

chapter ELEVEN

I finally fell into a restless sleep around dawn. My dreams were confused, dark shadows against a curtain of red. My phone rang off and on, and its ringtones wove themselves into my dreams, songs I already knew, alarms I couldn't shut off. Sometime late in the morning, when the sun had already stretched past the end of the bed and pooled on the floor near my desk, my mother shook me awake.

"It's almost eleven already, sleepyhead! Rise and shine!" Her highlighted hair was pulled into a ponytail, which curled gracefully and patted her on the back.

I rolled away from her, pulling the comforter around my shoulders and clenching it in fists near my face. "Mmarhgh."

"Looks like someone had a little too much fun last night!

Anything I should know?" She winked, and I recalled her suggestion that Jake might propose. Last night, it had seemed like the worst possible thing that could happen. If only.

"No," I said flatly. "Nothing happened."

She raised her eyebrows. "Nothing at all?" I didn't say anything. "Well, Stella needs me to pinch-hit for the caterers. Miranda and I are going over to stuff mushroom cups. Want to come?"

"No." I burrowed farther into my blankets. "I'm sick," I said. "I have a migraine."

The determined cheerfulness wavered. "Oh. You do? Oh."

I lay still, breathing into the pillow.

"You want some of my migraine medicine? Some coffee? Caffeine helps to constrict the blood vessels."

My voice was muffled. "I just need to sleep."

Downstairs, the house phone rang, echoing through the open rooms. My mother yelled for Miranda to answer it. Her voice drilled into my skull, and I groaned. "Sorry, honey," she said. "I'll leave my migraine medicine out on the counter just in case. And I'll fill up the coffeemaker, so all you have to do is turn it on if you want coffee, okay? Dad's on campus all day, so if you need anything, just call me and I'll see if I can sneak away. Okay?"

The sound of stomping in the hallway announced my sister. "Phone, Paige. It's some chick."

"Paige can't come to the phone; she's sick." There was

silence, and I imagined my sister staring blankly at my mother, either missing or ignoring the implicit instructions. My mother sighed loudly. "Oh, for heaven's sake, Miranda. Hello? This is Mrs. Sheridan! No dear, I'm afraid Paige is ill and can't come to the phone. Mmhmm, I'll tell her. Of course. Okay, you too. Okay. Buh-bye." There was a click as she set the phone down on my desk. "Sun Dee? Is that the little Kim girl? She wanted me to tell you that she and Ellen are working on their English homework today and you're invited to join them if you feel better."

"Great," I mumbled.

She leaned over me, smoothing my hair with gentle fingers. "Okay honey, we have to get going. Make sure to call me if you need anything, okay? Get some beauty rest; your skin looks a little gray." I stayed perfectly still, and after a moment I heard her walk away from the bed. "Come on, Miranda, those mushroom cups aren't going to stuff themselves!"

My sister didn't follow. Instead, she walked over to my bed and picked my phone up off the bedside table. "You have like a hundred new voicemails."

"Give me that." I swung my arm at her.

"Texts too. Do you want me to read them to you?"

"No! God, Miranda!"

"It's Mirror," she said. The phone vibrated in her hand, and she tossed it onto the bed.

"You can leave now."

"Rawr. Calm down, princess." She picked up a stuffed

dog from the floor and sat down on the edge of the mattress. "Hi, Mister Dog."

I sat up slightly. "It's Zeke. Remember, Zeke and Zia?" Miranda had a matching dog, somewhere, that was lighter in color, a tawny sand to Zeke's dark cinnamon. When we were little, we used to make houses for them out of the couch cushions in the living room.

She nodded. "Oh yeah." Next to me, the phone buzzed again. "Aren't you going to answer that?" I shook my head, my eyes on Zeke. The phone buzzed again. Miranda reached over and picked it up. "It's Jake."

I grabbed the dog from her. "I don't care."

"I don't care either." She threw the phone back onto the bed. Our mother's voice floated up from downstairs, calling her name. "God," Miranda said. The phone stopped vibrating and we were quiet.

"So . . ." she said.

"Miranda! Let's go!"

"You'd better go," I said. "She's going to come up in a minute and start yelling."

"Whatever." She looked thoughtful, and then grinned. "Anyway, she likes to nag me. It makes her feel useful."

"I guess."

"Miranda!"

"In a minute!" my sister screeched, making me wince.

She rolled her eyes. "Look, I'm sorry about last night. About, uh, being such a bitch to you, when you had a bad night."

I hugged Zeke to my chest. "Did Jeremy tell you to say that?"

"Why, because I can't be nice on my own?"

Yes, I thought.

She picked at a thread on my comforter, and sighed. "Okay, fine! He did, but I would have said it anyway. I felt bad. Obviously you were having a bad night, and . . . whatever. I'm just sorry, okay?"

I let go of something inside me, a breath I didn't know I was holding. "Yeah, okay. Thanks, Miranda."

"It's Mirror."

"Right. Uh, thanks . . . Mirror."

"MIRANDA ROSE SHERIDAN!"

She stood up, groaning. "Jesus!"

"Those mushroom cups aren't going to stuff themselves," I told her.

"Shut up," she said, heading for the door. "I can't believe you're getting out of this. I hate going to the Austins'. Jake and his dad are always wrestling and calling each other fags. It's like, if you want to wrestle, whatever, fine, but you don't have to get all defensive about your sexuality."

"Mmm-hmmm."

She shook her head. "Migraine my ass."

I smiled angelically. "Have fun."

"MIRAN—"

"I'M COMING!" she screamed. She paused at the door and turned back toward me. In spite of her black-and-red hair, she looked surprisingly like our mother. "Hey," she

156

said seriously, "if I see Jake, I'll kick him in the nuts for you, okay?"

After they left, I got up and wandered around the house, my ankle twinging with each step. The events of the night before sat like a crater in my thoughts, and I walked around the edge carefully, minding the boundaries without acknowledging to myself what I was avoiding. I made myself some toast with jam, brewed the pot of coffee my mother had left for me, flipped through a magazine, and thought idly about cutting my hair. I took a shower and spent a long time shaving my legs, running the razor over and over my skin until it was all perfectly smooth. I turned on the TV and tried to immerse myself in a reality show about fashion designers. I glanced through some college brochures that had come in the mail: Swarthmore, Columbia, Grinnell, Lake Forest. I wandered up to my room and spread my physics homework across my desk and stared intently at the problem set while my good foot bounced against my chair. I stared out the window. I made my bed. I didn't check my voicemails.

Finally, late in the afternoon, I sat down with my creative writing notebook and turned to a blank page. The pen in my hand hung over the page, bobbing up and down like a glass bird trying to drink.

I remember . . .

I remember the party. It's late and the living

room is lit only by the glow of white Christmas lights around the windows, not carefully stapled flush against the wooden frames, like your mother would do, but draped lazily and held up with thumbtacks and duct tape. The room is thick with cigarette smoke and muffled voices and the awareness of how late it is, the voice in your head nagging that it's way past curfew and no matter how distracted your friend's mom has been recently she's definitely going to notice how late it is, but you're so tired and even though the couch is the most hideous pattern of brown-and-orange velour, it's comfortable, and maybe you'll just have one more cigarette before you finally rouse yourself and go find the girls.

And somehow your cup is empty again even though you've just been sipping it, seriously, because Prescott's mixing awfully strong drinks and you really should be drinking mostly just Coke and only a little rum, just enough rum to make you forget about how annoying it is to be sitting in the smoky living room on this ugly couch so you can be the designated driver for your best friends' booty calls. Prescott hands you another cup, plastic with a Hawkeyes logo on it, the kind that should hold a Bloody Mary with a stalk of green celery at a tailgating party, not mostly rum and some Coke, long after midnight on an ugly sagging couch in a shabby college house.

Prescott sits down next to you and goes, "Hey,"

and you're like, "What?" "I'm glad you're here," he says, and you kind of laugh because you're so tired and maybe you were glad you were here three hours ago when those cute soccer guys were checking you out, but now? Not so much. But you go, "Thanks," and he's like, "I'm so sick of these parties, they're so fake," and you're like, "Yeah, totally," even though this is only the second college party you've been to, and before everyone disappeared into their various corners and rooms it was actually pretty cool. And he says, "You're not like them; you're different," and you're flattered even though you shouldn't be because you've known him forever, since you were in seventh grade and he was still a short high school sophomore who couldn't even drive yet. "Sometimes I just want to take off, you know," he says, "just jump on a train or something and get out of here, head out west, away from all the phony bullshit and everything," and you light another cigarette and say, "Yeah, that would be awesome," mostly just to make conversation, because it's clear that Lacey and Nikki aren't going to just show up on their own anytime soon.

And then he's talking about New Mexico, how dark it gets at night and all the stars and camping in the mountains under the wide desert sky, but you're not really listening, you're wondering about Nikki and that dude she was hanging on and hoping she's okay because she looked kind of out of it and usually you and Lacey tag team to make sure Nikki's okay, because she's a little too sweet for her own good sometimes. "In New Mexico you can see what the weather's doing fifty miles away on the Sangres," he says. Does Lacey seem unhappy lately, you wonder. She was drinking more than usual and you had a weird feeling tonight when you were getting ready, like your friends were somehow slipping away, so you yelled, "Group hug!" and grabbed them around the necks even though Lacey was trying to straighten her hair and you almost made her drop her iron on the carpet but she didn't, she managed to set it down, and the three of you hugged like you used to and for a minute everything was perfect, the three of you in one sculpture of twisted arms and twining hair, like in Girl Scouts when everyone would reach into the circle and grab someone else's hand and then you'd have to figure out how to untangle yourselves as a team. But then Lacey laughed and asked if you were lezzing out on her and pulled away and Nikki gave you one last squeeze and joked about how she was usually the hugger of the group, and your arms untangled on their own like a knot that's been cut open.

The rum is making you sad, maybe, so you drink a little more to make the sad go away and you try not to think about how pathetic and lonely this stupid house is, this stupid party, how in a few hours it will just be empty cups and beer bottles on the floor, full ashtrays and random girls' left-behind sweatshirts and a lingering sense of disappointment, and you drink a little more to make those thoughts go away. Prescott's so nice to stay here with you, it would be much more depressing without him, and his eyes are pretty in the dark and it's kind of cool whatever he's talking about, God and the desert or whatever, and the house is lonely and pathetic and he's nice and he's close and then you're kissing him. He tastes like vodka and ash and mint and teeth and his hand slides up your arm and it's warm and it's different from being with Jake; his lips ask questions and his fingers trace the skin down your neck and wander back up into the forest of your hair and you haven't kissed anyone but Jake in two years and you really shouldn't be doing this. But he's so gentle and you're so sleepy and it's all brand-new, like you're exploring room after room of an infinite mansion, each room more beautiful than the last.

No, you can't do this. Say it. I can't—your voice is quiet, breath against his cheek, and he goes to kiss your neck and you want to let him but you can't. Really, I—

And then Lacey is there with unmistakable delight in her voice as she says your names. "Paige!

Prescott! I'm shocked!" And Prescott practically jumps to the other side of the couch, abandoning you to the cold center. "We weren't —" he says. "Nothing happened. . . ."

I put down the pen and shivered, staring at the words on the page. It was more than I wanted to remember.

Later that afternoon, my sister appeared in my doorway. "Hey." I hit the MUTE button on the TV remote, but she wasn't fooled. "How's the migraine?"

"Fine," I said. "How was mushroom cups?"

"As awful as you might imagine," she said. "But at least Jake and his dad weren't there."

I grabbed my stuffed dog. "Where was Jake?"

"I thought you didn't care." She waited, watching me. "Anyway," she said, "Jeremy wanted me to ask you if you want to come with us tonight. We're going to Iowa City for a poetry reading or something. . . . He said it's homework for the class you guys have together?"

"Crap." I'd forgotten all about it. "I don't want to impose . . ."

My sister rolled her eyes. "Whatever."

"Seriously, if it's like a date or something . . ."

"Funny," she said. "Anyway, we're leaving in a half hour, so if you want to come you should probably put some clothes on and curl your nose hair or whatever."

I weighed my options: continue with my plans to lie

around feeling sorry for myself and trying not to think about things, or get a homework assignment out of the way and maybe distract myself from my own thoughts for a while. "I'll come." I shut off the TV and swung myself out of bed.

Miranda looked surprised. "Really?"

"Sure, yeah. Just let me get dressed and, you know, curl my nose hair. I'll be ready in twenty."

The bookstore was downtown, with a huge metal awning that reminded me of some of the Métro stations in Paris. Jeremy led us inside and up a flight of stairs to where a bunch of people were already sitting in rows of green plastic chairs. At the front of the room, Mr. Tremont sat behind a solid wooden table, along with a guy in hipster glasses and a girl with short dreadlocks.

"You didn't tell me Mr. Tremont would be here!" I whispered to Jeremy. He grinned and nodded.

My sister rolled her eyes. "Oh boy. You didn't tell me *she* was in the Teacher Love Club, too."

"Trust me, you'll be begging to join in a few minutes," he told her.

The three of us grabbed chairs toward the very back of the room, shuffling awkwardly past an older couple to get to them. I was surprised by how many people were there. If many more showed up, it would be standing room only.

After a few minutes, a tall man with a salt-and-pepper beard and a soft-green shirt stepped up to the microphone.

He introduced himself, saying he had been privileged to teach the three poets who would be reading tonight. Jeremy and I looked at each other. Mr. Tremont had a teacher!

As the man talked, I jotted some of his phrases in my notebook, unsure of what I might need for my homework. "We have seldom been in such dire need of poetry." People nodded and murmured in agreement as he spoke. My pen flew across the page, trying to capture his words, while a tiny part of my mind was remembering the first time Mr. Tremont had appeared in our stale classroom. Now, as then, I felt the shiver of truth, a sudden understanding that life was so much more than Willow Grove, Iowa, bigger than a sale on bath towels or the price of gas.

The bearded man adjusted his round glasses and introduced Mr. Tremont. In the front row, a woman went, "Woohoo!" and the audience laughed.

Looking a little nervous, Mr. Tremont stepped behind the podium. "I only hope that I can live up to that generous introduction," he said, smiling at his teacher. "Honestly, I wouldn't be the writer I am without Mark." He shuffled through the pages in front of him. "And now I'm going to read a poem that he's never liked." The audience laughed again, but I sat tensely, poised like a runner at the beginning of a race, my fingers gripping my pen.

He read, and it was like falling through water, like spinning under a clear night's sky. I didn't understand a single one of his poems on a literal level; I was listening too hard for that. Instead, I felt the meaning in my veins, the same way I'd felt the music the night before when the dread-locked kid stopped me and held me still for once. Made me *listen*. Mr. Tremont's words had the fleeting perfection of the moon slipping in and out of cloud on an autumn night, deer paused at the edge of a wood, a flock of geese a moment before they fly.

The audience seemed to think the other two poets were good, too, but I hardly heard them. I was distracted by questions I had about Mr. Tremont: Did he ever write, like I did, without even knowing what he was going to say? Was he ever surprised when he got to the end of the page? After he wrote, did he feel lighter?

Afterward, Jeremy, Miranda, and I hung back and watched as everyone swarmed Mr. Tremont and the other poets. Jeremy had his camera out and was taking pictures of everything. The first person to reach Mr. Tremont was a woman, probably around his age, who looked like Shanti. I wondered if they were related. She wore an orange sari, the color of tiger lilies, with gold embroidery along the edges. "Do you think that's his girlfriend?" I asked Jeremy. He pointed the camera at her, watching, then lowered it and shook his head.

"Hi, strangers!" Shanti popped up from behind a bookcase, and I jumped. It was like I'd thought her into existence.

"Did I scare you?" she asked.

"Only in the straitjacket kind of way," Jeremy said. I put my hand over my heart to steady it. If Shanti was here, then chances were good that Ethan was, too. The events of the night before, which I'd spent all day so carefully ignoring, suddenly came flooding back to me.

"Funny." She looked at me. "So? What did you think? Wasn't it amazing?"

I nodded, not trusting myself to speak.

My sister shrugged. "It was okay. I didn't really get it."

Jeremy clapped his hand over her mouth. "Forgive her. She's been living in a cave. I'm doing my best to acculturate her, but it's slow going." He widened his eyes and staged whispered. "She's still thinks boy bands make actual music."

Miranda punched him in the arm. "I do not."

Ethan joined us, carrying Shanti's purse. "Don't mind me, I'm just the purse man." He glanced at me but I looked away before he could make eye contact.

"You're not just the purse man, Ethan!" Shanti said. "You're the *best* purse man."

"I'm touched," he told her.

"Anyway, you guys," Shanti said, turning back to us. "Don't you feel weirdly shy now? Like you're not good enough to talk to Mr. Tremont, you know? What is he doing teaching high school? He should be, like, the poet laureate. Of the world!"

We all turned to watch Mr. Tremont, who was still surrounded by his fans. A short man with a well-trimmed beard stepped forward to hug him. He whispered something in Mr. Tremont's ear and they both laughed. The woman in orange tapped the bearded guy on the arm and pouted at him until he hugged her. The rest of the crowd began to disperse. "Okay. I'm going to go talk to him," Shanti announced. "You guys coming?"

I could feel Ethan looking at me, so I kept my eyes on Shanti. "Sure," I said. "Let's go."

Mr. Tremont's face lit up as we approached. "Hey, you guys! What did you think?" Fumbling between shyness and adulation, Ethan, Jeremy, and I told him that we'd loved it. I pulled Miranda forward, introducing her as my sister. Mr. Tremont shook her hand, thanking her for coming. Shanti's praise was more articulate than ours, and within moments she was deep in conversation with him, discussing some metaphor and casually dropping words like "semantics" and "trope."

The woman in orange extended a hand toward me. "I'm Padma."

"Hi," I said, shaking her hand. "I'm —"

"This is Paige," Mr. Tremont interrupted. "A future workshopper."

Padma's eyebrows went up. "Oooh, a writer?"

"Not really," I said, blushing furiously. "I'm not . . ."

Shanti held out her hand. "I'm Shanti."

"And this is Ethan, Jeremy, and Mirror," Mr. Tremont added.

"More writers?" Padma asked Mr. Tremont, looking at

him while she shook Shanti's hand. Then to Shanti, she said, "Padma Madhuri. I thought Iowa only made white people."

Shanti laughed. "Right?"

"You guys came down just for Cam's reading? What did you think?"

"We loved it," Shanti said. "Mr. Tremont, you were the best by far."

"Well, I'm happy you guys made it," Mr. Tremont said. "And flattered."

"It was homework, after all," Jeremy said.

Padma laughed. "You give them homework? And the homework is to come hear you read poetry?"

"Not me," Mr. Tremont said. "Their teacher had assigned them the task of going to hear one of the readings around town this weekend. They didn't have to come to this one specifically."

"Of course they did!" Padma said, and Shanti nodded at her like they were old friends.

"Obviously," Shanti said.

Padma grabbed the bearded guy and pulled him toward us. "Mason, you have to meet these guys. They're Cam's students, and they are the coolest."

Mason shook our hands, smiling. "I've heard a lot about you."

Afterward, Jeremy, Miranda, Shanti, Ethan, and I went to Perkins, where Shanti industriously built a sculpture with silverware and creamers while Jeremy and Miranda colored pictures in Jeremy's notebook with stolen crayons and Ethan dipped his french fries in ranch dressing. I'd waited until everyone else was seated before I slid into the booth, so I could be certain not to sit next to him, but I couldn't stop sneaking glances at him, worrying he might say something about last night. But he seemed content to joke around with Shanti and Jeremy, and he didn't catch me looking at him.

It was the first time I'd hung out with Miranda, outside of obligatory family functions, and I was surprised by how well she got along with everyone. For once in our lives, she seemed perfectly comfortable, while I felt like a total outsider. Everyone else was so aggressively individual. I felt like Molly Ringwald in *The Breakfast Club*—no matter what happened tonight, on Monday I would go back to being the pretty girl and once again have nothing in common with any of these people.

Jeremy and Shanti suddenly jumped out of the booth, throwing bad insults at each other. "I'll claw a stuffed kitty so fast it will make your mom look slow."

"Yeah? Well, I'll claw your *face!*"

Miranda slid out of the booth after them, and I looked at Ethan for an explanation. "Claw machine competition," he said.

"Ah." I went back to not looking at him, pretending to be very interested in the syrup jars instead. They looked a little bit like baby penguins, I thought. Clearly they needed to gather near the coffee pot, which looked like their mama.

"Um," Ethan said. "About last night . . ."

"Right," I said quickly. "I'm sorry about the sweatshirt. If I'd known I would see you tonight, I totally would have brought it back to you."

"Not the sweatshirt. The . . . you know . . ."

I braced myself and looked up at him. His eyes were warm and dark. "It didn't—it was just a mistake. I was drunk. I have a boyfriend."

It was a lie, of course: I'd been totally sober by the time I saw him. I waited for him to call me out on it, to argue with me, to try to convince me that it meant something. But he just nodded. "Right."

"And, um," I said, feeling like an asshole. "Could we just keep it between us? Because . . . boyfriend. And if it got out . . ."

"I get it," Ethan said. "No worries. It didn't happen."

"I'm sorry." I peeked up at him. "Are we cool?"

He smiled. "Of course."

"Good." I felt surprisingly relieved. One less person I would have to avoid in the hallways. "Thanks. And I promise, I'll bring your sweatshirt to class on Monday."

"Don't bother," Ethan said. "It's yours."

On Sunday, my mother insisted on taking me to get a pedicure. "Nothing like some TLC for your feet to perk you up!" She herded me into her yellow SUV, whistling to herself, and adjusted all her mirrors before backing out into the street. I reached out and fiddled with the radio, searching for something good. She flipped her blinker on half a block before the stop sign at the end of our street. "Did you hear about the Lanes? Of course, it makes sense after last spring. I don't know if Brenda will ever forgive herself. But still, it's sad. Poor Lacey."

"Yeah." In the side mirror, my lips stretched into a grimace.

"Stella says that Jake's been helping Lacey work through this terrible time. I suppose he understands how she's feeling, after what happened with his father." Her voice dropped conspiratorially. "Not that Stella said anything about that, of course. Even at the time, she wouldn't say a word about it. Of course, that was the summer we were working on the Owens wedding, and no one had a single moment to think about anything else."

The morning was overcast, and pale-gray clouds sat against the flat-white sky. I pulled at the zipper on my hooded sweatshirt, running it up and down. My cell phone was still at home, sitting on the table by my bed. They'd all called me the day before: Lacey, Jake, Nikki. I still hadn't listened to a single message.

"Marriages take work, you know," my mother said. "That's what they don't tell you, beforehand. They take a lot of work. You have to be willing to give up on a lot of things to make a marriage work."

I wondered what she had given up. Everyone loved her.

In the summers, on her rare days off from trying to get ahead at Stella Austin Events, my mother swam laps at the club pool. Afterward, she sat in a beach chair under an umbrella, her face in the shade, her long legs stretched out before her in the sun. From her chair she held court, trading secrets with the other women, laughing with the men. It wasn't until I was in middle school that I'd started to recognize the looks they gave her, the openly appreciative glances, the secret smiles. She soaked it all in as if it fed her.

"Jake asked about you yesterday," my mother said. "Did you have a fight?"

"No," I said. "I don't want to talk about it."

She slowed long before the turn. "Is it about Lacey?"

Her shoulder against his — the way she leaned into him, for protection — the way he leaned over her, a shelter —

"I hope you're not acting jealous, Paige. Jealousy makes women ugly."

"I'm not being jealous."

"You know, Delia Easton always had a jealousy problem. It made her into something of a shrew. It's sad."

"Mrs. Easton? Her husband was screwing every woman he could! She wasn't jealous; she was married to an asshole!"

"Language, missy. Princesses never cuss."

I crossed my arms. "Whatever."

"Anyhow," my mother said. "Delia is a perfect example of what I'm talking about. We have responsibilities in

172

relationships, Paige. The deal is, you stick together for better or for worse, but if it's all worse and no better, you're not holding up your end of the deal. You can't expect someone to be there for you if you're never there for him, and that means sometimes you have to set aside your own petty grievances." She pulled into the parking lot of Willow Grove's little strip mall and eased the SUV into a spot marked COMPACT CARS ONLY.

"I wouldn't exactly call infidelity a 'petty grievance,'" I said.

She turned to me. "Infidelity is only a symptom of a bigger problem, Paige. And maybe it's not fair, but when there's a problem, it always falls to the women to fix it." She shrugged. "We come by it naturally. We're nurturers; we nurture. I don't know the exact details of Delia and Charlie's marriage, but I do know this: he's not going to come home if there's nothing to come home to." She lowered the rearview mirror to check her eye makeup and wiped away a tiny smudge under her lower lashes. "I'm not going to pretend it's easy, honey, because it's not."

I wondered what Mr. Tremont or his friend Padma would think of this little lecture. The thought made me feel weirdly embarrassed.

My mother patted my knee. "You ready? We deserve a little pampering!"

At Jolie, we settled ourselves into adjacent chairs while a heavyset woman hovered over us, adjusting the massage

173

chairs and filling the tubs with hot water for us to soak our feet. "My daughter has a good shot at being the homecoming queen this year," my mother told the woman. "Isn't that exciting?"

I buried my face in my hands. "Mom."

The nail lady's name tag said, I'M KARLA! ASK ME ABOUT OUR REVLON SPECIALS! She kneeled at my mother's feet, smiling up at me. "Oh gosh, you must be real proud there! That's a very big deal, isn't it!" Her Minnesota accent was so thick that it took my ears a few seconds to translate her words into English.

My mother looked pleased. "It is a very big deal! We've been working toward this for years!"

Karla nodded, pulling my mother's right foot out of the water. "I had a girlfriend in high school who missed getting onto the prom court by three votes, and you know what? She never forgot it. To this day, she blames her first divorce on the fact that she was three votes shy of being pretty enough." She lowered her voice and glanced over her shoulder, as if her high school girlfriend might walk into the nail salon at any moment. "Of course, I say it has more to do with the fact that her first husband loved his six-packs of Schlitz more than he loved her, don't you know."

"I was the homecoming queen myself," my mother said. "In high school *and* college, if you can believe that! Of course, that was a long time ago." She shook her hair slightly, as if she couldn't quite believe it herself, but I knew that she was waiting for Karla to tell her how she could believe it, of course she could.

Instead, Karla looked at me. "You know, I always thought it would be fun to ride in the parade. It goes right past the store there, you know." She pointed, and I tried not to notice the folds of her arm swinging under the fabric of her sleeve. "Those girls always look so happy."

My mother looked at me, triumphant. "It's a real honor, Paige." She looked off toward the slatted windows, where potted plants and venetian blinds disguised the view to the parking lot outside. "These are the best years of your life, Paige. They really are. Enjoy them while you can."

I wasn't sure why she was arguing with me when I hadn't said anything to contradict her, but suddenly I wanted to. I pulled my feet out of the water, shaking them gently. "I know it's an honor, Mom. But isn't life actually supposed to get even better than this? Shouldn't the best years of my life still be ahead of me? I mean . . ." I closed my eyes, searching for the right words to say what I meant, even to know what I meant, as if I could find them etched across the insides of my eyelids, but the slate was blank, and by the time I opened my eyes, Karla had come back with a selection of nail polish, and my mother was deeply engaged in a discussion of the merits of eggplant versus mauve, and she never answered my question.

chapter TWELVE

"All hail the power of the blue dot!" A circle of people were standing outside the newspaper room as I walked to my locker Monday morning. They laughed and pushed one another, reaching for a piece of paper floating above their heads. "Gather round, all ye infidels, and worship the awesome power of the mystical blue dot!"

"Praise be! Praise be! The blue dot is printed!" someone shouted reverently.

Jeremy stood in the center of the crowd, holding the paper and yelling. "The blue dot knows all, tells nothing! It has the power to heal! It has the power to reveal!"

Without really meaning to, I slowed as I approached them, looking for my sister. She was rarely far from

Jeremy these days. I recognized some of the people from creative writing, as well as some of my sister's friends, but I didn't see her anywhere. Elizabeth Carr stood next to Jeremy, leading the crowd in its praise of the blue dot through hysterical giggles.

Jeremy called to me. "Hey, Paige! Come worship the mystical blue dot!"

"The mystical blue dot heals all woes!" Elizabeth added. "Praise be!"

"Oh," I said. "Um." I could feel the curious eyes of the crowd on me, wondering whether I'd join them or hang back, and I thought of Shanti on Friday night, laying out the social strata I'd never even thought about. Jeremy wasn't a popular kid, not in the way that Lacey and I were popular, but he was the president of the senior class and widely liked.

An amused voice spoke in my ear. "The blue dot knows all, tells nothing." I jumped in surprise. Ethan stood beside me, smiling. "Sounds like someone I know."

I rolled my eyes. "Hardly."

"The blue dot grants the truest wishes of your secret heart!" Elizabeth called, still giggling.

Jeremy looked at me. "What about it, Paige? Behold the power of the blue dot? What lies in your heart? Fame, fortune, and a bag of Skittles? Homecoming queen? One touch and the throne can be yours."

For a moment, homecoming queen sounded wrong, but then I shook myself. What else could it possibly be? Though I wouldn't say no to Skittles.

"Behold its majestic power!" Elizabeth cried. "Worship the blue dot!"

Six months ago I would never have touched a stupid blue dot just because the weird kids were yelling at me. In fact, I wouldn't even have slowed down, and I definitely wouldn't have been singled out as their target. Then again, if my friends had been yelling about something in the hallway, I would have stopped to listen. What was the difference? Just that the weird arty kids were yelling about a piece of paper, while my friends would have been yelling about some kegger they were planning?

Jeremy smiled at me, and I made a decision. "Fine." I glanced at Ethan and tried to match Jeremy's royal tones. "I shall grant thy wish, but henceforth I warrant the blue dot should, um, behold the awesome power . . . of me." I reached forward and poked the paper, and the crowd applauded.

I turned back to my place at the back of the crowd, but Mr. Tremont was standing in my spot, next to Ethan. "Nice," he said. "Whitman would approve."

Shanti joined us. *"I celebrate myself, and sing myself,"* she said, her voice lilting up and down with the lines. *"And what I assume you shall assume, / For every atom belonging to me as good belongs to you."*

"I'm impressed," Mr. Tremont said. "But not surprised."

Shanti's round cheeks turned pink, and she shook her dark hair over her shoulder. "That's all I know, actually. My dad made me memorize tons of poems when I was little, but I only remember the beginnings of most. I can do the first few stanzas of 'Prufrock' for you, if you'd like, or all of 'Ozymandias,' or most of 'Stopping by Woods,' or—"

"Yeah, yeah, we get it," Ethan said. "You're a genius." He smiled at me, as if this were some inside joke we'd been passing back and forth for years.

Shanti ignored his teasing tone and answered him seriously. "Only insofar as your average African gray parrot is a genius. I was my father's little parlor trick, that's all."

"Parrot?" Ethan asked. "Don't you mean cuckoo?"

She shook her head. "Poor Ethan. You try so hard, but you're just not funny."

Behind us, Jeremy and Elizabeth were still yelling about the dot. "All hail! All hail the power of the blue dot!"

Mr. Tremont laughed. "You guys remind me of my friends in high school."

I took a half step back, knowing he didn't mean me and not wanting to intrude. I could hardly follow the conversation, much less start quoting Whitman. Anyway, I had to get to my locker before history, and even though Elizabeth was in my class and didn't seem concerned about the time, I didn't want to be late.

But Mr. Tremont looked at me and asked, "How's the writing going? Going to be ready for workshop?"

I cleared my throat. "I don't . . ."

"Of course she will be," Shanti said. "We all will. Class guinea pigs. First to fly, first to fall. Like Laika the Space Dog."

Mr. Tremont looked confused, and Ethan said, "She means Muttnik. *Sputnik II* had a dog in it."

"Actually, the Russians sent nine dogs into space, all total," Shanti said. "I like to think that they flew off and started their own planet. A dog planet." She caught my eye and shrugged. "I did a research project on it in seventh grade. Sputnik, not the dog planet."

Mr. Tremont said, "Well then, yes. You'll be our Space Dogs, and you can tell us how the view is from up there."

"Laika died of stress and overheating a few hours into the flight," Shanti said.

Ethan rolled his eyes. Mr. Tremont said, "Let's hope my class isn't quite that bad." He looked at me and smiled. "I know you're up to it, though. You're tough."

The five-minute-warning bell rang, and the crowd around Elizabeth and Jeremy began to disperse. The hallway flooded with people, and Nikki appeared, grabbing my forearm. "Paige. I have to talk to you." Before I could protest, or even say anything in apology or thanks to Mr. Tremont, she dragged me off to a corner between a fire door and the end of a bank of lockers.

"Ow." I rubbed my arm where she'd pulled on it, wondering if it would bruise. I imagined a tiny black-and-blue circlet above my wrist. It would match the one on my ankle from Friday night. "Jeez, Nikki."

"Did you talk to Lacey?" Her eyes shot back and forth, locking first on my left eye, then my right, and back, so quickly I felt a little dizzy. She glanced over her shoulder, into the crowded hallway.

"No," I said. "I haven't talked to anyone."

"Oh yeah," she said. "Where were you all weekend? I called you, like, six hundred times."

"I was sick." Across the hall, Jeremy and Elizabeth were taping the paper with the blue dot to the door of the newspaper classroom, laughing and yelling, "Praise be!"

Ethan and Shanti walked past, laughing. They didn't look at me.

I turned back to Nikki, who was still doing the darting-eye thing. "Paige. Listen. Please don't say anything to Lacey about Friday night, okay? Because she would be mad. And I really can't handle that right now. She can't know. Okay?"

There was only a minute or so before the last bell, and the teachers in their doorways started shooing kids off to class. "Hurry up, folks! Let's go! Get to class!"

Nikki grabbed my hand. "Paige. Please."

I nodded, distracted. "Yeah, fine. I promise I won't say a word to Lacey."

Nikki sighed, relaxing her hold on me. "Oh gosh. Thanks, Paige. You're the best. Okay. Thanks. I have to go. Okay. Thank you!" She took off down the hallway, skipping lightly on impossibly high heels. I watched her until she disappeared, and I didn't move until the final bell rang.

• • •

I avoided Lacey and Jake all morning. In Contemptible History, I sat on the other side of the room, behind Jason Anderson, who always smelled like the pigs his family raised. I watched with satisfaction as Lacey craned her neck, searching the room for me. The look on her face — confused, troubled, cracks in her usually serene mask — made sitting behind Pigboy utterly worth it. Between classes, I took different routes down the hallways, avoiding the rooms I knew they'd be coming out of or going into.

At lunch, I hid in the library, idly flipping pages in physics books so the librarian wouldn't ask questions. Halfway through the period, I heard familiar voices and peeked through the stacks to see Nikki hunched over a computer, sitting with Jeremy. I tried to remember if they had a class together. Nikki took notes as Jeremy moved the mouse, clicking and pointing to the screen. I leaned in closer, trying to see what they were doing, but managed to knock a dictionary off the shelf and had to duck as they both turned in my direction. Embarrassed, I slunk back to my carrel, gathered up my things, and spent the rest of lunch in the English hallway bathroom.

As usual, the best part of the day was creative writing. "If you'd be so kind as to focus your attention on the board here," Mr. Tremont started, pulling a white screen down from above the chalkboard and wheeling an overhead projector into the front row. "Jenna, could you please hit the lights for us? And, Paige, could I get you to scoot your desk over just a bit?" I did, and he maneuvered the projector in next to my desk.

"Great. Okay, guys, today I want to talk at you a little before we write, if you don't mind." The class murmured its consent. Mr. Tremont turned the projector on, and a hazy field of haystacks appeared on the screen before us. "How many people have heard of the Impressionists?"

A few people raised their hands, and Mr. Tremont asked Jenna French to share what she knew about them. "Well," she said, "the Impressionists were a group of artists in the eighteen hundreds who took their canvases outside and tried to capture the landscape by painting really fast. They used colors in new ways, and their brushstrokes were visible in their finished paintings." I twisted in my seat to see if she was reading from a textbook. Her cheeks were pink in the reflected light of the projector, and I caught her smile before she glanced down at her desk to hide it.

"Perfect," Mr. Tremont said. "The Impressionists realized that in order to capture the truth of the landscape in that particular moment in time, they had to paint quickly to get the light right, because light was everything. They began to understand that everything that we see, at every moment, is just light bouncing off everything."

He slid a new painting onto the projector. Another hay field. "The light changes at every second, so you have to work pretty fast to capture the truth of any given moment."

He showed us another haystack, and another, and another. They all looked similar, but none of them was exactly the same. "Anyone know who painted all these haystacks?"

A couple kids shouted out in unison. "Monet!"

Mr. Tremont smiled. "You guys are awesome. That's right, Claude Monet." He put up another haystack and turned to us. "So here's the deal. In order to capture the truth of a moment, you have to work fast. The painters used big brushstrokes. We'll use pens. For the next twenty minutes, I want you to find a spot in the school, anywhere on campus, and capture the truth of your setting as well as you can. Write fast. Write big. Get every single moment. Notice the details: not *a kid walks down the hall* but *a dog-faced boy with red high-tops and a Lisa Frank binder swaggers down the hall.*"

We laughed.

"See?" he asked. "Original details tell the truth. That's all we're trying to do here, folks. We're just trying to tell the truest truth we can. Push through the voice in your head that says, 'You can't write that! It's not allowed!'" He smiled at us. "I'm giving you permission to write whatever you want, as long as it's true. Okay? And really, don't think too hard, just write."

He clapped, and the class started gathering notebooks and pens. "Oh, and one more thing—as you grab the truth and splash it on your page . . . do so quietly, okay? Don't get me in trouble." He smiled. "Twenty minutes! Go!"

I settled myself on the floor in a quiet corner of the school, at the intersection of the English and history hallways. The floor was cool under my legs. A freshman girl walked past, her boots squeaking against the polished linoleum. I thought about the painters, slapping on their paint to capture the truth of a moment. I thought about Mr. Tremont, encouraging us to write what we saw, what we heard, what we felt.

I feel . . .

It's cold on the floor, and dark in the corner. In the room behind me, I can hear Mrs. Bailey talking about the Treaty of Versailles. She wants people to understand its importance. Across the hall, they're watching a video on the Seven Wonders of the Ancient World. A girl with long red hair strides down the hallway in tall black boots. Her footsteps squeak loudly in the quiet hum of the halls. She sees me looking at her and looks back, probably wondering what I'm doing on the floor in this dark corner. The second someone sees me, I'm aware of nothing else but being seen, and all my attention is taken up by what I look like and how I hold myself. It's not until she disappears into a gray classroom that I can go back to watching the world, and forget about being watched. I let myself relax against the wall, relax like the first time Jake kissed me under the cool green trees. I sank into him, and every kiss said you are important because I choose you, you are precious because I want you, you are safe because you are with me. With every kiss he said here you are and here is home, and our bodies matched together, each curve and concave fitting together like we were meant to be that close, like we'd been invented merely to belong to each other . . .

The pen paused in the middle of the line, hovering. Down the hall, they were both in film appreciation together, watching some art film as Lacey flipped her hair around and flirted with Jake until he agreed to rub her shoulders in the classroom's cool darkness, as she planned the next step in her campaign to make him forget me entirely.

Slowly, methodically, I drove long lines through the sentences, one after another.

After class, Jake was waiting for me. "Paige."

"I'm late."

"You don't even have a class this period," he said, and smiled, as if pleased with himself for proving how well he knew me.

"Well, you do. You should go." Jake didn't move. I sighed. "I have homework."

He pulled a gift from behind his back, a slim rectangle wrapped in his mother's signature silver paper. "Well then, you'll have to open this later, I guess." When I didn't reach for it, he slid it onto the stack of books in my arms. "Paige, about Friday—"

"I really need to go."

"I'll walk you to your locker," he said, catching up with me. "A little bird told me you went to a poetry reading this weekend?"

"It was homework," I said. "For creative writing."

"You like that class, huh?"

"You're going to be late for gym."

He stepped in front of me, cutting me off. "Hey."

I stopped.

Jake reached out to put a hand on my arm. "Look, I just want you to know, okay, that even though everyone else says that that class is really gay, I know you're a really good student, and I totally respect that. And maybe it's a good thing you ended up in creative writing, you know, because you are a good writer, like when you helped me with my history paper last year. And I just—"

"Who told you where I was this weekend, anyway?"

"Your mom." He said, and laughed, like it was the punch line to a raunchy joke. *God.* I pushed past him and headed toward my locker.

"Paige, wait. I'm sorry. It actually was your mom. When you wouldn't answer your cell, I called your landline, and she said you went to Iowa City with your sister."

"Fine," I said.

"Nothing happened, babe. I know what it looked like, but I swear, I was just . . . Lacey just needed a friend. The divorce . . . And her mom is still really screwed up about the accident. . . ."

I bit my lip, wanting so badly to believe him. He *was* a good guy, and he and Lacey had basically grown up together. Was it possible that he was just being a friend? Just trying to do the right thing?

"Hey," he said softly. "I missed you." He moved in and kissed me on the cheek. His scent washed over me, the familiar blend of warm and clean and skin, and I closed my eyes, wanting to erase everything else.

And then the bell rang, and the hallways were full of running kids and closing doors. "I have to go," I said, and turned away, leaving him standing in the middle of the hallway.

It was a book of poetry, a slender edition of the complete sonnets of William Shakespeare. Even though I was fairly certain that Stella had picked it out for him — and obviously had wrapped it for him — I was still touched. I opened it in my car in the parking lot, idly flipping through it and trying to make sense of the sonnets. They didn't have much to do with the kind of writing we were doing in Mr. Tremont's class, but still. Jake had noticed, and he made an effort. That counted for something. It wasn't enough, not nearly, but my anger, like the pain in my ankle, had faded over the weekend. He was a good guy. He was probably just trying to be nice when I caught him with Lacey. It wasn't his fault, it was hers: she was the one manipulating him. We'd talk later, get everything out in the open. Work through it. It wouldn't be the first time.

I didn't drive out to my secret springs hoping to run into Ethan. I went because I craved the peace of the lapping lake and the silence of the afternoon woods. It was the only place I could escape from everyone else in my life, the only place I could think of where I wouldn't be watched, scrutinized, studied. Judged.

Somehow, though, I didn't mind when his feet appeared at the top of the path, hesitating before scrambling down the hill to the tiny clearing. "Am I intruding?"

I was perched on a thick tree root, dangling my feet in the water. My notebook sat closed in my lap. "No."

He half ran, half jumped the last thirty feet. "You *have* to tell me how you do that gracefully."

"I'm very talented."

"Obviously." He stretched, turning to crack his back. "Are you sure I'm not interrupting you? I was just running, and I thought I saw you down here — or I thought I saw someone, and since the only person I'd seen before was you, I guessed it might be you again. And — well, it is."

I surprised myself by gesturing to the roots of the tree next to me, an invitation. "It's okay. I wasn't doing anything to interrupt."

He stepped from rock to rock, making his way across the

pool to the far shore where I sat. "Sometimes you need to do nothing, just to recharge. Especially writers. We really need to do nothing."

I ignored the comment about being a writer. "It's hard," I said.

He nodded, hoisting himself onto the protruding roots of the tree next to mine. "It's an art."

"I mean, it's not hard. It's just—it's hard to find time when you can just be yourself, away from everyone—"

"Are you *sure* I'm not intruding?" he asked, and I surprised myself again by insisting.

"No, seriously, it's totally fine."

And it was. It wouldn't have been fine with anyone else—Lacey would have judged, Nikki would have gossiped, Jake would have wanted to make out—but Ethan and I just sat there peacefully, talking about nothing much, kicking our feet in the water, listening to the birds, until the shadows overwhelmed the sunlight and I had to leave. He stayed on the tree, leaning back against the trunk, eyes closed in the last of the afternoon light. I paused at the edge of the clearing, hesitating before I headed up the hill. "Hey, Ethan?"

He opened his eyes. "Yes?"

"Thanks."

"For what?"

"For, um." I gestured to the pool, the trees, the birds dipping from tree to tree. "For this."

"For doing nothing?"

"Exactly."

"I'm a do-nothing champ. Anytime you need someone to do nothing with, I'm your man." He smiled. "Anytime."

chapter THIRTEEN

On Tuesday, I avoided everyone. Again. The only thing on my mind was my piece for creative writing, which I had to turn in first thing the next day. At lunch, I secluded myself in the farthest library carrel, opened my notebook to a fresh page, and . . . stared at it. For the entire period. I probably picked up my pen fifty different times, but when the bell rang at the end of lunch, all I'd managed to write on the page was *September 21. Library.*

God. I was so screwed.

In class Mr. Tremont showed us these slides of modern art, including a urinal hung upside down and labeled as a sculpture, and something called *The Bride Stripped Bare by Her Bachelors, Even,* which he was so excited about that he got the whole class talking about it, just this one sculpture, for almost a full half hour. Of course, in Mr. Tremont's class, every discussion became a lesson in how enough tangential lines can eventually create a circle around something, and after touching on physics, math, what a chocolate grinder is and why it was part of a sculpture, space, robots, World War I, the French, labels, what is art? and how do you define it? the power of words, surrealism, Dadaism, New York, the 1930s, and who gets to decide what is or is not art?—all in less than an hour—by the end of class, it was clear to everyone that we'd gone pretty far in depth about . . . something. When Mr. Tremont talked I kept having flashes of something bigger than me, bigger than Willow Grove, and when I looked around the room I could see it on the other faces, too. It was like prom, where the same kids you see every single day put on tuxes and ball gowns and suddenly become something more, and the people they'll be as adults cling to them like shadows all night long. The room was full of the same faces I'd seen a thousand times, bored in algebra or laughing at lunch, but as everyone nodded with Mr. Tremont and jumped into the discussion, I could see what they'd look like in a year or two, taking notes in a lecture hall or struggling with a paper in the student union. We'd all been getting shiny college brochures for months, ever since the PSATs, but for the first time it actually seemed real, and I understood that when the year was over we'd all leave home and go our separate ways and become the people we were meant to be all along. And the spell wasn't broken until after the bell rang and we stumbled out of class into the fluorescent hallways and turned into the same shallow teenagers we'd been before class. Leaving class was like walking out of a movie theater after an amazing film, when part of you still thinks you're in Denmark or Mexico or a Nazi war camp or on a Southern plantation, and you resent the popcorn smells and the car noises and the cold night air of the real world for intruding on your dream.

Disoriented, I wandered off toward the library again to work on . . . whatever. When the bell rang, I had a page covered with doodled daisies and little stars, but still nothing I could turn in. I lectured myself through the crowded hallways. "Okay, Paige. Focus." I pushed through the doors into the cloudy afternoon, still muttering to myself. The sky was white and textureless, hanging right behind the contours of the lampposts and trees. Halfway to my car, I heard a shout behind me. "Paige! Wait up!" I closed my eyes, briefly, and thought about pretending I hadn't heard. I couldn't deal with Nikki or Lacey right now, I didn't want to make flyers for homecoming or meet with Dr. Coulter or answer questions or pretend to be friends. I just wanted to go somewhere nice and quiet and write my piece for creative writing so Mr. Tremont wouldn't think I was an illiterate moron. "Paige!"

I turned around, slowly, preparing myself to explain as nicely as possible that I couldn't do anything but WORK until I was finished with this assignment.

It was Shanti. Nikki would have been hunched over, panting and swearing that she was going to quit smoking, Lacey would have been rolling her eyes and looking supremely irritated that I would even think of making her call across the parking lot after me, especially now that she was crippled, but Shanti caught up to me easily and smiled. "Are you done with your thing for workshop?"

I thought about lying, about telling her it was all covered, no sweat, but before I could compose myself, my mouth opened and I heard myself saying, "God, no. I'm freaking out about it."

She beamed. "Oh, that's great."

I shifted my bag on my shoulder. "Well, I'm glad someone's enjoying my pain."

Her face tilted up to the sky, squinting against the vast whiteness. She shook her head a little, jingling her earrings. "No! I mean, I totally understand, of course, because it's like, high stakes here, right?"

I smiled. "Right. Muttnik."

"Right!" She dug around in the side of her bag and pulled out a cell phone. "Hold on a sec, okay?"

"Um," I said, and stood there while she texted someone with both thumbs. When she finished, she glanced at the phone once more before flipping it into the bag's larger pocket. "So," she said, and looked at me as if waiting for an answer.

"Yes . . . ?" I asked.

"Yes? Fabulous. Do you mind driving? I would, of course, but my car is an absolute disaster and I'm completely embarrassed to let anyone set foot in it."

I shifted my weight. "Um . . . what?"

"Or we could both drive," she said thoughtfully. "Bigger carbon footprint, but then you wouldn't have to bring me back here on your way home. And then afterward, if . . . Yeah, that works better. So you want to meet there?"

"Meet where?"

She stopped. "At Starbucks? To write? You said yes?"

"You didn't ask," I said, sounding more petulant than I meant to.

Shanti squinted up at me. "Really?"

I shrugged. "Nope."

The parking lot was mostly empty already, and it was quiet between us for a moment, until Shanti burst out laughing. "*Really?* I didn't? God, no wonder you look so confused! Am I going senile or something?" Stress bubbled in my veins and I couldn't smile. I had to get this goddamn thing written. I had to.

"Okay, anyway," Shanti said, still smiling to herself. "You should come write with me. I'm going to go work on my story for class, and you should come with me. Yes?"

I took a deep breath and nodded. "Sure."

Being with Shanti was as different from being with Nikki and Lacey as being with Ethan had been. I couldn't stop comparing them in my mind. Nikki would have talked the entire time, Lacey would have spent half the time leaning over the counter, flirting with the college guy who was pulling espresso shots, but Shanti sat across from me, leaning so far over her notebook she was practically resting her face on the paper, and worked. Her pen scratched through lines, she chewed her bottom lip, and sometimes she muttered to herself, making faces at her book. She wrote and she revised, and across from her I wrote and I revised, and after an hour or so Ethan walked through the door and tapped a finger on our table as he passed us on his way to the counter. Shanti smiled without pausing in her writing or looking up.

"Hey," I said.

"How's it going?" he asked quietly.

I looked across the field of Xs and lines. "I don't know, actually."

"Sometimes that's the best way to do it. Just let yourself write whatever. Don't think too hard about it."

The words were familiar, and I squinted at him. "That's what Mr. Tremont said."

Ethan shrugged. "He learned it from me."

"You wish," Shanti said, balling up a napkin and throwing it at him. "Don't you have work to do?"

He sighed. "A true intellectual's work is never done."

"Yeah, it takes a lot of intellectual capacity to froth milk," Shanti said.

"You see what I have to put up with, Paige?"

I nodded seriously. "Hey, Ethan?"

"Yes? You wish to thank the guru for his wise words?" He pressed his hands together as if in prayer.

I brushed my finger against my cheek. "You have a mint chip . . . right there."

He laughed.

"A what?" Shanti asked, but neither of us answered. "You're both weird," she announced, and turned back to her notebook. "Get frothing, Guru Man."

Ethan winked at me then headed back behind the counter. I turned to a clean page, took a breath, and started writing.

> "My baby, I killed my baby, I killed my baby." The voice was a siren looping around and around, echoing off the black tree trunks and keening back to itself. "My baby, my baby." I opened my eyes, tried to resolve the blur into a forest, to focus on the spaces in the sky where the stars should be. I rolled over, not dead, not broken, covered in wet leaves and mud. "Lacey?" I called and my voice tripped in my throat. "Lacey? Nikki?" My hands were brushing at my hair, my arms, my knees, finding dents and bruises, wincing with each discovery but also gleeful, almost giddy, with relief. Alive!
>
> The weeping voice stopped and asked for me in the darkness. "Paige?"
>
> I squinted up the hill, back toward the road where

the lights of another car, not ours, spilled through the fog. Two shapes. "Lacey?" I asked. "Nikki?"

"Paige? It's Brenda! Are you okay?"

Slowly, achingly, I put one leg in front of the other and pulled myself up the hill toward the headlights. "Mrs. Lane?"

She was bent over her daughter, her hands twining Lacey's hair around her fingers. "What are you doing here?" I asked. "What time . . . ?"

"I didn't see you!" she cried. "I was watching for the turn into the neighborhood, you know, it comes up so fast, and then the car was there—you were there!—and oh, my baby! My baby!"

"Mom?" Lacey blinked and blinked and Mrs. Lane collapsed over her weeping, "Oh Lacey, you're alive. I'm so sorry, I'm so sorry."

"What happened?" Lacey asked. "Where's Nikki?" She tried to sit up and immediately cried out. "Fuck! My leg!"

"Is it broken? I'm so sorry, sweetheart, my angel, it was all my fault. . . ."

Her fault? my confused brain asked. Lacey held my gaze, her eyes fierce even through the fog of alcohol and pain and fear. "Where's Nikki?"

"I don't know," I said, and Lacey grabbed her mother. "Mom. Mom. Stop crying. You have to find Nikki."

"I called 911," Mrs. Lane wept. "Before I got out of the car . . . I didn't realize it was you girls. . . ."

"I'll go," I said, and carefully turned back down the hill. The car's nose was pushed up against a tree like a pug dog, snub-nosed and wheezing. Beneath it, the ground sparkled like diamonds. Broken glass in the foggy light. "Nikki!" I called. "Nik!"

"Nikki!" Lacey's voiced floated behind me like we were all underwater.

"Nikki!"

Mrs. Lane tripped down the hillside behind me, still weeping, and we found Nikki tucked behind the steering wheel. In the distance came the sound of sirens, and we shook her shoulders to wake her up and patted her face, and her eyes blinked open and my eyes filled, for the first time, with tears.

It was after dinner by the time I turned into the driveway. The first thing I noticed was the lights. Every bulb in the house, it seemed, was blazing bright into the chilly autumn night. The house was lit up like the tacky ceramic houses my grandmother always set out at Christmas, gathered in a tiny village atop synthetic snow. Even with all the lights on, my house didn't look warm.

The second thing I noticed was the car, parked under the ash tree at the curb next door. The car in which I'd ridden to a thousand school dances and trips to the mall, the car with a long scratch colored in with Sharpie where Lacey had misjudged the distance between the passenger door and a mulberry tree (but with no traces of the accident last spring, as though it never happened). It was the first car I'd ever driven, long before my parents even dreamed of letting me get behind the wheel. Brenda Lane's car. My fingers curled tight against themselves.

Inside, they were all sitting in the living room: Brenda, my mother, Lacey, and Nikki. Brenda was hunched over under my mother's arm, shaking so hard that she bounced slightly against the firm sofa cushions, and at first I couldn't tell if she was crying or laughing. Lacey's face, though, was streaked with red and as frightened as I'd ever seen it. For a moment I saw her as she was last spring, crawling up out of the ditch, confused, crying, covered in wet spring leaves and sparkling squares of glass.

Something close to nausea crept up my throat, and I searched my mind for what I'd done wrong. There was nothing specific, no rule I'd broken, no law I'd breeched, nothing that would upset Brenda Lane. Was there?

My mother looked at me, and I braced myself for the tirade. *Where were you? Why didn't you call? Why didn't you telepathically sense that you were needed here?* I hugged my notebook against my waist, its cover tucked against the soft fabric of my shirt.

She held my gaze, staring at me until I grew uncomfortable and looked away. When she spoke, her voice was soft. "There you are, dear." Her thin hand rubbed against the sharp shoulder blades that stuck out of Brenda Lane's back like stumpy wings. The gold and diamond rings on her left hand caught the light of the reading lamp behind her and scattered tiny rainbows through the room. She cleaned and polished them every week so they'd do just that. "Honey," she said, almost whispering over Brenda's shaking skeleton, "would you do me a big favor and bring me out a box of Kleenex?" By the time she got to the end of the sentence, she was merely mouthing the words.

I nodded quickly and fled the room. The kitchen was dark by comparison, lit only by the faux-vintage chandelier hanging over the island in the center. In here, the air was cooler, like slipping out of an overcrowded party to sneak a cigarette and look at the stars. Someone must have died. Mentally, I scanned through every person we knew, looking to match a face with a funeral, a morbid game of Go Fish. Lacey's grandmother? Grandfather? Oh God, Prescott? What if it was Prescott? Would I have to speak at the funeral? I had only ever been to one funeral in my life, in May of my freshman year, and it wasn't someone I knew well: my grandmother's sister, who had lived in Pennsylvania. Miranda and I were fascinated by the hard wax of Great-aunt Earlene's white body, the unmoving ridges of her breasts and knuckles and chin. Miranda dared me to touch the body, and I did, glancing over my shoulder first in case anyone in the receiving line was watching. I poked the corpse on the arm just above the wrist, and Miranda and I grabbed each other's hands and rushed out of the room into the humid night air.

"Paige?" my mother called, her voice quiet still but insistent, and I grabbed a box of tissues and hurried back into the living room. Brenda was shaking even harder, rolling her face in her hands and making noises halfway between a mumble and a moan. I stretched my arm as far as I could to hand the box to my mother, unwilling to get any closer to Brenda than I had to. She'd been like a mother to me as long as Lacey and I had been friends, which was, essentially, our whole lives. The whole of our lives that mattered, anyway. I'd seen her thrilled and I'd seen her angry, had seen her sleepy and sick and drunk and stressed out and giddy and hungover and plain pissed off. In all the years she'd been my second mother, I had never seen her like this. Not even last spring, though maybe the difference now was in me, standing sober and unmoved as Brenda fell to pieces.

A part of my brain, the part that was still sitting at the coffeehouse with Shanti, still hunched over a notebook, searching for words, wondered: Is seventeen too old to be afraid of the adults around you? Because if I had to put a finger on what I was feeling, I would have to say *afraid*.

My mother looked up at us, me standing like a statue as far from her as possible, Lacey sitting stiff and red faced in the chair by the windows, Nikki puddled on the floor at her feet, looking uncertainly sad and sympathetic. Nobody, I could tell, knew what to do with this grief.

"Paige," my mother said, "why don't you take the girls up to your room for a while."

I nodded mechanically and they stood, and we all trooped up to my room, closing the door a half second after Brenda's voice started wailing below.

In my room, there was a second of silence in which we all shifted, turning over the questions of who we'd been to one another and who we'd be tonight, before Lacey perched her fists on her hips and announced, "He's getting *married*."

Nikki rushed over to her as if to hug her, but at the last minute Lacey turned away and Nikki ended up behind her, standing solemn like a bridesmaid. "Who is?" I asked.

Lacey scowled at me, lips pinched together, and I knew the answer to my own question before the sound of my own voice faded from my ears. "Oh."

"That fucking asshole," Lacey said, and burst into tears.

She didn't want to talk about it, no matter how much Nikki hugged and cajoled her. Lacey got ahold of herself quickly, and her face set like plaster. My heart was divided: half accusing and angry; half sorry for her, and sorry that I couldn't do anything to help. Even sorrier that I didn't really want to.

She wouldn't talk, so finally I turned on the TV in my room and we fell into our usual positions without thinking, Lacey on my bed, Nikki on the floor resting her back against the mattress, and me in the high-backed chair by the window. On TV, people spoke earnestly into a confessional camera. "I'm sorry, but I'm not here to make friends. I'm here to win."

On the floor, Nikki nodded to herself. Lacey remained impassive. I couldn't shake the stress about my creative writing assignment and wanted to get out my notebook, but I thought it would look bad.

Nikki sneezed into her hand, three times in a row, like a cat.

There was a pause. "Bless you," I said. Lacey stared straight ahead, seemingly engrossed in the TV. She had the tiniest smudge of mascara under her left eye, and I almost pointed it out to her. But then I softened, thought, *So what?* Instead, I grabbed my notebook.

"What are you doing?" Lacey asked.

"Nothing. Just something for school."

"School," she echoed, sounding almost like she had no idea what I was talking about. Even though her face was impassive, her voice betrayed her: I could hear the loss. The ache.

Nikki reached over to squeeze Lacey's hand, and I felt stupid. Why hadn't I thought of that? Why couldn't I drop the barbs of resentment and be there for my friend, my best friend? God, I thought, no wonder Lacey turned to Jake. He knew how to be there for someone.

"Is that the hand you just sneezed into?" Lacey asked.

Later, Brenda appeared at my doorway, pale but composed. She stood for a moment with her arm, thin like a dancer's, outstretched to hold the doorframe, and she surveyed the room. "It's so good to have you girls all together!" She smiled widely at us, blinking her watery red eyes.

"Yeah," I said. Nikki nodded. Lacey stayed still, staring at the TV, which was crowing about the Top 100 dance hits of all time. "Oh, I love this one!" Nikki gasped. She watched the screen with bright eyes, singing along. "Dancing queen, eat a bean off a tambourine . . ."

Brenda covered her mouth with a slender hand, just barely stifling a giggle.

"Those aren't the words, Nikki!" Lacey snapped, ignoring her mother. "Are you even listening to yourself?"

Nikki stopped singing. "What?"

"Eat a bean off a tambourine?"

"Yeah, like, they're in a band, so they just use their tambourines as plates," Nikki explained.

Lacey rolled her eyes. "I don't even know what to say in the face of such retardedness."

Brenda moved into the room, picking up the trinkets on my vanity: a clay dish from third grade, filled with change; an empty mascara tube; an origami paper crane, slightly crushed; a framed picture of Nikki, Lacey, and me at the Iowa State Fair in ninth grade. "How great is it that you girls are still so close, after so long?" she asked, staring at the picture as if the happy girls smiling into the sun would be the ones to answer her. "And you're all going to be on homecoming court together." Brenda had been homecoming queen herself, of course. Lacey was following in her footsteps perfectly. I imagined them like snow prints across a yard, fitting together so exactly that they look like one set. Of course, Lacey's prints would have a line of tiny cane holes alongside it, so maybe it wasn't a perfect metaphor.

"Oh, I'm so sure everyone's going to vote for the cripple," Lacey said bitterly.

"Of course they will," Brenda said. "They look up to you. You're so strong and brave."

My mother materialized in the doorway. It was like a convention of queens.

"You girls have been planning this since middle school, and here you are with all your dreams about to come true." Brenda's voice sounded watery, and I worried that she was about to start crying again. "How wonderful is it to be able to see your dreams become reality . . . all those years of hard work, and your whole youth . . . putting him through law school. . . ."

"It's really great," I said quickly. My mother shot me a look. "I mean senior year."

Nikki nodded in agreement. "It's so exciting!"

"So, what's the gossip these days?" my mother asked, changing the subject.

Brenda's eyes lit up. "Yes. Lacey never tells me the juicy stuff. What's going on, girls?"

"Well, there's a new English teacher," Nikki said gamely, stretching her legs out before her. "And he's totally hot!"

Lacey leaned back against my pillows, examining her nails. "Yeah, if you like that kind of thing."

"What do you mean?" I asked.

"He's totally gay."

The mothers exchanged a quick look. Nikki gasped. "What? How do you know?"

Lacey rolled her eyes. "It's totally obvious."

Mr. Tremont wasn't gay. Was he? He was perfect. He was clean lines and warm sweaters and freewriting. He was dark jeans and silver watch and Space Dogs and fine art. Most of the other male teachers wore sweatshirts and running shoes and . . . oh. Was he gay? He was awfully clean. . . . I shook myself. So what. So what if he was. He was still wonderful. "Even if he were, what's wrong with being gay?"

Nikki said, "Yeah, gay guys are the best! They actually like to go shopping!"

"He's a teacher," Lacey said. "It's just wrong."

I opened my mouth but a look from my mother shut it. Mirroring her, I crossed my arms and frowned.

Lacey clutched her cross pendant and said, "The Bible says Adam and Eve, not Adam and Steve."

"Ever since they passed the gay marriage thing, the gays have been overstepping their bounds," Brenda agreed.

Nikki said, "I think it's cute. When they had all those gay couples on the news, it was like, they all looked so happy! And they were so cute together!"

"Marriage is a sacred vow between a man and a woman," Brenda said, blithely unaware of the irony of her comment.

"Anyway, he's still hot, even if he is gay," Nikki said.

Lacey raised an eyebrow. "Well, we all hate him."

My voice burst out of me like pressured water. "What? Why?" My mother looked at me warningly. *Her father's getting married. Don't make it worse, Paige.*

Brenda said, "Lacey, love the sinner, hate the sin."

"I know, Mom. I do hate the sin, but he kicked Randy, Chris, and Brian out of class."

"He did?" my mother asked. "Why?"

Lacey didn't look at me. "For no reason. I think he's just totally prejudiced against good-looking guys because he's afraid . . ."

I pushed up from the high-backed chair. "Whatever," I said, barely containing my anger. "That's bullshit and you know it."

"Paige." My mother's voice was sharp.

"I don't know," Lacey said, "Jake's pretty worried that he'll be next."

"He's not even in creative writing!" I said. But in the next instant it hit me — she wasn't talking about getting kicked out of class.

Nikki looked extremely confused. "I don't get it. What is he afraid of?"

"Now, Lacey . . ." Brenda said, sounding like a real mom for once. But her daughter ignored her. As usual.

"He's afraid Mr. Tremont will fall in love with him, obviously. Just like he did with Chris and Brian and Randy."

I laughed disbelievingly. "Fall in love?" The absurdity of it was too much. Brilliant Mr. Tremont, who talked like a professor and looked like a movie star, fall in love with stupid Randy Thomas? Or anyone else in Jake's group, for that matter, even the girls? How could someone as intelligent and talented and perfect and *adult* as Mr. Tremont possibly have romantic feelings for a dumb teenager? The idea was absurd. Anyway, he was probably dating some Pulitzer Prize–winning supermodel. I was sure of it.

"He kicked those guys out of class because they were screwing around and being disrespectful, not because he was in love with them," I said.

Lacey ignored me, looking meaningfully at Nikki. "Well, you know, that's just how they are."

"You mean gays?" I asked furiously. "Are you trying to say that all gay men want to fall in love with stupid, homophobic teenagers? That's insane!"

"Well, yeah," Lacey said, in her Lacey-explains-it-all voice. "So they can convert them."

Nikki's eyes were wide, tracking us like tennis players. Lacey's mom smiled vaguely. My mother looked concerned, but she didn't take her eyes off me.

"Convert them? So, what, so they can form covens?" I laughed bitterly. "Gays aren't like vampires, Lacey!" My voice sounded painfully jagged in my own ears. I couldn't help it: I was trembling with outrage.

"Well, I don't think it's appropriate to have such people in our schools," Brenda said. "Teachers can be incredibly influential in a child's life, and I certainly wouldn't want our children's moral values to be polluted by such an influence."

Lacey looked happy for the first time that night. Any sympathy I'd had for her disappeared. So her father was getting married. That didn't give her the right to be such a judgmental bitch. She didn't even know Mr. Tremont. I wanted to scream. I wanted to punch her know-it-all face. I gripped my notebook and walked out the door, leaving everyone behind me. "I can't deal with this."

I sat on the back porch, in the dark, refusing to go back inside until everyone was gone. The stars were bright and thick above my head, but I felt mean and dark. Brenda shaking on the couch, Lacey's tight, angry face. How could she spread such ridiculous rumors about Mr. Tremont? Did it take her mind off her own problems? Was she congratulating herself on having smaller problems than he? Was she telling herself, *Well, my dad's getting married but at least he's not gay? Maybe I walk with a limp but at least I'm not gay!*

God.

She didn't even know him. She didn't even know who he was. All she had were rumors from Randy and Chris and Brian and maybe Jake, but not Jake, because he was better than that; he could be crude, but he was kind, better than his friends, and he was only spending time with Lacey because she needed a friend right now, because even her own father couldn't stand her stupid bullshit and took off to find a new family, a better one.

I caught myself, shocked at the depth of my own malice. That wasn't fair, I knew. It must be awful to have your family torn apart like that, and then to find out that your dad's already getting remarried, that this is something he's been planning for a long time? I couldn't even imagine it.

Still, that didn't give her the right to talk shit about Mr. Tremont.

A bat swooped across the wide triangle of light from the garage, its path jittery like the lines of a heart monitor. Behind me, a tree shifted and sighed in a slight wind, and I wished that I could wash my mind like a chalkboard and scrub out all the black thoughts. I wanted to write but I wouldn't go inside until I heard the *thomp-thomp-thomp* of three doors shutting, the growls of an engine turning over, the lonely noise of three people driving away.

chapter FOURTEEN

Wednesday morning, I quickly typed the final draft of my essay from my notebook. It was about the day we found the bat in fourth grade, a story version, about a little girl standing up to the rest of the school just to save a little bat. Feeling as though I were flinging myself from the top of some enormous cliff, I typed my name at the top and printed it out. It would have to do.

The whole drive to school, I worried about creative writing. *What if they don't like it? What if they read the bat story and know it's really about me and remember what a nerd I was in elementary school? What if Mr. Tremont pulls me aside after class and tells me I'm not up to par for this class?* Finally, the fear and self-doubt got the best of me, and I made my way sheepishly to Mr. Tremont's classroom. "Mr. Tremont—"

He was sitting behind his desk in a russet sweater-vest that shouldn't have worked but totally did. The desk was covered with papers, books, and manila folders, and anchored by potted plants at two of its corners. "Morning, Paige." He took a sip of coffee. "Rough night?"

"God, is it obvious?" I looked down at my outfit, old jeans with a T-shirt that had a picture of a little tiger and said HUNTINGTON ELEMENTARY IS PURRRR-FECT! I'd had to sneak past my mother while she was bringing my father his coffee; she would have had an aneurism if she'd seen me like this. "I didn't get much sleep," I admitted.

"Been there," he said. "Is everything okay?"

"Um." My hands fiddled with the straps of my bag. "I don't have anything to turn in."

"Ah." He took another sip of his coffee. "Because you haven't been writing, or because you're afraid of what you've written?"

"Afraid?" I echoed. He shrugged but didn't say anything. "I just can't . . . I don't have anything. I didn't finish the assignment."

Mr. Tremont nodded. "Okay. Well, we'll just schedule you in for later in the quarter, I guess."

"Okay," I whispered. He was disappointed in me, I could tell. It was awful. "I'm sorry," I said, my face flushing. I turned to leave.

"Hey, Paige?" Mr. Tremont asked behind me. I turned

214

back. Lacey's words from the night before swirled in my head like heavy clouds. Was he gay? Did it matter? Did he somehow know that we were talking about him? Did he think less of me for dating Jake, for being friends with the jocks he'd kicked out of class? Or was Lacey right, was he jealous of me for dating Jake?

Mr. Tremont smiled at me, among his plants and his books. "Go easy on yourself, okay?"

I'd discovered that I could fit quite comfortably beneath the carrel in the far corner of the library, and if I pulled the chair in after me, I couldn't be seen. Maybe it was totally childish, but it reminded me of the forts that Miranda and I used to build with pillows and sheets and tables, and there was something strangely comforting and even defiant in it, like I was thumbing my nose at anyone who said I had to grow up.

At lunch Wednesday, I curled up with my notebook and my pen and filled five pages with freewriting when I should have been in the commons flirting for votes. It was strange: in all my anxiety about my creative writing assignment, I hadn't even thought about the homecoming vote, and now I discovered that I could hardly make myself care. In the cafeteria, I knew, the members of the student council social events committee would be passing out sheets of paper with the names of every senior in the school, separated into columns by gender. "Circle five in each column!" they'd say perkily, handing out pencils and waiting patiently for people to make their choices. It was the same every year. The only difference about this year was that the names on the list were ours.

At the end of class that day, Mr. Tremont set two stacks of paper on the front table, instructing us to take one of each on our way out the door. He made no mention of the fact that there should have been three stacks, but I felt as though every eye in the room was on me, judging me, wondering why I hadn't turned in my assignment. We were supposed to read and comment on each story in time for Friday's class, Mr. Tremont reminded us. A tinny voice on the PA interrupted him, some reminder about the last chance to vote for homecoming court tomorrow at lunch, something about the bonfire Friday, something about basketball tryouts maybe. I wasn't listening; I was focused on the stacks of paper. Mine should have been up there. I was such a coward.

When the bell finally rang, I jumped out of my seat and grabbed a copy of the stories before hurrying to my locker. I had to get away before Ethan or Shanti could stop me, ask what happened to the story I'd been working on at Starbucks, call me out on not turning anything in. Moments later, I was speeding through the crowded hallways toward the front doors, the stories clutched in my right hand. I hadn't even taken the time to stuff them into my bag. I pushed through the door into an autumn afternoon of groaning gray clouds and skittering red leaves.

Outside, I finally slowed my pace and took a deep breath, feeling something like relief. As I walked, I glanced down at the top paper in my hand. *I knew this strange girl once*, it began. My eyes flicked up to the top of the page. *Fairydust*. It was Shanti's story.

> I knew this strange girl once.
>
> Lithe and mysterious, she kissed me under the autumn moon and said, "Look quickly, for the clouds only cover the stars for a time. The clouds will disappear and you will leave, but you won't forget."

"Paige!"

Ripped from my reading, I realized I had stopped moving altogether and now stood under an oak tree by the edge of the school's lawn.

Lacey caught up to me, leaning heavily on her cane. "What are you reading?" She reached a well-manicured hand toward Shanti's story.

Instinctively, I whipped the papers away, stuffing them in my bag. "Nothing. Just something for class."

"Oh."

We stood still in the middle of the moving swarm. Faces, bags, bits of conversation, and laughter all pushed past us in a flood of color and movement and sound as we stayed silent. As usual, Lacey surveyed the crowd as if at any moment she might see someone more interesting. I watched her, trying to see a hint of the person she'd been the night before, crying in my bedroom. There was nothing. Her face was an airbrushed portrait of itself. My mother's voice scolded me in my head. *She needs a friend right now, Paige. She needs you.* After all, who knew better than I the difference between the face you showed to the world and what you were feeling inside your heart? Lacey looked perfect because she cultivated it, not because she was.

"Hey." I took a deep breath. "About yesterday . . ."

Lacey jumped, turning to me as if caught. "There's a homecoming committee meeting tomorrow during eighth. I need you to be there." It was the voice she used when she talked to Dr. Coulter, the voice of a helmet-haired newscaster.

"Oh." Why couldn't I be like Nikki? Endlessly forgiving, endlessly sweet, Nikki would reach out, would ask, *Do you want to talk about it?* or, *Is there anything I can do?*

"Hey," I said again. "Do you—"

"I have to go," she said abruptly. She turned away and limped toward the front doors of the school. I watched her shuffle through the crowd, nodding to some, greeting others, until the top of her head disappeared behind a group of band geeks carrying their shiny plastic cases. The band moved slowly, laughing, and I turned before they dissipated, but through the forest of WGHS MARCHING BAND sweatshirts and utilitarian ponytails, I could have sworn I caught a glimpse of my boyfriend in the space of Lacey's wake.

I drove out to the springs to read the stories. The drive was full of questions, of voices and doubts, and my own words echoed in my head as I walked down the path. *You move through the world, see yourself being seen . . .* I wasn't hoping to be seen. I wasn't imagining how I'd look walking down the path from the perspective of someone sitting on the tree roots, his back leaning against the trunk, his feet planted firmly against the water-splashed stones. . . .

The springs were empty; no one else was in the secret clearing, and I told myself I was relieved. I settled myself against my usual rock with the stories, and soon the rest of the world fell away.

Ethan's was good. It was very good. His story was long, but I hardly noticed. Once I started reading I was pulled into his world, a world where a computer had a sense of humor, and maybe even a soul, and gangs of Christians roamed the streets, committing acts of terrorism in the name of the Lord. Normally, I didn't like sci-fi, but Ethan's story was different. It wasn't just about a computer; it examined the question of what it means to be human in the face of the technology we create. The story was dark and funny and sad. I was hooked from the very first sentence. Hooked, and intimidated.

Shanti's story was just as good. Maybe even better. It was more like a poem than a story, just a few ephemeral moments in time, woven together in the language of magic and stardust. An accountant falls in love with a girl from another world, and when she goes away, the sun and the moon switch places. Not understanding what he has, he misses the wet little footprints in her room after a dream of water. He tries to hold on to her but he cannot, and she disappears in the echo of a speeding train.

> . . . The door appeared for a moment and she slipped through, as quickly and silently as moonrise. She'd spoken of doors, of stars and the voices she could hear on the other side, but I'd taken her talk for poetry, not fact, until I saw her slip through the door and lost her forever.

The words hung in my head, slowly revolving like wind chimes. Just like that day in Mr. Tremont's class, I had a flash of what my life could be. I wanted my life to be more than what my mother had planned for me — more than *I* had planned for me. I wanted to walk through that door. *As quickly and silently as moonrise.* . . . Alone in the woods, I sat watching little bugs skate across the creek's surface until shadows stretched across the water.

Quiet piano on the radio accompanied me on the drive back to town. The music matched the afternoon. I drove with windows down, savoring the cool breeze against my skin. It was tinged with sharpness and smelled like distant fires, autumn smoke. Someone somewhere was burning leaves in their backyard. The long gray pavement stretched before me, curving around farmhouses. Deep-red barns stood out against the tawny sunset cornfields, and dove-colored clouds gathered behind the long bank of orange-and-gold leaves.

Something more. The something I had been looking for without exactly knowing it, the sense of the universe unfolded before me. Shanti and Ethan had found it, they'd captured it in their writing, and I couldn't tell how I felt about it. In awe of their talent and a bit intimidated? Absolutely. Inspired? Excited? Maybe.

But most of all, I felt found.

In creative writing on Thursday, Mr. Tremont handed out pages photocopied from Ovid's *Metamorphoses,* and he instructed us to write something new using only the words from Ovid. "It's good to push yourself beyond your usual vocabulary," he said.

Jenna raised her hand. "What if you don't know some of the words? Like, what's Phaethon?"

"I'm actually not that interested in meaning; I just want you guys to start experimenting with language outside your comfort zone." He smiled. "But since you asked, Phaethon is just your average teenager — borrows his dad's car, which in this case happens to be the chariot of the sun, and then crashes it, killing himself and setting half the world on fire."

"Typical," Jeremy muttered.

Mr. Tremont laughed. "Anyway, I chose Phaethon because I love the scene where his sisters are so paralyzed by grief that they start turning into trees, and their mother is trying to rip the bark off to save them, and they're weeping because the bark is their skin: 'The tree you tear is me!' Amazing."

I skimmed the poem on my desk to see if it was the one he was talking about, but mine was about Narcissus and Echo, not Phaethon.

"You really should read *Metamorphoses*," Mr. Tremont said. "It's like a soap opera: everyone's always having secret babies and affairs, and then the gods get angry and turn them all into trees and birds. It's the best." My classmates must have looked as confused as I felt, because he laughed. "Anyway, for now, just pretend it's a puzzle. Circle the words that jump out at you. Rearrange them, repeat them, see what you can come up with. And . . . go."

We spent the rest of the hour working while Mr. Tremont walked around the room, looking over our shoulders and encouraging us. At first I was hesitant, worrying that I wasn't doing it right, but by the end of class I was grabbing words and phrases from Ovid without worrying if they made sense, and by the time the bell rang I felt like I'd created something beautiful.

After class, I headed outside. I'd walked to school that morning, so I thought I'd run home, grab my car, and head to the springs. I would use the momentum from class to redeem myself in workshop. Mr. Tremont said he'd schedule me for later in the quarter, and this time I wouldn't disappoint him. I walked slowly, maybe half hoping that someone would catch up to me and ask if I was headed out to the springs and maybe offer to drive us both.

But it was Nikki who caught up to me. She grabbed my arm. "Where are you going? We have a meeting with Dr. Coulter during eighth period, remember?"

I looked longingly at the parking lot. Other seniors were getting in their cars and driving away to eat Pop-Tarts and watch TV. I wanted to be one of them. I wanted to be walking away from school, not dragged backward by a girl who was shockingly strong given that she only ate things that were orange. Her fingers were bulldog teeth pinched around my arm. "Nikki. Hey. Arm . . . losing circulation."

She strode forward without relaxing her grip. "Hey, Cindy!" she called. "Nice jacket!"

"Nikki! I'm coming! You don't have to drag me."

She didn't look at me. "Oh really?" Her voice was low, pressed against her teeth. She sounded like Lacey. "Well, forgive me for worrying that you might run away again! After that night at your house!"

"Um," I said.

"Hi, Nate!" She waved with her free hand, blowing a kiss that may or may not have been ironic, before switching back into iron-jaw mode. "I don't know how to say this," she hissed. "But you are like a different person lately! It's like you're . . . you're not nice! You are not nice, Paige!"

"Whoa." I wrenched my arm out of her scrawny claw. "*I'm* not nice?"

"That's right, I said it! Lacey's life is like, falling apart! And all you can do is give her mean looks! And you won't talk to her! And she just really needs a friend right now!" Her voice got louder and louder, until she was practically shrieking. "And maybe I DO, TOO! IT'S NOT ALL ABOUT YOU, PAIGE!"

"Whoa," I said. People were staring. "Calm down, Nik—"

She patted her hair nervously, suddenly aware of so many faces watching. She took a breath and gave me a giant Stepford smile. "It's just," she said. "I don't like being in the middle. And I don't like it when you fight. And Lacey really needs us both right now, Paige. But especially you. I don't know how to talk to her. I mean, you were always her best friend. I know that."

I started to interrupt, but she held up a hand.

"No, it's true. I'm just, like, the sidekick. I know."

"Nikki," I said.

"Paige. Just, please. Come to this meeting. Be yourself again. Be nice. Okay?"

"Sure, Nik. Of course." I tried not to think about Pop-Tarts or soap operas or the quick sweep of my pen across a blank page or anything but the light that came back into Nikki's eyes the moment I nodded at her. She hugged me hard and led the way back into the dark school.

chapter FIFTEEN

Lacey presided over the gathering of members of the homecoming committee and student council. Her face was perfectly smooth as she guided everyone through a neatly typed agenda, speaking to Dr. Coulter as an equal. Next to her, student council president Jeremy kept his finger on the bullet points as we moved through them.

"Next point," Lacey said. "Bonfire tomorrow night."

Randy and Chris threw their fists in the air and whooped. Jake caught my eye across the room and grinned.

Lacey smiled. "I know we're all excited about it, because it has the potential to be one of the biggest nights of our lives. I want to go down the checklist, real quick, to make sure everything's taken care of." She glanced up at us, steely eyes above her wide smile. "One: JV team is in charge of gathering wood and building fire. Check?"

"Check," Geneva said.

"Great. Two: Chaperones?"

"Coach Ahrens, Coach Wickstrom, Mr. Berna, Ms. Hoeschen, and Ms. Bailey," Jeremy recited.

"That's not enough," Dr. Coulter said. "You need to have at least six."

"Mrs. McConnell was supposed to chaperone, but I guess something came up in her family and she has to go to Wisconsin this weekend." Jeremy checked his notes.

Dr. Coulter looked slightly startled, as if he hadn't realized that his teachers had lives outside the walls of the building.

"So we need one more," Lacey said. "Any suggestions?"

"I think we should ask Mr. Tremont," Jeremy said.

Nikki leaned against me and giggled. Tyler and Chris looked at each other and smirked. *God.*

Lacey frowned. "Why don't we ask Mrs. Moore? I bet she'd—"

Jeremy shook his head. "I already asked her. Her kid's birthday party is that night." Jenna French spoke from the back of the room. "Mr. Tremont will do it. He's really cool."

"Fine," Lacey snapped. "Who wants to take care of that?"

"I will," I said, surprising myself. Tyler snorted, but the look on Lacey's face was worth the weight of everyone else's stares. Jake gave me a questioning look, and I shrugged. "I just want to help," I said sweetly.

226

"Fabulous!" Jeremy said. "That's taken care of."

Lacey's voice was razor sharp. "Get that done today please, Paige."

"Great." Dr. Coulter sighed and settled back in his chair. "What's next on the agenda, Lacey?"

Nikki raised her hand. "We need to talk about DIEDD."

Across the room, Geneva leaned over to whisper something to Randy, who looked at me and laughed. I dug my fingernails into my palms and didn't look up again for the rest of the meeting.

We wrapped up a minute before the period ended, and people moved around the room, chatting. Nikki turned to me, slinging her heavy backpack across her frail shoulders. "Thanks for coming."

"No problem," I lied.

"Can you do me a favor?"

"What?"

"Can you write a eulogy for the DIEDD thing?"

I frowned. "What? A eulogy? Like, for a funeral?"

"Yeah," she said, "it's going to be really intense, and, like, we're going to have this thing where people are—" The bell rang, cutting her off, and we moved toward the door.

"You know, I'm really busy," I said. "And I have to go talk to Mr. Tremont about the dance or whatever, so . . ." I swung my arm to include the whole room, as if the entire world were encroaching on my free time and ability to do favors.

Nikki looked away. "Yeah, no problem, that's fine," she said, and released at last, I left.

Out in the hallways, the entire school population pushed toward the parking lot like water sucked to sea before a tsunami. I fought my way upstream, trying to lose my thoughts in the noise of the crowd. As I moved, head down, my ears began to pick up a familiar note buried beneath the swell. My cell phone. I leaned against a pillar for a second, out of the current. The number was one I didn't recognize, but I answered anyway. "Hello?"

"Hi! It's Shanti!"

"Oh," I said. "Hi."

"I'm across the commons. Look up! I'm by the pop machines!" She stood between the water-and-juice machine (available all day) and the soda machine (available after school only) and waved. Her voice came through my phone as she walked toward me. "Hi! So, what are you doing?"

"I'm talking to you," I said into the phone.

She stood in front of me, grinning. "So, when do we hang up?"

"Now." I put the phone back in my bag. "What area code is that?"

"Madison. I'm on my dad's plan, from when I stayed with him last summer," Shanti said. "The 608 forever, man." She shook her head to flip her hair behind her shoulder. "So seriously, what are you doing right now? Because you should come hang out with me."

She interrupted herself, pointing at a poster on yellow butcher paper. "Why can't anyone in this school use an apostrophe correctly?"

I looked to where she was pointing. HOMECOMING TICKET'S $20, the poster announced. Next to it, a glittery poster encouraged us to SUPPORT YOUR CLASS! BUY SPIRIT LINKZ, LEI'S, T-SHIRTS!

"It's not that hard!" Shanti said. "Are any of these words possessive? No!"

Jeremy walked up to us. "Okay, okay. Settle down, girl." He looked at me. "Wanna take bets on how soon she'll be locked up in a padded room, rocking back and forth and muttering about grammar?"

"Isn't it weird how big of a deal homecoming is here?" Shanti asked, ignoring him. "It's like we're still in the Eisenhower administration or something."

"It's a tradition," Jeremy said, "and people love traditions. It makes them feel like they have roots, which is really hard to do these days, when the economy is in shambles, the family farm is dead, and the cornfields are all turning into condos and McMansions."

Shanti squinched up her mouth. "I guess. It's just, sometimes I feel like I'm in a John Hughes movie or something. But not in a good way. In a weird way."

Jeremy put his hands on his hips. "Girl, if you're going to be a writer, you're going to have to learn how to empathize with all kinds of people, which includes the good people of Willow Grove."

"Praise the Hornets, America, and Jesus, in that order!" She saluted, and he whacked her.

"I guess it gives people a chance to feel like they're a part of a legacy," I said. "Like, my mom was homecoming queen a million years ago, and now she wants me to be, too."

Jeremy nodded. "Like mother, like daughter. Except . . . not exactly." He smiled at me.

Shanti shifted her weight impatiently. "I guess. Anyway, I think it's sexist and dumb. But that's not the point. The point is, what are you doing right now, Paige? Because I really think that you should hang out with me this afternoon."

"I don't know," I said.

Shanti wiggled her eyebrows. "I'll buy you a latte. . . ."

Jeremy laughed. "Is that a bribe?"

"Maybe." She looked at me. "Is it working?"

"I have to talk to Mr. Tremont," I said.

"I'll wait for you here," Shanti said. "But really? You have no choice. I'm kidnapping you."

"It's a talent of hers," Jeremy told me.

I nodded. "I'm noticing."

"Go work your magic for me, girl," he said. "Show a little leg if you have to."

I laughed and started walking backward across the commons.

"Okay," Shanti said. "I'll hang out here—and inveigle you when you get back."

"Inveigle?" Jeremy asked.

"Shut up, it's an SAT word." She punched him and called after me. "See you in a few, Paige! I'm not above using duct tape if I have to!"

"Oooh," Jeremy said. "Kinky!"

It was the first time I'd talked to Mr. Tremont outside class since yesterday morning, when I hadn't turned a story in, and I had a moment of fear that he would turn on me and demand to know why I was thinking about homecoming when I should be writing. But of course I needn't have worried—another teacher might guilt-trip me, but not Mr. Tremont.

He seemed interested in the bonfire. "Walk me out to my car." He neatly zipped a stack of papers into a black briefcase, slipped in a yellow legal pad, and surveyed his desk for anything else. "Keys? Wallet?" he asked himself.

I hung back, watching his hands through the arms of his plants. There was an ink stain on his right index finger, and what looked like words at the base of his hand near his watch. He wore a plain silver band on his right ring finger. His thumbnails were square and broad.

"So, a bonfire? How does that work exactly? As I recall from my long-ago high school days, teenagers and fire don't exactly mix."

"Hence the chaperones," I said.

"Ahh. So my job would be to prevent self-immolation?" He ushered me through the door, flipping off the lights and locking the door behind us.

"Self-immolation's fine, as long as no school property is damaged," I said.

Mr. Tremont laughed. "Oh, of course. Priorities!" He headed toward a back door, and I matched his pace along the waxed tile. "It's weird. I pretty much stayed away from school-spirit-type events when I was in high school, and now someone wants me to be a chaperone?"

"Did you guys do a homecoming bonfire?"

He squinted. "I don't think so. . . . We definitely had a dance, and I think we had a half day with a parade and a pep rally, because my friend and I skipped out to go to a diner and then got rear-ended, and it was as though the School Spirits themselves were mad at us."

"Well," I said, "this would be your chance to make it up to them. Good karma and whatnot."

"Good point. I make it a personal policy to piss off as few spirits as possible." He pushed the door open and held it for me, nodding to the wide sky. "Looks like rain, huh?"

I followed his gaze to the broad white canvas stretched out above the sullen highway. "Yeah," I said. "This has been a weird fall."

"*Wild nights—wild nights!*" He grinned to himself. "I'll do it."

"You will?" I asked. "Really?" He nodded. "Okay, cool. Thanks, Mr. Tremont." It took me a second to realize that I was standing half in and half out of the school, awkwardly close to his outstretched arm. He smelled like soap, with a hint of sandalwood. I hopped backward over the threshold, catching myself on the shiny floor. "Okay, great. Thanks."

Mr. Tremont looked amused. "Hey, Paige?"

"Um, yes?"

"In all seriousness, would it be inappropriate to bring a friend?"

Friend? Like . . . a *boy*friend? My heart thumped in my chest. *Shut up*, I told it. *Settle the hell down.* "Of course not," I said without breathing. "No problem."

Mr. Tremont smiled. "Awesome."

"See you tomorrow," I said, waving like a dumb girl until the door closed between us and I could safely flee. I hurried down the empty hallways toward the other end of the school, my cheeks hot. Mr. Tremont probably thought I was . . . God, I didn't even want to think about it. I'd been askew all year, like I was standing just off center and couldn't catch my balance, and now I was forgetting how to talk to teachers without completely embarrassing myself. I used to be good at this. I used to be charming, convincing, smiling, fun. I used to be like Lacey . . . but, then again, so did she. She used to be smiling and fun; now she was brittle glass, unyielding. No wonder Nikki was freaking out. We'd both changed.

I slowed, my feet measuring steps in inches. Who knew it would all come to this? All those years of working and strategizing and showing up to the correct parties and never saying too much or too little and paying strict attention to the cut of our jeans and the texture of our hair and being nice to everyone to their faces and then cutting them down with a single observation the second they left the room, and wooing the teachers and the administration and holding one another up and checking one another, constantly, for stray hairs and uneven hems and smudged lip gloss and cakey foundation and food in our teeth and things in our noses and weird breath and clumpy mascara and the slightest hint of body odor . . . all the business of popularity, and in the end, it had eclipsed our actual friendship. What had happened to the house of Lacey and Paige, built on a foundation of shared secrets and inside jokes, of notes signed LYLAS, of late-night confessions and endless walks through the dusky spring streets, and of promises never to let a boy get between us?

"Hi, babe." Jake materialized from nowhere, appearing before me in the empty hallway.

I jumped. "Jesus!"

"No, Jake. But I can see why you'd get confused." He kissed me on the cheek. "What are you doing down here? You're like, just standing in the middle of the hallway."

"Um." I blinked twice. "Sorry. Lost in my thoughts."

Jake leaned against a bank of lockers, spreading his fingers in a fan against the aqua metal. "Planning tomorrow's outfit in your head?"

"No," I said, more forcefully than I'd intended.

"Hey," he said.

"What?"

Abruptly, he reached out and grabbed my face, his hands rough against my cheekbones, and kissed me.

I wobbled when he pulled away, but managed to find my voice. "Where did that come from?"

He shrugged, staring into my eyes. "I miss you. I feel like I haven't seen you in forever, between school and working at my dad's office and everything."

Everything meaning Lacey, my mind whispered, but I ignored it. "I miss you, too." I reached for his wrist, which was wider and flatter than Mr. Tremont's. Junior year, we used to drive around for hours, talking and listening to music and pulling off the road in secluded clusters of trees to make out. Everything seemed so simple back then: Jake liked me and I liked him, and nobody hurt anyone else and nobody kept secrets. Maybe it wasn't too late to reclaim those days, and the simpler, happier person I'd been. Maybe it was like my mother said: it was up to me to make things right with us.

"Hey," I said, running my hand up the back of his neck. "We have a whole afternoon in front of us. We could go back to my house, if my mother isn't around, bribe Miranda to get out . . ."

He sighed. "I'd love to, but I have to run," he said. "Extra practice."

"Really?" I pouted, twining my fingers through his hair. "We haven't hung out in forever, and you have a bye tomorrow. Can't you skip?"

He smiled at me, tugging on the edge of my shirt. "I wish."

"What about after?" I leaned into him, trapping his hand between us.

He squinted and glanced somewhere behind me. "I can't, babe. I told Lacey—"

My bones calcified beneath my skin, turned to stone. I pulled back. "Oh. Lacey."

"Paige, don't be like that."

"I'm not being like anything."

"She's just really having a hard time lately."

If one more person said that, I was going to scream. I took a breath. "Well, I actually have plans anyway. So it's cool."

"You do?" He sounded surprised. "With who?"

I crossed my arms. "Just a friend."

Jake seemed suddenly present, a laser of attention pointed at my face. "A friend? Which friend? Nikki?"

"Shanti Kale." He didn't react enough, so I added, "Maybe some other people, too. Like Jeremy Carpenter, Ethan James—"

Jake raised his eyebrows. "That freshman dude?"

"He's not a freshman," I said, and looked at him slyly. "Are you jealous?"

"Should I be?" he teased. "Are you going to leave me for a freshman?"

"Maybe," I said.

"Well, I guess I'll just have to kick his ass, then," Jake

joked. His voice softened. "God, babe, I really do wish I could hang with you. Lacey's drama is getting old." He ran a finger down the inside of my forearm, making me shiver. "But she really needs a friend right now."

"So I've heard."

Jake looked at me with all the intensity of the first time, and for a moment it was that day on the bleachers in the sun, and no one else existed.

"I have to go. Call me later, okay?" And though I actually reached out to hold him there, he turned more quickly than I could grasp, and was gone.

Shanti was sitting cross-legged on top of a lone cafeteria table, scribbling in her notebook. At my footsteps, she looked up and grinned. "Yay!" She jumped from the table and took off down a side hallway, tucking her notebook into her bag as she walked. "I just have to grab something," she said over her shoulder. I followed without paying attention, eager to be gone. At the blue dot, she swung through the open doorway of the newspaper room. "Hi! Sorry— sorry—excuse me." She wove through kids hunched over computers in tight rows and stopped behind Ethan. "Hey, Jeremy!" she called.

Jeremy looked up from a computer near the front of the room, where he was sitting with Nikki, of all people. She sat with her back to me, staring intently at the screen, where a video of what looked like a car accident was playing. "What now, Kale?" Jeremy asked.

"I have to borrow your op-ed man," Shanti announced.

Jeremy grinned. "You mean kidnap?"

"Toe-may-toes, toe-mah-toes," she said, and poked Ethan in the back as he shut down his computer and grabbed his bag.

"Be careful, Paige," Jeremy warned. "Them's crazy folk."

At my name, Nikki glanced up in surprise and caught my eye. I gave a stupid, sheepish half wave, embarrassed to be seen leaving with Shanti and Ethan—and hating myself for feeling that way.

"Anyway," she said, turning back to Jeremy. "The bonfire's Friday night and the dance is the next Saturday. Should we do the funeral on Friday morning? Or Saturday night?"

"Saturday night? Girl, you crazy."

Shanti excused her way back through the tangle of legs and backpacks and reappeared at my side, flushed and smiling, with Ethan following behind. "We're kidnapping him, too."

We all piled into Ethan's beat-up old Jeep, though Shanti insisted on driving. "I'm an excellent driver!"

Ethan laughed, teasing her. "I'm an excellent driver. I like to drive in the driveway. I'm an excellent driver."

"Okay, Rain Man," Shanti said, rolling her eyes. She pulled the seat all the way forward and adjusted the mirrors. Clearly, this was not the first time she'd driven the Jeep. Ethan offered me the front seat but I declined, preferring to observe from the back. Shanti flipped through a mess of jewel cases in Ethan's glove box, then pulled a CD out and popped it in the CD player. "Do you like Dar Williams?" she asked, glancing at me in the rearview mirror.

"Yeah, sure," I lied. I'd never heard of it. A voice filled the back speakers, soft and crooning and entirely unlike the music I usually listened to. It sounded like the singer was just singing the word "Iowa" over and over again.

I watched the silver-green corn flash by the window, the red barns somehow more striking standing against the deep-gray sky than they would be against summer blue. Telephone poles blinked by as steadily as the rain that Mr. Tremont had predicted.

The Iowa song ended, and the next song began with a simple guitar line. Ethan sang along, his voice matching the singer's perfectly. Shanti harmonized on the chorus.

"So, where are we going?" I asked.

Ethan deepened his voice like a game show announcer. "Where are we going, Shanti?"

"Um, did you not hear me state quite clearly that you are being KIDNAPPED? And when you kidnap someone, you do not TELL them where you are going, because then they might call their rescuers to come find them, and then you do not get all the glorious lovely ransom money." Downshifting, slowing the car, she waved through the window toward a broad bank of trees, a low valley among woodsy hills. "Obviously!"

Ethan stage-whispered, "She has no idea."

"I do so!" Shanti protested. "I know exactly where we are going! And it's going to be amazing!"

Ethan shook his head slowly, mouthing, "No. Idea." I laughed.

Shanti merged onto the highway without signaling, sweeping in front of a giant semi before darting into the next lane while the truck flew by laying on the horn. I gasped loudly and was immediately embarrassed, dropping my head so my hair fell across my face. My fingers twisted around the middle seat belt, turning white.

Ethan glanced back at me and turned to Shanti, his voice light but serious. "Could I ask you a favor? Could you maybe *not* get us killed today?"

"I'm an excellent driver!" she yelled.

Ethan turned back to me and mouthed, "Sorry," rolling his eyes. "I'll drive on the way home . . . if we live that long," he said aloud, and Shanti yelled, "Look at these hands! Ten and two!" but she eased off the pedal and kept her eyes on the road. "I am an excellent driver!" she said again.

I took a deep breath, forcing myself to relax and listen to Ethan and Shanti sing. Shanti seemed to be channeling the ghost of Ethel Merman, while Ethan crooned in an excessively twangy cowboy voice. It made for a strange duet, but they seemed to be enjoying themselves. It was strange: they both seemed to take each other as they were. I'd never heard either of them comment on what the other was wearing or doing, and when they teased each other it was always friendly, without a razor's edge of warning underneath. I tried to remember the last time I'd allowed myself to say everything that was on my mind without worrying what someone would think.

The Jeep crested a hill and suddenly a whole field of gold rose in my vision, hill after hill of tangled sunflowers. They were so bright against the blue-slate clouds, raising their dark-brown faces to the sunless sky like hope. "Wow," I whispered, and Ethan reached back and tapped the ashtray near my feet, a silent agreement.

The Merman/cowboy duet came to an earsplitting finale, and Ethan turned to me. "Hey, how was the homecoming committee meeting today?"

"What?" I asked. "How did you know about that?"

"I'm on student council."

Shanti hooted. "Loser!"

"Shut up, Shan," Ethan said easily. "I was drafted."

"How did that happen?" I asked.

"I have drama lit first period," Ethan said.

"Ohhhh." The theater crowd wasn't exactly known for its school spirit.

"Ila Grayson nominated me, and apparently everyone in that group does whatever she tells them to."

"Lacey nominated me."

Shanti's eyes flicked up at me in the rearview mirror. "You sound less than enthused."

I shrugged. "It seems kind of pointless."

Ethan shifted so he could see us both, sitting sideways.

"I don't know," he said. "My committee is working on this presentation that will actually be pretty good, I think."

"Really," I said.

"Yeah, actually. You know Nikki Rosellini?"

I laughed. "Yes. She's—yes. I definitely know her."

"She's doing this thing," he started.

"DIEDD," Shanti interrupted. "With three *D*s."

"I heard," I said.

"That's not even how you do acronyms," Shanti said. "What does it stand for again? Dude, I Eat Dunkin' Donuts? Doctor, I Examine Diseased Dogs?" She laughed.

"Don't let friends drive drunk." Ethan and I said it at the same time, and I shot him a grateful look. Nikki might be annoying sometimes, and maybe she wasn't a superintellectual, but she meant well. And she was still my friend.

"It's really going to be a cool thing," Ethan said. "Nikki's gotten the police and fire departments to come in, and there's going to be this all-school assembly, and—"

"And it's all a bunch of emotionally manipulative bullshit so she can parade her guilt in front of the whole school," Shanti said. "It's sick. And sad."

I opened my mouth to disagree, but then closed it, thinking. Did everyone in the school feel the same way? The Jeep hung empty with quiet until Shanti finally asked, "What?" She sounded defensive.

"I mean, she's trying to do something positive," Ethan said. "She sees a problem and she's doing something to try

242

to fix it. So her solution's a little weird—at least she's doing something. It's better than cynical hipsters who sit around complaining and making fun of everyone without ever doing anything to help make the world better."

"Cynical hipsters?" Shanti asked, keeping her eyes straight ahead. "Speaking generally or specifically?"

I sat back, revising my theory about people who didn't judge. Maybe it was a universal problem after all. Maybe no one lived up to the expectations of their friends.

"I'm just saying that it's easier to criticize than it is to put yourself out there and try to do something," Ethan said. "You know I'm right. We're all guilty of it sometimes."

"Do you disagree that spending hundreds of tax dollars on a *danse macabre* designed to manipulate the emotions of a bunch of stupid high schoolers while you reenact your own guilt complex on a public stage is a little fucked up?"

"All I'm saying is—"

"Do you disagree?" Shanti pressed.

"It's better than doing nothing. I mean, it's something."

"But it *is* fucked up."

Ethan caught me in the rearview mirror and rolled his eyes, but he was smiling. "Yes, it's a little fucked up."

"Thank you."

"Do you *have* to have the final word? Is that, like, a remnant of your privileged childhood?"

Shanti grinned. "Hey, it's not easy being right all the time, but I make it work."

A minute later, they were singing to the radio again, this time with opera voices on an '80s power ballad. I marveled at the jumps from banter to argument and back again, amazed that they could disagree so vehemently and still be friends.

Almost an hour after leaving Willow Grove, Shanti announced, "We're here!"

"A truck stop?" I asked.

"A truck stop? A truck stop?" She cranked the wheel and we rumbled off the highway, turning from off-ramp to overpass almost without slowing.

Ethan and I braced ourselves against the doors. "Whoa, Shan," Ethan said. "Go easy on my car; it has to last me the rest of the year, at least."

"It's fine," Shanti said. "You worry too much."

"Would you like to buy me a new one? Because in case you thought otherwise, I don't actually work for the sheer pleasure of making lattes."

She ignored him, angling the Jeep across two spaces. She pulled on the parking brake, dropping the clutch so the engine died with a jolt. "My dear Paige, this is not *a* truck stop. This is *the* truck stop! The Iowa 80! Glorious cathedral to Kitsch Americana!"

"The World's Largest Truckstop in Walcott, Iowa," Ethan read. "Does that mean it's the largest truck stop in the world, which happens to be in Walcott, Iowa, or is it the largest truck stop of all the truck stops in Walcott,

Iowa? And if so, just how many truck stops are there in Walcott?"

"I have never actually been here," I said as we jumped from the Jeep. "I've driven past it a million times and never once stopped here."

"Oooh, she's an Iowa 80 virgin! Time for your deflowering!"

"Shanti!" Ethan said.

I giggled. He shook his head. "It's happening more quickly than I feared. We're corrupting her."

Shanti ran ahead of us and turned back, beckoning me. "Great! Come toward the light, Paige! You can do it!" Ethan rolled his eyes, but I ran toward her in slow motion.

"You're a bad influence, Shanti!" he called.

"Maybe I want to be influenced, Ethan," I said. "Ever think of that?"

He quirked an eyebrow and I blushed.

Shanti paused at the front doors and turned to us. "Your mission, if you choose to accept it, is to find the best, most stunning, most awesomely and hilariously and perfectly Iowan item in this vast kingdom of weird touristy crap."

"What do we get if we win?" I asked.

She thought a moment. "If you win, I will purchase said item for you and you can wear it home."

"That sounds more like a punishment than a prize."

"Yeah," Ethan agreed. "I think you should purchase said item and YOU can wear it home."

"Okay, but if I win, then one of you has to wear it."

"Deal." He held out his hand, and they shook.

Shanti looked at me. "Paige?"

I hesitated for a moment and then nodded. "Deal." I held out both hands, crossed in front of me like the Scarecrow giving directions, and shook both their hands at once. "But I have to warn you, I am a master shopper."

"Oooh, she's throwing down the gauntlet!"

"The gauntlet has definitely been thrown," Ethan said. "Nice."

I shrugged. "That's how I roll."

"Ready?" Shanti asked. "On your marks . . . get set . . ." And then she ran into the truck stop without us.

"What a dirty cheater," Ethan said, pretending to be shocked.

"Actually," I said, "I don't know if you've heard this? But cheaters never win, and winners never cheat." A little breeze picked up from the parking lot and stirred my hair, blowing strands across my face. Though we weren't more than a quarter mile off it, the highway seemed strangely distant, and the breeze carried the quiet hum of cars flashing past the autumn green grass and yellow fields of soybeans.

Ethan reached over to brush the hair out of my face, slipping into a John Wayne drawl. "That's some intense philosophizing there, little lady."

I batted my eyes modestly. "I learned it from McGruff the Crime Dog."

He laughed. "So basically, we have to kick her ass."

"It's a matter of honor."

"Exactly," he said, and held the door open for me. "After you, ma'am."

"Thank you kindly, Sheriff."

The Iowa 80 Truckstop was enormous. It had a food court and a sit-down restaurant, a trucking museum, truck washes, a movie theater, a laundry, a barbershop, and apparently a dentist.

"Really?" Ethan asked, studying the map. "Because I know when I'm driving across the country, I think, 'You know, I have to pee. Maybe get a cup of coffee. And while I'm at it, maybe I'll get a root canal.'"

I nodded seriously. "Oh, yeah. You know, truckers have the highest rates of gum disease of any profession."

"Is that a fact?"

"I read it in *Periodontists Daily.*"

It took him a moment. "You are so lying. I can't believe Paige Sheridan is lying to me. Do I have to call for a royal tribunal?"

"Your gums are very important," I said.

He laughed. "God, we *have* corrupted you."

Or maybe I'm just good at lying, I thought as we ambled along, looking for the ultimate in Iowa trucker kitsch. He held up a Daniel Boone hat, complete with raccoon tail, and when I couldn't stop laughing, he decided to wear it around the store, occasionally stopping to direct other customers to find their manifest destiny on the western side of the store. "It's pretty good," I told him.

"But good enough to beat Shanti? She needs to be put in her place once in a while, and we are just the people to do it."

"I don't know," I said. "Maybe if it had a raccoon tail *and* an American flag?"

"You're right. That must exist, right?"

I shrugged, laughing, as he Daniel-Boone-marched up to a store clerk and asked for the patriotic rodent section. "Raccoons aren't rodents," I whispered, and he quickly corrected himself. "I'm sorry," he said to the clerk, "how embarrassing. What I mean to ask is: Can you direct me to the patriotic *small mammal* section?"

Twenty minutes later, the three of us reconvened near the front doors. I held my find behind my back, hiding it from both of them. Ethan was still wearing his coonskin hat, but he had added a bunch of American flag pins to the front, and he had a small stuffed eagle with pinch wings dangling from the end of the tail. "Points for creativity," I said.

"Yes, but the assignment was not to *construct* the kitschiest item, but rather to find it," Shanti said. "Fail."

"Let's see yours, then," Ethan said.

"Gladly." She eyed us. "Though I'm not sure you're ready for this degree of awesomeness."

"We're ready."

"Are you sure? Because it's pretty awesome."

"I think we can handle it," Ethan said.

"If you're sure . . ."

"Shanti!"

She whipped a T-shirt out from behind her back and draped it across her chest. "Ta-daa!" The shirt was purple with an airbrushed rainbow underneath the words I LOVE MY IOWA GRANDMA. Ethan and I nodded appreciatively.

"Points for the airbrushing," I said.

"It does say Iowa," Ethan said.

"What?" Shanti cried. "How can you two sound so blasé? Look at the craftsmanship! The hideous shade of violet! It's perfect!"

"I don't know, I saw a shirt over there with lipstick marks and pig faces that said 'Hogs and Kisses from Iowa,'" I said.

"There's one with corn wearing sunglasses that says 'Another Iowa Tourist,'" Ethan agreed.

"Iowa Grandma is far superior to Hogs and Kisses!" Shanti shook her shirt at us. "Airbrushed rainbow! It's kitschy *and* gay friendly!"

Two women with unnaturally tan, prematurely wrinkled smoker's skin, dressed identically in sleeveless denim shirts and extremely tight mom jeans, gave us hostile glares as they passed, and we all cracked up. "It's like looking into the future," I said, and Shanti shuddered.

"No way. I am getting the hell out of here before I ever

go the big-hair-tight-jeans-denim-shirt route." She looked down at her find happily. "Though of course I am proud to be an Iowa Grandma."

"Wouldn't wearing that shirt signify you were the grandchild?" Ethan asked. "It seems like a grandma would buy that shirt for her grandchild. Right, Paige?"

I nodded. "I think that's how it works."

"Yes, but I won't be the one wearing this shirt," Shanti said. "You will."

Ethan raised his eyebrows. "That depends on Paige, I think."

"True," I said, with my best poker face. "But I don't know. . . ." And then I pulled my find out from behind my back. "Is this better than the grandma shirt?"

Shanti gasped and Ethan guffawed. My find was a camouflaged trucker hat with a poorly rendered picture of a flying pheasant and the words IOWA IS BIG COCK COUNTY emblazoned across the squishy front. "For the win!" Ethan said.

"No way," Shanti said, but you could tell she knew she'd lost. "No, that's just standard misogynistic frat-boy crap."

"Points for Iowa," Ethan said.

"Is a male pheasant even called a cock?" Shanti asked.

I nodded. "Good question. I have no idea."

"All part of the charm," Ethan said. "Your average 'misogynist frat-boy crap,' as I believe you called it, would definitely have a more standard rooster. The pheasant really elevates its regional Iowan charm."

"Male peacocks are called cocks," I offered. "Females are peahens."

"There you go," Ethan said, and then: "Wait, *county*? Don't they mean *country*?"

"There is an Iowa County," I said, "just to the west of Johnson."

"There's also an Iowa County in Wisconsin," Shanti said. "You drive through it to get to Madison."

"The existence of counties called Iowa is not the question here," Ethan said. "The question is whether or not the hat should read 'big cock *country*,' and I would argue that it should, because 'Blank is blank country' is a common construction, whereas 'Blank is blank county' is not."

"Agreed," I said.

"Shanti?"

She looked resigned. "Agreed."

"Misspellings, a pheasant that may or may not actually be a cock, the word 'Iowa,' and camo on a trucker's hat? It's like the perfect storm of Iowa kitsch!" Ethan grabbed my hand and held it up above my head. "Paige wins!"

"Grandmas are way kitschier than cocks," Shanti grumbled, but she took the hat and headed up toward the cash register.

"Tell them you want to wear it out!" Ethan called after her. She turned and gave us the middle finger. "She loves us," Ethan said.

• • •

Shanti convinced us to buy her dinner at the sit-down restaurant inside the truck stop, the Iowa 80 Kitchen. "Best diner fries ever," she said. "Seriously."

"Only if you wear the hat," Ethan said, and she grudgingly smashed it on her head, where it pushed her bangs out into little fingers around her face. The hat was horrendous, but Shanti managed to make it look edgy, even while she glowered at us in a fake sulk.

"Very Iowa hipster," Ethan said.

"Not helping."

"Those trucker hats were totally trendy," I said. "Like, when we were in third grade."

"Great."

"What's up, kids?" Our waitress was tall, with boxy glasses and appealingly messy curls.

"Hey, Carrie," Shanti and Ethan said together.

"What brings you all to the 80 today?" she asked. "Nice hat, by the way."

Shanti blushed. "Not my fault."

"Actually, it's all your fault," Ethan said. "Unless (a) kidnapping us, (b) driving us halfway across the state, (c) proposing a ridiculous contest, and then (d) losing said contest somehow count as 'not your fault.'"

Carrie laughed. "Same old, same old."

"This is Paige," he said. "Also kidnapped."

Carrie's familiarity with Ethan and Shanti reminded me that I was still an outsider, and I felt my ability to keep up with Ethan and Shanti's banter slipping away. "Hi."

"I feel for you," Carrie said.

"She's a princess!" Shanti informed her.

I shook my head. "No, I'm not."

Shanti made her hand into a wall in front of her face and stage-whispered, "She's going to be!"

"So you're going for the king's ransom?" Carrie asked.

"Nice," Ethan said.

It was an easy joke, and I felt dumb for not thinking of it myself. "Anyway."

"Anyway," Carrie echoed. "What can I get you all? The usual?"

Shanti's usual was grilled cheese, Ethan's was a turkey burger, and they talked me out of the salad bar and into meat loaf, claiming you weren't allowed to visit a diner and not try the meat loaf.

"Carrie was in our summer class," Shanti explained after the waitress left.

"Class?"

"Yeah, Ethan and I both took a summer writing class at the U. That's how we met."

He nodded in agreement.

"Apparently she's writing a novel that takes place in a diner, and that's why she's working here for the year. Then she's going to apply to MFA programs. But over the summer she had terrible writer's block and couldn't write one word of her novel. Instead, she spent the summer writing poetry about famous paintings." I must have gotten a strange look on my face, because she said quickly, "It sounds weird, probably, but some of them were really amazing. She wrote the most incredible thing about this Mark Rothko painting. I can't even explain it, but it was one of those things that just gets stuck in your head for days, you know?"

I did know. Before I lost my nerve, I admitted, "Your story was like that for me."

"Really?"

I nodded.

"Wow, thanks," she said. Behind her, a long beam of light, hung with dust motes, bounced off her pheasant hat and got tangled in her dark hair, bounding through the strands until they sparkled maroon and purple. "I have to admit I'm a little surprised. I wouldn't have pegged you for a fantasy person."

"I've been surprising myself a lot lately," I admitted. "I'm surprised to be here."

"Why?" Ethan asked.

Shanti looked at me, and it was like I could feel her peeling away the layers, trying to see who I was beneath the veneer of perfection. "You've changed a lot, haven't you? And not just from when I first knew you. Like, you seem different now from who you were at the beginning of the school year."

Nikki had said nearly the same thing to me just a few hours ago, and yet when Shanti said it, I didn't feel embarrassed or defensive. I felt almost *proud*. "I'm working on it," I said.

"What were you like when Shanti first knew you?" Ethan asked.

I caught Shanti's eye and smiled. "I was a nerd."

"I find that hard to believe," he said. It was neither an insult nor a compliment, the way he said it. Just a statement of fact.

"And then I was perfect," I said. "But it was always someone else's idea of perfect."

Shanti nodded. "You were a magazine picture, not a person."

"That's a little harsh, Shan," Ethan said.

"No, she's right," I said. "I wasn't a person. I was like a walking cardboard cutout."

Shanti picked up her coffee and looked thoughtfully at me again. "But you're different now. I noticed it that night at the game. You were by yourself, first of all. And then you actually talked to me when I sat down. You didn't give me the popular girl brush-off. That's when I knew you weren't the person everyone else — and I — thought you were."

Seeing myself, my old self, through her eyes, I looked even worse. The girl she had just described was the girl my sister still saw: shallow, phony, basking in the attention of teachers and parents, playing perfect for them, while treating my peers with a mixture of polite disinterest and carefully disguised contempt. But Shanti also saw a side of me that no one in my family had ever witnessed: a girl who was smart enough to keep up with lightning-quick conversations, and who was sometimes even funny enough to make people laugh.

She smiled at me and I grinned back, feeling a connection between us, an unspoken understanding. "Working on it, huh?" she said, and I nodded.

Ethan opened his mouth to say something, and she held up a hand, pinching her fingers together like a clam. "We're having a moment here," Shanti said. "Eat your turkey burger."

After eating, Shanti herded us to the Jeep. "We still have some daylight," she said, nosing the Jeep out of the parking lot and back toward the highway. "I vote that we make one more stop. And since I'm driving, my vote's the only one that matters."

I sat shotgun, with Ethan perched in the middle of the backseat, leaning forward to talk to us. "What stop, Sarge?"

She kept her eyes on the road and smiled. "Secret."

"Can we guess?"

"You can try." She tugged at the brim of the hat she still wore, moving it to block the western sun.

"Okay," Ethan said. "Is it bigger than a bread box?"

"Where we're going?"

"Yeah."

Shanti snorted. "Um, wouldn't it have to be? Or how could we all fit inside?"

"So it's inside!" Ethan said.

"We could stand around it," I said.

"Around what?"

"The bread box."

"It's not a bread box!" Shanti said.

"We're really making progress here." Ethan rubbed at his chin, and I remembered the day he'd interviewed me, playing the cub reporter. It had been only a few weeks ago, but it felt like part of another life, like the memory of a story I'd heard or a movie I'd seen. "So," he asked, "what you're saying is it's bigger than a bread box?"

"Stop with the goddamn bread box!"

"Is it bigger than a *cake* box?" I asked. "Or a hatbox?"

"What about a black box . . . theater?" Ethan asked.

"A hotbox?" I asked, and Ethan laughed.

Shanti rolled her eyes. "You two are impossible."

"-ly awesome," Ethan finished.

"I meant annoying."

"-ly awesome," I said, and she laughed.

chapter SIXTEEN

We arrived in Iowa City around six, about an hour before
sunset. Shanti veered into a parking ramp, hit the brakes
with gusto, turned off the Jeep, and jumped out. "I'm going
to go write by the river for a while," she announced, taking
off the hat and slipping on a pair of oversize sunglasses.
"You two can entertain yourselves, I trust?"

I nodded; Ethan saluted.

Without planning to, we followed Shanti to the river,
where we saw her sitting with her notebook at the top of
a hill overlooking the water. Ethan and I meandered along
its banks, kicking at the first fallen leaves. Little kids rode
past us on bikes decorated with handlebar streamers and
little personalized license plates, often followed by parents on larger, undecorated bikes. Other people passed us,

too: college-aged joggers with Greek letters on their shirts, middle-aged couples holding hands, conscientious roller-bladers with knee and elbow pads. Ethan told me stories from the summer, how he and Shanti had met, the day trip the class had taken to Maquoketa Caves. I told him about my summer in Paris—not interviewing taxi-driving poets, as he'd once suggested, but trying to keep the baby from crying while the Eastons fought in the next room.

The sky was a crisp shade of blue, and you could almost watch the leaves turning colors. This time last year, we'd decorated the junior class float out at Brian Sorenson's house, and afterward he and his father had built a campfire for us down by the pond. It was an afternoon just like this, and Lacey and I had wandered away from the group around sunset to go walking along the uneven shore. Hung in mist, the trees looked blue against the pink sky, like the mountains in Kentucky and Virginia. Lacey and I ambled out to the edge of a small wooden pier, where we sat down and took off our shoes without discussion. I remember we laughed about that, how we just knew. We dangled our feet in the water and smoked cigarettes, flicking them into the pond. She'd just been dumped by this guy Jason, who'd graduated the previous spring and gone off to Iowa State, breaking up with her less than two weeks into his freshman year. Though normally Lacey never talked about her feelings—we always used to joke that she had a heart more like a guy's, getting mad but never sad, punching things but never crying—on the pier that day she let down her

259

guard for an hour, admitted that she had been completely shocked when Jason dumped her. I was surprised by the raw honesty in her voice as she ground another cigarette into the wood. "I really think my heart's broken, Paige," she said. "I'm not sure what to do about it." I pushed our shoes aside so I could scoot across the boards and sit next to her, my shoulder pressed against hers. We sat like that until the last cigarette was gone and the sun was low on the water.

Ethan was teaching me how to skip stones across the surface of the water when a group of tanned guys carrying water bottles and Frisbees called his name. He looked up in surprise, and I watched as his face relaxed into recognition. "Hey!" he yelled back, waving. "I played Ultimate with those guys this summer," he explained. "Do you mind if I . . . ?"

"Oh, of course," I said. He grinned at me and jogged after the Frisbee guys, and I watched him for a moment, his green T-shirt clinging slightly to his broad shoulders. . . . I blinked, shook the dust out of my head, and wandered off to find Shanti.

She was sitting near the top of the hill, her back resting against a wide oak tree. Her notebook lay open in her lap, and the pen in her hand rested slack against the pages. A yellow leaf balanced in the book's gutter. Though I couldn't see her eyes behind her giant Audrey Hepburn sunglasses, I could tell that she was gazing off to some unseen horizon.

I walked up the hill slowly, my hands wrapped around the strap of my messenger bag. Despite the connection I'd felt with Shanti earlier, I was shy, worried I'd disturb her or disrupt her thoughts. As I watched her, she abruptly reappeared in the present moment, and her face lit up. "Hey!" she said, patting the grass beside her. "Did you get dumped?"

"Ha," I said, wondering why the word gave me a pang.

"I saw those guys playing Ultimate earlier," Shanti said. "I figured it was only a matter of time before they found Ethan."

"Hmm." I dropped my bag in the grass and eased myself down beside Shanti, following her gaze to the edge of the river. We tracked Ethan as he loped along the path, throwing and catching a red Frisbee in increasingly challenging ways as the boys worked to impress one another.

"This reminds me of this summer," Shanti said. "I can't even tell you how much time I spent watching Ethan play."

For the first time, I wondered if there was—or had been—something more between Shanti and Ethan. I studied her, looking for clues.

"That sucks," I said. The disc flew between the boys like a special effect in a school play, as if suspended by fishing wire from some invisible ceiling. The tallest of Ethan's friends jumped up with his arm stretched all the way over his head, and the disc seemed to slow in its approach until it was just floating there, hanging obediently above his head for him to pluck, effortlessly, from the air.

"Not really," Shanti said. "I got a ton of writing done." Absently, she fingered her notebook. "After this summer, there's a part of me that could totally see myself going here for college, but then there's the part of me that always vowed I'd go as far away as possible for school."

"Yeah," I said. I tried to imagine myself here as well, writing under trees overlooking the endless parade of jogging strollers and squirrel-chasing dogs, but in my family it had always been a given that I would go to Northwestern, as my parents had. I imagined telling my mother that I wanted to go somewhere else for college. She'd tilt her head like a spring robin and the skin would crinkle between her eyes. "I don't understand," she'd say carefully. "Why would you want to go anywhere but Northwestern?" I sighed.

"You guys were pretty cute down there, skipping stones." Shanti's dark eyebrows rose over the black frames of her sunglasses. There was something in her voice that I couldn't quite read. Was it jealousy?

"It's funny," I said neutrally, "how we grew up around so many lakes, and yet I never learned to skip stones." On the other shore, a large black dog threw itself into the river after a tennis ball. I ripped the grass at my side into little piles, scanning the bushes and trees along the river. In my peripheral vision, I could see Shanti taking up her pen again, the nib hovering above the handmade page for a moment before scratching its lines of ink across the surface.

Without looking at her, I said, "Can I ask you something?"

"Sure," Shanti said, stopping her pen.

"You aren't—" I started, and tried again. "I mean, you're not—you and Ethan aren't—"

"A thing? A couple?" She smiled. "No. Not at all." She paused, as though weighing her words. "Actually, I have a boyfriend."

"You do?" I asked, unable to temper the surprise in my voice.

She didn't seem offended. "I met him at the summer writing workshop. He and Ethan were roommates, actually." She smiled behind her glasses. "He lives near Omaha, but we're talking about going to school together next year."

"Omaha," I repeated lamely. "That's . . . not close."

She smiled again. "No, but we write each other almost every day. He writes the most incredible emails."

"Why don't you ever talk about him?" I asked.

Shanti shrugged. "I don't know. I guess I don't feel the need to shove my personal life in people's faces. I mean, like those people at school who are always making out in the hallways, pushed up against lockers. . . . It's like, what are you trying to prove?"

"Um," I said, unsure of whether she was insulting me.

She noticed my look. "Not you."

Down near the river, Ethan was drinking from his teammate's water bottle while the guy next to him stretched his quads.

"And he doesn't mind about Ethan?" I thought grimly about my own relationship. "He's not jealous?"

"No," Shanti said. "He's very enlightened. And anyhow,

263

he knows I'm not Ethan's type." Her voice was dryly amused, sweetly self-deprecating, as if she were making an inside joke with herself.

I couldn't help myself. "What's his type?"

Shanti raised an eyebrow. "Princesses," she said, and went back to her writing.

We were quiet for a while, Shanti writing while I people watched. We'd been sitting in sun, but now the tree's wide shadow stretched across us. I shivered, wishing for more than my thin hooded sweatshirt. Shanti looked up. "Ethan probably has an extra jacket in the Jeep," she said. "He usually does."

"Oh, I don't —"

"I'll go with you," Shanti said, and yelled down to Ethan. "We're going on a walk!"

He looked up and waved.

"We'll come back for you!" she called.

He cupped his hand around his ear, shook his head, shrugged.

Shanti just waved and turned back to me. "I'll text him."

She hummed as we walked, and her steps were bouncy, but she was more subdued than she'd been earlier in the day. "So." Our feet stepped off the curb together. "Can I ask *you* something?"

My breath caught in my throat. She was going to ask me about kissing Ethan. Had he told her? "Maybe?"

"What's up with you and Jake? Half the time you look

like you want to push him into traffic, and the other half you're like, three seconds away from jumping him."

"Oh!" I said. "Jake!" My mind ran a quick montage of his face: winking from across the room, gritting his teeth as he dug a grave for the Austins' cat, softening the moment before he kissed me, wincing in the thunder of his dad's voice, looking down at Lacey, protective.

"Jake," I said again. "I don't know." Shanti was quiet, and I knew she was going to respect my privacy and leave it at that. But I found myself elaborating, telling her about Jake and Lacey and Mrs. Austin and my mother and how easy it all used to be, and how hard it had been since I got back. I talked and talked, realizing that I hadn't talked to anyone, not really, not like this, for weeks. It was such a relief. I felt my shoulders loosening as we strolled around Iowa City, aimlessly now, turning random corners and wandering down side streets. Shanti asked questions but didn't say much else, and I talked until we'd gone all the way to the Jeep and back and the sky had turned smoky blue with dusk.

Driving home, Shanti glanced at me as we passed beneath the glow of a streetlight. "What are you thinking about?" Ethan shifted in his seat to look back at me.

I dug my chin into my knees, pulling them more tightly to my chest. My thoughts were pictures rather than words, a whole reel of scenes and moments from the day. "You know," I said slowly, the realization moving through me like sunrise, "I think I'm actually . . . happy."

Ethan laughed. "You sound so surprised."

"Yeah," I said. "I guess I am."

As we drove through the quiet center of town, I felt all the years I'd spent there, all the versions of myself layered inside me like Russian nesting dolls. I saw myself like a ghost, years earlier, walking with Lacey on a night just like this one. We wandered to the school yard, swinging idly and talking about everything in the world as the moon crossed the sky above us.

"I'm dropping myself off first," Shanti announced a moment later, passing my house. "My car's still at school."

"That was my house," I said, pointing behind us.

"Sorry," Shanti said, not sounding very sorry at all. A few minutes later, she pulled up next to her car in the school parking lot. We all hopped out of the Jeep, and Shanti hugged me. "Thanks for coming with us today, Paige."

"Thank *you* for kidnapping me," I said.

She drew her eyebrows together, looking stern. "Yes, and as your kidnapper I demand that you write at least three pages tomorrow. I want them on my desk Monday morning, Sheridan!"

I laughed, holding my hands in the air. "Okay, okay, just don't hurt me."

Shanti handed the keys to Ethan and kissed him on the cheek. "Thanks for letting me drive."

"No prob. See you tomorrow." He swung up into the

driver's seat and looked at me, standing awkwardly in the nearly empty parking lot. "You didn't drive today?"

"Sometimes my global warming guilt complex kicks in," I said, and shrugged. "It's only a ten-minute walk."

"Well, the planet thanks you," Ethan said.

"I can walk now, actually," I said, "if it's too much trouble . . ."

"The planet doesn't thank you that much." He grinned. "It's my pleasure."

I hopped into the passenger seat. He waited until Shanti was safely in her car and pulling away before he shifted the Jeep into first and pulled out after her. Moments later, we were pulling into my driveway. Ethan shifted into neutral and set the parking brake. My house was dark, save for the dim light in my sister's bedroom window. Green numbers glowed on the Jeep's dashboard. 11:31. My parents were probably sleeping; they'd stopped waiting up for me years ago.

"Well," Ethan said. "Here we are." The cool night air smelled like campfires and pumpkin spice, and the Jeep's speakers still murmured the sounds of Shanti's mix.

"Thanks," I said finally. "For everything."

He nodded. "It was a great day, wasn't it?"

"It was." A long crack across his windshield caught my neighbor's porch light and flashed like a diamond ring. "Are you going to the bonfire tomorrow night?"

"Probably not," Ethan said. "I offered to work tomorrow afternoon, so I'll probably be pretty tired by then."

"Mr. Tremont will be there. He's chaperoning."

"I know," Ethan said. "Jeremy told me."

"I'll be there."

He looked at me. "With your boyfriend."

I hesitated. "Well . . . yes."

Ethan reached for the volume on the stereo, turning it up a notch.

"You know," I said. "I never interviewed you."

He looked up, squinting. "Hmm. True."

"Well, I'm not doing anything right now."

"Fair enough." He turned the key in the ignition so the engine turned off but the radio stayed on.

Unbuckling my seat belt, I grabbed my notebook and a pen and turned toward him. "Okay." I hunched over my book like he had that day in class, playing the ambitious cub reporter. "First question: Are you or are you not a freshman?"

He laughed, as I'd hoped he would. "We're still dwelling on that?"

"Answer the question."

He laughed. "Sorry, Ms. Reporter. No, I'm not a freshman."

"But you're new to Willow Grove?"

"Yes." He turned the radio back down. "We moved over the summer."

"From?"

"Just outside of Omaha."

"Isn't that where Shanti's boyfriend lives?"

Ethan nodded. "Yeah. Aaron. He's my best friend. We grew up together."

"Why did you move?" I asked quietly.

He looked away, through the driver's side window to the rippling shadows of dark trees moving under streetlights. "My mom. Her boyfriend moved and she followed him. He had a buddy here who could get him a job, he said, so my mom sold the house we'd been living in since I was a baby and dumped almost all our furniture and clothes and my brothers' toys at a garage sale. I was in Iowa City at the time, at the summer intensive. She told me she thought I'd be happy."

I bit my lip.

"She thought I'd be happy that she got rid of my entire childhood and traumatized my brothers so she could be closer to Ed." He shook his head.

"What was the job?"

Ethan's laugh was ragged. "Yeah, the job. I can't say I know, because so far Ed hasn't done a goddamn thing but lie on the couch and drink beer and yell at my brothers while my mom busts her ass working double shifts at the hospital to support him."

"She's a nurse?"

"Yeah." He leaned back against the seat. "I'm going to take my little brothers and raise them myself. After college. I'll get an apartment and a job, a real job, and I'll take them to school in the mornings and help them with their homework at night. Dave Eggers did it, he raised his little brother. I'll be like that."

My notebook sat slack in my lap, all pretense of cub reporter forgotten. "How old are they?"

"Andy's six and Sam is four. Their dad left after Sam was born, said he couldn't take the commitment." Outside it had started to rain, and Ethan flicked the windshield wipers on. "I know Starbucks is the corporate man, blah blah blah, but they do health insurance, and if I stay with them all through college they might give me my own store when I graduate. And then once Andy and Sam are old enough to watch themselves, in eight or nine years, maybe I'll have time to go to grad school and get my MFA."

"God, Ethan. I'm sorry."

He looked away. "It's not your fault." The rain faltered and the windshield wipers groaned against the glass. "Hey, I'm sorry," he said abruptly. "Way to put a damper on a great evening, huh?"

"No." I reached for his hand without thinking, but then stopped halfway, my fingers hanging in the air above the stick shift. He glanced down and I tucked my fingers into my palm. "I'm glad—"

He cut me off. "Don't tell anyone, okay? I don't want anyone to feel sorry for me. I don't want sympathy."

"Of course."

He sighed. "I shouldn't have said anything." He shook his head. "Just forget it, okay?"

"Hey," I said.

"It's late." He closed his eyes, massaged his head between his fingers and thumb.

I got the hint. "Okay." I swallowed hard and swung from the Jeep, landing lightly on the driveway. "Thanks for the ride."

"Oh," he said. "Sure. Of course."

"Well." I hung in the door for a second, looking back at him. "Drive safe."

"Yeah." His voice was thick and his hands wrapped around the steering wheel. "Have fun at the bonfire, Paige."

I bit my lip and shut the door. I stood watching as he backed out of the driveway, wondering what I'd done wrong, how I'd managed to ruin the only good night I'd had in months. Even as he pulled to the end of the street and turned out of sight, I stayed frozen in place, staring at the empty spot in the driveway.

chapter SEVENTEEN

In class on Friday, we did our first round of workshopping with Ethan's and Shanti's stories. Mr. Tremont led
the discussions, facilitated them, but didn't contribute
that much about any of the stories. His rule was that the
writer couldn't talk, couldn't defend her piece or explain
anything, until everyone was finished discussing it. He
had this way of completely validating everything we read.
He didn't make many comments, but the few he did make
about each piece brought them to life in new ways. It was
like putting glasses on for the first time, when the world
you thought you knew is suddenly clearer and more beautiful than you'd ever imagined. I almost wished I'd turned
my bat story in after all, even though it was so stupid and

banal compared to what Ethan and Shanti had written. But I almost believed Mr. Tremont could find something worthwhile even in my dumb little piece.

I wanted to catch Ethan and Shanti after class and tell them again how much I'd liked their stories, but they both seemed a little shell-shocked from the workshopping experience and wandered into the hallway with private, dazed expressions. I'd talk to them later, I decided. Shanti would be at the bonfire, and Ethan—well, if I didn't run into him this weekend, maybe I'd stop into Starbucks on Sunday. I headed out to my car, smiling at the thought.

After school, my mother was in a complete panic over the latest Stella Austin event, and she forced Miranda and me to roll a million napkins with pieces of burlap and tie them with long strands of colored raffia. "Stella's been so edgy lately," she kept saying. "Everything has to be perfect."

At one point she went tearing into the garage to find extra double-sided tape to keep the ribbons around the vases, and Miranda whispered, "She's psychotic. You better not break up with Jake."

"What?"

"I mean," she said, looping raffia around her fingers, "you *should,* because he's a loser and you can do better, but you shouldn't, because Mom's head will explode."

"Jake's not a loser," I said. "Anyway, why would you even say that?"

Miranda rolled her eyes. "I'm not an idiot, Paige."

"We're not going to break up," I said. "And even if we did, Mom would be fine."

My sister snorted. "Sure, Paige. And your actions never affect anyone else." She shook her head. "If you and Jake broke up, I bet Mom would get fired."

"What? No she wouldn't. Stella wouldn't do that."

My sister raised her eyebrows. "Wouldn't she?" Just then, my mother came tearing back into the room, clutching double-sided tape like grenades in both hands. My sister looked at me meaningfully and went back to tying raffia.

Around five, my mother looked at the clock and screeched. "Paige! What are you doing?"

"Rolling napkins?"

"Look at the time!" she cried. "The bonfire starts at eight!"

"It's three hours away," I said.

"Aren't you going to Lacey's to get ready? You have to do your hair!" She yanked the yard of burlap from my hands. "Did you steam your dress? You still have to take a shower!"

I raised my hands in defeat. "Okay, okay, I'll go shower."

"Tonight's the announcement, Paige! When's the final vote, next Thursday? You have less than a week! And you have *not* been dressing to impress lately, that's for certain!"

I glanced down at my worn jeans and threadbare green hoodie. Under the hoodie I wore a T-shirt that said NOT EVERYTHING IN IOWA IS FLAT, but I supposed that didn't count as 'dressing to impress.' She'd been so wrapped up in

Stella Austin drama all week I was kind of surprised that she'd noticed my wardrobe at all.

"Why don't you jump in the shower and I'll call Brenda to let her know you're on your way over," my mother said.

"I wasn't going to—" I started.

"Cool, can I be finished too?" Miranda asked.

"Is that a joke?" my mother asked Miranda. "We need to finish these napkins before tomorrow morning! And I still have to do my hair and put on my face for the bonfire!"

"You look fine, Mom," I said.

My mother gritted her teeth. "Girls, please try to cooperate for once! Paige, get in the shower! Miranda, please finish these napkins!"

She was still screeching when I got out of the shower, so I finally packed my things and headed for Lacey's. My mother shouted after me to be patient with Lacey. In case I wasn't aware, she was having a "really rough time right now."

At the Lanes', Brenda was just as psycho as my mother had been. She grabbed my arm at the door and pulled me up to Lacey's room, where the girls were both standing in front of Lacey's mirror, examining their reflections. "It's good there's no game this year," Nikki said. "This way my hair will still be perfect."

"You never know," Lacey said. "There's always a chance it could get messed up."

"How?" Nikki asked reasonably. "If I'm not making out with anyone before the bonfire, my hair will be fine."

"Look who's here, girls!" Brenda announced.

"Hi, Paige," Nikki said.

Lacey continued talking to Nikki as if I weren't there. "Oh, I don't know, maybe the wind? Maybe a random spark will just fly out of the fire and ignite the product in your hair, turning your head into a giant fireball?"

Nikki clapped her hands over her head, stricken. "Oh my God! I never thought of that!"

"I'm sure it will be fine, Nik," I said, dropping my bag on the bed and hanging my dress over the door.

"Right," Lacey agreed acidly. "As long as you don't have a chance to whore around under the bleachers, I'm sure it will look fine."

"Jesus," I said, and Lacey flipped her gaze to me.

"Speaking of whoring, what did you do yesterday, Paige?" She sat on a small bench in front of her faux-French vanity, her bad leg sticking out awkwardly straight in front of her. She watched herself in the mirror, pulling a comb through her fine hair, following it with a curling iron.

"What the hell is that supposed to mean?" I kept my voice steady as I pulled my dress from its bag and stepped behind the closet door to change.

Lacey's voice was innocent. "I'm just asking what you did yesterday."

"Nothing." I slipped the dress over my head. The fabric was soft against my skin, and I stepped back into the room, enjoying the swish of material against my bare legs.

"Nothing?" Lacey asked. "Really? That's weird, because I could have sworn I saw you in Iowa City."

"Why were you in Iowa City?" I asked.

Nikki looked up from her bottle of nail polish and blinked at Lacey. "I thought you had physical therapy, and that's why you couldn't hang out."

"But let me ask you this," Lacey said to me, ignoring Nikki. "Where was your boyfriend yesterday, when you were running around with those queers? Are you too good for him now? Huh? Just like you've been too good for the rest of us ever since you got back from Paris?"

Nikki tried to interrupt. "Lacey —"

"Doesn't it bother you, Nikki? Doesn't it bother you that ever since Paige got back from Paris she hasn't wanted to hang out with us?"

"More like every time I tried to hang out with you, you were 'comparing physical therapy notes' with my boyfriend —"

She raised her voice over mine, speaking to Nikki. "How about spending your summer in the hospital while Perfect Paige went to Paris? While you were stuck here watching your family fall apart?"

"I was exiled!" I said. "My parents were so embarrassed of me that they sent me out of the country!"

Lacey put down her curling iron and spun around to look at me. "Right. Exiled. We're all supposed to feel so sorry for you because your life is so difficult. Well, guess what: without us, your life would be a hell of a lot worse. So think long and hard before you throw it all away."

Her eyes were cracked with summer lightning. She turned to Nikki. "Doesn't it bother you even a little bit to see her treating Jake like shit, taking him for granted, when he does nothing but fawn all over her and she doesn't fucking deserve him? Hmm?"

"And you do?" I asked.

Lacey hit me with the full force of her glare. "Maybe I do. Because you haven't fucking been there for him one minute, and I have."

"You've been there for him?" I shouted. "I thought it was the other way around! Because it seems to me that all I've heard from the second I got back this summer was all about how you need help, you're going through a rough time, you have it so hard, you you you! I haven't heard one thing about Jake having a hard time, even though he's obviously so sick of your drama he could scream!" I was screaming now, my arms pulled tight across my chest like safety straps.

Lacey yelled, "Maybe that's because you haven't taken one second to think about anyone but yourself!"

Nikki stood, reaching between us. "Girls—"

"Since when are you Miss Do-gooder anyway, Lacey?" I yelled. "I thought you left that act to Nikki!"

Nikki's face dropped, and her outstretched arms fell to her sides. "Act?"

"Oh, Nik," I said. "I didn't mean—"

"No," she said. "I don't really want to hear your apologies anymore, Paige."

She turned and walked out of the room.

"Nikki!" I called.

"Let her go," Lacey said. "And get used to it. Because after tonight, nobody's going to want to listen to your shit anymore. You're done."

I stared at her until she became unfamiliar, like when you repeat the same word over and over until it seems like the most unlikely combination of consonants and vowels and you wonder how it ever could have had meaning for you. Her eyes were small in her face, her cheeks flushed and hot. The longer I looked, the more monstrous she appeared, until I was overcome by it. How could Jake have chosen her over me, even for one minute?

"You know what?" I finally said, grabbing my bags and makeup and the clothes I'd worn over to her house. "You are a small, judgmental, mean little girl. You think no one else sees that? They remember who you were, and so do I. You were the bully on the playground, the one who had to scare people into playing with her. And now you're a bitch!"

"I'm a bitch?" she hissed. "Look in the mirror, Miss Paris!"

"No wonder your dad left. I would have left you, too!"

My words rang in the air, clearly marking a line between before and after. A line I couldn't cross back over, even if I wanted to. But I didn't—and as though to prove it, I kept going. "Jake doesn't like you; he just feels sorry for you," I said. "But I don't. You deserve everything that's happened to you."

"You deserve ten times that!" she yelled. "You should have been the cripple! The accident was all your fault! If you hadn't been such a slut . . . You ruined everything!"

My throat was tight, but I forced the words through. "You know what? I take it back. I *am* sorry for you, because you're going to end up all alone. Too bad you didn't die in the accident; everyone would forget what a bitch you are and make you into some kind of hero."

"I wish I *had* died!" she screamed. "I wish we both had!"

I stood in the doorway of her room, shaking, as the words echoed through her and she collapsed in on herself, weeping.

And then I left. Left her sitting all alone in the middle of her room, barefoot, boobs shoved into a strapless Wonderbra to create the illusion of a chest in her satiny dress, the curling iron dangling in her right hand, half her hair still hanging straight and limp across her shoulders.

My flight brought back memories of the previous weekend: running down the wide front steps, taking them too fast even though my ankle still winced at the memory of its last journey down these stairs. I darted across the open doorway toward the dining room, hoping to avoid Brenda. The house was eerily quiet, and I imagined I could sense the gaping absence Lacey's father had left behind him. I was burning with pure adrenaline and anger, hearing the ugly echoes of my own voice reverberating in the house's gaping silence, shaking and shocked by my own capacity for evil. Maybe I *was* the bitch. Maybe we both were.

In ninth grade, Lacey and I saw this dumb made-for-TV movie where the girl comes home to find her boyfriend in bed with another woman. The boy sits up in bed, looking vaguely embarrassed, and the girl grabs this framed picture of them off the dresser and hurls it at his head, scattering glass everywhere, while the other woman grabs her things and runs from the house. The movie was terrible, but there was something about that scene that struck us, and we spent weeks afterward discussing it: In the girl's place, would we do the same thing? Would we scream, break things, make a scene? Lacey said yes, but I worried that I wouldn't, that I'd just run from the room without a word, silent and crying. Lacey laughingly agreed.

Well, now we know, I thought wryly. I should tell Lacey.

And then it hit me.

I couldn't tell Lacey. I couldn't tell anyone. The adrenaline drained from my body. "I just broke up with Lacey," I whispered to myself. She would never forgive me. Our friendship was done. I couldn't remember a time I'd felt more out of control — or more alone.

I had to get out of there.

Jake's. I'd go to Jake's. I nodded, glad to have made the decision, because a person who could still make decisions wasn't totally lost yet, was she? Armed with a plan, I headed toward the kitchen door. And then I was gone, realizing only much later that it might be for the last time.

Five minutes later, I pulled up in front of Jake's house, my heart throbbing in the base of my throat. The radio went off with the ignition, and for a moment I sat in the car's clicking silence as the engine cooled and tree branches bobbed against the windshield. The night was cloud tossed and windy. *"Wild nights!"* I whispered, remembering Mr. Tremont smiling to himself. The thought calmed me. I reached for my makeup bag and took a few moments to do my eyes in the rearview mirror. My hair looked surprisingly decent, considering I hadn't managed to curl it or put it up or do anything but run my fingers through it on the drive to Lacey's. A dab of my favorite lip gloss and I was good. Good enough, at least.

My hair was ruined the second I stepped out of the car; it whipped across my face in fierce strands like something living. Nikki wouldn't be happy, I thought, before remembering that I'd messed up with her, too. Could I stay friends with Nikki after breaking up with Lacey? Would she choose Lacey over me? Would we make her choose?

I went in through the garage, mindlessly punching the numbers into the keypad. I knew this house as well as my own. My mother had been working for Stella Austin Events since the summer before eighth grade, and even before that I had come with Lacey, who'd been friends with Jake since they were little. The summer after seventh grade, my mother finally got her invitation to join the Willow Grove Country Club, and she immediately signed me up for tennis lessons. Afterward, Lacey and I would play doubles against anyone she could tease into joining us. Most days we played Chris Jensen and Jake. I spent the summer feeling strong and loose, savoring the way the sun warmed my suddenly long legs until I was sleek and tan and unstoppable.

That summer, for the first time in my life, I felt like everything was right. Lacey and I were inseparable. Any leftover loneliness from elementary school had faded away. Grown-ups started treating us differently, looking at us with something like respect, listening when we had something to say. Brenda started asking us for the latest gossip, and Lacey and I would tell her, crowded around the kitchen table with magazines and diet sodas. My mother never missed a chance to introduce me as her daughter.

At the end of that summer, Lacey and I snuck out of her house in the middle of the night and ran around the golf course's perimeter, clinging to the wooded edge for cover, to meet Jake and some of his friends on the sixteenth hole. Five of us sat at the base of an old oak tree, in a circle like it was story time. Chris brought his iPod and tiny speakers. Jake brought a bottle of vodka-spiked Sprite. Lacey brought the skinny menthol cigarettes that Brenda pretended not to smoke. I sat between Lacey and Jake, watching the shadows shift on the blue grass in moonlight, shivering in the chill of the evening and the excitement of sneaking out. Jake took off his sweatshirt and draped it over my shoulders. And when, almost two years later, he kissed me under the misty trees in Lacey's backyard, I remembered that moment, the scent and warmth of his sweatshirt against my summer skin.

I took a deep breath and pushed open the garage door. I paused in the mudroom between the garage and kitchen, listening. Jake's house was almost identical in layout to Lacey's, the same kitchen–dining room–foyer–living room pattern across the first floor. I always knocked, in case someone was in the kitchen; one time I'd startled Mrs. Austin and she'd screamed and dropped a very expensive wineglass on the Mexican tile. All was quiet, and I leaned my forehead against the door's cool surface for a moment before opening it. The kitchen was dark, but I could hear voices in another room. Jake's house always smelled light green, clean and sagey. I slipped out of my shoes and left them by the kitchen door, padding across the dark floor toward the front staircase. The voices got louder and my steps slowed, the back of my neck tight and prickling. I rested my fingers on the banister and silently lifted myself up the stairs, one at a time.

"I don't care if it's for a girl," Jake's dad was saying. "You are going to be a lawyer, not a damn poet! The only writing you do will be legal briefs and client letters, and most of the time you won't even write them, your secretary will. You understand what I'm saying, son?"

I stopped, hardly daring to breathe.

Jake's response was too quiet for me to hear, but his father's rumbled back. "Then buy her something nice! Take her out to dinner; buy her flowers! I won't have my son writing poetry like a damn faggot!"

A door slammed, and I sprinted back down the stairs and slid across the polished wood of the dining room. Heavy footsteps followed, tromping down the stairs, and my heart jumped against my rib cage. I quietly opened and loudly shut the kitchen door and turned the light on. "Hello?" I called.

Mr. Austin's voice answered. "Hello? Is that Lacey?"

I bit my lip, but called back cheerfully, "No, it's Paige!" I bent down like I was taking off my shoes and pressed my hand to my chest, trying to slow my breath.

I stood up just as Mr. Austin appeared in the kitchen. "Haven't seen you in a while, Paige. How have you been?" He walked over to the fridge and peered inside. "Do you want something to drink? Diet something? Juice? Beer?" He took one for himself.

"Water's fine," I said. "I can get it myself."

He ignored me and grabbed a bottle of water from the refrigerator door, setting it next to his beer on the counter. "You don't need ice or a lemon, do you?" I shook my head. "No, you're low maintenance. It's a rare quality in a woman, I tell you what."

He passed the water bottle to me and leaned against the sink, tapping his fingers against his beer.

"Jake will be right down."

I nodded. The bottle was wet with condensation in my cold hands.

Mr. Austin's voice was sudden in the empty room. "You don't like poetry, do you? You want something concrete: flowers, chocolate, jewelry."

"Um." I took a sip of water. Something outside triggered the motion-sensor light, and sudden shadows skipped across the wide kitchen window. A raccoon, maybe. Or a cat.

"When I was your age, I was working my ass off to get into college. I had focus. I was going pre-law and then law. We wrote papers. We had to study Latin for chrissakes. We didn't have time to lie around writing *poetry*." He spit the word out like it was poison.

"Well . . ." I said.

"My brother used to write poems. He was always inside when we were kids. We were running around the neighborhood, whatever, but he stayed inside and wrote little stories. And then he goddamn went off and disappeared, never even called until the day he got sick." He shook his head, staring out the window, and I wondered if he was even talking to me anymore.

I took a step toward the dining room. "I'm just—"

Mr. Austin turned back toward me. "Jake shouldn't be wasting time trying to 'express his feelings.' He can't even spell. He's eighteen and he doesn't even know how to spell 'you' or 'to.'" He looked at me. "Do you do that? Abbreviate everything with letters and numbers? Teenagers." He slammed the bottle down on the counter near the sink and grabbed another one from the fridge.

"Maybe I should—"

"Why don't your teachers teach something worthwhile, like how to spell a damn word? We had to diagram sentences and read the classics. *Tom Sawyer. The Old Man and the Sea.* Goddamn *Moby Dick.*"

I set the water bottle on the counter. "I'm just going to—"

Mr. Austin beat me to it, striding over to the foot of the stairs. "Hey, Allen Ginsberg! Your girlfriend's here! Get your ass in gear!"

I kept my eyes glued to the kitchen floor, hoping it would keep Mr. Austin from continuing our conversation. The tiles were perfectly clean, perfectly shined, except for a toe print just in front of my feet. I inched my right foot forward and pressed my big toe down on top of the print. It matched perfectly.

Jake clattered down the stairs and I looked up, seeing him much younger in the shadowed hallway. He was twelve, thirteen, eager to show me and Lacey his newest game console. He was in baggy blue shorts, ready to teach me how to sink a layup. He was surreptitiously checking his face for zits in the hallway mirror; he was shoving books into a duffel bag. He was damp from the shower; he was sneezing into a paper towel; he was tugging at a new tie. He was tired, uncertain, proud, nervous, eager, disappointed, pleased. He was everything I'd ever known him to be. He was five years of Jake all at once.

Mr. Austin shook his head. "See if you can do something with him."

Jake scowled, but I smiled my first genuine smile of the night. "I will." I held out my hand to Jake and he crossed the room to meet me. He looked tired and grumpy. I slid my fingers into his hard hand and held tight.

"We're taking the truck," he told his father, and pulled me out the door.

In the truck he didn't talk, and I pressed my fingers against my knees. Jake drove through the neighborhood and turned onto the slow country highway that stretched between the gates of Sauvignon and the edge of town, twelve miles of empty hills and paper stalk cornfields. The moon hung low over distant trees, a circle of deep orange.

Jake slapped the steering wheel. "Goddammit!" His voice was deafening in the quiet night, and I imagined entire fields of geese waking to startled flight. "That fucking . . . He had no fucking right." I wanted to reach over and place my hand on his leg, to comfort or maybe distract him, but in his voice I heard something of his father, and I stayed still.

"Fuck!" he said, and pulled over to the side of the road. "I'm sorry."

"It's okay."

We sat in silence for a moment, staring straight ahead. The engine murmured beneath us. Jake reached across me and flipped open the glove box. Inside, a silver flask glinted in the low-wattage light. He grabbed it and took a long swallow, and another, and then handed the flask to me.

I drank without thinking. "Jake," I said. "Is everything—"

He shook his head, staring through the dark. A last, late firefly glowed briefly and disappeared. "He found my—I was trying to—I wanted—"

For one crazy second, I thought of Ethan in his Jeep, staring out the window and talking about his mother's boyfriend, his little brothers. Is this how boys confess? Staring through windshields into darkness? But thinking of Ethan made me feel guilty. I turned my focus back to Jake.

"It's so fucking stupid. I was just . . . I wanted to write something . . . for you. . . . I know how much you like that stuff, and Lacey said . . ." He shook his head. "He fucking ripped it up."

"God," I said. "I'm sorry."

He punched the steering wheel. "Never mind. It's so fucking stupid. My dad's right."

I spoke quietly. "No he's not."

"Yes, Paige, he is. Poetry is for chicks and fags." His voice was heavy with disgust, and he sounded like his dad.

"Jake—" I ached to think of his first, fragile attempts at writing, real writing, ripped apart and sagging in strips against the sides of his wastebasket.

He didn't look at me. "Lacey says some girls just go for gay guys, but I thought if I could—"

Lacey? She was behind this? I suddenly wanted to punch something myself.

"Fuck it," Jake said. He shifted the truck back into first gear and revved the engine.

I wanted to make him feel better, but I didn't know any words that could temper the strange severity of his tight fists and sharp voice. My hand reached for his and faltered in the space between us, hanging, until it felt unhinged from my body. The headlights stretched down the dark road before us, catching bits of leaf and dust blowing through the blustery night. "At least let me drive," I said, but he shook his head.

"I'm fine."

"Jake," I said softly, choking on my own voice. He didn't look at me, just moved the flask to his lips again and again until there was nothing left.

We pulled into the orange-lit student lot, parking in the far corner where Jake always parked, to minimize the potential damage that came with parking among the masses. He clicked off the ignition and sat still for a moment. "Do you have gum?" I asked. "If anyone smells alcohol on your breath, you'll get benched for the next game."

"I know." He reached across me and popped open the glove compartment. "See?" he asked, pulling out a tin of mints and a tiny bottle of cologne. He popped a mint into his mouth, spritzed the cologne on himself, and then turned to me with a sudden realization. "Hey, where were you yesterday?" His voice was already thicker, slower.

"Nowhere."

"Lacey said she saw you with that freshman. Evan."

Guilt washed through me, and I searched my mind for an excuse. "No, I was—" But then a thought struck me: What if Lacey somehow had evidence, if she'd snapped pictures of us with her camera phone or something? What the hell was she doing in Iowa City anyway?

"Yeah," I said, trying to keep my voice even. "I was hanging out with some people from my creative writing class. I told you that."

"You picked them over me," he said.

"What? You said you were too busy to hang. You said you had plans with Lacey." I fought the urge to add *Again*.

"She ditched me. Said she had to help her mom with something. Lawyer stuff, I don't know. I called you, but you didn't answer."

"So you get ditched and then come looking for sloppy seconds?"

He looked stung. "No! I just wanted to see you. Things have been so messed up lately."

I softened. "I know."

"You like him more than me." He sounded surprised, like he'd plugged everything into an equation and come up with a different answer than he'd expected.

I sat back, feeling my face burn. "What? That's ridiculous."

"Yeah. You like him more than you like me. Because he can write poetry. You think I'm a dumb jock." He looked away, and I imagined those strands of scribbled lines, tentative phrases and measures to match up to some ideal in his head, ripped and thrown to waste. Shit.

"You're not—"

"Lacey says you're going to leave me for him!"

"What?" My mind whirred. We hadn't done anything in Iowa City that would arouse suspicion. Except for skipping stones, I'd spent more time with Shanti than I had with Ethan. Unless—oh my God. The night of the party. Had she been there? Had she seen us? How was that possible? She'd been too drunk to leave the house, much less sneak silently through the dark forest. How did she know?

"She says I'm too much man for you," he said.

Fucking Lacey! I reached for Jake's hand. "Lacey's just a . . . she's confused." I leaned across the truck's bench, pulling at his face to make him see me. "Jake, listen. I'm not going to leave you. I love you." The kiss with Ethan flashed before my eyes, but I shook my head. That had been a mistake, it didn't count.

He held my gaze. "Lacey said she saw you in his classroom. Alone. With him."

"With—wait, with Mr. Tremont? You think I'm going to leave you for Mr. Tremont? That's ridiculous," I said.

"You weren't alone in his classroom with him?" Jake asked.

"No!" I said. "I mean, yes, I was, but I was just—"

Jake pushed my hand away. "So you lied." His voice sounded suddenly like his father's. Dangerous.

"What? No! You're confused. This is crazy."

"I'm crazy?" Jake asked menacingly.

"No, I didn't mean—" My heart was hammering my throat. I felt like I couldn't breathe. "He's gay!" I blurted.

Jake sat up. "He's what? No way. How do you know?" He narrowed his eyes. "Are you fucking with me?"

I took a breath, hating myself. "I mean, it's kind of obvious. He's so . . . clean."

"Oh, shit! No way, man, that's crazy! I mean, Randy and those dudes said it, but I thought they were just being dicks. Mr. fucking Tremont's a queer!"

"God, Jake," I said, but he was already reaching for the door handle, jumping down from the truck.

I was a terrible person. I was just as bad as Lacey, spreading rumors to manipulate people. Worse! Because unlike her, I actually had a conscience; I knew it was wrong, and I did it anyway. I prayed to everything and anything holy that Jake would forget about it before we reached the back lot, that he wouldn't immediately tell every person he saw. That it wouldn't get back to Ethan and Shanti and Jeremy and my sister that I'd joined the dark side, that I could possibly spread rumors like this.

Suddenly, an even worse thought hit me: What if it was true? Mr. Tremont *was* very clean! He had asked about bringing a friend to the bonfire—what if he brought a guy? Jake and his friends would kill him!

"I can't believe it," Jake said, shaking his head. "Lacey said something, but then she said you . . ."

He slammed the door and walked around to my side,

opening my door for me. "It's crazy," he summarized, and held out his arm. "You ready, babe?" I nodded and pushed myself out of the cab, wobbling the moment I stood up. He caught me. "Careful."

At least he wasn't thinking about his dad anymore, I thought weakly. "Jake —"

"Yeah?"

I had to distract him. Make him forget. I pushed him against the truck, leaning the length of my body against his. I could feel the square outline of the flask in his jacket pocket. "Hey," I said.

He inhaled sharply. "Whoa."

"I would never leave you for anyone," I whispered, and ran my tongue up the side of his neck to the base of his ear until he shivered. "You're the only one. You."

His hands moved down my back, pulling me even closer. "Are you sure?" His breath was whiskey hot on my bare skin, and I shivered in the cold night air.

"I love you," I whispered, and kissed him until I was convinced.

Jake was the first to pull away. "We should go."

I was shivering still, rubbing my arms as I lost his heat. "We don't have to," I said, and for a moment I really believed it. We could go — not back to his house, where his father was drinking alone, and not back to my house, where my mother was constructing centerpieces like a terrorist building letter bombs, but somewhere — somewhere

294

alone, where we could forget about the rest of the world, forget Lacey and Mr. Tremont and Ethan, where we could stay wrapped in each other's arms and perfect and happy for the rest of our lives. We could skip the rest of our senior year and drive to Mexico, find a little house on the beach and do only the things that made us happy and ignore everything else, fall asleep together at night and wake together in the morning, sweaty and happy and together.

"I promised Lacey," Jake said, and Mexico disappeared. The night was still cold, I was still shivering, and I had no choice but to follow him around the side of the school.

chapter EIGHTEEN

The sky was dark, with tall wispy clouds sweeping in front of the nearly full moon, catching and releasing its light as they rolled over and over themselves like ocean breakers. I half expected to see some ghostly clipper ship appear through the parting shadows. There was something in the air, a wildness in the breeze as it whiffled through the trees, snatching at the driest leaves and sending them spinning to the ground, pushing at my hair and the hem of my dress so I had to hang on as I walked, slightly off balance.

We turned the corner and saw the bonfire, leaping orange against black skeletons of trees and shooting sparks up into the rolling night sky. Shadows of students, teachers, and parents swarmed like evil spirits and witches dancing around a fire. The sky suddenly flashed twice and thunder ripped through the heavy air, unapologetically loud.

I jumped and gave a short scream. Jake leaned over and whispered into my ear, his breath warm. "You're drunk."

"No I'm not," I whispered back, suppressing the urge to grab his hand and run—fly—away from our classmates and into the night.

Laughter floated from behind us, and I turned to see Lacey and Nikki crossing the parking lot with Randy, Chris, and Geneva and her suck-up friends. Lacey looked perfect, in stark contrast to when I'd seen her last: every hair in place, dress clinging in all the right places, eyes glittering dangerously.

"What up, man," Randy called to Jake. "Post party at Jensen's!"

Chris nodded. "It's gonna be dong. Three kegs, no 'rents."

I laughed. "Dong? Who says that?" Out of habit I glanced at Lacey, but she stared straight past me. Nikki just stared at the ground. The junior girls looked everywhere but at my face, and I marveled at how quickly Lacey's machine worked. Only the boys acted like nothing was wrong. "You know what I mean, Paige. It's gonna be hizzle." I could have sworn I saw Lacey roll her eyes.

Jake found my hand and pulled me toward the bonfire, and I had to trot in my ridiculously high heels. As we approached, the laughing and yelling turned to murmurs, and a few random people clapped. And then Lacey and Nikki stepped into the light, and the clapping turned to cheers and screams. The girls waved and blew kisses.

"Oh God." I felt suddenly panicky, but Jake put his arm

around me and we moved closer to the fire. Off to the side, the pitifully small pep band had set itself up in the bed of a pickup truck, just next to the flatbed trailer where Dr. Coulter stood with his hand shading his eyes, apparently staring directly into the fire. The pep band was butchering a Journey medley, and a few people were dancing ironically, or not so ironically, near the truck. I scanned the crowd for Ethan, even though I knew he was working.

I should have been standing next to Lacey and Nikki, blowing kisses to the crowd. I should have been thrilled to be here at last, after so many years of planning. So why did I keep thinking about stones skipping across water in the afternoon sun?

"I'll be right back!" I untangled myself from Jake's embrace and pushed through the jungle of arms and faces and letter jackets and beer breath and cologne and hair and heels and elbows and expectations and desires. Behind me, Jake was swallowed up in seconds, my trail erased as if I'd never been.

From the fringes, I saw a side of the school I'd rarely seen before. There were the geeks and weirdos you might expect, but there was drama, too: groups of girls rushing off together, couples making out in the shadows, people on cell phones with fingers in their ears to block the ambient noise, a couple of boys kicking around a hacky sack. Teachers stood on the edges of the circle, laughing with one another and ignoring the students. Closer to the flames,

Mr. Berna was trying to polka with the home ec teacher, Ms. Hoeschen, while she laughed hysterically. I saw flirting and fighting, relationships renegotiated, love, hate, and indifference. All this on the outside of what I'd known, beyond the edges of anything I'd cared about before, and tonight it seemed more interesting than whatever was happening in the center.

Then I spotted Mr. Tremont. He was dressed all in black and was scribbling notes on a legal pad, glancing up at the bonfire and down at the page, up and back, up and back.

Oh God, was he alone? I had to warn him. I would tell him that Lacey was spreading rumors. It was Lacey's fault!

"Hey, Paige."

I shrieked. Jeremy stood beside me, and I put my hand over my pounding heart. "Jesus Christ!"

"Are you okay?"

"Oh my God, Jeremy! Lacey! She is telling everyone that Mr. Tremont is gay!" The ground tilted and I reached for his sleeve.

He caught me, and the ground steadied. "Are you drunk?"

"No," I said. How much had I sipped from Jake's flask?

"Girl, are you crazy? They're about to announce court."

"Screw court!" The pep band stopped and my voice was too loud. "Jeremy," I said more quietly. "Lacey is spreading rumors that Mr. Tremont is gay! And she's evil!"

"Let's get you some water," he said.

"I'm not drunk!" I said. "I mean, okay, maybe I'm a little tipsy, but it's still true! Lacey will tell Dr. Coulter! She'll get him fired!"

"For what?" he asked. "For being gay? Honey, that's illegal."

I shook my head. "Not in Willow Grove. You can't be gay here. Everyone hates gays here."

Jeremy's face shattered. "Oh really."

"Yes!" A muscle in his jaw jumped. It took my foggy brain a second to realize that he was furious — and another second to grasp why. "Oh. Oh! No — Jeremy . . ."

"You know what, Paige?" He shook his head. "No, never mind. It's not even worth it. I'll see you later." He turned and walked into the fray.

"Jeremy, wait!" I called, but he was gone and I was alone. "Shit!"

I'd have to fix things myself. Where was Mr. Tremont? He wasn't standing with his legal pad where I'd seen him before. I had to find him. No, I had to find Jake! Find him before he said anything about Mr. Tremont. I'd distract him, pretend to fall, pretend to sprain my ankle, make him drive me home. But he was drunk. Maybe I would drive myself home. I wasn't drunk. I was fine, I just . . . Shit.

Mr. Tremont reappeared behind a group of bouncing freshman, and I headed for him. He was still writing, still watching the crowd, the fathomless clutter of colors and sounds, the squeal of clarinets and the thumping of the tuba and the tangle of faces in the flickering orange light.

"Now, am I supposed to keep them from throwing themselves into the fire," Mr. Tremont was saying, "or just pull them out after they've gone in?"

The woman next to him laughed. "Did I ever tell you about the time a car spontaneously combusted in the parking lot of my high school?"

I knew that voice! It was Padma, his friend from the reading! And she was a girl! My pounding heart slowed. Everything was okay. Mr. Tremont wasn't gay.

Mr. Tremont turned toward Padma, and the fire highlighted his profile. He was so beautiful. Of course he wasn't gay. But so what if he had been. He was still the best teacher I'd ever had. He was still gorgeous. It didn't change anything.

"I'm sure you haven't," he told Padma. "That sounds like a story I'd remember."

I stepped forward until I was in his line of sight. Mr. Tremont saw me and waved. "Paige! I'm glad to see you!"

"You are?" I grinned, but then thought of Jake's accusations. Was it wrong for me to feel so happy whenever Mr. Tremont paid me a compliment?

"Can you clear something up for us?"

"I can try." Up on the flatbed, Dr. Coulter tapped the microphone. There was a loud screech of feedback.

"So, am I supposed to be preventative or punitive?" Mr.

Tremont asked. "Keep them from going into the fire, or just give them detention once they have?"

Padma punched him. "You cannot let children catch on fire, Cam!"

I laughed, still giddy with relief. "As long as no school property is damaged," I said, "you're fine."

He pointed. "So I should probably go stop that kid?" Near the front of the blaze a kid from my Spanish class swung a textbook like a shot put.

I shrugged. "It's an older edition. I wouldn't worry about it."

Coach Wickstrom appeared out of nowhere and grabbed the book. "See?" Mr. Tremont told Padma. "The grown-ups have it under control."

"You are supposed to be one of them!" Padma said.

He smiled at me and matched my shrug. "I'm not supposed to worry about it."

On the flatbed, Dr. Coulter tapped the microphone again and this time a *thump thump* reverberated across the gathered crowd. "May I have your attention please? Folks? Up here, folks." The crowd ignored him. "People?" Next to him, Coach Ahrens blew his whistle into the mic, and its shrill tweet shot across the night, piercing our ears.

"Thank you, uh, Coach Ahrens," Dr. Coulter said. "Before we announce the members of this year's homecoming court, I have a few announcements to make. . . ." The crowd murmured and Dr. Coulter raised his voice.

"First of all, please remember that we have a zero-tolerance policy at this school. Any student caught with alcohol, tobacco, or any other restricted substance will be suspended, no exceptions."

Coach Ahrens grabbed the mic. "And I will not hesitate to search backpacks and persons, so don't think you can sneak anything past me!"

I shivered and rubbed my arms. If anyone caught Jake . . .

"Are you cold?" a voice whispered, and I turned, expecting to see Jake, as if he'd heard my thoughts and come to find me. But it wasn't Jake.

"What are you doing here?" I asked, fighting goose bumps that had nothing to do with the cold.

Ethan smiled. "It was dead at work, so they let me go." He took a step closer, and I could feel the warmth of his arms, just inches from mine. "You're shivering."

"I'm fine." I locked eyes with him and shivered again. "Hi."

His voice was quiet. "Hi."

There was a loud crash as Dr. Coulter managed to wrench his mic back from Coach. "Uh, thank you for that reminder, Coach Ahrens. As I was, ah, saying. Second, Nikki Rosellini, the members of, uh"—he glanced down at his notes—"of her group D-I-E-D-D, and the members of the student council have asked me to remind you to drive safely tonight and every night." He gazed out over the student body as if he could gauge how seriously we were taking his warning and, seeming satisfied, nodded and went back to his notes.

"Third, the Bee Boosters are selling hot chocolate, cider, and popcorn as a fund-raiser to continue to support our teams. They can be found, uh"—he looked up and pointed—"at that table over there."

"This is agonizingly uninteresting," Shanti said, appearing on the other side of me. "Why did we come, again?"

"It was your idea," Ethan told her.

"Yeah, but that was before I knew you'd have to ditch work to be here," she said.

Ethan blushed. "I didn't ditch. They let me go. It was very slow tonight. . . ." As they talked, he moved infinitesimally closer to me until the fabric of his jacket was skimming across the skin on my arms.

"Riiiiight," she said. "Well, I've seen enough. Wanna go?"

"Paige is about to be named to homecoming court," Ethan said.

"But we don't care about that," Shanti said. "It's just part of the hierarchical high school bullshit that perpetuates stereotypes and poor body images. Right, Paige?"

"Be nice," Ethan said. I felt like I could hear his heart beating. I resisted the urge to move just an inch closer.

"Paige doesn't care about the announcement." Shanti grinned at me. "I bet she'd come with us if we asked."

Ethan looked at me.

"I . . ."

I was saved from answering by the sound of Dr. Coulter clearing his throat. "And now it is my honor to announce the members of this year's homecoming court." The crowd immediately shushed, and I felt a sudden impulse to head up to the flatbed and find Lacey, to stand next to her and weave my fingers through hers, squeezing in excitement at each name. My hand actually reached out looking for hers, and I balled my fingers into a tight fist at my side to keep it in check.

"The five senior boys on court will be Tyler Adams, Jake Austin, Chris Jensen, Brian Sorenson, and Randy Thomas." No surprises there. One by one, the boys hopped up onto the trailer, making a sloppy line behind Dr. Coulter. In front of us, a group of sophomore girls squealed and clutched at one another's arms. "Oh my God, he is soooooo hot!"

"Which one?"

"Does it matter? They're all hot!" Giggle giggle giggle, squeal shriek snort. I wanted to vomit.

"Congratulations, boys," Dr. Coulter said. "Now for the girls." A warm hand covered my fist, and for a hallucinogenic moment, I actually thought Lacey had come back to prove that no fight would get in the way of who we'd always been to each other. I glanced down in surprise, but of course it wasn't Lacey's hand. Shanti smiled at me. "What? I can hate the populocracy bullshit and still root for you."

"The five senior girls on court will be Jenna French, Katrina Hoffman —"

I blinked in surprise. Katrina and Jenna were much like Nikki, Lacey, and I, but they each had one fatal flaw in the eyes of Willow Grove's elite: Katrina's family was poor, and Jenna's mom was a black Haitian immigrant. She'd met Jenna's dad when she was cleaning his office. I wasn't sure if it was the black thing or the cleaning lady thing that irritated Willow Grove. Jenna accepted Jake's offered hand, but Katrina leaped lightly onto the trailer, unassisted.

Dr. Coulter cleared his throat again, and I had a sudden, vivid flash of a world in which the next three names he called weren't ours at all, but some completely random girls', and all of Lacey's scheming was for nothing.

"Lacey Lane—"

I sighed. The real world was so mind-numbingly predictable.

"Nikki Rosellini—"

A part of me was relieved that my mother had been wrong. Maybe our school was more forgiving than she thought. Lacey and Nikki moved to the front of the trailer, and Jake and Randy leaned over, reaching arms down to help pull them up onto the flatbed. The crowd applauded, and Nikki blew kisses while Lacey leaned on her cane with a huge Miss America smile.

"—and Paige Sheridan. Congratulations, girls."

The girls in front of me bounced like popcorn under a hood. "Woo, Paige!" Shanti shouted, throwing her arms around me. Behind us, I thought I heard Mr. Tremont laugh. Shanti released me, and Ethan extended a fist toward me.

"Um, princesses don't *fist bump*," I said, jokingly disdainful. And before I knew what I was doing, I was hugging Ethan, my arms wrapped around his neck, my body flush against his.

He spoke so only I could hear. "Congratulations." I closed my eyes.

"Paige!" I jumped and pulled away from Ethan. "You have to go up there!" Shanti said.

"So it's all bullshit?" Ethan asked her.

"Shut up," she said, shoving me. "Go on, Paige!"

I made my way through the crowd slowly, wondering at the utter lack of excitement I felt in this moment. This was it. This was what we'd been working toward since forever, what we'd talked about and planned every single autumn since junior high. This was supposed to be the pinnacle of my high school career. And yet in my head, where there should have been fireworks and party horns, there was just the fuzz of static between radio stations. My mother's voice cut through the static in my head (*Smile, you never know who might be falling in love with you!*) and I fixed an obligatory smile on my face.

Where was my mother, anyway? I realized I hadn't seen her anywhere, not standing with the huddle of parents near the Bee Boosters booth or clutching a cup of hot coffee near the front of the crowd, determined to catch every detail. The only thing that could keep her away was Stella

Austin and her hundreds of raffia-wrapped napkins and centerpieces. I imagined a call from Stella—*The bride changed her mind; they want burnt umber and merlot raffia, not cinnamon and crimson!*—and my mother, alone in her workspace, surrounded by rolls of brown and red string. I felt a momentary stab of sadness at the thought.

When I reached the trailer, Jake leaned over to help me up, and he didn't let go of my hand as we walked back to the line. Lacey's eyes were icy, and almost unconsciously I leaned closer to Jake.

"This year's homecoming game will take place next Friday night, October first," Dr. Coulter announced. The trailer bed vibrated with his voice. "And the homecoming dance will take place the next night, Saturday, October second. Voting for king and queen will take place at lunchtime during the week." He glanced down at his notes and back at us. "And, uh, congratulations again to the members of the Willow Grove High School homecoming court."

The crowd applauded and quickly turned its attention back to itself and the fire, while on the trailer the girls hugged one another and the boys shook hands. Jake pulled me to him and kissed me, in front of the whole school. I blushed and pushed him away. "People are watching," I whispered.

"Fuck them," he said, and kissed me again, hard and boozy. Whiskey fumes stung my eyes.

"Get a room," Randy said, and Chris said, "Hey man, party at my place afterward, okay?"

308

"Of course," Jake said, wrapping an arm around my waist.

"Party?" Coach Ahrens interrupted. "What kind of party?"

Chris stood straighter under his gaze. "Just a small group of friends, sir, mostly just the court and a few dudes from the team."

"No alcohol?" Coach asked, and Chris put a hand across his heart, a vow.

"Of course not, sir, not during season!"

Coach Ahrens folded his arms. "I didn't think so."

Randy leaned over and whispered something in Jake's ear. Jake nodded and turned to me. "Hey, I left something in this fool's truck. Meet me in like ten minutes?"

"You what?" I asked, but he was already following Randy, jumping off the trailer like it was a skateboard ramp, and jogging off across the parking lot. Jenna caught my eye and grinned.

"Are you going to Chris's?" she asked.

I nodded. "Apparently."

"Cool," she said. "We'll see you there." She and Katrina stepped lightly off the trailer, leaving me alone with Nikki and Lacey and the principal.

"I, uh," I said, and realizing I sounded just like Dr. Coulter, I spun around and jumped off the trailer bed. Behind me, I heard the principal ask, "Do you know 'There's No Beer in Heaven?'" and just before I plunged back into the crowd, he said, "It's a *song*."

I ended up back where I'd been, standing with Ethan and Shanti and Mr. Tremont and Padma. "Princess Paige!" Shanti cheered, and Padma gave me a hug. "Are you so excited?"

"I guess," I said. The pep band started up a surprisingly accurate rendition of "Poker Face," and the handful of people dancing turned into a mob.

"Oh my God." Padma laughed. "This song takes me right back to senior year of college. Remember?"

"Did you go to school together?" I asked.

Padma shook her head, her eyes sparkling with reflected light. "No, we met in the workshop, but we're almost exactly the same age."

"She's three days older," Mr. Tremont said. He looked at Padma. "You want to go dance, don't you?"

"Nooooo," she said, trying to suppress a smile. "Yes. Totally."

"So, go ahead," Mr. Tremont said.

Shanti stepped forward. "I'll join you."

Ethan looked at her in surprise. "You're going to dance?"

"Always keep them guessing." She cocked an eyebrow at him. "You wanna come?"

He shook his head. The three of us stood and watched as Shanti and Padma made their way into the jumping fracas. Mr. Tremont said, "I hope that's not too weird."

"It's a little weird," Ethan said. "But so what. No one's paying attention anyway."

"She was really excited about coming tonight," Mr. Tremont said. "She's the one who should be teaching high school, not me. I'm totally out of my element."

"You can't tell," I said, and Mr. Tremont smiled at me. "Thanks, Paige."

Ethan gestured toward Mr. Tremont's legal pad. "What are you writing?"

Mr. Tremont tilted the pad so it caught the light and skimmed a field of small black lines. "Just notes about the whole bonfire, homecoming court, pep-band-in-a-truck thing. Padma wants me to do a sonnet cycle about high school. She thinks it would be funny."

"Ah," Ethan said, "but what do *you* want to write about?"

Mr. Tremont laughed. "Nice," he said. "Very wise. If I'm not careful, you'll take over my class for me."

Ethan seemed to color slightly, but it might have just been the firelight. "No way. I could never . . ."

He sounded so earnest it almost hurt me. Normally such reverence in any other person — for any other person — would disgust me, but this I understood. Mr. Tremont was on a whole different level than the rest of us. Logically, we knew that he was only a few years older than we were, and a student as well, but intuitively we knew that he was so much more than a mere substitute teacher or grad student. He was real in a way that most adults weren't.

"Oh boy," Mr. Tremont said suddenly. We followed his gaze to see a kid pointing a bottle of hair spray at the flames. "I should probably—" he started. The noise of the crowd carried the rest of the sentence away as he pushed through bodies toward the firebug, leaving Ethan and me alone.

We were quiet for a moment, just standing together, letting the floods of noise and light wash over us. I caught sight of Jeremy in the crowd, with a group of kids from the paper. My heart clenched when I thought about what I'd said to him. I'd find him on my way out, apologize, explain that I'd just been panicking. I'd just wanted to protect Mr. Tremont. And okay, maybe I'd been a teeny bit drunk. But I hadn't meant it.

"So, you're a princess," Ethan said.

"Apparently." I was a princess, Lacey and Nikki were princesses. . . . Despite everything that had happened last spring, this summer, even these last few weeks, everything had turned out just as we'd always planned. I could see Lacey, still standing up on the flatbed, her blond curls blown slightly back, like a photographer was carrying around a wind machine just for her.

The wind shifted directions, blowing the warmth of the fire away from us and pushing at my bare skin. I shivered.

"You're cold," he said. "Do you want my jacket?"

"No, I'm fine." I smiled, feeling strangely shy. "Anyway, I still have your sweatshirt. You can't let me steal all your warm clothes."

"Good point," he said. "You're quite crafty."

"I really can't be trusted," I said. He looked at me

strangely, and I wondered if I meant the warning for him, or for myself.

We were quiet again, lost in our own thoughts, until Ethan nudged me with his shoulder. "What are you thinking about?"

"Nothing." I nodded at the fire. "This."

"Yeah," Ethan said softly. "Me too."

The crowd was thinning out as parents left, taking their youngest children with them, leaving a core of middle and high school students who were getting increasingly hyper and crazed. Pretty soon Jake would be back from whatever errand he'd run to Randy's truck for—I really didn't want to know—and would come looking for me. I sighed.

"Look," I told Ethan, "about last night—"

"Yeah," he said. "I wanted to apologize for that—"

"No," I interrupted. "It was my fault. I'm sorry I brought it up." And I was. He was turning into a good friend, and I hated the idea of making him feel weird or mad about anything. I made a mental note not to mention his mom or her boyfriend again.

"No," he said. "It wasn't you. It's just . . . I haven't really told anyone else, and I was surprised—I didn't expect to—" He took a deep breath and looked at me searchingly. His voice came out in a rush. "Paige, I have to tell you something. I don't—I've been practicing how to say this in my mind all day, but I haven't come up with the right words, so I'm just going to say it." His eyes were the darkest brown, so dark you'd almost think they were black at first—unless he was holding your gaze and you couldn't look away, you couldn't see anything but his dark-brown eyes.

"I came tonight because I wanted to see you."

A tiny black hole opened at the center of my solar plexus and pulled everything in toward it. *No no no,* I thought. *Don't say anything to ruin what we have. We're such good friends and you're going to ruin it. Please, don't.* "Ethan—"

"Paige, I've never felt a connection like this with anyone else, not even Shanti. I don't even know how to explain it. I feel like I already knew you before I met you, and the first time I saw you, the first time I talked to you, was incidental, because the connection was already there—" He inhaled sharply and looked away. "God, I'm saying this badly."

"Ethan . . ."

He looked at me again. His eyes were the deep earth, the forest and the trees and the leaves and the wild autumn night. "Please don't get upset," he said. "I'll completely understand if you don't feel the same way, but I just had to say it. I feel like you see a version of me that no one's ever seen before. A truer version of myself. Does that make any sense at all?"

It did. I knew exactly what he meant.

Being seen. Feeling found.

"And I know I agreed to forget about it, but I just can't, Paige. Kissing you . . ."

"Don't," I said, and winced at the way he flinched in response. "I'm sorry," I whispered.

His shoulders sagged, but he smiled faintly. "It's okay," he said. "I was stupid to think—"

"No," I said. "It's just—I have a boyfriend."

Ethan frowned. "But you're not like them. Look at— ugh. " He gestured to the flatbed trailer where Nikki was grinding on a junior boy, her face flushed with alcohol. "You're not one of them, Paige. You're a real person."

I bit my lip, fighting the pull of the collapsing star behind my sternum. "Ethan, listen. You're a great friend. But I—" I thought of Mr. Austin's hard voice and Jake's attempt to write a poem, the strips of notebook paper leaning against one another along the sides of the wastebasket, broken trees after a windstorm. I thought about the warmth of Jake's side in the parking lot, the night on the golf course, his shouting father, my crazed mother. We were cut from the same cloth, we belonged together. Ethan was wrong. I wasn't a writer at all. I belonged to my family and the Austins and even the Lanes. I was a princess, for chrissakes. "I can't leave Jake."

For the first time since we'd met, Ethan looked at me without a single flicker of recognition. I was un-seen. Un-found.

The bonfire sent up a sudden shower of sparks, and everyone started screaming and laughing, but Ethan's eyes went dark. He was about to walk away. Just like Jeremy, like Nikki, like my sister, like everyone. Pretty soon he'd be looking past me too, like Lacey, and eventually I wouldn't even exist. No more quiet moments out by the springs. No more kidnappings or crazy adventures, no more river walks or booths at Perkins or trucker hats or inside jokes.

"Ethan, wait." I reached forward and grabbed his arm. He turned — and for a flash it was back, the recognition in his gaze. "Wait."

"Get your hands off her."

I jumped and dropped Ethan's arm like it was venomous. "Jake!"

"Stay away from my girlfriend." He stepped up close, snaking his arms around my waist and sticking his face in Ethan's. "Faggot." His breath burned with the sharp tin smell of alcohol.

"Jake," I said. *So that's what you left in Randy's truck? More liquor?*

"You're drunk," Ethan said.

"Fuck you, punk."

"Come on." I tugged on Jake's arms, trying to untangle myself and pull him away. "Let's get out of here."

"No. This little fairy needs to be taught a lesson." He pushed his face closer to Ethan's. Ethan was a little bit taller, but Jake was heavier.

I pulled at Jake's sleeve. "Jake, come on! Let's go!"

Ethan reached up to brush his hair from his eyes, and Jake knocked his hand away.

Behind us the carnival of fiery light and twisting limbs

paused, suspended, a photograph of blurred motion. Ethan looked down at his hand with scientific interest. "Really? It's so clichéd." He almost sounded like he was talking to himself, but I knew Jake would take offense. At this point, anything would piss him off.

"Jake —"

He reached forward and grabbed Ethan's shirt. "Clichéd? You smug mother fucker, I'll show you fucking clichéd."

"Jake! Stop it! This isn't you!" Desperately, I slammed my heel down on his foot, and he loosened his grip on Ethan.

"Fuck!" he yelled, hunching over. A crowd was gathering around us, chanting and clapping. *Fight! Fight! Fight!*

Mr. Tremont pushed through the crowd and grabbed Jake from behind, pinning his arms against his sides. "Come on, son." His voice was firm. "Nothing to see here, folks." Jake struggled in his grip but Mr. Tremont held tight.

Mr. Berna shoved in behind Ethan. "What's going on here?"

Mr. Tremont said, "It's okay, Carlos. I got it." He pushed Jake ahead of him, keeping his arms locked so Jake couldn't get away.

Shanti ran into the circle, shrieking. "Oh my God, Ethan! Are you okay?"

Ethan looked at me. "I'm fine."

I met his gaze and for a second I thought I could hold that connection forever, I could hold both ropes and not let go. But of course I couldn't. Tonight I was destined to break everything in my path.

"I have to go," I said.

I found them in front of the school, standing in the shadows of a sickly neon floodlight. Mr. Tremont's voice was low and insistent; Jake was slumped against the concrete brick. He was going to get kicked off court, he was going to be benched, his team would hate him, his father — oh, no —

"Mr. Tremont," I said, running up to them. "It's all my fault. It was me."

"Paige." Mr. Tremont looked surprised. "What's all your fault?"

I swung my arm wide, feeling wild. "Everything!"

He didn't say anything. He seemed disappointed and I hated it. My heart ached like hands were wringing it, twisting, but I stood my ground. I had nothing left to lose. Jake had everything. "It's all my fault," I repeated.

Mr. Tremont sighed. "Take him home," he said finally. "Don't let him drive."

"Really?" I asked, then shook myself. "Yes, okay. Thank you, Mr. Tremont. Thanks. Thanks." I grabbed Jake around the waist and propelled him toward the parking lot. I couldn't bear to look back.

Away from the fire, the night was wilder than we'd left it. The clouds were black now, glowing from behind, lit by the icy moon. Jake broke free of my hands and strode ahead,

318

shoving his hands deep in his pockets. A cold wind twisted across the parking lot, pushing though skeletal branches and clattering the leaves.

I wrapped my fingers around my arms, shivering. *Are you cold?* Ethan would have noticed, would have insisted I finally take his coat, but Jake pushed forward without me. Above the dark football field, a jagged arm of lightning ripped the sky from zenith to horizon, followed by a crash of thunder. I was aching to ask what had happened back there, whether or not Mr. Tremont was going to tell Dr. Coulter, whether or not Jake would have a place on the team next week, but I was afraid to hear the answers.

A plastic cup scuttled across the pavement like a startled cockroach. The long black horizon flashed once, and as if in reply, a distant car alarm started beeping. Ahead of me, Jake stopped and ducked against the wind to light a cigarette. I was the one who let him drink on the way here. I should have taken the flask from him, should have thrown it out the window when I had a chance. If I had just followed him out to Randy's truck, I could have stopped him from drinking on school grounds, could have kept him from getting so wasted that he felt the need to start shit with Ethan. And Ethan—if I hadn't grabbed him, if I hadn't tried to hold them both . . .

More garbage whipped through the parking lot. A hamburger wrapper bounced against Jake's truck and hung there, quivering against the silver metal, until it finally shook itself free and went flying away into the sky.

"Jake." My voice disappeared quickly into the black wind. "Jake," I said again, louder, but he didn't look back. Shadows from the orange streetlight danced darkly on his face, and he stubbed his cigarette on the bumper of a red car, charring a sticker with stars that said WE FIND MAGIC EVERYWHERE. Over the football field, lightning zipped between dark clouds, striking sideways. Thunder followed, booming so low I could feel it in my bones.

The first time Jake and I went out, Lacey spent hours helping me get ready, plucking my eyebrows and shoving tooth-whitening strips in my mouth. Jake showed up early and we both panicked, screaming as we pulled curlers out of my hair and spritzed perfume into the air for me to walk through. On the way down to answer the door, I caught the hem of my brand-new jeans under the heel of the boots Lacey made me wear, and I tripped, sliding all the way down the stairs on my butt, earning myself giant bruises on my thighs and back. At the bottom of the landing, I jumped up and brushed myself off, trying to appear dignified. At the top of the stairs, Lacey's mouth was an O of horror. I opened the door as gracefully as possible, trying to suppress the inevitable blush that would outshine Lacey's careful work, praying that he hadn't seen me, that he wouldn't suddenly change his mind and decide to go out with someone a little more coordinated. Months later, Jake told me that he'd seen the whole thing through the windows alongside the door, but that day, he said nothing but *You look beautiful.*

"Jake," I said.

In the silence after the thunder, Jake looked up at me. He reached for my face, his thumb sliding along the lower part of my jaw. His other hand reached in his jacket and pulled out a familiar silver square, unscrewing the cap and draining it without taking his eyes off mine. He dropped the empty flask into a front pocket and leaned into me, and the entire evening slipped away—everything I'd broken and ruined and wrecked—and in that moment, nothing mattered but his skin against mine, the heat of his breath in the freezing night. I sank against him and let everything go. We belonged together. I wasn't a writer; I couldn't tell the truth like they could. I'd never fit in with people like Ethan and Mr. Tremont and Shanti. I was made to be with Jake. We matched. It wasn't him fighting back there, it was his father talking through him. It was all the tiny darts of disappointment from a father he'd never be able to please, a mother so busy with work she hardly saw him. I knew him, really knew him, and at his core he was a good person.

"Let's go to Jensen's," Jake whispered, sliding the tip of his tongue along my earlobe, and in that moment I would have followed him anywhere in the world.

chapter NINETEEN

Chris lived a few blocks from the high school and I managed to convince Jake it would be easier to leave the truck in the school parking lot, so we joined the stream of people wandering away from the bonfire and winding up the little street that led to Chris's cul-de-sac. The street was lined with cars all down the block, and Jake muttered something about how we should have driven after all.

The windows of Chris's basement were flashing with strobe lights, and people spilled out onto the brick patio in the backyard. We went in through the garage, the quickest way to the extensive wet bar in the basement. Jake went down the stairs first, and the room erupted into cheers. "Austin! What's up? Austin's here!" He had already been swallowed up by the time I got to the bottom of the steps.

It was the parking lot before the bonfire all over again, but louder. Lacey had arrived, but looked straight through me, and Nikki rushed off to talk to someone else. Geneva and the juniors watched me like wolves appraising the weakest member of the herd. I took a deep breath and tried to stand straight. They wouldn't take me down tonight.

Tyler Adams was bartending. "'Sup, Paige?" he asked. "You look like you could use a drink."

I grinned. "Is it that obvious?" The boys still liked me, at least. I would hang with them tonight. They were easier, anyway. If they were mad, they punched someone and got over it. If they were sad, they punched someone and got over it. Easy. I stood in a circle of dudes and sparkled, cracking jokes and making them laugh. Tyler was all too happy to pour shots of tequila for me. Last spring should have taught me that it's never a good idea to drink when with every shot you're whispering, *Make it go away,* but tonight I didn't care. I didn't care. The guys gathered around me, egging me on or matching me shot for shot. Randy, Brian, Chris, and I threw the shots back and chomped on limes, grinning at one another.

At some point I left them and headed back toward Tyler for another drink. Lacey appeared out of nowhere and grabbed my arm. "You dumb slut. You got Jake benched for the next three games." Her breath smelled sweet like rum, and she had to put her mouth right up to my ear to be heard over the music from the next room. The air was stale and heavy with smoke. Nikki was there, too, I realized dimly.

"No I didn't," I said. "Mr. Tremont wouldn't—"

"Mr. Tremont! What the fuck is wrong with you? Mr. Tremont's the one who did it."

I was having some trouble focusing, I noticed. Maybe it was my contacts.

Some of the boys doing shots noticed I was gone. "Where'd Paige go?"

Nikki waved helpfully. "She's over here!"

Chris pulled me away from Lacey, back into the fray. "She's with us," he told Lacey. I hung on to him, leaning against his shoulder.

"That's interesting," Lacey said smugly, "because apparently Paige goes for older guys."

I shook my head, blinking hard, willing the room back into focus. Oh God, was this it? Was she finally going to tell everyone about Prescott?

"What older guy?" Geneva asked, as if on cue.

Lacey smiled sweetly. "Paige thinks she's in love with Mr. Tremont."

A junior girl cried, "Ooooooohh, Paige loves Mr. Tremont."

"No, I don't," I protested.

"And did Paige happen to mention that it was her darling Mr. Tremont who got Jake benched?" Lacey asked the crowd. "From the homecoming game?"

"That asshole kicked us out of class!" Randy yelled.

324

"I wonder if Paige actually asked Mr. Tremont to get Jake benched," Lacey said thoughtfully. "So Jake would be out of the way?"

"What are you talking about?" I asked her. "That doesn't even make sense."

Lacey pursed her lips and shrugged.

"What's wrong with you, Paige?" someone yelled.

Chris pushed me away and I stumbled toward the bar.

Someone else yelled out, "Slut!"

"Whore!"

"Cradle robber!"

"He's older than her, retard."

"I meant him. . . ."

"You're an idiot."

"Craftmatic Adjustable robber!"

The crowd laughed, closing in.

"No," I said, looking around desperately for something to hang on to. Suddenly, I was having a very difficult time standing up. "I'm not . . ."

Lacey's junior class doppelgänger cocked an eyebrow wickedly. "I saw Paige standing next to Mr. Tremont at the bonfire. They were probably planning the whole thing!"

Jake materialized from out of nowhere, pushing through the crowd to stand beside Randy. "What's going on, dude?"

Geneva pointed at me. "Paige was just telling us about her secret love affair with Mr. Tremont."

I held up my hands weakly. "I wasn't—I'm not—"

"She said you're not enough man for her!" Geneva

interrupted. Through the fog of alcohol, Geneva took on the appearance of one of those Puritan girls from *The Crucible,* proclaiming me a witch.

Jake kept his cool, laughing it off. He grabbed me around the waist, pulling me to him tightly. "I highly doubt that, Geneva," he said. I leaned against the warmth of his arm, grateful for the extra support. I didn't know how many shots I'd done, but it was unquestionably more than I'd drunk in months and months. "Maybe the problem is that I'm too much man, if you know what I mean. . . ." His friends laughed appreciatively.

"Anyway," Jake said, "Mr. Tremont's a fag, so I seriously doubt he's man enough for anyone."

The crowd went crazy. Voices jumped out at me from the swirl, gossiping and eager and too loud and drunk.

"He's gay? But he's so hot!"

"They always are. It's the shoes."

"Dude, he was climbing all over Jake tonight, did you see?"

"He was protecting that faggy freshman kid. Jake was about to throw down."

"Oh man, that's probably why he kicked you out of class, Randy. 'Cause he totes had the hots for you!"

"Sick, dude!"

"Mr. Tremont's gay?"

"I *told* you that, Nikki!"

I felt sick. The rumor would be all over school by Monday. It didn't matter that he'd come to the bonfire with a girl; no one would believe that he was straight now, even if he married Padma tomorrow.

"No worries," Jake said. "I let him down easy tonight." The crowd moved closer to hear Jake's voice over the music and chatter. "Yeah," Jake continued. "Dude was all, 'Jake, I wish I could get a dude as hot as you,' and I was all, 'Whoa, man, no offense, but you're not my type.'" Everyone screamed with laughter.

"Hell no!"

"You did not!"

"You're crazy!"

Randy held up a double shot, toasting Jake, and others followed suit. Chris handed me another shot — my fifth? Sixth? As usual, Jake had rescued me. He could always turn a bad scene good, like the time my sister broke her arm and he drove us to the hospital, calling my mom on the way. He was so nice. I snuggled into the crook of his arm while his friends tossed insults across the room like footballs. *You are. Shut up, dude, you totally are.* The music was loud but pretty, and I thought again of the guy with dreadlocks at Lacey's party, the one who made me listen to the Cure. Listen to that guitar. *They're like, so magical.* Jake held me against his side, because he was nice. He made problems go away. Another glass in my hand, full. And then empty. The room was getting strangely dark around the edges, but the music was so pretty. Jake's arm around me was good — it was good to help stand. Standing up was good, but I would like to lie down. Sleeping is good, too.

The music is so pretty, and I would like to sleep sleep sleep because standing is so hard when you're tired and everyone is so fuzzy and saying such funny fuzzy wuzzy woozy thingy thing things talky talky. Sleepy drunky. Beddy bed, sleepy sleep. Pretty music, pretty drunky, sleepy woozy. Giggly laughy, funny sleepy. So sleepy, so dark.

"Not enough man for you? Who's a fag now? I'll show you. I'm not a faggot. I'm not a fucking faggot." I opened my eyes slowly. Through the parted, woven threads of my eyelashes, I could see Jake's face inches from mine, red and twisted like it got on the football field when he needed all his concentration to dominate the game. "Who's a fag now?" His voice was pinched, hard, and he was talking so fast, so fast. My thoughts were coming so slowly, drifting across my mind like poky little clouds. I wrapped my arms around him; I held on to him. My mouth found his and stopped his words, and his kisses were hard and he was hard and my face was wet and his face was wet and my hands pushed at his cheeks to dry them. "You're not," I whispered desperately. "I love you." His face was hard and wet and it was dark under the trees in the black night in the wind in the grim moonlight and he was so sad—he was dark and familiar and sad and I held on to him, and his voice was broken it was raw it crumbled in the wind. *Why don't you love me?* asked his broken voice, and there was rain on his face it was raining. *Why don't you love me?* and he was reaching for me his hands sliding up my skirt ripping tearing pulling at his belt fumbling with the buckle pressing me against the tree we fall the sidewalk so hard so dark the wind and the clouds and the hard ground. *Ow Jake, that hurts, Jake, no please not here.*

"What's going on?" Strong arms wrap around Jake and pull him away in the rain. "Paige?" Jake struggles and it's all happening again. Mr. Tremont pulls him away and I'm scrambling backward, pulling at my skirt and my hair in the rain.

"Paige, are you okay? Was he trying—" And Jake pulls free and spins around, his arms swinging, his fist in Mr. Tremont's lovely face and Mr. Tremont bending over yelling, "Shit!" and Jake screaming, "Fuck you, man, you fucking faggot!" sprinting off through the dark thunder sky and Mr. Tremont holding his face and I should help him and I should help Jake he hit Mr. Tremont he was trying to hurt me and everything is broken and I'm running stumbling falling running running running.

chapter TWENTY

My head was pounding; every muscle in my body ached. My eyes were open and I was sitting, sitting and shivering and awake, and how long had I been sitting there? My arms were around my knees, wrapped around my knees, and I was sitting on the curb. On the curb. Where was I? My head was pounding. Oh, I hurt. Did I pass out? I was awake. Did I black out? Did I fall on the ground? Maybe I had a concussion. Everything was so fuzzy.

Gingerly, I tried to push myself into a standing position, wobbling in the street. My body cried out in protest, every muscle felt bruised. My hands did a slow inventory of my body, my arms, my forehead, my chest. My dress was ripped, but I was in one piece.

I stood up, wobbling in the street. Oh, I hurt. I hurt.

Where was Jake? What happened to Jake? We were outside, we were by the school, and then we were running. I lost him. I let him go. I had to find him. I stumbled toward the parking lot. Where was Jake?

I passed his truck in the parking lot and it was still there. Was the party still going? It started to rain and I tried to run but I was still drunk, too drunk, and I fell, gagging and choking, throwing up in the bushes until there was nothing left, nothing at all.

Up again and drunk and running, running blindly down the street through the pounding, freezing rain. I ran until my feet bled and my hair clung to my face and shoulders in heavy dripping ropes and sometimes I stopped to throw up again and I wasn't very drunk anymore but I was crying and I was aching and I was so cold and I had to find Jake and I couldn't think about what happened—where was he and why did I hurt and I was crying and I had to think about something else, *Think about something else, what time is it and when does Cinderella lose her coach, when do her footmen turn back into rats and when do her fancy glass slippers turn into running shoes and how long did she have to run and what if someone was chasing her, what if there was a car coming there's a car coming there's a car coming what if it's the police, they'll find me, they'll call my parents, they'll send me away again, they'll send me away, it's the police.*

Panicking, I threw myself over the embankment, rolling

to a stop at the base of a weeping willow, where I curled up into the smallest, tiniest ball I could become and held myself still like a little mouse. *Maybe they won't find me maybe I'll be safe.*

The car stops. Headlights in the rain. Footsteps crunch on gravel.

"Paige? Paige Sheridan?"

He's coming, oh my God he's coming down the hill, don't find me don't find me don't find me.

But he did find me and his hands were softer and his voice was softer. "Paige? Oh my God, Paige, what happened?" And it wasn't the police at all; it was Ethan. He helped me up the hill and put me in his car and I was shivering, so he wrapped me in his coat and I tried to make a joke but it didn't work, my words were wrong, and he tucked a blanket around my legs. "Do you need to go to the hospital? Oh my God, Paige." He pushed the hair out of my face — it was wet and heavy but his hands were light. "You're bleeding! What happened? Should I take you to the emergency room?"

"No!" What would my parents say, what would everyone say, I'm a princess, I can't go to the hospital. I was drunk, it was an accident. It's a bad dream, it's a memory, it's not happening, it's a dream. It was an accident. Another accident. When will you learn? What would my parents say? They'd never forgive me. They'd send me away again, forever. "No," I said again. "Please, just take me home."

He clicked my door closed so quietly and went around

to the driver's side door, slid into the car slowly, like he was worried that I'd be afraid but I wasn't afraid. Not of him. "Are you sure?" he asked softly.

I nodded, tucked in his coat. It smelled good, warm and safe, and I saw the stars through the window as the rain stopped.

"How can you drive?" I asked, turning to look at him.

He frowned, confused.

I pulled the blanket tighter around me. "You're a freshman."

"God," he said, and I was struck by how pretty his voice was, how much like warm syrup. "I'm a senior. You know that, Paige."

I spent some time with that, thinking about it and maybe dozing off a little, and then waking up with an answer, because I know that already and he can't know I'm drunk I'm not drunk. "Right." I nodded wisely, my eyelids heavy and my aching muscles finally beginning to unwind a little bit.

After a long silence, he spoke hesitantly. "Paige," he said, "may I ask — what happened —"

"No," I said softly.

"Okay," he said. "That's okay."

He drove and I drifted in and out of sleep. "Keep talking," I murmured. His voice was an anchor, keeping me safe in the warm car, keeping me out of the rain.

The drive seemed to last forever. ". . . went to Perkins with Shanti . . ." I heard him say, and I thought about how nice it would be to snuggle up against Jake, to lean myself into the warmth of his chest and arms.

". . . dropped her off . . . and thought I saw you running . . ."

Stars through the window, the window cold and the moon. My dad told me about stars. The Seven Sisters, also known as the Pleiades, are a sign of autumn. We saw them from the boat in Minnesota. Some Native American cultures used them as an eye test; if you could see the two stars in the double-star system, you had good vision.

". . . eyes were playing tricks on me, but then I saw . . ."

Uncle Roger is from Wisconsin, and he told me that Cassiopeia is a giant *W* for Wisconsin. The ancient Greeks said it was a queen who was tied to a chair, doomed to spend half the year dangling helplessly upside down as punishment. What was she punished for? I couldn't remember.

I don't know when we stopped driving. I vaguely remember telling him about the side door that opened almost directly into the back stairs. I struggled to stay awake.

An arm around my waist walked me up to my room, and he turned his back as I stepped out of my ruined dress. It was torn and stained, muddy and wet.

I climbed into boxers and a tank top. "Don't leave," I whispered, tugging on his sleeve.

He glanced up at the clock on my bedside table. "It's two in the morning."

I held on to his sleeve and forced my eyes to stay open. "Please. Stay."

He stayed.

He sat on the edge of my bed, holding my hand and telling me stories as I slept and woke and slept again. At one point I woke up and his voice had stopped. He was stretched out on the very edge of my bed, as far from me as possible. He looked precarious, like he might just roll off at any second. I pulled his arm toward me, tucked myself under it, and slept.

chapter TWENTY-ONE

The next time I woke up I was aching all over, throbbing headache, scabbed and torn feet—but feeling oddly peaceful. I slowly opened my eyes.

"Paige?"

I was alone in my bed, no safe anchor on the edge. I blinked, and my mother's head came into focus from the door. "It's almost noon, sleepyhead!" she trilled. "We're off to the club for lunch. I'd ask if you wanted to join us, but it looks like you had a little too much fun last night!"

"Mmrpf," I said.

"I had to swing by Stella's this morning and noticed your car in the driveway. I'm glad you didn't drive last night, honey! Very mature!"

"Thanks," I mumbled.

"Want us to drive it home for you? Miranda can do it."

"I guess."

My sister pushed past her, striding into the room. "Are you hungover?" Her voice dripped with disgust.

"So, no on lunch?"

"No." My voice was like pebbles under a bike tire. I coughed and cleared my throat. "I have to, uh, work on the homecoming float today, anyhow."

My sister looked down at me. "You're repulsive."

"Now, Miranda," my mother said, "you know as well as I do that the homecoming parade is very important to this town. Helping with the float is a community service."

Miranda sputtered, seeming torn between several different scathing remarks. Finally, she just huffed and stalked out of the room.

"Oh, dear," my mother said, looking after her, "I just don't understand what's not to like about homecoming."

I didn't make it out of my bed for another hour after that. When I finally dragged myself into the shower, I found dark-blue and pale-green bruises peeking up at me from my arms and legs. Every muscle in my body hurt. I huddled under the hottest possible water, scrubbing at myself with a rough loofah as if I could slough off all my memories and start over with a new skin, a tougher skin, a smarter skin.

The day was cool, almost chilly, punctuated by an unsteady drizzle. I felt restless, and a little scared, like

337

I didn't want to stop moving. I still owed Mr. Tremont a story for creative writing, but I was afraid of facing the blank page. I was afraid of facing myself and my memories. I would study. I was behind where I wanted to be with my physics paper anyhow, I'd been so caught up in Mr. Tremont's class.

I stared at my physics notes for a half hour before giving up. Nothing made sense, and the words just hurt my head. I got a glass of water and went back to bed for the rest of the day.

Late in the afternoon I woke to the ringing of my phone. It took me a moment to place the sound and then another to remember where my purse was. I rolled to the side of the bed and grabbed for the strap peeking out from under it. There was a clattering metallic noise as everything dumped out onto the floor and rolled under the bed. "Goddammit," I muttered, patting my hand around for the flat shape of my phone. When I finally found it, I didn't recognize the number and stared at it for a moment before answering. "Hello?"

"Paige?"

My breath caught in my throat. "Ethan?"

"Yeah. Hi."

I felt myself smiling into the phone, and then I remembered the night before. *Shit.* "Hi." I fell back against my pillows and closed my eyes.

"Uh . . . how are you?"

What had I told him last night? What had I said?

Memories came to me in flashes: Ethan crouched next to me, backlit by headlights; the way his car smelled, like mint and warmth and spice; his reassuring weight on the edge of my bed. I thought of how I must have looked to him—pathetic and wasted—and I flushed with shame.

"I've been better," I finally said, cringing.

His voice was soft. "Are you okay? Really?"

The concern in his voice made me anxious. His words came back to me: *I've never felt a connection like this with anyone else.* . . . And where had that gotten him? I couldn't let him keep caring, because he'd only get hurt. I wasn't the person he thought I was. I couldn't be. I'd made my choice, and I chose Jake. I wasn't a writer, I was a fucking drunk. What had Lacey called me? *A dumb slut?* I was a dumb slut, not a writer. I didn't belong at a poetry reading or writing in a café; I belonged in the smoky basement of some party surrounded by people I hate.

"I'm fine."

"About last night . . ."

"Thanks for bringing me home," I said quickly. "You didn't have to do that."

There was a pause. "Of course I did."

"It was very nice of you, but I could have walked. I was okay."

Another pause.

I pulled at a string in my quilt. "I should—"

He interrupted me. "Look, I . . . I fell asleep. . . . I didn't mean to, but I did. When I woke up . . ." He paused. I

339

held my breath, squeezing my eyes shut. "You had curled up beside me, tucked yourself under my arm, and I thought . . ."

I didn't breathe. It was quiet between us, the long expectant pause of waiting to hear the thing you want the most. I swallowed heavily. "I was . . . very drunk."

Silence.

"I have to go. I'll see you around, okay?" Without waiting for an answer, I hung up the phone and threw it across the room.

On Monday morning I was drained like the morning after a night spent sobbing. I drove to school in a daze, not even bothering to stop and buy coffee. The air pushed against me like water, and I had a hard time hearing. I swam against the stream of people and headed to class. The week leading up to homecoming was designated "Spirit Week," with a different stupid theme for every day. Apparently it was Pajama Day. In the hallways, girls in pigtails and slippers whispered and pointed, and Lacey limped past me with a blank stare. *You're done,* her eyes said, but I didn't even care.

Halfway to history, the hallway traffic stopped moving, and the normal morning chatter and gossip stopped with a gasp. "What's going on?" asked the girl next to me.

I shook my head. "I don't know."

Voices spoke in a jumbled chorus. "I can't believe it — Who did it? — It's true, you know — It's awful — It's wrong—Did you hear?—Stonewall-type shit." Curious now, I pushed through the crowd to see for myself.

Sprayed across a classroom door in angry red letters, sharp like lightning, was one word:

FAGGOT.

The crowd swirled around me, shocked and whispering, people edging themselves into the drama as if to elevate themselves by proximity. Planning to lay claim to the celebrity of first witness, most horrified, most outraged. Boys scoffed and girls gasped and in my head voices from the weekend suddenly threatened to overwhelm me.

Everything blurred at the edges, and the people grew hazy around me, until the only things that remained clear were the jagged letters across Mr. Tremont's door.

Halfway through first period, the PA interrupted Mr. Silva's endless drone. "Excuse the interruption, Mr. Silva," the voice said. As always, everyone turned to look at the speaker box.

"YES?" Mr. Silva shouted. He didn't trust technology.

"Is Paige Sheridan in class?"

Twenty heads swiveled to look at me. Lacey gave me a huge, delighted smile. "YES!" Mr. Silva shouted.

"Could you please send her down to the office?"

"NO PROBLEM," Mr. Silva yelled, and gestured to me, then to the door. I gathered up my books and hurried through the class's stares and whispers into the silent hallway.

In the office they were ready for me. "Go right in," the secretary said, sounding sympathetic. I clutched my books to my chest and stepped hesitantly into Dr. Coulter's office.

"Paige," he said, "come right in! Have a seat!"

There were two chairs in front of the principal's desk. Coach Ahrens was already sitting in one; I took the other. My mind was running through a thousand possible reasons I could be here. Just a homecoming thing, I told myself. Princess business. But of course I knew Coach wouldn't be there on princess business, and my heart pounded in my throat.

"It has, uh, come to our attention," Dr. Coulter began, "uh, events on Friday night . . ."

Oh God, the fight at the bonfire! Were they going to kick Jake off the team? "Nothing happened!"

Dr. Coulter blinked. "Well, uh, we've had reports of an altercation between Jacob Austin and—"

"Nothing happened," I said again. Fighting fell under the zero-tolerance policy; if Jake got dinged on both drinking and fighting, he'd be off the team for the rest of the year. His dad would kill him. "They were just messing around. You know how boys are."

"Uh . . . huh. Well, we have various, uh, reports about the bonfire . . ."

"Seriously, it was nothing." I tried my best to find the innocent princess face that Lacey always used in order to get Dr. Coulter to do whatever she asked. "There was a misunderstanding but it was fine."

342

The principal looked at Coach Ahrens. "Okay, so what about afterward? There was a party. Was there drinking?"

"Oh! No." I laughed nervously. "I mean, maybe a few theater kids or something were drinking, you know, but no student athletes or members of court. We value our . . . school . . . too much. To drink."

Dr. Coulter smiled at me. "What about after the party? Where did you go after that?"

Flashes of thunder and rain. Running, stumbling. Losing Jake. Losing everything.

"Home?" I asked, and then decided. "I went home."

"With Jacob?"

"No, I walked. Jake, um, wanted to get home early to rest up for the big week, you know. Homecoming."

"So you weren't with Jake outside the school on Friday night."

"I—oh." What were they asking? Had we been outside the school? I had a sudden memory of Jake punching someone. Ethan? But he'd seemed fine later . . . hadn't he? I shook my head. "No."

Dr. Coulter leaned across his desk. "You didn't see Jake, uh, attack anyone?"

"What? No."

Coach Ahrens asked, "Did you see anyone attack Jake?"

"No!"

They looked at each other and sighed. "All right, Miss Sheridan, you may be excused. But, please, uh, feel free to come back if you, uh, remember anything."

"Sure." I clutched my books to my chest again and stood. "Jake's a good person."

Dr. Coulter coughed. "Thank you, Paige."

I hurried out into the empty hallways, keeping my eyes on the dirty linoleum tiles, not looking at Mr. Tremont's door as I passed it. Somehow I found my way to the library, where I fell into a corner chair and stared at the wall, trying not to ask myself the obvious questions. What was that all about? What happened Friday night? My memories were hazy and full of gaping holes. I didn't want to remember. I didn't want to know anything about it. I wanted to start the weekend over, maybe the whole year.

And poor Mr. Tremont. I hated to think about his reaction when he walked in this morning. Fucking Willow Grove! My throat tightened. Out of the corner of my eye, I thought I saw Ethan walk into the library. At least, I assumed it was him because the moment he saw me, he turned and walked out again. Awesome. I rubbed the flats of my hands across my face.

"Rough day?" Mr. Tremont asked, easing himself into the chair next to me.

I couldn't look at him, didn't trust myself to talk. "Mm-hmm."

"Me too." He sighed. "I guess I had the naive idea that things had gotten better since I was in high school."

"No," I whispered. "It's still terrible."

I sensed he was smiling in that way of his, as if he had

344

some inside joke with himself that he wouldn't mind sharing, if anyone asked. "The good thing is that it will give you something to write your sitcom pilot about."

I had to laugh. Any sitcom about my life would be set in hell.

"Use it, Paige," Mr. Tremont said. "Use it all. The pain and the anger and the stupid, shallow absurdity of it all. Use it. Write from anger, from love, to get revenge, to win dates, whatever. Just write."

He had the strange ability to say exactly the words that you needed to hear. "Mr. Tremont?" I looked up at him and gasped. His left eye was swollen and puffy, and there was a ring of dark red and purple around it, like an angry moon.

He smiled at me, just like the first day among his plants and his writing secrets, like nothing had happened. "Yes?"

"Oh my God," I whispered. Images flashed before me: Jake's hands under my skirt. Mr. Tremont pulling him away. Jake swinging his fist. "It was you! I mean, Jake punched you! I'm so sorry."

Mr. Tremont shrugged. "It's not your fault."

"Um," I stumbled. I thought about apologizing for the day, the week, for talking him into chaperoning, for not protecting him from Jake. I thought about what Shanti would say if she were here, or Ethan, or Jeremy.

"On behalf of the senior class of Willow Grove High, I'd like to apologize for the a-holes and d-bags." I gave him a tiny smile, the most I could manage.

Mr. Tremont laughed. "Thanks, Paige. That actually

means a lot." The morning sun spilled through the sky-lights above us, illuminating small patches of bookshelf here and there. Mr. Tremont laughed again. "A-holes and d-bags. Padma will love that."

I managed to avoid any encounters with the enemies I called friends, or vice versa, all morning. In trig, Nikki was too busy passing notes and making googly eyes at Marcus Truman to notice anything else. He grabbed her after the bell, ushering her out the door ahead of him. Lacey stalked past me in the halls like I didn't exist. Jake—well, I couldn't even think about Jake without feeling like I was about to implode, taking everything down with me as I fell.

I threw myself into my classes, diligently taking notes all morning and spending my lunch hour in the library, poring over an article for my physics project, thinking per-haps that if I could regain perfection in one area of my life, the rest would fall into line. By the time I emerged for my afternoon classes, the janitors had cleaned Mr. Tremont's door and the gossip had died down.

Shanti caught me before creative writing, snaking her arm through mine and holding me against her as we walked through the crowded halls. I braced myself for her anger, for choosing Jake over Ethan, for letting things go so far at the bonfire. She would lecture me. I actually cringed, waiting for the attack.

It didn't come. When she spoke, she just sounded sad.

"You picked Jake." It was half question, half verdict. We stopped in the hallway and let students flow around us. I couldn't look at her.

"Oh, Paige." Her voice nearly broke my heart.

There was nothing for me to say.

I left her to wait for Ethan while I hid myself in the back of the room, between Elizabeth and Jenna. "You okay?" Jenna asked.

I shrugged. "Monday." *Liar.*

She studied me a second. "You know, Mr. Tremont would say to use it." I had to smile. She didn't know how right she was.

"It feeds the muse," Elizabeth added. "Not to eavesdrop or anything." I nodded absently.

Jeremy walked in. The moment I saw him I remembered that I'd never apologized to him. At least, I was pretty sure I hadn't. A loud movie briefly played in my head. Leaping flames, loud music, and drunk Paige, yelling something about how everyone hates gays. God, I was such a *bitch*! I closed my eyes and dropped my head into my folded arms. I was practically as bad as whoever tagged the door.

Shanti and Ethan walked in with Mr. Tremont a second after the bell. Mr. Tremont quickly checked attendance while everyone got settled. There were gasps from the people who hadn't seen him yet, hurried conversations in whispers and passed notes: *What happened? I heard . . .*

Mr. Tremont clapped his hands to bring us together. "Okay, folks, let's get started."

The editor of the school's literary journal, Alison Conforti, along with a senior named Jessica Hudson, and Jenna were all up for workshop that day. "I'm nervous," Jenna admitted.

Elizabeth reached across my desk to squeeze Jenna's hand reassuringly. "You'll be great." Her gesture caught me by surprise. I hadn't known that they were friends. Then again, there was just something about this class that made people act different, better. Mr. Tremont's classroom was the truest place I'd found in four years of high school, and looking around the room, I saw that it was the same for my classmates. No wonder we sometimes felt like a family.

"I'm sure you all have some feelings about, or reactions to, the message on my door," Mr. Tremont said. The class looked around at one another, nodding seriously. Shanti's eyes flashed with anger. Jeremy stared down at his desk. I accidentally looked at Ethan, and he turned his head quickly to avoid my gaze.

Mr. Tremont smiled. "Use it." Jenna turned and grinned at me. I managed to grin back.

We started with Jenna's piece, a personal narrative about tutoring kids in Minneapolis over the summer. Her writing was vivid, full of colorful and surprising word combinations. "There's something really painterly about her use of language," Elizabeth said. "This writing reminds me of Frank O'Hara, his poems about New York." The group murmured its agreement, and Jenna smiled to herself, dark roses on her cheeks.

I was so deeply involved in the analysis of Jenna's writing that I didn't hear the classroom door squeak open, and when Dr. Coulter's excessive throat clearing interrupted our discussion, a couple of kids actually jumped. "Please excuse the interruption, children," he said, smiling squintily at us, "but I need to, uh, borrow your teacher for a moment."

Mr. Tremont unfolded himself from the student desk where he sat. "Sorry, you guys," he said, looking around the circle. "Keep going, I'll be right back."

He followed Dr. Coulter into the hallway. Jeremy cleared his throat. "Okay," he said, ever the editor in chief. "Back to the metaphor of the geese in Loring Park. . . ."

Halfway through our discussion of Jessica's story, our concentration fell apart. "Why hasn't he come back yet?"

Alison went to the door, first peering out the narrow window and then opening the door. "They're not out there," she said, returning to our circle.

"That's weird," Elizabeth said.

Shanti and Ethan looked at each other, having one of their silent conversations. Jenna frowned at me like she expected me to understand what she was thinking, but I couldn't read the sudden thunderclouds in her face.

"You don't think . . ." Jeremy said, trailing off.

"What?" Alison asked.

"Never mind," he said, shaking his head. "I'm sure it's nothing."

But we all sat silently until the bell rang.

chapter TWENTY-TWO

After class, I followed the force of the pushing crowd through the hallways to the commons and toward the front door. Outside, the day was fiercely bright and unusually warm for September. I squinted into the sun and waited for my eyes to adjust.

Jake was sitting on a bench, slumped over, with his elbows on his knees. "Hey," I called, walking over to him. "Where have you been all day?"

He stared at the ground. "I'm off the team."

"What?"

"Someone told them I was drunk on Friday night."

I sank down slowly on the bench beside him. "Oh, shit. Oh, Jake. I'm sorry."

"It's not your fault," he said woodenly.

Wasn't it?

I opened my mouth to say something, to find some word that could possibly make things okay, but before I could speak, Mr. Austin punched through the front doors and came out yelling. "Jake! Get your ass over here!"

Jake jumped to his feet. "I gotta go." He hurried to catch up with his father, and I heard slivers of conversation cutting through the air like glass. "No son of mine . . . How could . . . so *stupid* . . . That prob . . . aken care of . . ." They stood together in the parking lot, Mr. Austin's arms waving wildly, Jake curled over like a fern. Mr. Austin jumped into his truck, slammed the door, and peeled out of the parking lot. A moment later, Jake's silver car followed suit.

That night, Mirror refused to eat dinner with the family. My mother smiled gamely and served the green beans while my sister stalked through the dining room, holding the cordless phone to her ear. Pausing, she pushed the mouthpiece against her chest and screamed, "I hope you're fucking satisfied, Paige! You make me sick!" She ran upstairs.

My father looked at me questioningly. "Sister issues?" he asked mildly.

I shook my head. "I have no idea what she's talking about."

After school, I'd come straight home, holing up in my room. I'd tried to call Jake a number of times, but he hadn't been answering his phone. On the plus side, I'd made some progress on my physics research, with my personal insight into the problem of our expanding universe: *As the amount of dark energy in the universe increases, it pushes the galaxies farther and farther apart, meaning that every single day we become further isolated, increasingly alone in a universe of dark energy and evermore distant galaxies.*

My father and I got into a discussion of Hawking's theories while my mother whisked away the dirty dishes and reappeared with steaming cups of coffee, each in its matching saucer. "You two and your astrology," she flirted.

"Astronomy," I said.

"Speaking of which," she said, bringing her cup to her dark red lips, "I talked to Stella just before dinner."

My father winked at me over his coffee.

"You know, Stella . . . like star?" My mother laughed at her own little joke, impressed with her segue.

"We get it," I said, dreading the conversation we were about to have. *Kicked off the team! Did you know that Jake was drinking? Did you let him drive? After last spring?*

"Well," my mother said, "she told me that they finally did something about the problem at the high school."

"Wait, what?" I looked at my dad, but he shrugged.

"You know," my mother said conspiratorially, savoring the delicate flavor of gossip. "The gay teacher."

I struggled to breathe, as if the oxygen in my lungs suddenly doubled in density. "What?" I gasped.

"Yes," my mother said, "they fired him."

"Mr. Tremont?" I asked. As if I needed to hear it. As if there were any question.

"That sounds right. The substitute for Beulah Mueller."

"They can't do that!" I said, looking to my father for reassurance. "Just because he's gay?"

My father frowned. "That's discrimination. Homosexuality is not legal grounds for dismissal."

"Oh, of course not!" My mother's lipstick left red smears across the white china cup. "But this man was a pervert. Jake told his mother that this teacher attacked him after the school bonfire and tried to sexually assault him. Can you imagine? Richard went to the principal to demand his resignation."

"WHAT?" All the little boxes inside my heart flew open at once, releasing years of stuffed rage. I could feel it inside me, swarming like Pandora's thousand demons poised to wreak havoc on the world. "THAT FUCKING ASSHOLE!"

My mother's cup clattered into its saucer. "Language, young lady!"

I ran up the stairs to find my sister. She was tucked into the third-floor window seat, one of our favorite hiding places. I thrust out my hand. "I need the phone."

She glared at me like a cat. "Fuck you!"

"Mir, I have to call Jake."

Her eyes flashed blue diamonds. "Oh, in that case . . ." she said sarcastically. Into the phone, she softened her tone.

354

"No, it's Paige. I know, she wants to call her boyfriend."
Pausing a moment, listening. "I know, exactly."

"Fine!" I turned and clattered back down the stairs. *Cell phone, cell phone.* A part of my mind wanted to rehearse what I'd say to Jake, but all I could hear was my own voice in the dining room, filling the vaulted ceilings. The words became a mantra, pushing me through the house. *Fucking. Asshole.*

My cell phone was dead, its little battery box empty of bars. I punched at the POWER button, but all I got was a cheerful little message: PLEASE RECHARGE BATTERY NOW. I threw it on the bed. Where the hell was my charger? I ran upstairs again. "Where's my phone charger?"

Miranda held her hand over the phone. "Like I care!" And then, into the phone, "No, sorry. It's nothing. Anyway, what?"

I ran back down to my room and looked around as if I could will a phone into existence. On my desk, my car keys glinted in a sliver of moonlight.

Seconds later, I was running out the door, yelling over my shoulder as I flew. "I'm going out!"

The drive out to Sauvignon and Jake's house normally took about eighteen minutes. I made it in twelve. Before I knew it, I was marching up to his front door and smashing at the doorbell. The night glowed silver in moonlight, and I could see my breath. Doorbell chimes echoed dimly through the house.

Stella Austin opened the door. "Paige!" she said.

"I need to see Jake."

Mrs. Austin smiled tightly. "We're at dinner, dear." Her voice was calm, with the faintest trace of a Southern accent.

"It's important." I sounded like such a brat, I thought distantly. My mother would be horrified. I didn't care. I pushed past Mrs. Austin into the house.

Piped Vivaldi floated through hidden speakers. Candles flickered on the table. How many nights had I sat at this table, with this family, their evening ritual nearly a carbon copy of my own.

Jake stood, taking the cloth napkin from his lap and laying it on the table. "Paige."

"How dare you!" I yelled, surprising even myself. Mrs. Austin looked like she'd been slapped. "What is *wrong* with you!"

Mr. Austin appeared in the archway from the kitchen, nodding, a beer in his hand. "Here to dump his sorry ass? I don't blame you."

Jake's face turned white. Mrs. Austin held out her hands. "Now, Paige, dear . . ."

"You have no right!" I cried. "The world doesn't belong to you. You can't just destroy people's lives because you feel like it."

Mr. Austin grunted and took a step into the room.

I ignored him. "For years, I've forgiven you, all of you! I looked away, pretended not to hear you." I glanced at his parents, seeing a flash of myself in the ornamental mirror behind them. "The stupid racist comments, the snide, judgmental, self-satisfied conversations about *those* people—I never said anything because I was in love with Jake."

Vivaldi stopped, and my voice rang in the sudden silence. Jake held out his hands, echoing his mother's gesture. "Paige—"

"No!" I yelled, regaining my momentum. "You listen to me. I've looked away too many times." My voice was low, on the verge of breaking. I took a ragged breath. "I will not let you hurt other people. Mr. Tremont didn't attack you—*you* attacked *him!*" Somewhere in the distance, I thought I heard Stella Austin gasp. Ignoring her, I forced myself to keep going. To stay strong. "You lied to Dr. Coulter. I lied for you! I didn't know you'd say—" I sputtered. "Mr. Tremont is a good teacher, a good person, and you have no right—no right!"

"Paige—"

"No!" I yelled. "We're done, Jake."

The Austins all stared at me. In the mirror I looked like someone else. I turned to Mrs. Austin. "And *you.* You've been stringing my mother along for years! Making her jump through hoops for you! But we both know you have no plans of ever promoting her!"

Mrs. Austin's eyes were cold, her face unmoving. "Paige Renee Sheridan. You are out of control."

I spun on my heel and stormed out of the room. At the front door, I stopped and turned back. Jake had followed me halfway and stood at the edge of the dark foyer. "Paige,

357

wait. I'm sorry about what I said. And the door . . . I don't know what came over me —"

Flashes of the night in the rain came back to me. His face. His angry voice. *Who's a fag now?* I gasped. "It was you? On the door? You did that?!"

"I'm sorry, babe. I —"

"WHO ARE YOU?"

Stella Austin appeared behind him. "I think you'd better leave."

"I'm leaving!" I yelled. She took a step back, and I sucked in a breath. "I'm leaving."

When I got home, my mother met me at the door, her face ghost white. "Stella Austin just called."

I nodded, waiting for the wrath. *What is wrong with you? How dare you yell at the Austins! How dare you lose control of yourself! Are you on drugs? What happened to the perfect daughter I kept under my thumb all these years?* It didn't come. I looked up at her colorless eyes, her pale set mouth.

"She fired me."

chapter TWENTY-THREE

I was a ghost. I walked through the hallways Tuesday morning without creating a single ripple in space, without seeing myself reflected in anyone's face. By the end of homeroom, I wasn't even sure if my teachers saw me. I drifted back through the crowds to my locker. On the door, just below eye level, someone had written FAG HAG in thick black marker. My hands shook as I twisted the lock, and my mind tried to put together sentences to describe my situation. *I've never — I don't — This can't be —*

I ditched physics, heading to the office instead. I would report the vandalism to Dr. Coulter. He liked me; he'd fix it. I'd explain — reasonably, adult to adult — that Jake had lied, that Mr. Tremont would never hurt a student, that Mr.

Tremont was the best teacher we'd ever had. I clenched my jaw and focused on my mission. I could fix this. I could help Mr. Tremont. I had to.

Dr. Coulter's secretary wasn't there, so I went to the open door of his office and peeked in. "Hello there, Paige," he said. "I didn't hear you come in!"

"Hi, Dr. Coulter," I said, fighting nervousness. "Can I talk to you for a second?"

"Of course," he said grandly. "Come on in! What can I do for you? More streamers for homecoming? Worried that the float won't be pretty enough?" He winked at me.

"Um, no," I said. "Actually, it's . . ." My mother played tennis with Lydia Coulter. Stella Austin Events had done their twentieth anniversary party last spring. She was going to kill me. I took a deep breath. "You said to come see you if I thought of anything else? Last weekend? It's about Mr. Tremont."

Dr. Coulter frowned. "That's not anything you have to worry about, Paige. You're not in danger. We've, uh, taken care of the problem."

I was thrown off course. "In danger?"

"There's nothing to worry about, Paige," he repeated. "Now, why don't you get back to class? Mrs. Manning will write you a pass."

"Dr. Coulter," I said, trying to keep the note of urgency out of my voice. "Sir. What Jake said—it's not true. Mr. Tremont would never do anything like that. Jake lied."

His face pulled together in a hundred fierce wrinkles. "It's none of your concern, Miss Sheridan."

"But Dr. Coulter—"

"Mrs. Manning will write you a pass," he said again, and turned back to his computer.

Shaken, I stood and hurried out of the office. No one had ever called me "Miss Sheridan" in that tone of voice before. I'd always been one of Dr. Coulter's favorites. The hallways were empty, so at least I didn't have to hear the accusing silence of conversations ending as I went by. There was no way I was going to physics. I just wanted to get out. I headed for an obscure back door in the east wing, planning to slip out and drive around for a while. Maybe I'd write. Maybe I'd disappear altogether.

Jeremy caught me in the hallway just before I could escape. "What are you doing?" His voice was lower than normal, rougher.

"I, uh . . ." I said.

Jeremy shifted the stack of papers he was holding. "Running away?" He was accusing, the triumphant prosecuting attorney.

"No," I said. "I just—I talked to Dr. Coulter. I tried to help . . ."

He raised an eyebrow. "And?"

"And nothing," I said. "He called me *Miss Sheridan.*" My voice choked on the shame of it. The injustice.

Jeremy was quiet for a moment, looking at me.

"Someone wrote on my locker," I whispered. I looked down at my feet in their black boots.

"Yeah," he said. "I saw."

I bit my lip.

"This is what your friends do to people," he said. "It sucks, doesn't it?"

"Not just my friends," I said quietly. "About Friday, what I said—I'm so sorry."

Jeremy sighed. "Me too."

"I wish there was something I could do," I said. "I tried—but Dr. Coulter—"

"You want to help? You can start by getting over yourself." Tears gathered in the corners of my eyes. My throat was tight.

He softened. "We're going to fight for Mr. Tremont. Come help?"

I nodded, concentrating on not crying.

"Great," he said.

I followed him down the hall into the staff room. Five or six people were crowded around a central table, flipping through thick books and scribbling in notebooks. Several more were scattered at computers throughout the room, scrolling through pages online. I expected to see Shanti and Ethan, but they weren't there.

"I went to the law library on campus yesterday," Jeremy explained, gesturing to the pile of thick leather books. "We're going to fight this."

"Yesterday? How did you —?" I asked.

Jeremy smiled for the first time. "I have my sources. I'm not the editor in chief for nothing." He sat me down next to Elizabeth, who was scrolling through an online news site. "We're calling everyone," Jeremy said.

Without taking her eyes off the screen, Elizabeth nodded. Beside her hand lay a notebook, quickly filling up with precise notes. She glanced at me. "I'm compiling the names and numbers of influential people in the media and community. You can work with me, if you want."

"Who do you have so far?" I asked, pulling the list toward me. Many of the names I recognized, Iowa City news anchors and journalists.

"We need to talk to everyone," Elizabeth said. "The news media, the mayor, the city council, the school board, everyone."

"I can help find names and numbers. My parents are friends with most of them."

"Great! Can you call them?"

I heard my mother's voice from last night. *She fired me.* "No . . . I'm sorry, but I don't think I'm up to that."

"That's okay," Elizabeth said, her eyes turning back to the screen. "Just making a list will be really helpful."

It was nice of her to say. But making a list, I knew, wasn't enough. Ashamed, I ducked my head and pretended to look for a pen until I was sure I wouldn't cry.

• • •

Jeremy ordered pizza, and we all worked through lunch. Someone brought in a radio, tuning it to the college station out of Iowa City. The energy in the room was grimly festive; the reason for our gathering was terrible, but there was pleasure in the meeting itself, the rush of working toward a goal in a room of like-minded people. I tried to explain it to Jeremy, but he looked puzzled. "You're on student council, aren't you?"

"Just the social committee stuff," I said.

"Oh, right." He looked at me as if seeing two people at once, overlaid. I knew the feeling. "Well, the education committee is doing some really cool stuff. They're bringing in this presentation on Friday morning. . . ."

I remembered Ethan saying something about a project he was doing in his student council committee. Nikki's presentation. All my ex-friends teaming up to change the world. Before Jeremy even had a chance to finish, I smiled my princess smile. "Sounds really great!"

"Yeah," Jeremy said slowly, with a strange look. "Anyway, do you want to help me round everyone up for seventh period?"

Under Jeremy's leadership, we picked up the whole operation and moved it to our creative writing classroom. The room that—until yesterday—had been Mr. Tremont's. His plants were still on the desk, but the room had a slightly stale, empty feeling, like an old-time ghost town. "We should water the plants," I said.

"It feels so empty," Jenna said, rubbing her arms.

The sub, a young Asian woman named Ms. Chen, laughed. "He just left yesterday, didn't he?"

"She's right, though," Elizabeth said. "This used to be more than just a room."

Ms. Chen cocked an amused eyebrow at us and offered to take a seat while Jeremy addressed the class.

"Great," Jeremy said, taking charge. In the front of the classroom, he laid out his plans on the chalkboard, his authority more natural than the sub's. He delegated responsibilities quickly and efficiently. A few minutes later I found myself bowed over a large placard with Shanti, sketching out the letters of protest in light pencil.

"Where's Ethan?" I asked, overly casual, tracing a giant *H* across the tagboard.

Shanti didn't mince words. "Between you and Mr. Tremont, he's pretty devastated."

I winced, searching my mind for anything that wouldn't just make her hate me more.

"I'm sorry," I finally said.

Shanti sat back, perching on her heels. "What's wrong with you, Paige?"

I laughed bitterly. "Funny you should ask. . . ."

"I'm serious." She caught my eye, holding my gaze until I had to look away. "How could you reject him like that?"

I pulled the thick paint marker over shadowy outlines and shook my head, letting my hair fall across my face.

"He's a great friend," I told the tagboard. "I just don't feel that way about him."

"Like hell you don't," Shanti said. She walked away, leaving me on the floor with my traced outlines, empty words.

chapter TWENTY-FOUR

Lying in bed that night, I heard a faint tap on my door. "It's me," my sister said, pushing the door open a crack.

"Come in." I wiggled over, making space for her on the edge of the bed. "What's up?"

She looked sad. When we were little, she used to come into my room like this, late at night, when our parents would fight. She'd crawl under the covers and look to me to make everything okay, and I'd whisper stories to her, stories I'd make up on the spot, about princesses who didn't need any princes to rescue them, they could rescue themselves just fine, thank you. I hadn't thought of those nights in years.

Mirror settled herself nervously on the edge of my bed. "I heard what you did. At the Austins'? Sorry I wouldn't let you use the phone last night."

"Don't worry about it," I said.

"I'm serious," my sister said, looking like every word was a struggle. "I'm really impressed. I never thought you . . . you know."

"Thanks, Mirror," I said, genuinely touched. "That means a lot."

"You know," she said. "I think Mom's going to be okay, in the end." We were quiet for a moment, sitting together in my dark room, and all the walls we'd built between us in the last five years suddenly didn't matter, didn't even exist.

I pulled the quilt between my thumb and finger. "I hope so."

"She will. Stella was never going to promote her."

"Tell that to her."

Mirror grinned. "I think I'll leave that to you. I'm kind of enjoying being the good daughter for once."

I snorted, and she laughed, and then we were both laughing hysterically, pounding on the bed and falling on the floor and clutching our stomachs like we hadn't done since we were little kids, giggling after lights out, with our mother screaming from the living room for us to settle down and go to sleep. It was wild, helpless laughter, a paper-thin edge from crying, and we laughed and choked and gasped for breath and wiped away tears until we were both lying on the floor, side by side, rubbing our abs. "Shit," I finally said.

She nodded solemnly. "I couldn't agree more."

• • •

After she left, I lay in bed, feeling better than I had in days. At least I had my sister, I thought. I decided I'd ask her to blow off first period and go to breakfast with me the next morning. Maybe we could even get our dad to go with us.

A cool breeze brought the tapping of raindrops against my bedroom window. Far in the distance, I could hear the static buzz of traffic on the highway, wet tires through water, the occasional semi. *Here I am,* I thought. All the questions of loyalty and identity seemed so unimportant at that moment, and I wondered how I'd wasted so much energy on them in the last few weeks. How I dressed, who I kissed, what I forgave, who I loved — what did it matter under the comfort of the late September night?

My peace faded with the dawn. I woke up edgy, restless, dreading school and yet knowing that I couldn't stay away. Jeremy needed me, my creative writing group needed me. Mr. Tremont needed me.

I dressed in dark jeans and a black sweater. I couldn't explain it, but the black made me feel safer somehow, like I was shielded. The night before, I'd overheard my mother on the phone in the study as I padded downstairs for a glass of water. Her voice had been pinched. "Do you think she's gone goth?"

I had to tell Mirror that; she'd laugh and laugh.

I missed my sister by a minute. "She just left," my father said, lowering the *Iowa City Press-Citizen* and reaching blindly for his coffee.

369

"Shoot," I said. "I was going to take her out for breakfast."

"Can I make you something?" he asked, still holding the paper. "An omelet or something?"

I grabbed a granola bar from the pantry. "No thanks." I slung my messenger bag across my shoulder and hurried toward the back door, but then I stopped and turned. "Dad?" I asked.

His face appeared over the paper once more. "Yes?"

"I'm sorry about Mom. I didn't mean to get her fired."

He nodded. "I know. She'll be okay, eventually."

I sighed. "I hope so."

The paper went up again.

"Dad?"

"Yes?"

"I love you," I said.

He looked surprised, then pleased. "I love you too, honey." He looked up at the ceiling, seeming to pull his words from somewhere above his head. "Paige?"

"Yes?"

He smiled. "Give 'em hell out there today."

School was a circus of color and shouting, TV news vans, giant protest placards. Two angry camps separated by news anchors and cameras camped out in the circle of benches at the front of the building. On one side, people carried signs that said GOD HATES FAGS. In freshman history, our teacher made us watch a documentary about Matthew Shepard, a gay college student who was tortured, beaten, and then tied to a fence and left to die in the cold Wyoming night. As we watched the video, the horror of it crept over me until the uncomfortable plastic chair and loud ticking of the school-issued clock disappeared. The worst part of it was at his funeral, where a small group of people actually protested with signs that said things like MATTHEW SHEPARD ROTS IN HELL and AIDS KILLS FAGS DEAD. I remember some girl in my class raised her hand and said, "Yeah, people used to be like that, back when the KKK was around and stuff, but, like, we're not like that anymore, right?" Mrs. Fox shook her head sadly, "Kaitlyn, Matthew Shepard was killed in 1998." I couldn't believe that people could actually be that cruel.

The homophobic and hateful signs on the front lawn of Willow Grove High School shocked me. As much as the video about Matthew Shepard had upset me, I still felt safety in my distance. Matthew was killed in Wyoming, but I lived in Iowa, where people were kind. How could this be happening to us? These were our people, Midwesterners living under the same wide blue skies, standing on our school's front lawn with signs proclaiming ADAM AND EVE, NOT ADAM AND STEVE and HOMOSEXUALITY = DEATH. Iowa was supposed to be better than that.

Traffic past the school was slow, each driver craning his neck for a better view of the action. I was no different, searching the crowds as I drove, picking out the distinctive shape of Jeremy Carpenter standing under the flagpole near the Stonehenge circle of benches. A few feet away from him stood a camera crew, its young reporter smoothing her hair as the videographer fiddled with the equipment. I watched the media crews like you watch a crush at a party, not wanting to seem too eager, too interested. A few feet behind them, I saw Elizabeth and Alison with signs that said ERASE HATE and JUSTICE INDIVISIBLE. Warmth spread through my chest slowly, a feeling I finally identified as pride. We'd done this. Jeremy and Elizabeth and Jessica and Alison and Jenna and Shanti and everyone else, working through lunch, pulling together over paint markers and tagboard signs to make this happen. We'd done this.

I parked out by the back tennis courts and hurried across the parking lot to the heart of the action.

I couldn't get to Jeremy's side without passing through the God Hates Fags camp. I half jogged past them, trying not to look, trying not to be seen. I was nearly there when Jake grabbed me.

"Paige, wait."

"Don't touch me," I said, struggling to pull free.

He squeezed my arm harder, imploring. "Paige. Will you listen?"

With one good twist, I broke his grasp. "No! I can't believe you brought those people here!"

"Babe, I didn't. That's what I wanted to tell you." He reached out again, but I stepped back. Unable to look at his face, I trained my eyes over his shoulder instead, seeing Lacey and Geneva down near the street. They stood before a camera, earnestly nodding as a J. Crew–model type held a large microphone to their faces. Just feet away, a pale woman marched back and forth carrying a large sign. Her thin lips were pinched in a line. KEEP OUR STUDENTS SAFE, screamed her sign. Her body was rigid as she turned north, toward Jeremy's half of the school's wide lawn. The other side of her sign said SCHOOL DAYS, NOT SCHOOL GAYS.

"Look at this!" I said, sweeping my arm across the whole spectacle. The news vans, the protesters, the students, the worried teachers, the crowd growing larger every minute as curious neighbors and parents and townspeople joined the milling herds of students. "You did this."

Jake shook his head miserably. "I didn't mean to, Paige. That's what I'm trying to say. I never meant for it to get this big. My dad—"

"Oh, your dad? It's never your fault, Jake. It's your dad, your mom, it's Lacey, it's your friends, it's alcohol, whatever. Take responsibility for once."

He grabbed for my sleeve. "Paige, no—I didn't—my dad was the one who called these guys . . . I didn't mean for all this . . ."

"It was *you,* Jake. You told the lie that got Mr. Tremont fired. You caused all of this, even if your dad was the one who made the call," I said, then spun on my heel, leaving him alone in the hateful mob.

When I reached the other side of the yard, my sister dropped her placard (HATE IS NOT A FAMILY VALUE) and threw her arms around me. "You're here!"

"Hi!" I said, startled and pleased.

"Jeremy's over there, talking to the media," Mirror said, tossing a hitchhiker's thumb over her shoulder. "Isn't this great?"

I looked past her to where Jeremy stood, his red hair catching the morning sun as he spoke earnestly before the camera. Funny, on the surface he looked so much like Lacey and Geneva talking to that reporter, I thought. But Jeremy actually belonged in front of the camera, while Lacey and Geneva, I was certain, were butting their way into the spotlight merely for the chance to be on TV. "Great?" I echoed.

"Yeah," Mirror said, nodding eagerly. "Jake's bringing in the God Hates Fags people makes our position so much stronger."

Feeling sick, I thought about Jake's words. His voice had sounded so small, so lost. In fact, I couldn't remember a time when he'd sounded worse. It set me off balance, made me nervous. Since when was Jake smaller than the world he built around himself?

A familiar voice called for my sister across the quad. "Mirror! Mirror!" Ethan ran up, stopping abruptly when he saw me. "Oh."

"Hi," I said.

He took a long breath and looked at my sister. "Mirror, Jeremy needs you over by the Channel 27 people."

My sister's ocean eyes searched the crowd. "Okay," she said, smoothing her dyed hair. "I'll be right there."

Ethan ducked his head. "Great." Without looking at me—looking anywhere but—he said, "Catch you later," and hurried off.

Mirror sighed. "Not good, huh?"

I shook my head unhappily. "Not good."

She glanced toward the Channel 27 van. "I would stay—"

"Jeremy needs you," I said. "You'd better go."

"Okay," she said, looking as though she wanted to say something else. After a moment, she shrugged and ran off across the lawn.

The crowd had to be more than a thousand strong now, between the students and the bystanders and the teachers and the protesters. Above my head, I heard the low *chop-chopchop* of the news helicopter. I shivered, pulling my jacket more tightly around my shoulders. Jeremy was still talking to the Channel 27 people, still nodding solemnly. The picture would be appealing to TV viewers, I thought, Jeremy standing beneath the flag and the turning autumn leaves.

Shanti snuck up on me a moment later, startling me. "When did you get here?" she asked.

"Twenty minutes ago?"

"It's terrible, isn't it?" She gestured to the circus around us.

"I hate it." My voice was bare, stripped clean of its defenses. "I don't think I can stay." I didn't mean to say it, but the moment I did, I knew it was true.

"You want to go find Mr. Tremont?" Shanti asked. Far overhead, a vee of geese flew across the rich-blue sky, muttering and honking.

I nodded. "Yes."

"Great," she said. "I'll go get Ethan."

chapter TWENTY-FIVE

But of course Ethan didn't come with us. How could he, when he couldn't even stand to look at me? I'd been a little ways away when Shanti asked him; he was on board until Shanti mentioned that I'd be coming. Then he stammered and stuttered his way back out of the invitation. Jeremy needed him. Jenna wanted his help on a donut-and-coffee run for the gang. I had tried to fade into the tree I stood behind, had tried not to feel so thoroughly rejected.

"So how are you, really?" Shanti asked now.

Over the next rise, I knew, was a falling-down old barn, collapsing more into its gray center with each passing day. Every time I drove this road, I waited to see the barn with the thrill of things falling apart, half welcoming and half dreading the day it would finally be gone. Eventually someone would demolish it completely and clear out the rubbish, maybe build something new in its place, but for now it remained: wound in vines and wildflowers, bowed in the middle with outer beams pointing to the sky, splintered and deteriorated but remaining. I sighed. "I'm here."

She looked at me from the driver's seat, and for a second it was there: the recognition, the understanding, the feeling of being on the exact same page. She smiled faintly. "Me too," she said.

Mr. Tremont wasn't at the Java House or Prairie Lights or the Thai restaurant where Shanti said she'd run into him once before. Nor at the university library, the bagel place, the funky little record store. "This is stupid," I said, kicking at a squarish rock on the sidewalk. I was embarrassed for us both, thinking we could just wander around downtown and magically run into him. A flock of pigeons suddenly took to wing, casting shadows against the September-bright buildings.

Shanti sighed. The sun glinted off her black sunglasses, flashing like cameras. "I don't know," she said, and I got the feeling that she was talking about more than whether we'd been stupid to come.

She kicked a rock next to me, and we scuffed our way down the street. Fat cinnamon squirrels hopped across the sidewalk in slow parabolas. A plane droned overhead, followed by a lazy white tail. Shanti and I matched our feet together. *Scuff, scuff. Scuff, scuff.* A man rode his wobbly bike past us, its wire basket packed full of junk. Lights turned green, red, green. Cars paused, drove. People strolled by in ones and twos, students mostly, in sunglasses and baseball caps, with their faces to the sky. It didn't seem right that people should be moving through their daily lives like nothing was wrong.

And then we found him. He was sitting on a bench near the river, sandwiched between Padma and the bearded guy from the reading, Mason. They were watching some little kids feeding ducks by the river and didn't see us until we were practically in their laps. Shanti cleared her throat loudly, and they all looked up together.

"Oh," Mr. Tremont said, drawing in a breath. He looked anxious, older.

Padma clapped her hands together in delight. "Our friends!" She beamed up at us, but she looked older, too, the skin around her eyes darker and more crinkly.

"Hi," I said, lifting my hand awkwardly, like a wave or a gesture of peace.

Mason smiled at us. "Hello, girls."

The five of us stayed quiet for a moment, wondering how honest we could be. Shanti broke the silence at last. "Mr. Tremont," she cried. "This sucks!"

He nodded gravely. "Indeed."

"People are marching at school today," I said.

Mr. Tremont sank slowly back into the bench. "Oh, God."

379

Padma looked at me searchingly. "People?"

"They have signs," I said. "They say things like 'God hates fags.'"

"Oh my God!" Padma was indignant, horrified, but Mason and Mr. Tremont looked resigned.

"We've seen this before," Mason said sadly. "In college."

"One of our professors was going to marry her partner in the university chapel," Mr. Tremont added. "People were protesting outside their wedding."

"People suck!" Shanti said angrily.

"It can be difficult," Mason agreed. A breeze kicked up, ruffling the leaves above our heads and tugging the river into long ripples.

"But it's illegal, Cam," Padma said. "They can't just fire you for being gay!"

Mr. Tremont shrugged. "Allegations were made . . ."

"But they're lies!" I said.

"Yes," Mr. Tremont said, "but parents were calling, and Dr. Coulter . . . Well, it doesn't matter. The point is, I chose to leave."

Shanti's voice was pleading. "Mr. Tremont, we need you. It's not the same without you."

"It's not," I agreed, thinking of the postapocalyptic feel of his classroom, when he hadn't yet been gone a full day. "You made school mean something, Mr. Tremont. You changed us."

He sighed, smiling faintly. "None of us is delicate enough to touch anyone else without hurting them a little bit." His voice had a hollow, reflective quality, as if he were reciting a quotation only he could recognize.

Padma dabbed at her dark eyes. Mason reached down and squeezed his hand. My gaze seemed to get stuck there, staring at Mason's furry little hobbit hand wrapped around Mr. Tremont's perfect one. There was a tiny glint of silver from the band on Mr. Tremont's hand, and I searched Mason's for a matching one, but his hands were jewelry free.

"Mr. Tremont," Shanti said again. "We *need* you." Blocks away, the faint sound of a siren oscillated through the early-afternoon streets, bouncing off buildings and skipping across the river. I ripped my eyes from their hands and tried to focus on the conversation.

"I'm sorry, Shanti."

"How can you stand the injustice? The hatred? Why don't you take a stand — you could make a difference in the world! You could make the world a better place!" She planted her fists on her hips, looking just like she had on the playground in fourth grade.

"Shanti," he said quietly, "even if they asked me back, I wouldn't go. I couldn't. I don't want to be a political figure. I just want to finish grad school and live my life."

"But you owe it to —"

"I owe it to myself to finish my dissertation. Who I love shouldn't be a political issue. I don't want to be a poster child for gay rights. I just want to write, to write . . ."

"A sonnet cycle about high school?" I asked.

He smiled. "Exactly."

Shanti stomped her foot. "But it's not fair!"

"No, it's not," he agreed, and looked at us. "So use it."

He gave us his email address and phone number before we left, offering to write college recommendation letters, as if that somehow made up for abandoning our cause—*his* cause! Shanti and I took his offered scraps reluctantly and tucked them into our pockets before heading back to the car for the disappointing drive home.

We sat in silence for a long while, each of us lost in our thoughts. Finally, I gave voice to the question that had been on my mind since I saw them holding hands. "So," I said. "Is Mason, uh . . . ?"

"Mr. Tremont's boyfriend?" Shanti asked. "Yeah, I'm pretty sure."

"So he actually is gay."

Shanti gave me her fiercest look, her eyes sparking and snapping. "Yeah?" she asked. "And?"

The *and* was that it was slightly jarring to see it up close. I'd never known a real gay person before, and while I would fervently defend Mr. Tremont to all the small-minded people in Willow Grove, it was just kind of . . . weird, I guess, to see it for real.

"Who he loves doesn't change who he is," Shanti said, "and if you aren't cool with it in two seconds, I will seriously kick your ass and dump you on the side of the highway."

I smiled sheepishly. "No, I'm cool. You're right," I said. "He's still Mr. Tremont, right? Even if his boyfriend is kind of . . . boring."

Shanti giggled. "Okay, I wasn't going to say it. But Mr. Tremont is just so . . . It's hard to imagine anyone being good enough for him. But you'd think it would at least be, like . . ."

"A prince?"

She laughed. "Yeah, or like, a Nobel laureate."

"Who's devastatingly handsome."

"But totally humble."

"Of course!"

"Who goes to Haiti twice a year to build hospitals."

"Who speaks seven languages and can write love poems in each one."

"Who built his own ark before Noah and saved the unicorns."

We were laughing at our own stupidity and at the senselessness and futility of the entire day. Everything was so messed up—and so surreal. Our giggling finally died down, and we both sighed at the same time. "Mason's just so . . . normal," I said at last.

"And so short!" Shanti cried, and we were both off again, giggling and guilty and slightly crazy. It was awful, but God, was it a relief just to laugh.

• • •

We got back to Willow Grove around dusk, and Shanti pulled up alongside my car in the school parking lot. I reached for the door handle but she shifted her car into park. "Wait."

I turned to look at her. She bit her lip. "I have to tell you something." The radio suddenly blared the opening bars of a bouncy dance song, and Shanti reached forward to turn it off. "Um."

I braced myself for another lecture about Ethan. She'd been mercifully silent on the issue all afternoon, and I assumed she'd gotten it out of her system. I sighed and leaned back in my seat.

Shanti looked down at her hands. "I, um."

The last sliver of red sun disappeared behind the tree line. Out on the highway beyond the football field, the cars had their lights on, a string of traveling stars.

"I was the one," she said at last. "Who, um, told."

"Told what?"

Her face was creased with shadow in the fading light. She sighed. "On Jake."

I turned. "What?"

"Don't hate me," she said. "It's just . . ."

"What? It's just what?"

Her voice came out in a flood. "He was drunk! And he could have hurt Ethan, seriously hurt him—he was out of control! He could have hurt *you*! And it's not fair that people like him get away with everything, and they can just ignore the rules and everyone else just kowtows

384

to them—it's not fair! And he's a real asshole, Paige. You should have heard what he said to Ethan when you weren't around in school, in the hallways. He's an asshole and you can do better and you're in love with Ethan not Jake!"

I knew I should argue, should put her in her place. Should say: *It wasn't your right to tell.* And: *Who are you to decide who I love? Shouldn't I get to decide who I date, just like Mr. Tremont?* But silence fell across me like velvet, heavy on my shoulders, and I kept my mouth closed.

"You hate me, don't you? Paige, look, I'm sorry. Dr. Coulter probably wouldn't have even acknowledged it, but Mr. Berna was standing right there and he'd seen Jake push Ethan, had heard him yelling, and you know how strict he is about the zero-tolerance policy with the cross-country runners, and I bet he's tired of seeing the football dudes get away with shit, too, so he jumped on it and it was out of my hands and . . . I'm just tired of watching the jocks get away with everything."

I wasn't mad. I wasn't anything. I felt like a little piece of me was floating above, watching the scene, taking notes for later. Analytical. *Look at Paige. She's not reacting at all. She's just sitting there. That's kind of strange.*

"God, I'm sorry, but I'm not, because Jake's a real asshole and he has, like, no redeeming qualities and I have no idea why—well, whatever, it doesn't matter—but, Paige, seriously, I'm sorry. I am."

I nodded. "I'll see you later," I said, and let myself out of the car.

• • •

I drove aimlessly, unwilling to go home, in love with the empty freedom of driving. Mr. Tremont didn't want to be a political figure; he just wanted to be a poet. It was my fault he had to make the choice. I was the cause of the whole mess; I was at the tangled center of the web. It was my fault Jake had been drunk, my fault he fought with Ethan, my fault he got caught. My fault Shanti told on him, my fault he tagged the door, my fault he thought Mr. Tremont was gay in the first place.

I was the cause, and I could be the solution.

Twenty minutes later, I was pounding on the Austins' red front door, with its fox-shaped knocker slamming his little chin against the metal plate behind it until Mrs. Austin appeared with her face of ice. "You're not welcome in this house."

"I have to see Jake."

Her fingers curled in fists against her skeletal hips. "You are not welcome here. You may leave of your own accord or you may leave with a police escort. It's up to you."

"Will you please tell him to call me?"

Mrs. Austin frowned. "I don't think so. Please leave now."

I sighed, letting my shoulders drop. "Okay. I'm leaving."

She slammed the door and I got in my car and pulled away from the house, but halfway down the long driveway I parked behind an old oak and jumped out, dashing behind trees and hurtling over bushes through the woods until I came out behind the house. I ran up the side yard and threw my keys at Jake's window. They clattered to the ground, and just as I threw them again the window slid open and Jake's face appeared. "Hey." He snatched the keys from the air in front of him and looked down. "What are you doing?"

"I have to talk to you," I said, and I must have sounded desperate enough, or maybe just crazy, because he nodded and slid the window back into place. I stood on one leg as I waited for him to reappear, counting the seconds I could hold my balance, until I thought I saw a flash of movement in the kitchen window and bolted back into the safety of the trees.

Jake showed up a moment later, moving slowly through the damp autumn forest. "Paige?" I watched the way he walked, carefully, mindful of each step. He seemed stripped of something, exposed.

"Hey," I said.

He settled himself down on the crumbling log beside me. "What's up?"

"Jake." *We stood in the misty trees talking about nothing until he laughed quietly and I asked, "What?" and he said, "I was just trying to think of an excuse to kiss you" and I said, "You don't need an excuse."*

I dug my fingernails into the center of my palm, into the health line, the life line, the love line. "Jake. You have to tell the truth about Mr. Tremont."

He glanced over his shoulder. "I shouldn't be out here," he said. "If my dad knew . . ."

"Jake, listen." I wanted to grab him, shake him, but I was afraid, for the first time in my life, to touch him. "You *have* to tell the truth. You can't just fuck with people's lives like that! You have to fix it!"

His eyes stayed trained on the ground before him: twigs poking up through wet yellow leaves, a mossy rock, a crushed rusting can. "I can't."

"But Mr. Tremont!"

"I'm not like you, Paige. I have too much to lose."

I laughed harshly. "Not like me? Nothing left to lose because I've already fucked up beyond belief?"

He didn't say anything for a long time.

"Brave."

The word shocked me into speechlessness and I couldn't look at his face. Finally I stood up. "I have to go." He stood, too, and impulsively I reached over and hugged him. "I'm sorry. About everything."

He hugged me back tightly, burying his face in my shoulder. We stayed like that for a long minute, entwined, until I unwound his arms and stepped back for the last time.

"I have to go," I said softly, and walked off into the quiet trees.

That night, I sat in my wing chair by the window, staring at the places where the stars should be. I couldn't save Mr. Tremont, couldn't save Jake, couldn't even save myself, so what was the point of trying anymore. I searched the sky for a star to wish on, not that I had anything to wish for anymore, but the sky behind the moon was smooth, jewel blue, and the night clouds were surprisingly white. It was a strange sky, a daytime sky transposed onto night. I stayed by the window, drifting in and out of dreams, until morning.

chapter TWENTY-SIX

The local news channels picked up the story of the protesters, but since Mr. Tremont refused to talk to the media, and
since he'd willingly resigned, the story fizzled out pretty
quickly. It turned out that many of the God Hates Fags
protesters weren't even from Willow Grove — they'd been
bused in from Kansas. Still, that side had had its share of
locals, more than enough to leave a bad taste in my mouth.

On Thursday, Dr. Coulter stationed the school security guard and the local truancy officer outside to usher
students in to their classes, and the protests dwindled
without the energy and numbers of the students. By late
that afternoon, there were just a few people left, and they
weren't even carrying their signs — they'd propped them
up against trees and were sitting on the benches, chatting
with one another.

I heard all this secondhand from my sister. I'd hardly slept at all after talking to Jake Wednesday night, and I decided to take a mental health day on Thursday. I got my dad to sign an excuse for me. My mother never would have allowed me to stay home only two days before the homecoming dance, but she seemed to be taking a mental health day of her own and didn't come out of her room until dinner. I wasn't even sure that she knew I was home. I stayed in my room, napping and watching bad daytime TV, and she stayed in hers, and the house beyond our doors seemed emptier than it would have if no one were home at all.

On Friday morning, already running late, I stopped for a latte on the way to school. It was October 1, the day we'd been looking forward to since middle school. The parade, the game, and somehow I'd managed to break up with my potentially-homecoming-king boyfriend just days before. If my eighth-grade self could see me now, she'd punch me.

But I didn't care. I was listless and slow from strange dreams and too much sleep, and I was only half awake in the crispness of early morning. Flashes of dreams from the night before came to me as I shuffled across the student parking lot — snippets only, and nothing that added up to any kind of narrative logic. But I remembered driving, remembered long highways unwinding before me, and the sense that no matter how much I drove, I couldn't get to where I needed to be. Wherever that was.

As I neared the school, I saw flashing blue-and-red lights

bouncing off the brick walls of the field house. I slowed my pace, not wanting to burst on the scene like a voyeur. What was going on that they needed police at school this morning? Not the protesters; only a few persistent marchers were still out front by now, and anyhow, if the school had wanted to call the police on them, they would have done so the first day.

I turned a brick corner to reach the parking lot behind the auto shop and immediately saw that I needn't have worried about standing out as an onlooker. A swarm of students and teachers gathered on the boundaries of the lot, watching the proceedings in the muttering quiet of a concerned crowd.

In the center of the circle of bystanders and authorities sat a car, crushed in the front like a crumpled beer can. Two firefighters dressed in black worked together with a large tool to cut away at the roof of the car, peeling it back. With growing horror, I made out a dark figure in the front passenger's seat, hunched over and unmoving. The car must have hit something—the heavy steel Dumpster? The brick wall beside it?—and bounced back.

The car wrenches sickeningly across the country road, everything out of control, slow-motion, flipping over an embankment and falling, turning, an eternity through space to the riverbed below.

A couple of EMTs leaned over a body on the ground, checking for a pulse. Flashes of red and blue lazily swept the crowd, and though it was a sunny day, the enclosed lot seemed to be lit only by the spinning lights.

Over near the cruiser, a police officer stood behind a person in a yellow sundress, pressing her up against the car with one hand against the back of her neck and slapping a pair of handcuffs around her wrists with the other hand. I could just make out the officer's voice reciting the familiar Miranda rights. Keeping a hand on her head, the officer turned and shoved her down into the backseat of the car, and I gasped. It was Nikki. I turned to the girl in front of me, a short blonde I didn't know. "Why are they arresting her?" I whispered.

"She's drunk," she whispered back.

She's half dressed and barely conscious and you grab her purse and keys and shirt and drag it all out of the frat house with your other best friend, the bitch, at your shoulder saying "What about Jake? How could you do that to him?"

"What?" Nikki couldn't be drunk, it was eight in the morning — this wasn't real. It couldn't be real. The blond girl nodded, keeping her eyes on the scene unfolding before us. The firefighters were nearly finished cutting away the car, and one of them called for an EMT. Inside the destroyed car, the girl slumped in the front seat looked a lot like . . . "Is that my sister?" I pressed my hand over my mouth, feeling sick. Mirror's soft black-and-red hair fell in strings across her face, and her white tank top was covered with blood.

My sister. My awesome, stubborn, beautiful, bitchy, passionate, funny, amazing sister. Covered in blood. I wanted to rush the scene, pull her up, take her place. If one of us was going to be hurt, it should be me. I was the one who deserved it. I was the awful one.

It wasn't real. Of course it wasn't real. It was Nikki's presentation, the one she'd been working on since last spring, since the real accident. It was what everyone had been talking about at the edges of my awareness all month, what Shanti had called emotional manipulation, something about reenacting your guilt complex on a public stage, the public theater of fright, to scare kids away from drinking and driving after the dance tomorrow night. DIEDD. And Nikki had cast herself as the culprit, the reprehensible drunk who kills all her friends. My God.

It wasn't real, I knew it wasn't.

But it felt real.

One of the EMTs rushed over to Mirror from where she'd been working on yet another body, this one lying on the rutted pavement. "She was thrown from the car," whispered the blond girl.

Lacey staggers out of the car, crying and crawling up the hill, her bare knees damp with spring dirt. Nikki's unconscious in the backseat, the driver's seat smashed back and pinning her to the seat. . . .

"Oh my God," I whispered again. Nikki was in the backseat. Lacey and I were both thrown from the car because we were both in the front seats. Because *Nikki wasn't driving.*

Nikki wasn't driving. "Oh my God!"

The body on the pavement was wearing khakis spattered with blood and a stained pink sweatshirt. Elizabeth Carr. Her hair fanned across the rocky parking lot, rippling slightly in the breeze as an EMT bent over her, giving her mouth-to-mouth respiration.

The girl pointed, still not taking her eyes from the scene. "And that guy."

He was lying on the pavement near the car's smashed hood, sprawled on his back. I had been too distracted by the firefighters cutting the car up to notice him earlier, but now that they were strapping Mirror onto a stretcher, I could see him. It looked like he had been flung through the windshield onto the pavement in front of the car. There were no words for the feelings flooding through my system, the terror and sadness and shock. The whole drama was carefully orchestrated to trigger panic and sorrow and fear in us, the innocent onlookers; I knew this, and yet my body reacted as if it were real, as if my eyes and chest and heart and skin simply refused to listen to what my brain told them. Emotional manipulation, a modern passion play— whatever you wanted to call it, it was working. I just kept whispering the same words over and over, hardly hearing myself. "Oh my God, oh my God."

Screams hang suspended as the car swerves sickeningly across the country road. . . .

. . . Lacey's fingers grip the wheel, desperate to regain control. . . .

395

The EMT kneeling over the boy stood up slowly and shook her head at one of her colleagues. She looked sad. One of the other EMTs walked over and pulled a white sheet over the body, patting the first EMT lightly on the back. She reached down and pulled the sheet all the way over the boy's scratched and bloody face, and as the white linen covered his features, I suddenly recognized them beneath the bruises and blood. It was Ethan.

Everything stopped. The sun stopped in its trek across the sky, hanging between motionless clouds. In the cage of my ribs, the ventricles of my heart stopped pumping, the blood completely still in my veins and arteries. Ethan.

Ethan, keeping me out of the cold night rain. Ethan, stretched out along the farthest edge of my bed, staying all night just because I asked him to. Ethan, bent over his notebook writing, his sentences opening into entire galaxies of meaning and light. His brown eyes, seeing me.

Time unfroze as the sad EMT gently zipped Ethan into a body bag and dragged him over to a hearse parked behind the fire truck. I was shivering, I realized, trembling to such a degree that I thought I might lose my footing and fall to the ground, scrape my knees on the same pavement that had cradled Ethan's body. "God," the blonde said quietly, "that hearse is so creepy."

Nikki. Elizabeth. My sister. Ethan. I couldn't breathe. I couldn't stop shaking. And then I was crying, choking and gasping as tears ran down my face.

Next to me, the health teacher nodded grimly. "Pretty terrible, isn't it?"

I nodded hysterically, breaking into fresh sobs. The police cruiser put on its sirens and pulled away. Through my tears, I saw Nikki looking forlornly out the window, her forehead pressed to the glass.

The black hearse followed the cruiser, slowly carrying Ethan away. I couldn't breathe.

"Keep *that* in mind the next time you kids want to drink and drive," the health teacher said gruffly. Was she talking to me specifically? Did she know that I was in the accident last spring?

The ambulance pulled out of the parking lot after the squad car, lights and sirens going. I rubbed my eyes with my long black scarf. As the crowd began to stand, stretch, and disperse, I noticed for the first time that some people had been seated on metal bleachers.

The health teacher gestured to the scene. "Let this be a lesson to you. You could kill the people you love! You could end up in prison for the rest of your life!"

It spells DIEDD, because we could have DIED.

I took a deep breath, looking at the toad-faced health teacher. "It wasn't real."

"Oh, it's real, all right," the health teacher said, frowning at me.

"But Ethan and the others aren't really dead." I clenched my scarf in my fists.

The health teacher crossed her arms, looking morbidly satisfied. "They would be, that's for sure!"

A girl behind her said, "They wouldn't have a hearse in real life. That's not accurate."

"Yeah," her friend agreed. "They load bodies into ambulances, not hearses."

The health teacher shot them an evil look. "Get to class."

"Everybody knows you shouldn't drink and drive," the girl said. "I can't believe the school spent so much money trying to scare us."

"Ethan's not dead," I said again, just to make it perfectly clear. Not dead. He wasn't dead.

"He will be, if you kids drink and drive. . . ." the health teacher said, but I was hardly listening. I had to see for myself. I had to find him.

He tastes like vodka and ash and mint and teeth and his hand slides up your arm and it's warm and it's different from being with Jake; his lips ask questions and his fingers trace the skin down your neck and wander back up into the forest of your hair and you haven't kissed anyone but Jake in two years and you really shouldn't be doing this. But he's so gentle and you're so sleepy and it's all brand-new, like you're exploring room after room of an infinite mansion, each room more beautiful than the last. . . . "Paige! Prescott! I'm shocked!" And Prescott practically jumps to the other side of the couch, abandoning you to the cold center. "We weren't—" he says. "Nothing happened. . . ."

Lacey ignores him and says, "It's time to go. Where's Nikki?" and you don't know and she acts like somehow that's your fault, like you can't do this one simple thing, "Are you such a slut that you put your snatch before your friends?" and you protest that nothing happened—nothing happened!—you try to catch her to make her listen, you want to grab her by the shoulder and spin her around and make her believe that nothing happened but she's not listening, she's stalking through the halls opening every door in the house, startling couples in compromising positions and surveying piles of passed-out bodies before she finds Nikki half naked and being licked from navel to neck by some creepy dude you've never seen before.

"Time to go," Lacey announces. "Sorry, Charlie." She crosses her arms until Creeper backs off and Nikki rolls off the bed, giggling. "Moooomm, do I have to?" She laughs and Lacey nods without smiling and you're gathering Nikki's things and she's like, "My shirt, where's my shirt?" and you throw a T-shirt off the floor at her and she's like, "That's not my shirt. I need my shirt, my shirt. I got it at the Mall of America last summer," and Lacey lets out a loud huff and bends down to look under the bed. Creeper starts snoring and Lacey flings a shirt at Nikki, who hugs it and squeals and then hugs Lacey and says, "You're such a good friend, thank you so much for that," and Lacey nods and says, "Time to go," and pushes her out the door.

In the living room Prescott is sitting on the arm of the ugly couch, leaning against the wall. "Hey," he says, "maybe

I could give you a call sometime?" Lacey shoves him and says, "She has a BOYFRIEND," and he looks at you like he wants to say more but Lacey's there between you, holding up Nikki who's half asleep and daring you to choose her brother over your best friends, over your boyfriend, over your whole life. So you shrug unhappily and leave without saying a word, wandering out into the quiet Iowa City night.

You spend the two-block walk to the car encouraging Nikki to keep walking, while Lacey repeatedly refuses her requests to be carried. When you finally get there, Lacey digs the keys out of her purse and throws them at you, but you don't catch them and they fall in the street. "Dammit, Paige," Lacey says, and you're fumbling around trying to find them and it occurs to you that you're not really in any state to drive. "Maybe I shouldn't — Prescott was making —"

You realize your mistake immediately but Lacey jumps all over it. "Prescott was what? I can't even believe you were kissing my brother. That's so wrong. Jake is going to be crushed."

"You're not going to tell Jake. You can't tell Jake."

She's under the streetlight and her face is full of shadows. "I think Jake has a right to know, don't you? I know I would want to hear if my boyfriend were making out with another chick. . . ."

Nikki complains about how cold and tired she is, and you finally manage to unlock the car and help her crawl into the backseat, where she curls up like a dog and promptly passes out.

Lacey stares at you, waiting. "Anytime now."

"Wait, I'm driving?" you ask. "But I was drinking. . . ."

"Oh for fuck's sake, Paige. You're the designated driver, so drive. Get in the goddamn car."

"I don't know, Lace. I don't think . . ."

"What did you drink? Half a Corona? You never could hold your liquor."

"Pres—your brother kept spiking my Cokes. I didn't mean . . . but you and Nikki were missing, and . . ."

"Fine," she says. "I'll drive. Give me the keys."

"Have you been drinking? Are you drunk?"

"Give me the fucking keys, Paige."

"Are you drunk? Maybe we should just call someone. . . ."

"We're not fucking calling someone. If we're not home by the time my mom gets back from Meskwaki, she'll flip out, and I can't even deal with that. Give me the keys."

"My dad always said we could call him anytime and he'd pick us up, no questions. . . ."

"Give me the keys, Paige."

I gave her the keys.

chapter TWENTY-SEVEN

Ethan had disappeared. Shanti hadn't seen him. Jeremy hadn't seen him. I followed some student council members down the hall, hoping to find the dead. When I saw my sister, I shrieked and threw my arms around her, surprising both of us. "Don't you ever do that!"

"Do what?"

"Die! You can't die! I need you! Who else understands how crazy Mom is?"

Mirror laughed. "I'll see what I can do." She touched the fake blood by her temple. "Isn't this makeup cool?"

"No, it's creepy!" I said. "Just—don't die. Okay?"

She held up her hands, laughed again, and promised. Clearly, she had no idea how awful she looked, or how upsetting it was to see your sister be fake dead.

"Listen, Mir, have you seen Ethan?"

"Not since he got carted off in that hearse."

I shuddered involuntarily.

"It wasn't real, Paige."

"I know that," I said. "But it still freaked me out. After . . . you know."

"Sorry," she said, more gently. "All the dead kids have the rest of the day off, so that it seems more real—he might have taken off already."

"Oh," I said. "Right."

"I'm going to wash my face," she said. "If I see him . . . ?"

"Tell him I'm looking for him." My voice was strained, and even I could hear the edge of desperation in it.

My sister smiled. "Yeah. Of course."

I found Nikki in the back hallway, near the auto shop. "Paige, you're not supposed to be back here." She rubbed her wrists where the handcuffs had been.

"Sorry, I was just looking for—are you okay?" Her eyes were sunken into her face and ringed in dark circles. She looked as bad as my sister, but she wasn't wearing any makeup.

"Me? Yeah, I'm fine. I just—put a lot of work into this thing, you know? Like, I've been up until one or two in the morning every night for the last two weeks, going over details, getting all the permission slips from everyone, watching online videos of how other schools did it, emailing with SADD people from other schools. . . ." She stopped and waved her hand. "Well, you don't care."

"I do, actually."

She shook her head. "No you don't. You think it's stupid."

"Nik, I —"

I stopped, remembering all the times I'd refused to participate, teased her about her acronym, didn't listen when she tried to tell me what she was doing, didn't speak up for her when other people made fun of her, accused her of being a hypocrite. Shit. I was an asshole.

"Nikki, I seriously don't think it's stupid. I think it's great."

"You don't have to say that." She slid down the wall until she reached the radiator, settling her weight on her skinny elbows and knees. She looked so little.

I squatted beside her. "I'm not just saying it, Nikki. Really. I think . . . well, it's hard to put yourself out there and actually try to make a change for the better." With a pang of regret, I heard Ethan's words in my own. Why hadn't I listened more closely? Why hadn't I paid attention?

"Then write Mirror's eulogy."

"What?"

"If you really care, help me out by writing your sister's eulogy. Jeremy was supposed to, but he got overwhelmed by the whole Mr. Tremont thing and flaked on me."

"Oh," I said. "I don't know . . ."

"We're doing the mock funeral tomorrow night, before the crowning of the homecoming king and queen. I'd need you to deliver Mirror's eulogy then."

"You're doing the funeral at the dance?"

Her face was set. "The whole town turns out to see the crowning ceremony, and I want this message to reach as many people as possible."

I thought of Nikki at Lacey's party, not so long ago, how fragile she'd seemed. She seemed so forceful now. She'd changed so much. We all had.

"Nikki—" I started, and then stopped.

"Yes?"

"It wasn't your fault, you know. You weren't driving that night."

She nodded. "I know."

"You do?"

"Yeah. It took a while, but I remembered. I wasn't driving."

"Nik, I'm so sorry," I said. "I don't know how—"

She held up a hand, stopping me. "It wasn't my fault. But it could have been."

I sat back on my heels, studying her, and then nodded. "I'll write my sister's eulogy."

The afternoon sky was dark and colorless as I trudged out to where the homecoming float was parked, behind the football field. I'd stumbled through the day in a haze. Ethan was nowhere to be found, and classes seemed weirdly empty without the missing kids. Nikki had actually been taken to court where she would be yelled at by a real judge, and I heard Jeremy was going to film it for her. And so, after everything, she wouldn't even be on the homecoming float with us.

Only four princesses climbed up on the trailer, and we settled ourselves carefully atop the giant papier-mâché beehive. I sat on a little bench with Jenna, who looked beautiful in a white wool coat and perfectly tailored gray wool slacks. I felt like a slob next to her in my old black peacoat and jeans. A month ago, my mother would never have let me out of the house looking like this, but since she'd lost her job, she hadn't been getting up in the mornings with us. I wondered if she'd even be watching the parade today.

The wind started to pick up as we rolled down the street behind the wheezing marching band, and I watched the teachers and parents along the sidewalks look at the sky and mutter to one another while the kids waved their hands and yelled for candy. Down in one of the chairs closest to the trailer hitch, Lacey waved regally to the crowd, letting the football player next to her throw candy for the both of them. As always, her hair was perfectly curled and falling just so over her school-spirit-yellow sweater. She had white gloves and white earmuffs but no coat. She was probably freezing, but she didn't show it. Elbow, elbow, wrist wrist wrist. Serene, secure, waving to the crowd just as we'd always imagined.

I watched the people clustered along the curb, searching for two girls, middle schoolers, holding hands. One keeps her eyes fixed on the float, her face strong and determined.

The other tries to focus on the parade but her eyes keep darting back to her friend. One day they'll be up there, they promise, riding the float down the center of Main Street, surrounded by good-looking boys in letter jackets, perfect hair and perfect smiles, waving to an adoring crowd.

But of course I didn't see them. Those girls existed in memory only. I tried to make myself feel something, tried to enjoy the moment we'd dreamed of for years, but all I felt was emptiness. After a few blocks I stopped waving, and I tried to focus on writing my sister's eulogy in my head. I had no idea where to start. How the hell do you sum up your sister in three minutes? She's your twin and your polar opposite. She's your constant companion and your competition. She's your best friend and the biggest bitch in the world. She's everything you wish you could be and everything you wish you weren't.

Halfway down Main Street the sky started spitting rain. Two blocks later, there was a deafening CRACK of thunder. And then it started hailing. We princesses jumped out of our chairs and tumbled down the float, running for cover. The football boys followed suit, and frazzled elementary school teachers herded their charges toward any shelter they could find. Up and down the street, garage doors opened and neighbors called to the children through the blinding rain and stinging hail. I followed the other girls toward the lights of the gas station.

Inside, it was surprisingly still. Customers stood frozen, listening to the snare drum *rat-a-tat* of rain on the metal roof. The fluorescent lights buzzed overhead, and behind the register a woman clicked her teeth as the hail bounced against the plate-glass windows. My hair lay heavy and wet against my neck, and my heart pounded from the run. A second later, the door pushed open again and Lacey fell breathlessly into the store beside me.

"Hey," I said.

She leaned her cane against a donut case and stood on one leg while wringing her wet hair like a dish towel. She must have lost her earmuffs in her flight.

Another crash of thunder shook the windows, and Lacey and I both jumped. I grabbed her cane and handed it to her. "So . . ." I said. "Was it everything you always dreamed it would be?"

Lacey glanced at me. Her mascara was running down her face in dark streaks, and I realized that mine was probably just as bad. We both reached up to run fingers under our eyes at the same time, using each other as mirrors, just as we'd done a thousand times before. For the first time in weeks, I smiled at her. She shook her head and smiled back. Outside, the ridiculous papier-mâché beehive float listed to the side, slumped over the edge of the flatbed trailer, and finally collapsed in the street.

chapter TWENTY-EIGHT

I started my sister's eulogy a hundred times. A hundred lines scribbled, a hundred lines scratched out.

> Drinking and driving can lead to terrible consequences. . . . You shouldn't drink and drive because . . . When I first met my sister, she was a baby. . . .

Nothing was right. Nothing would do. I tried exercises from Mr. Tremont's class:

> I remember . . .
>> I remember seeing my sister lying dead on the pavement, blood spattered across her white tank

top. The next class period, I was hugging her in the hallway . . .

I remember when she picked me up because no one else would, and in the end we have to be there for each other. . . .

My sister is the nicest . . .

My sister . . .

An hour later I was lying on the floor of my bedroom, staring at the ceiling and remembering how I used to imagine it was the floor. You would have to climb over the walls above the doors to get in and out of rooms. You could sit on the ceiling fan like a merry-go-round, and the ceiling lamp would be like a little electric campfire where you could warm your hands in winter. The ceiling was so appealingly bare, without rugs or furniture. It invited you to roller-skate across it, do cartwheels, have a ceiling dance party, make ceiling angels.

I was losing my mind.

Downstairs, my mother's heels clicked across the floor, back and forth, back and forth, as she paced and talked to her sorority sisters from Northwestern. She'd been on the phone all afternoon. When one sister got tired of talking to her and hung up, she dialed the next one. Her voice curled up through the vents like smoke, the words indistinct but the tone perfectly clear: both her daughters had failed her, she'd failed as a mother, nobody loved her and she'd die alone.

410

My mother's voice floated up again, and I scooched across the floor on my back and slid under the bed. It was built higher than a normal bed to fit a rolling trundle under it, but for some reason I'd never actually gotten a trundle. Underneath it was like an abandoned fort, dusty and stuffy and littered with objects that had fallen behind the bed or gotten kicked under it. I sneezed once and hit my head on a spring, but then settled down and breathed deeply. It was quiet. Peaceful.

Mirror and I used to lie under our parents' bed, side by side, on our backs, staring up at the dusty bedsprings. Later they traded in their bed for a Japanese-style bed that was too close to the floor to hide under, and Miranda and I grew up and stopped hiding together, and then we stopped talking. *I remember my sister, hiding under the bed with me. . . .*

I closed my eyes.

I wished I could stay under my bed forever. Or fall asleep and wake up to a world where people were good and things weren't so complicated. My stuffed dog, Zeke, was half under the bed, and I pulled him in with me, hugging him against my chest.

I remember the accident today, how real it felt even though I knew it wasn't real, how bitterly, horribly, awfully real it seemed, and Ethan was dead, and Mirror was dead, and how could they be dead when there's so much I never told them. . . .

I remember the accident last spring, how we dragged

411

Nikki away from the party and threw her in the back of the car and drove away under the bloodred moon, and we both stayed silent when she awoke in the backseat all alone, surrounded by glass and blood and blame, and we raised up our heads for a moment to see that she was alive and dropped them back into the cold, wet grass. . . .

"Paige?" My sister's feet appeared beneath the bed skirt. "Are you here?"

"Yeah."

"Where? Under the . . . ?" Her feet moved slowly toward me, and then she knelt down, pulling at the sheets. "Oh, hi."

"Hi."

"Scoot over." She lay down and squeezed under, next to me. "Hi, Zeke."

My mother's voice haunted the pipes.

"Mom just asked me if I've ever tried meth." Mirror sighed. "This week sucks. Remember when we were little and I used to sneak into your room when they were fighting?"

"Yeah," I said. "I remember."

I remember . . . there was no way we could beat her mother home but Lacey tried anyway, muttering about how Brenda was always late coming back from the casino and we could still make it. I couldn't tell if she was drunk or not; she didn't seem drunk, but she rarely did. When Nikki drank, she got loud and happy and giggly and clumsy. When Lacey drank, she got quiet and dangerously thoughtful.

She leaned forward over the steering wheel, as if it would help us go faster. We were already doing 75 down a two-lane country highway and I wanted to warn her about deer and coyotes and raccoons who might appear in the headlights at any moment, eyes reflecting the light like spooky beacons. Last year a boy hit a deer on this same road and completely totaled his car and broke both arms where he tried to protect his face from the air bag. He didn't come back to school after that, and people mostly forgot about him, but something about the story haunted me, and I strain my eyes for hints of suicidal woodland creatures.

Everything feels abstract, like I'm not 100 percent in my body.

"I can't fucking believe you," Lacey suddenly says. We're close to home now, turning onto the winding road out to Sauvignon.

"What?" you ask, and then blush as it all rushes back and you're embarrassed that you already let yourself forget. No, not "yourself": myself. I can't hide behind you, it wasn't you. It was always me.

I kissed Prescott. I'd never kissed anyone but Jake in years, and the worst part was I liked it. He was a good kisser, attentive and fully present, like the kissing was enough, was more than enough, like he'd be happy to stay there kissing me all night and never complain that we weren't going any further.

But it was wrong. I should not have kissed Prescott. I love Jake. "I love Jake," I say.

"What?" Lacey asks. "You take Jake for granted. You're disgusting. You don't even deserve him." Her fingers are white around the steering wheel and her foot smashes down on the accelerator and the needle inches toward 80.

"And you do? Is that what you're trying to say?"

"Yes!" The word explodes out of her. "I do! I wouldn't fucking cheat on him, that's for sure. I would know what I had and I wouldn't just throw it away."

She's staring through the windshield like she could burn a hole through it with her eyes, and I'm suddenly filled with this crazy rage, like all these little hints she's dropped all spring and all the times I've bitten my tongue to keep her happy suddenly just swell up inside me and I just reach over and grab the tiny millimeter of flab under her upper arm that she's totally self-conscious about, and I pinch it as hard as I can. "Ow! You bitch!" One of her hands flies off the steering wheel and punches me in the leg. "Fuck!" I punch her in the leg, an eye for an eye, and she reaches out to block my arm and suddenly everything is bathed in light. Her arms, my arms, the steering wheel, the gear stick, all become strange puppets in the garish light, and Lacey's face is a mess of shadows and geometry and fear, because it's a car coming straight at us, out of nowhere a car, and Lacey wrenches the wheel as hard as she can and we go spinning off the road . . .

and hit the ground, bouncing, rolling. The windshield is gone and Lacey is gone and then I'm gone, flying through the open door and landing, finally, a hundred yards away, a collection of limbs and bones and skin, and the car slides to a stop with the sound of screeching, crunching metal.

I don't want to remember.

I don't want to remember how small Nikki looked when we finally found her smashed behind the front seat, unconscious. Or the silence after the crash, when I held my breath as long as possible, listening for Lacey and Nikki, and the forest held its breath with me, the leaves hanging silent on the trees and the animals stopped in their paths and the rain paused on the tips of branches, everything silent and still and then the sound of sobbing from the road above.

I don't want to remember kissing Prescott just because I was bored and drunk, and how Lacey stood over me, smirking, and held it over my head like a bully the whole way home, taunting and threatening and driving too fast around the curves. . . .

I remember wanting to smash Lacey's face in, wanting to push her out the door, wanting to hurt her, destroy her, shut her the hell up, punish her, punish her. . . .
. . . I remember grabbing the steering wheel . . .

. . . twisting it . . .

I grabbed the steering wheel . . .

. . . twisted it . . .

. . . I was the one . . .

. . . spinning out of control. . . .

I wanted to hurt her—
to stop her—push her out the door—make her shut up
about her brother and Jake and the whole awful night—to
stop—

I was the one . . .

*. . . wrenched across the road, the world upside down, wait-
ing for the terrible crash. . . .*

My fault.

All my fault.

Oh God.

Oh my God.

I pushed against my sister.

"I have to get out of here!" My fault. All my fault.

"Paige, what's wrong?"

"I can't—I have to go! I have to get out of here!"

I slid out from underneath the bed, got up, and ran.

chapter TWENTY-NINE

I ran down the stairs, grabbed my bag, grabbed my keys, ran out the front door to my car, and then stopped. What was I doing? I couldn't drive, I could hardly see straight. But I needed to escape, to outrun the voices in my head. I needed to fly. I ran into the garage, grabbed the bike I'd ridden all over town back in middle school, before Lacey told me it made me look like the witch from *The Wizard of Oz*. Good. Maybe I'd be sucked up into a tornado.

The physical exertion felt good, punishing and true, and I rode faster than I'd ever gone in seventh grade, as if I could outdistance my own terrible thoughts. I didn't want to remember. For months I'd blamed other people for my own mistakes. First Nikki—how I'd resented her while cooped up in the breathless Paris apartment all summer, bouncing the crying baby in my arms while Mrs. Easton lay crumpled in her bed, holding pillows over her head. *If only Nikki hadn't gotten in the car, if only Nikki weren't so careless, if only she weren't such a stupid drunk, I'd be home with them right now, stretched out beside Lacey at the pool, driving around the countryside with Jake under the glittering Iowa stars.* Then I blamed Lacey, who'd chased me from the party with her awful accusations and her constant air of waiting for me to trip up so she could pounce. She lied to Nikki, she pulled Jake away, she never told the truth about anything. It was her fault, Nikki's fault, but never my own, no, because Princess Paige was perfect.

I sped out of town, trying not to choke on my own self-loathing. Suddenly, I could understand why Nikki felt the need to replay the accident in front of everyone we knew; I was half tempted to drench myself in fake blood and stand before the school, declaring myself a monster and begging for forgiveness.

On the other hand, maybe it would be better to disappear altogether, to keep pedaling until I crossed into Illinois. I'd go to Chicago and lose myself among the anonymous crowds, start over with nothing to live up to and nothing to live down. Or I'd go farther than that even, east through Indiana and Ohio and Pennsylvania, until I reached New York, and if I still hated myself when I got there, I'd turn straight around and keep going until I hit the Pacific Ocean.

I'd never go back, and at home they'd wonder about

me, and someone would write an article called "Whatever Happened to Princess Paige," and they'd document my perfect life, my straight As and my great tan, and people would tell all sorts of lies about how nice, how sweet, what a good friend I was, and they'd publish my senior pictures and maybe do a whole spread in the yearbook about me, but eventually they'd forget I ever existed, except in a Willow Grove legend warning girls who wanted to grow up to be princesses to be careful or they, too, might disappear.

What was so great about being a princess anyway? Why had we pinned our entire identities to this one stupid word, not just since middle school but forever, since we were toddlers in tutus and tiaras, with pink Cinderella birthday cakes and fairy wands? Who wanted to be a princess? Real-life princesses were constantly being killed in horrible ways: Princess Di was killed in a car accident; Princess Grace, killed in a car accident; Princess Anastasia, murdered with her family. . . .

Why hadn't my mother protected me? She'd been homecoming queen in high school and college, she knew the strain of trying to be perfect. She was still aiming for perfection and slipping wildly, she must have known on some level that it was an impossible task. . . .

Then I caught myself: I was blaming other people again.

Goddammit! Why couldn't I just accept responsibility for the wreck I'd made of my own life? I was the one who agreed when Lacey gripped my hand and declared we'd do anything to be up on that float; I was the one who smiled

419

to people's faces and cut them down behind their backs; I was the one who protected Jake at any cost; I was the one who listened to my mother's endless litany of ways to be beautiful; I was the one who studied fashion magazines like they were the key to unlocking some holy code. I was the one who turned the wheel.

I was the one who caused the accident.

I was the one who got myself exiled.

I was the reason everyone was unhappy. I was the reason our senior year had careened so wildly off the tracks. It was my fault; everything was my fault. Me. Paige Sheridan. My head pounded with each accusation of my internal tribunal. My fault. All mine. I gripped the handlebars, practically standing on the pedals. Everything was my fault, and mine alone.

I was worse than the Wicked Witch. I wished a house would drop on me.

chapter THIRTY

I ended up at the secret spot in the woods. I hadn't meant to; I'd been riding blindly, consumed by my thoughts. Once there, I dropped my bike at the trailhead and took off down the trail, running. The sky above me was pebbled and gray. My leg muscles burned with exertion, but I pushed them around the final turn and down the hidden path to the spring.

It was only when I saw that it was empty that I realized I'd been hoping it wouldn't be.

I wanted him to be there. He would be sitting on our boulder, writing in his notebook, waiting for me. I didn't deserve his forgiveness but I would beg for it anyway, because I couldn't imagine going through the rest of the year without him. And he would listen; he had to.

I would find him. I would jump back on my crappy bike and speed back to Willow Grove. I'd make Shanti tell me where he lived. I'd go to his house, I'd make him listen. I would tell him the truth. I spun around to run back up the trail.

And then I heard it: a slight movement in the bushes, the faint brush of leaf against leaf. I froze, waiting.

The whole woods took up a breeze and trembled. I held my breath until the red-and-gold leaves resolved themselves into a shape, a face, with bright, intelligent black eyes, a long sharp nose, bat ears tipped with black: a fox. I stood, silent and still, as we made eye contact. He looked strangely familiar, though I couldn't remember ever seeing a fox before, other than perhaps in a zoo or as roadkill. But here he was, with his white muzzle and grayish chest, a long black sock up the leg he held out, as if any moment he would step forward and continue on his way. He was the size of a small dog, smaller than you'd think, almost feline in the delicacy of his features.

From behind me, the sounds of voices on the lake floated into our clearing, and the fox's ears swiveled, straining, and it was only when he looked back to me that he seemed to remember himself. He turned, flashing his thick tail, and disappeared into the bushes. I released my breath.

I was sick and tired of running. Ever since Paris—ever since the accident—I'd been running, running, from the guilt about Prescott, from the truth about Jake, from the memories of that night. I'd been too rushed to stop and notice that the happiest I'd been in ages had been right here, perched on this boulder, leaning against this tree. Writing, or talking, or sitting in silence, listening to the water and the birds.

I took a deep breath, trying to find the center my mother had talked about in her yoga phase. Breathed again. All that I was rushing toward or running away from would wait. I settled against the tree and pulled my notebook from my bag.

I remember . . .

I remember my sister the night we camped in Michigan and there was a crazy thunderstorm and we sat up all night telling each other stories about our elementary-school teachers, imitating their voices and the way they yelled at the dumb kids. I remember the time she and I stood in the front yard with a Wiffle bat, hitting black walnuts off the tree and into the street so cars would run over them, until the mean old lady next door called the police on us, and my mother had to sweet-talk us out of trouble. My mother was always doing that: I remember when she drove me back to school in sixth grade to demand that my teacher raise the grade on my report about South Dakota from a B+ to an A. I hid behind her, embarrassed, knowing I didn't deserve it, I hadn't worked that hard. But it was only ever the appearance of perfection she cared about. After that, though, I always made sure I did deserve the A.

Even after the accident last spring, my mother did everything she could to cover it up, until I couldn't remember what happened myself. *Dark road, raining, swerved to save a dog, lost control.* We'd never spoken aloud the truth of what happened that night, never acknowledged what we could have done, how much hurt we could have caused. My mother sent me away to sweep up the aftermath, to save face for all of us.

I paused. *Tell the truest truth you can,* Mr. Tremont had told us. *You must be enormously afraid. But keep going.*

I kissed Prescott last spring. I did. It was a mistake, but I did it, and I never told Jake, never confessed to my own moment of stupidity and weakness.

And then I kissed Ethan.

I told Jake that Mr. Tremont was gay.

I let Jake get drunk before the bonfire.

I blamed Lacey for everything.

I twisted the wheel.

I caused the accident.

I was an awful person.

But.

None of us is delicate enough to touch anyone else without hurting them a little bit, Mr. Tremont had said.

Mr. Tremont doesn't want to sacrifice his privacy to further a cause.

Jake decided to drink before — and during — a school function.

Jake started the fight with Ethan that got him kicked off the team.

Shanti told on Jake.

Jake lied about Mr. Tremont.

Jake's dad got Mr. Tremont fired.

Lacey lied to Nikki about the accident.

Lacey tried to steal my boyfriend.

Nikki drank too much.

Mirror can be a total bitch sometimes.

I can be a total bitch.

But.

Mr. Tremont taught us how to write.

Jake tried to help Lacey through her parents' divorce.

Shanti stood up for what she believed.

Nikki worked hard to make a difference.

My sister picked me up when I was utterly alone.

And Lacey . . . Lacey hadn't told Jake about

Prescott. Not even when things were the worst they'd ever been between us. And while I knew it was probably for Jake's benefit and not mine that she didn't tell him, it was still a nice thing to do.

As for me . . .

I tried to help Mr. Tremont.

I tried to help Jake.

I'm going to help Nikki by writing Mirror's eulogy. . . .

I will apologize to Ethan.

I will take responsibility for my actions.

And suddenly, I knew what to do.

chapter THIRTY-ONE

I prepared for the dance alone, standing in my bathroom, closing my eyelashes over the mascara wand, blending blush and translucent powder across my cheeks and forehead. I'd always loved doing my makeup. Attending to my eyes and skin and lips almost felt like a form of meditation, a cleansing ritual. I thought of the night, less than a month earlier, when I'd stood before this very same mirror, shadowed by my mother. Tonight she was the one on a date, at the club with my father. He'd been more attentive to her lately, brushing his fingers across the small of her back, kissing her softer face.

It was only a few minutes past six when I finished dressing. Normally I'd be going out to dinner before the dance, eating at the club with Jake and with Lacey and Nikki and their dates. Without dinner plans of my own, I didn't quite know what to do with myself. I checked my phone again, irrationally hoping that Ethan had called and I had just missed it. 6:13. Nothing else.

Mirror was gone already. I wondered what Shanti was doing right now. I wondered what Ethan was doing. I checked my phone again. 6:14. I drummed my fingers against the top of my vanity. 6:15.

I sighed and flopped into the wing chair by my window, careful not to mess my hair, and went over my notes one more time.

Shanti caught me at the door of the gym, pressing her cold fingers against my bare skin. "Have you seen Ethan?"

"No," I said. "He wouldn't answer my calls."

"He said he'd be here."

"He did?" A momentary warmth swept through my chest, rushing through the nervousness like ocean waves.

Her earrings tinked as she nodded. Beneath the twinkling lights strung along the walls, her eyes glowed with spots of gold glitter at the inside corners, and her full lips were lined darkly in red. She looked beautiful.

A dark figure appeared behind her, tall like Ethan, and my heart jumped. He came closer, into the light. It wasn't Ethan, not at all.

Gently, he placed his hands over Shanti's eyes, kissing her on the crown of her head. "Guess who."

"Aaron." She spoke with the certainty of someone who understands that she deserves the good things she has.

"You must be psychic," he said, smiling.

She laughed. "Everyone else here is afraid to touch me."

Stepping around Shanti, the boy held out his hand to me. "I'm Aaron," he said. "And you must be Paige."

I smiled. "You must be psychic."

"Everyone else is afraid to talk to Shanti," he said.

She nodded. "It's true."

"You drove all the way from Omaha?" I asked.

"Yeah," Aaron said. "Two-hundred-plus miles just to go to a high school dance."

Shanti twined her fingers with his. "Must be love." She seemed distracted, glancing past me toward the door.

"So you're a princess, right?" Aaron asked. "How does that work?"

I sighed. "It's a pain in the ass."

Shanti laughed. "This is why we like her." Looking at me, she asked, "So, did you have to do the parade thing yesterday?"

"Yes," I said, "and it sucked."

Aaron grinned. "Best princess ever."

"Speaking of which," Shanti said, nodding her head toward the stage. I turned, following her gaze to where Dr. Coulter stood, captive in the glow of a double spotlight.

"Shit," I said. Around us, the crowd began to murmur and the houselights seemed to dim. "Where's Ethan?"

"He'll be here," Shanti said. "The real question is —"

The music died abruptly, and the sound of Dr. Coulter's fingers tapping against the microphone echoed through the gym. "Good evening, Hornets," he said cheerfully.

I felt a stab of panic. "Oh God. Can I leave?"

Shanti shook her head. "Sorry, Your Highness."

Aaron laughed. "I like her," he told Shanti.

"Best princess ever," she agreed.

"First off, I'd like to congratulate the football team on their win last night against the Newton Cardinals." The gym swelled with screams and cheers. "GO, HORNETS!" Mostly you could hear the first syllable: Go, Horrrrrrrrrs!

My heart was pounding, but I tried to play cool. "We're known as the Willow Grove Whores, for short," I told Aaron. "You know, like a nickname."

He laughed. The heavy gym doors opened every few seconds to let another straggler in, and each time I turned, expecting—hoping—to see Ethan.

When the screaming died down, Dr. Coulter glanced at a card in his hand. "And now, I'd like to invite one of our princesses onto the stage. Miss Rosellini?"

The gym fell silent as Nikki stepped from the shadows. She wore a shimmery pink dress, glittering and ephemeral in the lights. She looked like a fairy princess. Except for the handcuffs clipped around her left wrist.

"Thanks, Dr. Coulter," she said, with more authority than Lacey or I had ever had. She turned to the mic and cleared her throat. "Yesterday I killed three people," she said. "And I'm really sorry."

"This is so fucked up," Shanti said, and added for Aaron's benefit, "She was in a car accident last spring, a drunk driving thing. Her car was totaled. And now she's reenacting it in front of the whole school, to air her guilt."

"It wasn't her fault," I said. "She wasn't the one driving."

"That makes it even weirder, then," Shanti said.

"What would you have her do?" I asked. "She's making a positive effort for change, even if it is weird. Maybe it's not what you would have done, but it's something. Better to do something than run away and pretend nothing happened."

"You sound like Ethan," Shanti said.

I blushed. "Well?"

Aaron chimed in. "I agree with Paige."

I grinned at him. "Thank you."

"So please, please don't drink and drive. . . ." Nikki was finishing up, wiping under her eyes with her handcuff-free hand. Her voice was wobbly but firm. I wondered where Lacey was, whether she was watching Nikki with the same mixture of fondness and pride.

"And now I'd like to invite Paige Sheridan up to say a few words," Nikki said. Shanti shot me a questioning look, but I just smiled and pushed through the crowd to find my place beside Nikki onstage.

From the stage, the gymnatorium was lovely. In addition to the tiny white lights on all sides, giant paper lanterns hung from each of the folded basketball backboards, glowing like round moons. I leaned into the microphone. "Hi. So I was supposed to write a eulogy for my sister, who 'died' in the crash yesterday." Scanning the crowd, I found my sister's face and grinned. "I was going to tell you about how awesome she was, and what a brat she could be. I was going to make jokes about her joining the legions of the undead." Mirror rolled her eyes, but she looked pleased.

"I started making a list of all the people who would be affected by her loss, and then I realized—everyone would be." I thought of Shanti and her whole hierarchy of cool, the band kids and the theater kids and the tech kids. A tech kid was running the spotlight right now, and another tech kid was running the sound for us. "It's like what Mr. Berna's always saying, when he starts ranting about 'global temperature change.'" I heard a few chuckles. "We all affect one another. We're all connected."

Down on the gym floor, Mr. Berna started clapping enthusiastically, and the kids around him giggled. Ms. Hoeschen leaned over and grabbed his hands to silence him.

"Nikki took the blame tonight for killing my sister, and my friends Elizabeth and Ethan. Just like she took the blame for the accident we were in last spring. And though obviously it was her fault yesterday—I mean, you were there, you saw—" I smiled, and the crowd kind of laughed. "But last spring it wasn't her fault. I mean, we all made bad decisions that night, and when I think of what could have come of those decisions . . . when I think about losing people like Elizabeth Carr or Ethan James, or my—my little sister—I can't believe we were that irresponsible.

"I realize you probably don't care about one stupid accident that happened months ago, and I'm not really asking you to. The point is, Nikki cared. She realized how lucky we were to have survived, and she saw that the mistakes we made weren't incredibly unusual or strange. Anyone could have gotten behind the wheel that night."

The far doors finally opened, admitting a long sliver of yellow light from the hallway as a dark figure slipped into the dusky gym. I squinted through the darkness and the crowd, willing myself to see Ethan, staring a moment too long at the back of the room before regaining my place.

"The rest of us tried to forget about it, but Nikki decided to try to keep other people from making the same mistakes. She spent the whole summer planning with local police, fire, and emergency services to stage yesterday's crash. She went to every business in town to get funding, and she spent her own money to fly out to Maryland for a training session in late July."

Nikki's eyes widened slightly, and I smiled at her. Thanks to Jeremy, who as editor in chief of the paper made it his business to know everything, I'd discovered that there was a lot I'd never thought to ask about.

"She even got the director of the national mock-crash program to consult with her personally," I said, and the crowd murmured. "She helped to write the script for yesterday's accident and personally helped train each of the student actors."

Nikki blushed and tried to wave the comments aside,

but I continued. "We all screw up, and it's hard enough to take the blame and apologize to the people you hurt when you do. But Nik went one better: she worked to keep other people from making the same mistake."

I reached out my hand, and Lacey stepped out of the shadows and limped up to the mic. Nikki looked shocked, and I stretched out my other hand to pull her toward me, until it was the three of us standing center stage, together. Just as we'd always planned.

Lacey smiled at the crowd. "In honor of Nikki's hard work and contribution to our community, the student council has agreed to donate the proceeds of tonight's dance to a local teen substance abuse counseling program." She looked around, and her junior doppelgänger, Geneva, stepped forward with an overlarge check made out to Willow Grove House. "Nikki, on behalf of the student council, senior class, and student body, thank you."

Geneva stepped forward to hand her the check, and Nikki waved at her face so her mascara wouldn't run. She looked at me and mouthed, "Thanks," and I grinned and gave her two thumbs-up. Collecting herself, she turned to wrap things up with a final message about how Elizabeth, Ethan, and Mirror weren't really dead, but they could have been, and that she hoped people would keep DIEDD's message in mind after the dance tonight.

Dr. Coulter reclaimed the mic from her, clearing his throat. "Very nice. Very nice. Thank you, everyone. Quiet down please. Quiet down."

And then I saw him. He was standing at the other end of the gym, dressed in a suit and looking ridiculously handsome. Our eyes locked and I lifted my hand to wave, but suddenly Jake was hopping onstage and picking me up in a strangling hug. "That was amazing, Paige!"

He leaned in to kiss me but I pushed against him, struggling out of his arms. "Jake, no." I looked past his shoulder to where I'd seen Ethan, planning to signal him somehow to wait for me—

"It's not too late, babe," Jake said. "We could still be king and queen—just like you've always dreamed."

I looked into Jake's eyes. He used to make me weak in the knees with one look. He used to be able to talk me into anything. But he no longer had that kind of power over me. "You know, I think I'd rather be a commoner," I said.

I turned back to find Ethan, but he turned away, and I couldn't catch his eye. Was he leaving? Where was he going? I looked around, desperate, and inched toward the edge of the stage, wondering if I could jump in these heels.

"Paige, wait." Jake grabbed my hand. "I fucked up, I know that. But I can change—I can be the person you want me to be."

"The person I want you to be?" I asked. "Jake, I spent the last two years trying to be the person *you* wanted *me* to be—you, my mother, Lacey—and I was never good enough. And now? I feel like I hardly know who I am. So maybe you should focus on trying to figure that out—who *you* are, not who I or Lacey or your parents think you should be." I held his hand, feeling the familiar weight of his fingers, rubbing my thumb along his rough skin. "You're a good guy, Jake. Deep down. But you have to stop listening to everyone else."

He sighed. "So. This is really it, huh?"

"Yeah, it is."

Jake looked resigned. "I guess I knew that already." He hugged me again, hard, and then let me go.

When I turned back to look for Ethan, he was gone.

The rest of the princesses were onstage now. I edged forward, still thinking of jumping, but Nikki caught my hand and pulled me back. "Where are you going?" she whispered. "It's time for the Rose Ceremony!"

"I—" I looked at her, and for once I was the one who couldn't keep a secret. "Fine," I whispered. "I'm here."

Dr. Coulter finally got around to the traditional pomp of the homecoming ceremony, calling everyone's names and handing each of the princesses a red rose, brilliant against the dark curtains at the back of the stage. The thorns had been carefully removed, probably by the mothers of the Bee Boosters club. I accepted my rose, smiled for the cameras, and then squeezed Nikki's hand. "I hope you win!" I whispered.

Dr. Coulter was clearing his throat into the mic, and I crept backward as smoothly as if my tottering heels were moccasins. Toe, heel, toe. Just like Sacagawea, but backward. As the boys made their way forward, my hands parted the curtains behind me and I was free, disappearing into the heavy black.

I snuck through the hallways and back into the gym to find Ethan. Shanti and Aaron were standing approximately where I'd left them.

Aaron saw me first and gave me a thumbs-up. "Awesome!" he whispered.

"Nice speech," Shanti said.

"Really? I felt like it was so long."

"It was great." She grinned. "Go, Space Dogs!"

I felt a pang of regret that Mr. Tremont couldn't be here. My speech wasn't much, maybe, but I never would have been able to write even that without him. I should have been turning in my story to him next week. Technically, I still could; I did have his email address, after all. But I knew that I'd lost my chance to redeem myself to him, to show him that I could make myself vulnerable in front of my peers. At Northwestern—or wherever I decided to go—I resolved not to let fear stop me.

An arm slid around my waist, and Jeremy's voice spoke in my ear. "That was crazy, girl. Was that a eulogy, or a campaign speech?"

"Shut up," I said, and he laughed. I felt a sudden rush of affection for him. Thank God I hadn't ruined things between us for good. "Listen, Jeremy, I just want to say again how sorry—"

"I know."

"No, seriously," I said. "You've been nothing but nice to me, even when I totally didn't deserve it. And all the work you did for Nikki and for Mr. Tremont . . . You're amazing, and if anyone says otherwise, I will kick their ass." I grinned at Shanti, who was obviously eavesdropping. "I learned that from Shanti," I told Jeremy.

He nodded wisely. *"Meeting Intolerance with Violence: The Shanti Kale Story."*

Out of the corner of my eye, I saw a familiar face. I turned, and Mirror smiled at me. Her gown was deep-red velvet and vaguely Victorian in style. She looked amazing. I beamed at her. "I'm glad you're not dead."

"Hey, I don't mean to interrupt," Shanti said, tapping me on the shoulder, "but shouldn't you be running after a certain Prince Charming right about now?"

"What?"

She pointed at the door. "He just left."

"Shit!" I said, and ran, weaving around clusters of my classmates until I reached the back of the gym, where I pushed through the heavy wooden doors — and flew.

One thing the storybooks never make clear enough is the moment between the spell and its conclusion. Is it sharp, like the crack of ice on the spring equinox? Or does it fade slowly, almost imperceptibly, like night fading into morning? Was there a moment when Cinderella sat in her pumpkin carriage, surrounded by sticky innards and giant pumpkin seeds, when her beautiful glass slipper got caught in the sludgy orange goo?

Outside, black clouds darted across the moon like schools of sleek fish, and a drizzly breeze pushed at my bare arms and pulled my hair out of its updo. The school yard was empty. I ran toward the student parking lot, searching for Ethan's Jeep. My expensive high heels sank into the mud, and the hem of my dress collected rainwater as I ran, but I didn't care. "Ethan!"

Princesses don't yell, my mother's voice reminded me. "ETHAN!"

At the far end of the parking lot, I saw a dark figure walking away, a black shadow under the orange lights. I gathered up my long, wet skirt in one hand and sprinted across the lot, darting between cars as the drizzle turned into a shower. By the time I reached the far end of the lot, my shoes were utterly useless. I kicked them off and hurried through the grass along the sidewalk. "Ethan!"

It was him. I was close enough now to see for sure, and even from behind I recognized his long stride. The rain was pounding against the sidewalk, against the windshields and hoods of cars parked in the street, against the tin roof of the equipment shed out near the soccer field, but still I was fairly certain he could hear me. He kept walking.

"Ethan, goddammit, I want to talk to you!"

He spun around, pushing a hand through his wet hair. "Why? What more is there to say?"

"Let's see," I said. "How about I'm sorry, for one?"

"Are you asking or telling?"

"Telling. I'm sorry. You've been so great to me, and I've been an asshole to you."

He shrugged. "Whatever."

"I mean, you *are* great," I said.

"Fine," he said. "Thanks."

"Really great," I said, getting desperate. His eyes were dark.

"Look," he said, not unkindly. "I just don't think we can be friends. We tried, it didn't work, fine. Let's cut our losses and move on."

I flinched, raising a hand to my cheek as if I'd been slapped. The rain poured down my face. I didn't even want to think about what I looked like—my carefully applied mascara was probably running in rivers under my eyes, my hair a limp, wet version of Medusa's snakes. Princess Paige would have left it there, would have gathered what poise she had remaining and made the most dignified exit she could.

But I was no longer that girl. "Ethan," I said, and then stopped. What could I possibly say to convince him? *I didn't realize—not until I thought you were dead. . . . I spent the last two days looking for you.* Everything I thought sounded so trite, and yet I couldn't stop running through every cliché I knew. *You had me at hello. You complete me.* Shit.

"I missed you," I finally said.

"Look," he said impatiently, "I saw you with Jake—"

"On stage? That wasn't—Ethan, listen to me." I reached out a hand and grabbed him, and even through the freezing rain a spark of electricity jumped between us. "Listen. That wasn't anything. We're finished."

"Which explains why he was kissing you. . . ."

"Which explains why I punched him in the junk and ran away."

He laughed unexpectedly. "Really?"

A strand of wet hair flopped across his eye, and I had to restrain myself from brushing it back. My heart was shivery and nervous, but I tried to play cool. "No, but would I seriously be standing, barefoot, in the middle of a torrential rainstorm if I was still with Jake? I mean, logically, wouldn't I still be inside, dancing and . . . um . . ." I looked around, desperate for inspiration.

Ethan gave me a small smile. "And eating princess cake?"

"Exactly. And floating on fairy castles. . . ."

"Riding unicorns into the sunset. . . ."

I laughed and shivered.

"Look," I said. "I have a lot of things I need to figure out. But with you, I feel like it's okay that I don't exactly know who I am. Because you don't make any demands of me. You don't expect me to be anyone but myself." I sighed, frustrated that words were failing me when I needed them most. "Am I making any sense at all?"

He grinned. "You mean, other than the part where you seem to think that being with me is better than riding unicorns?"

"Other than that."

Ethan's eyes locked with mine. "Absolutely."

We were built on words; the words we'd written together, the things we'd told each other that we hadn't said to anyone else. But there was also something between us that transcended words: the connection, the understanding, the times we had looked at each other and really *seen* — all those moments of silence were just as important. All this time I'd been holding myself back, keeping myself between the lines other people had drawn for me, because I couldn't see myself as anything more than princess. But with Ethan, I *had* been more. I had been myself. And while I knew that I would continue to be myself with or without him, I wanted to be me with him. If he'd have me.

He reached for my hand. I grinned, tears mingling with cold rain on my cheeks, and laced my fingers through his. I leaned against him and he leaned against me, and we walked until the rain stopped falling, the clouds evaporated, and one by one the stars appeared.

acknowledgments

This book was written in six years, five houses, four jobs, three cities, two states, and with the help of one incredible community. Because my gratitude is as vast as a continent, allow me to give my most geographic thanks.

In Publishing Land: I am overwhelmingly thankful for Secret Agent Becca Stumpf, who in addition to being a visionary editor and a relentlessly cheerful champion is also an excellent dancer. I am equally thankful for my brilliant editor, Kaylan Adair, whose editorial wisdom has far surpassed my every expectation. I recently read that they don't make editors like they used to; apparently Kaylan didn't get that memo—and thank goodness, because I don't know where I'd be without her keen eye and sharp green pencil. Hogs and kisses, Kaylan!

In New Mexico: Lisa Aldon, in whose house this book began, Jennie Lee, Tony Forbes, Rory Cobb, Kelly Williams, and my students at Moriarty Middle School, who inspired and challenged me, with special thanks to fellow writers Elizabeth Carpio, Liz Spalding, and Anaztasia Borrego.

In Chicago: StoryStudio has been the kind of writing community most writers only dream of, and I owe huge thanks to everyone, especially the members of the Advanced Fiction Workshop, who saw early drafts and asked all the right questions. I am particularly indebted to my mentor, teacher, and friend, Jill Pollack, without whom I would not be the writer I am today. Thanks also to the Ragdale Foundation and to my fellow residents for the champagne and daffodils.

In Iowa: Ali Brown and Cameron Gale were this book's first readers and cheerleaders. You're both okay, I guess. Dan Beachy-Quick and Mark Baechtel shaped me as a writer and teacher, and provided Mr. Tremont's best lines and lesson plans. Em Westergaard Hamilton, Jennie Wheeler Rothschild, Adrienne Celt, and Carly Schuna read early drafts and convinced me to keep going. Molly Rideout read a late draft and talked me off the ledge. Nick Wagner has been my favorite writing buddy, and Chris Rathjen was my consultant on Iowa topography and flora. Melissa Torres, Dana Watson, Sarah Aswell, Kate Herold, Hudson Heatley, Rick Heineman, Carrie Robbins, Nadia Manning, and Mary Hoeschen: you're all wonderful. And the entire Grinnell and Plans community, without whom I could hardly face the world each morning, much less write a book. Thank [you] all.

In Wisconsin: Lifelong gratitude to Gail Gregory, Karen Ludvigsen, Camille Farrington, Michele McConnell, Debe Van Steenderen, Dan Williams, Heather James, and especially Nat McIntosh, who understood from the beginning.

At home: My giant, wonderful family, including several hundred cousins, aunts, uncles, steps and halfs and once removeds. Thanks especially to Val, Justin, Elodie, Helene, and all the Hestads, to Roger Backes and Sally Hestad for their unflagging support, to my whip-smart sister Megan, whose incredible eye for detail helped this book immeasurably, and to Eileen Backes, for everything. Finally, my deep and lasting gratitude to Natalie Kossar, for the thousand ways you support me every day. Thank you for putting up with me and all my envelopes.